The Night Stalker

of

Vietnam

By

Henry Nichols

Copyright © 1997 by Henry Nichols

ISBN 0-7414-0905-4

Published by:

INFINITY
PUBLISHING.COM

Infinity Publishing.com
519 West Lancaster Avenue
Haverford, PA 19041-1413
Info@buybooksontheweb.com
www.buybooksontheweb.com
Toll-free (877) BUY BOOK
Local Phone (610) 520-2500
Fax (610) 519-0261

Printed in the United States of America

Printed on Recycled Paper

Published May, 2002

I wish to dedicate this book to Crystal, Vanessa, Victoria, Brandon, Jonathan and Andrew my Grandchildren. The real meaning of love.

A special thanks to Mrs. Ava Delorenzo for Editing this book.

I've lived near the water most of my life. I've always found comfort just sitting there, looking out over the water. I've always been able to think clearly listening to the water. On this particular day I had good reason to be there. I was thinking about my mother. I knew that there was something wrong. Whenever I asked her about it, she would give me the same answer. I could feel it inside; she was holding back something from me. She is like that. She never complains about anything.

My mother is the only parent I've ever known. My father left us when I was a baby. My mother never really spoke to me about him. I never asked her why he'd left. I figured she would tell me when the time was right. I love my mother; she was a proud and beautiful woman. She worked hard and always took care of me. She's always worked two jobs and never complained. She never asked anyone for help. I can't think of any time when I heard her complain.

She works long hours, for very little money. When I was little, she worked a job where she could keep me with her; her boss would let me stay with her while she worked. As I looked out at the water, I thought, She is working a second job and it really bothers me. I can see her second job is really getting to her. I wish she would quit and stay home at night. One day, I'd asked her to quit the second job but she just smiled and said everything was all right.

I knew I had to do something. I wanted to make life easier for her. I wanted to ask her if I could quit school and help out. But I knew she would never let me do that. I also knew that I had to try.

I decided to go home and talk to her about it. As I walked up the sidewalk, I could see my mother sitting on the porch. She was just sitting there enjoying the summer air.

She looked so nice. The sun was out and shining on her golden hair.

"Hi Mom!"

"Hi love, did you have a nice day?"

"Sure did, Mom." I sat down next to her on the swing. I was sitting there trying to find the words to ask her if I could quit school. We just sat there, together, silently. My mother looked at me and asked, "Tim, is there anything wrong? You're being very quiet, you know."

"Mom, I have a question to ask you. I guess you know I have been worried about you. Lately, you have been tired, almost all the time. You never seem to have time to rest. You are working two jobs. I've been wondering if I could quit school for awhile and help out around the house." I was looking at my mother and could see her eyes filling up.

"Tim, I live for the day you will graduate from high school. You must realize I want you to graduate and make something of yourself. That is the day that I am working for. After you graduate, you can go to work. If I have to, I will work three jobs to keep you in school. You have a whole lifetime to work. It takes an education to make something of yourself. Staying in school is the only way you can do that. Tim, I want you to promise me that you will stay in school and graduate."

I looked up at my mother and smiled, "Okay Mom, I promise I will stay in school." All the time I was saying I would stay in school, I knew I had to do something. I started thinking about getting a job after school, but would she agree? I was looking at her and she reached over and put her arm around me and gave me a big hug.

"Tim, don't worry; everything is going to be all right. I promise you, I will start taking better care of myself."

"Okay Mom, I think I will turn in now."

"Goodnight, Tim."

The weeks went by and I could see my mother was getting worse. I knew there was something wrong.

Seeing her like that was really getting to me. I had to find a job and help out. This time I wasn't going to take no for an answer. I was going to find a part-time job. I just didn't want to hurt her.

"Tim, get ready for supper."

"Okay Mom." I sat down and looked at my mother sitting across from me. I sat there, staring at my supper.

"Tim, is there something bothering you?"

"Yes Mom, I am worried about you. I was wondering if I could look for a job after school. That way I could help out and still stay in school. I really want to do this."

"Tim, everything is all right. I appreciate your wanting to help. We are doing fine. I think your time after school would be better spent doing your homework. That's all I need. Everything is going to be all right. I promise you."

She knew that I was hurting inside as I continued to look at her. I loved her more than anything in the world. I also knew she wouldn't give in, but I'd made up my mind to keep on trying.

I decided to look for a job. The only question was what kind of a job? At sixteen there wasn't that much available. School was another problem. What kind of job can I get that won't interfere with school? I wondered.

I decided to walk to the waterfront. I knew that I could think there. I climbed up to the top of a piling. As I was looking out over the water, thinking about my mother, I was also thinking about the docks. I wondered if there was anything available on the docks. Suddenly, I heard a noise. Turning around, I saw Tom coming towards me.

Tom said, "Hi Tim."

"Hello Tom. How are you?"

"Fine, how about you? You look like you have a problem. Is there anything that I can do?"

"Nothing much, Tom. I am just worried about my mother. She has been working too hard lately. It is really bothering me. I feel that I should be doing more for her at home. That's why I'm here. It's nice and quiet, and I can think clearly. Tom, do you know if there are any jobs available on the docks?"

"Tim, listen to me. Everything is going to be all right. It just looks bad now. Just give it some time and you'll see."

"Well, I guess you might be right. I sure hope so."

I watched Tom walk away. He turned around and looked at me.

"Tim, I hear Captain John is looking for someone to watch his boats at night. Maybe he can use you. I don't think it's that hard a job."

"Thanks Tom. I'll look him up."

I walked over to Pat's Bar. Pat's is a bar where all of the fishermen hang out. I'd never been in there, but used to see the fishermen go in there all of the time. I looked in the window and saw Captain John sitting at the table in the corner with his crew. I opened the door and walked in. Everyone was watching me. I was quite nervous by the time I reached Captain John.

I was standing next to the table when one of the crew saw me and yelled, "Tim, you old enough to be in here?" He started laughing.

I heard Captain John tell him to shut up.

"Hi Tim, what can I do for you?"

I was standing there wondering how to ask him about the job when I heard him say, "What's up Tim? Don't just stand there, say something."

I took a deep breath. "Captain, I heard you are looking for someone to watch your boat at night."

The crew started to laugh. When they saw the Captain wasn't laughing, they became very quiet.

He sat there watching me. He remained quiet for a minute, then asked, "Tim, aren't you still in school?"

"Yes Sir, but I can still work part time at night."

"Sit down for a minute."

I pulled a chair out from under the table and sat down. I heard the bartender yell, "You guys know he can't be in here."

"Relax! He'll only be here a few minutes. Just bring him a Coke."

The bartender gave me the Coke and I said, "Thanks, I won't be here long, Sir."

"Tell me something, kid. Why do you want to work?"

"Captain John, I am worried about my mother. She's working two jobs and I want her to quit one of them. I just want to help out so she can start to take it easy. If I get a job, I will be bringing money into the house. That way she can quit the other job. Sir, I'm sixteen years old and I can work nights after school. This job means a lot to me. I will do a good job; I promise I won't let you down."

"I know Tim. What about your mother? Does she know you're looking for a job?"

"No Sir, if you give me the job, I am sure she will let me do it. She might not like the idea, but I think I can talk her into letting me work."

"Okay Tim, you have the job. That is, if she agrees. There is one condition that goes along with the job."

"What's that Sir?"

"You will have to stay in school, and your marks better be good. If they go down, you will be out of work. Do you understand?"

"Yes Sir! Thanks a lot Captain. I'll ask my mother tonight during supper. I'll let you know tomorrow morning what she says. I know she will let me do it. Captain, I will not let you down."

"Okay kid, now get out of here before the bartender has a fit. You're too young to be in here."

"Thanks again, Captain." I turned around and started to leave. When I reached the door, I looked back and smiled at the Captain. He just sat there smiling. I opened the door and left.

"Captain, that's one hell of a kid. Not too many kids care today about anything. His mother sure has done a great job with him."

"Carl, you sure have that right. The only thing that scares me is the number of break-ins we have had on the docks. I sure wouldn't like to see Tim get hurt."

"I wouldn't worry; that kid has a head on his shoulders."

"I guess you're right, Carl."

I ran all the way home. It was only a few blocks. I cleared the front steps and was opening the door before I knew it. "Hi Mom. I'm home!"

"Hi Tim, wash your hands. Supper will be ready in just a few minutes. Now get moving." She always said that to me smiling.

"You've been down to the docks again, huh?"

"Yes Mom. I've been talking to some of the guys. They're a great bunch of guys. I enjoy their company. They are always nice to me. I'll wash and be right back." I sat down at the table with my mother.

I was sitting at the table playing with my food, wondering how I was going to tell her, when my mother said, "Tim, is there something wrong? You look like something's bothering you."

"Mom, I have a favor to ask you."

"Go ahead, ask away."

"I know you are against me working. I really want to help out around here. Before you say anything, let me finish. I was on the docks today. I heard about a job. It's not a dangerous job. Captain John is looking for someone to watch his boat at night. I asked him if I could have the job. He said yes, but only if you agree. I can handle it. I promise you that it will not interfere with school. He also told me that if my marks dropped, he would fire me. I will work part time at night during the week, and all night on the weekends. It wouldn't be every day either. The boats only come in for four days and then go back out to fish.

"Mom, I am really worried about you. I just want to help out. I love you, Mom. Can I tell Captain John you will let me have the job? I really want to work."

My mother started to cry. I got up from the table and walked over to her. "Mom, please don't cry. I really want to do this. I promise you, everything will be all right."

"Tim, you know what school means to me. I want you to graduate. I live just for that day."

"I know. I promise you, I can handle it. Mom, you know I always keep my promises. I will finish school at the top of my class. The job is not dangerous; besides, everyone knows me. There are people walking around the docks all night long. I'il be safe, Mom. You don't have to worry."

"Okay Tim, you can try it out. Remember, if your marks drop, you will have to give up the job. Do you agree?"

"Yes Mom. I promise my marks won't drop. Don't worry, I'll be the smartest kid in my class."

She didn't say anything, and I watched her get up from the table and go into her bedroom. I could hear her crying. I waited for a few minutes, then knocked on the door. I was standing by the door when I heard my mother tell me to come in.

When I opened the door, she was sitting on the edge of the bed, wiping her eyes. I sat down next to her.

"Mom, are you okay?"

"I'm okay, Tim."

"I just want to be the man of the house"

"I know that. I just don't want you to grow up too fast."

"Awe Mom, I will always be your little boy."

"No Tim, you're a man."

We sat on the edge of the bed holding each other for a long time. I asked her to come back to the table and finish supper. She smiled and said, "It's probably cold by now."

"It doesn't matter; it will still be good. After all, you cooked it." We laughed and went back to the table to finish supper. We didn't say much during dinner. Afterwards, we did the dishes and went into the parlor to watch television together for awhile and then both went to bed. I didn't sleep too well. I was anxious to tell Captain John I could start working for him.

When I left the house in the morning, I ran to the docks. I could see Captain John on his boat. He was smiling; he knew my mother had agreed to let me take the job. I guess he could sense it.

"Well kid, I guess your mother agreed to let you work."

"Yes Sir. I can start tonight. Since it's Friday, I can stay all night until you come in the morning."

"Okay. Be here by nine. I will meet you here and tell you what I want you to do.

"Tim, remember what I said, low marks, no work. I mean it. I don't want your mother mad at me. Do you understand what I'm telling you?"

"No problem. I will be the top man in my class. I promise!"

"Okay, just make sure you have your homework with you!"

"I won't have to. My homework will be finished before I get here." I yelled goodbye and ran to school. I felt good—I had a job and was going to be able to help my mother.

It seemed like the longest day of my life. I could only think about starting my job. The bell rang and I ran out of the school all the way home. When I arrived home, I went straight to the kitchen where my mother usually was at that time of day. She was standing near the kitchen counter making supper, and I grabbed her and yelled, "I have the job. I start tonight at 9 o'clock!"

"That's great, Tim. I'm happy for you." We ate supper then I cleared the table and did the dishes. I could hardly wait for nine o'clock to come, so I could start my job.

A little before nine, I got up and told my mother I was leaving for work. I felt good. I had a great big smile on my face. "Mom, I'm a working man now." She laughed and handed me a snack. I kissed her and gave her a great big hug. "I'll see you in the morning, Mom."

I left the house and walked toward the docks. It was a beautiful night and I was feeling great. I turned around and saw my mother standing on the porch, watching me heading off to work. I waved and continued on.

As I approached the docks, I could see the fishing boats all lined up. Captain John was standing next to his boat, watching me.

"Hello Captain. I'm ready to start work."

"Hi Tim. Glad to see you. I want you to be careful. If you see anything, call the police right away. I don't want you getting hurt. Do you understand?"

"No problem. I'll be careful."

I felt great. My first job. I kept thinking about my mother and how much the extra money would help her out. I could hardly wait to give her my first paycheck. I sat down on the forward hole and looked out over the water. It was calm and the night was beautiful. The moon was out and lit up the area. All I kept thinking about was what a wonderful night it was. All night long, I watched the boat. It was about three in the morning when the police cruiser showed up. The cruiser stopped alongside the boat.

"How are things going, Tim?"

"Fine Sir, it's been quiet all night. What brings you down here?"

"Captain John asked us to check on you. So here we are. Can you use some coffee?"

"I sure could!"

"My name's Chuck, Bill is my partner."

"Glad to meet you. Do you take your coffee black, Tim?"

"Black will be fine, Sir. I heard you cops like your coffee and doughnuts."

Bill laughed and handed me a bag. "You get use to them."

I opened the bag. Bill and Chuck were laughing. They said they would be back in a little while to check on me. "Tim, be careful. What time will Captain John be here?"

"I'm not sure. He didn't say. I guess, I should be finished around seven thirty."

"We'll be back to give you a ride home."

"Thanks a lot. It's not out of your way, is it?"

"No problem kid."

I watched them drive away. They were pretty nice guys. They'd worked the night shift for years. Everybody on the docks liked them because they never pushed their weight around. I'd seen them go out of their way to help the fishermen. They were always helping someone. That's what made them good cops, respected by everybody on the docks.

It was seven thirty when Captain. John arrived, just as Bill and Chuck were pulling up.

"Hi Tim, how did it go last night?"

"It was quiet Captain. Can I go now? Bill and Chuck are giving me a ride home?"

"Sure, get out of here. I'll see you tonight."

"Thanks again, Captain." I opened the door to the cruiser and sat in the back. It was my first time in a cruiser. It seemed funny. When we arrived at my house, my mother was waiting for me on the porch and waved. "Thanks guys, I appreciate the ride."

"How did it go, Tim?"

"Great Mom. Everybody kept checking on me all night. It was a lot of fun. Bill and Chuck came by and brought me coffee and doughnuts. They are really nice guys."

Working and going to school really made the time fly.

Before I knew it, I had completed my first week of work. I was on the boat, getting ready to go home to sleep before school started when the Captain arrived. I waved at him. When he climbed aboard the boat, I asked him how he was doing.

"Fine Tim. It's payday. I came to give you your money." I watched him reach into his pocket and retrieve his wallet. "You know, Tim, we never did discuss your wages."

I didn't know what to say. "Well Captain, I guess that's up to you. It doesn't really matter. I just want to work to help my mother. Just pay me what you think I am worth. I will be satisfied with whatever you give me."

"Let's see, from what I understand, I not only have a watchman, but I have my own police force. I hear Bill and Chuck spend a lot of time down here."

"Yes Sir, they check on me all the time."

"Then I better pay you. I'd hate to get into any trouble with the law."

I laughed. I watched as the Captain opened his wallet and took two one-hundred-dollar bills out. I was shocked. I'd never expected that kind of money.

"What's the matter Tim? Not enough money?"

"No Sir, I never expected that much money."

"Well, you're worth every penny of it. Your ride is here. You know something kid, not everybody gets to ride home in a cruiser. You're a lucky kid. I'll see you in about a week when the boat is back in. Thanks for everything, Tim."

"Thanks Captain." I reached down and picked up my gear. Waving to the Captain, I yelled, "See you next week. Thanks for the money." I opened the door to the cruiser and sat in the back seat.

Bill looked at me and asked if I was ready to go.

I had a big smile on my face.

"What's that smile for Tim?"

"I just got paid. Captain John gave me two hundred dollars. I can hardly wait to give it to my mother."

"Well, I guess we better get you home fast. Chuck, hit the siren and lights."

I laughed. It didn't take long to get home. The neighbors were outside laughing as we drove up. I ran up the stairs and hugged my mother. I waved back to Bill and Chuck. We went inside the house and I gave my mother the money.

"Tim, I can't take this money. You worked for it." Her eyes were filling with tears.

"Please Mom, it's yours. That's why I went to work. Now, I can be the man of the house."

"Tim, you are the man of the house; you always have been. I told you, without you, I never would have made it. Why don't you put the money in the bank?"

"Please Mom, it's yours. Now, it's time for me to take care of you. What I would like is for you to go buy something nice. Like a new pair of jeans. You look nice in jeans."

My mother smiled and said, "Look nice in jeans, huh? You're getting too big for your britches."

"Well Mom, I see how the men look at you."

"Tim, you better get some sleep before you have to go to school."

"Okay, when I get home from school this afternoon, I want to see you in a new pair of jeans."

Later, when I came downstairs to go to school, I smiled and told my mother to buy a new blouse also. Giving her a hug and a kiss, I ran out of the house.

When I arrived home after school, my mother was standing there in a pair of new jeans. She'd even bought a new blouse. She looked great. "Mom, I think you are the most beautiful woman in the world." We both stood there smiling at each other.

At the end of the year, my marks had been higher than ever. I knew it pleased my mother. I could see in her face, she was proud of me.

During the summer I was able to watch more boats. I made a lot of money. I was even able to talk my mother into quitting her second job. When she did, I was thrilled.

I only had a few weeks to go before school started again and I would be a senior. I noticed that my mother was becoming more and more tired and was losing weight. I could see it in her face.

"Mom, can you do me a favor?"

"Yes Tim, what is it?"

"I am worried about you. Will you make an appointment with a doctor? I will feel better if you do."

"Okay, man of the house. I will call today for a physical. Will that make you happy?" I hugged her and told her yes. I felt a lot better.

I left my mom in the kitchen and was very worried about her. She just didn't look right. I could see that she was still losing, weight and didn't have the energy that she usually had. When I asked her how she'd made out with the doctor, she said fine and that made me feel better. Time was going by fast. I would be a senior soon. My mother was pleased; I could see it in her eyes. She was always talking about my graduating from high school.

In the fall after school had begun again, as we were sitting at the table together one evening, my mother said, "Tim, I want you to promise me that you will finish high school, no matter what happens." Between work and school, we were not able to spend much time with one another so these moments meant a lot to me.

"Mom, is there anything wrong?"

"No Tim, everything is fine. Maybe I worry too much."

"Don't worry. I promised you a long time ago that I would. Have you forgotten already?"

"I guess I have"

We finished supper then I cleaned the table and did the dishes. My mother went to watch TV. When I heard the clock strike eight, I said, "Well, it's that time again. I have to go to work." I kissed my mother and left for the docks.

As I was walking toward the docks, I began to think about my mother and what she had said about high school. Something was not right. I was worried about what she had said.

"Hey kid! You want a ride"?

"Yes, Sir," I replied as I opened the door to the police cruiser and got in.

"Tim, are you feeling okay? You look as if something is bothering you."

"No, Bill, everything is fine. By the way, where is Chuck tonight?"

"He called in sick. I guess he wanted to spend some time with his wife."

I just smiled.

"Pretty smart, aren't you kid?"

When we arrived at the docks, I got out and thanked Bill for the ride, saying "See you later."

"Sure thing, kid. Catch you later."

I was halfway through my shift when I saw the cruiser coming. I watched as Bill got out and walked toward me.

"Hi Bill, you're early, aren't you?" I asked puzzled.

He didn't answer me. This isn't like Bill, I thought. "Is everything all right?" I asked. But he still didn't answer; that made me uneasy. I heard a noise and saw Captain John coming over to me. Now, I am really worried, I said to myself.

"Tim, we have some bad news for you. It's about your mother."

"What are you talking about?"

"I just left the hospital. It's about your mother."

Before he could say anything else, I asked Bill if she was all right.

"Tim, I'm really sorry but your mother died earlier tonight. That's why we are here. One of your neighbors called the station. She thought there was something wrong because your mother never leaves the lights on this late. So, I went over to check the house. I rang the doorbell but there was no answer. Then I tried the front door and it was unlocked. When I called for your mother, there was no response. I checked the house and found her lying on the floor. I called for the ambulance right away, but she was already gone so I had them take her to the hospital. I wish I didn't have to tell you this.

"Tim, get in the cruiser and I will take you to her. Captain, you can come with us?"

Captain John sat in the back seat with me. No one spoke as we drove to the hospital. Once inside they showed me to my mother's room. I entered the room and could see my mother lying on the bed. I just stood there looking at her. She was so still. I felt like grabbing her and shaking her. I wanted her to wake up.

"Bill, what's going to happen to Tim? He has no one now that his mother is gone?" Captain John asked.

"I don't know. I guess he will have to go to the Detention Center and then to a foster home."

"That sucks! You know it, don't you?"

"I know, but what can I do? I can't keep him. They wouldn't allow it."

"What about me? Do you think they would let him stay with me?"

"I don't think they will allow that either. You're single, just like me. The people at Child Services frown on that kind of thing."

"We'll see about that. Tim is not going to the Detention Center; I promise you that."

As I stood next to the bed holding my mother's hand, I just kept staring at her. I wanted to cry but felt numb. I couldn't believe that she was gone.

"Tim, my name is Doctor Thompson. Are you all right?" I heard someone say, startling me as I stood next to the bed.

"Yes Sir. Can you tell me what happened? I knew she was tired lately, but thought she was getting better. When she quit her second job, everything seemed to be getting better."

"Tim, your mother had a tumor on the brain. That's what killed her. She was scheduled for a series of x-rays next week. I guess the tumor was too far along. I'm really sorry. I wish I could say something else to you. Tim, listen to me. I want you to cry and let it out. That will help you."

"I'm okay, Doctor. Can I stay for a few more minutes?"

"Sure, go ahead—take your time."

"Bill, Tim's taking it hard," Captain John said very concerned.

"I know. We have to get him out of here."

"Tim, we have to leave now. You can't stay here," Captain John said to me quietly.

"Tim, I have to take you to the station. You can't be alone. Captain John wants you to stay with him for now. I don't know if they will allow it because you are a minor and the law is very clear in situations like this. I am going to talk to my supervisor. Maybe he will let you to stay with the Captain. Just remember, however, he could say no."

"Okay Bill, whatever will be will be," I answered as I leaned over my mother and kissed her goodbye.

When we got to the station, I sat down on a wooden bench next to the wall. I watched Bill and Captain John walk to the Captain's office. Bill knocked on the door and they both went in.

"Captain," Bill said, "I have a problem. Tim's with me. His mother died tonight and Captain John wants to take Tim home with him."

"Bill, you're putting me in a tough spot. Child Services will be bullshit."

"We know. But the kid shouldn't go to the Detention Center. He's a good kid and doesn't deserve to end up there. Can't you do something? The kid will be better off with Captain John for now."

"Let me make a call."

"Thanks Captain."

Captain Johnson picked up the phone to make the call as Bill and Captain John left the office.

"Hello Ann, this is Captain Johnson. I have a slight problem and need your help."

"What's wrong, Captain?"

"I have a young man here. His mother died tonight. He's sixteen and has no family. I have his boss here and he wants to keep the kid with him. The kid works on the docks with him and he's no troublemaker. If any kid needs a break, it's Tim. Officer Bill wants Tim to go with Captain John also. Nobody wants to see him go to the Detention Center. This is not a run-of-the-mill kid; he goes to high school and is at the top of his class. What can you do for us?"

"Captain, you're putting me in difficult position. You know the law."

"I know! But believe me, this is not your usual kid. Let's bend the rules a little this time. The kid needs a break."

"Okay, but if I go down, so will you. He can go with Captain John."

I saw the Captain beckon to us through his office window. As we went into his office, I began to get a little nervous.

"John, my neck is sticking way out. If anything happens to Tim, a lot of guys will swing. Tim, you can stay with Captain John tonight, but I don't know how long you'll be able to stay there. Ann from Child Services will be around to see you. Until then, you can stay with Captain John."

"Thank you, Sir."

Captain John and I went to his house. About three days later, as we were having breakfast, we heard a knock at the door. Captain John answered the door. A lady was standing there.

"My name is Ann Reynolds. I am from Child Services."

"Come in, Ann. Would you like some coffee? Tim and I were just having breakfast?"

"Yes, I'll have some coffee," Ann replied.

"Please sit down and I'll get it."

"You must be Tim. I've heard a lot about you," Ann said turning to me.

"Mrs. Reynolds, can I ask you something?"

"Sure Tim, go ahead. Ask me anything."

"I will be seventeen in a few weeks. I work and I have some money. I would like to stay at my mother's house. I can support myself. My mother raised me to be responsible. I can make out by myself."

"Tim, I have checked on you and what you say is very true. However, there is just one problem. You're a minor in the eyes of the law. The law says I have to place you in a foster home. When you turn eighteen, you can be on your own. I wish I could do it for you, but I have to follow the law. I have no choice."

"Ann, what if he stays here with me?" Captain John asked as he brought her some coffee.

"Captain, I wish he could. There is a problem with that also. You're a single man and that alone disqualifies you. I will let him stay here until I find him a suitable home. But first, I will have to talk to my boss about Tim staying here with you. He might not agree with it. A lot of people are sticking their necks out already."

"Thanks Ann. We appreciate it."

We finished breakfast and Ann left to go back to her office.

The day of my mother's funeral came; everybody was there. It was a beautiful ceremony. My mother looked nice. I knew she would be happy. We had a lot more friends than I'd thought. After the funeral we went to Captain John's house. Right after we arrived at the house there was a knock on the door. It was Mrs. Reynolds.

"Tim, I have found a nice home for you. Their name is Mr. and Mrs. Baker. They have no children. They are anxious to meet you. I'm sure you will like them. I promise you, Tim, you're life will not change. I told them you have a job and you go to school. Remember, if you ever need me, just pick up the telephone and give me a call. I will be coming by from time to time to check on you."

"Mrs. Reynolds, thanks for everything. I guess, Captain, this means I will have to go now. I will make sure I get to work on time."

"Tim, don't worry. Your job will be waiting for you. Take a couple of days off to get acquainted with your new home."

Ann and I drove to the Bakers. Ann introduced us and they seemed to be nice people.

"Tim, I want you to know how sorry we are about your mother. We will do everything we can for you. I hope we will be more than foster parents to you. If there is anything you need, just ask. Okay?" Mr. Baker said.

"Thank you. I will try not to be a bother to you."

"You won't be a bother to us. We want you here. Follow me and I will show you your room," Mrs. Baker said and turned to leave the room.

"That would be nice." I turned around and thanked Ann for all of her help.

"You're welcome, Tim. Keep in touch with me. As I said before I will be coming by to check on how you are doing."

I gave her a hug. She looked at me and said, "Tim, I have been in this business for fifteen years and you are the first youngster that has ever hugged me. Thank you, so much."

I saw Ann's eyes start to fill with tears as she turned around and left the house. I was alone with the Bakers.

"Tim, that was a nice thing you did. I think my husband and I will love having you here."

"Follow me and I will show you your room." We went upstairs and she said, "This is where you will be staying. I hope you will like it. When you get settled in, come downstairs and we can have lunch and talk."

"Thank you, Mrs. Baker. I would enjoy that." I watched her as she left the room. I felt totally alone. I kept thinking of my mother. Then I thought that she would probably like the Bakers.

"Honey, I think Tim is going to work out. He's so polite. His mother did a fine job with him," Mrs. Baker said to her husband when she went downstairs.

"Dear, he appears that way to me too. I was scared at first, but now I feel better about Tim and his being here. I think he will be good for both of us."

The Bakers and I had had several talks together. It was nice. They were very nice people. They told me how their son had died and what it had done to them. I felt sorry for them. I think they looked upon me as a son. I was glad. I was comfortable with them.

When I went back to work it felt good. Ann was right—my life didn't change. Everything was going well. I was a senior and at the top of my class. I had made a promise to my mother and was determined to keep it. I knew my mother would be very proud. Even though she wasn't with me, I felt her presence every minute of the day.

One night when I went to work, I climbed aboard and asked Captain John how things were going.

"Things are getting bad, Tim. It's getting harder to make a living. The fish are scarce and the regulations are killing us. We're all feeling the crunch."

"I know. I have heard the fishermen talking about it. They are all hurting. It's worrying me also."

"Tim, talking about the future. What are your plans? You have to start thinking about it."

"I have been giving it some thought. I know you can't keep me on so I was thinking about trying to get a job at one of the fish processing plants. That way I can save more money for college."

"That's a good idea. Why don't you try Ocean Fisheries. The owner seems to be a nice guy. Most of the men he hires stay with him. That says something about him."

"I think I will take a walk over there. Thanks Captain."

I walked over to the fish house, which was just a few blocks from the docks. I went up to the door that said "Office" and knocked. Hearing someone say "come in," I went inside. I looked around and saw a girl sitting behind the desk. I'd seen her around school. She was always quiet and seemed to be a nice girl.

"May I help you, Tim?"

"How do you know my name?" I asked, surprised.

"We go to the same school. I've seen you walking around the school. What can I do for you?"

"I would like to apply for a job. May I fill out an application?"

"I'll get you one. You can fill it out at the desk over there."

I watched her walk to the file cabinet in the corner of the room and retrieve an application.

"Fill this out and I will have Tom talk to you."

The door opened and a tall, distinguished-looking man came in, saying, "That's okay, Jill. I was waiting for him to come by. Tim, follow me."

"Have a seat," he said when we reached his desk.

"How did you know I was coming?"

He laughed and answered, "I spend a lot of time on the docks. There is no one down there I'm not aware of. I received a call about you coming to see me about a job. I have been watching you for some time. I'm sorry about your mother, Tim. I knew her and she was a nice lady.

"Why do you want to work in a fish house?"

"I love the docks and I want to work down here until I finish college. That's why I am looking for another job. I want to make some money for college."

"Okay Tim, you're hired. I will introduce to my daughter Jill. That's her sitting at the desk. You know, the cute one."

"That's for sure!" I replied. I watched him smile.

"You go to the same school, I believe?"

"Yes Sir. I have seen her there."

"Come with me, Tim. Jill, Tim is going to be working with us. Fill out the necessary papers; he doesn't need an application. Tomorrow is Saturday. I'll see you at 6:00 A.M."

"Thank you, Sir." As he walked away, he turned and asked me if I had any rubber gear.

"Yes, Sir."

"Okay, fill out the papers and get out of here. Unless you two have something to talk about."

Neither one of us said anything, but we both smiled. Jill helped me fill out the papers. After the papers were finished I said goodbye.

"Goodbye Tim, I'll see you tomorrow morning. Stop here first so I can tell you where you're going to work."

"Thanks Jill. I'll see you tomorrow."

I closed the door behind me as I left. I felt good about going to work in the fish house.

"Jill, you know Tim from school, don't you?"

"Yes Dad. He is a nice boy. I know he was very close to his mother. He went to work to help her out. Everybody seems to like him even though he keeps to himself and studies all the time. I understand his marks are the highest in the school. He takes school very seriously. I think he made a promise to his mother he would get high marks.

"I've seen him in the back seat of the police car several times. He's very friendly with the police. They give him a ride home every morning. Like I said, he's a nice boy."

"I think I like him. Team him with Mr. Chin."

"That's a good idea, Dad. Mr. Chin and Tim will be a good team."

"You like him, don't you honey?"

"Yes, I do. We have never really spoken to each other before today."

I arrived at work at 5:30 A.M. Tom was waiting for me. I punched in and he told me to follow him. We were walking toward the freezers and I noticed an oriental gentleman standing there.

"Mr. Chin, this is Tim. He is going to be working with you. Show him the ropes."

Mr. Chin and I shook hands.

"Follow me, Tim. I will show you what to do."

"Yes Sir." We worked together all morning. He was a nice guy, very quiet. He never raised his voice. It was like he wasn't there. At lunchtime, we punched out and went outside to have lunch.

"Mr. Chin, may I join you?"

"Yes, Tim. Please, sit down next to me if you like."

After lunch, we punched in and went back to work. It wasn't long before it was time to go home.

As we were punching out, Mr. Chin said, "It was nice working with you."

"Thank you for everything, Mr. Chin. I'll see you tomorrow."

While walking home, I thought about Mr. Chin. He was a strange man. At least he seemed that way to me. Of course, I had never met an oriental man before. Maybe, I was the strange one. All I knew was he was a nice man.

We had been working together for a few weeks, when I noticed that none of the other guys ever bothered with him except to pick on him. But, he never said anything back. He just took their insults. It bothered me to see them pick on him.

One day as we were sitting on the pier having lunch, Big Al started to give Mr. Chin a hard time. I got mad and yelled for Al to cut it out.

Al turned toward me and grabbed me by the shirt. I tried to break his grip, but couldn't. He was too strong.

"Look kid! I do what I want. What are you a gook lover?" he yelled as he pushed me down and walked away. I yelled after him, "He's a man just like you." Al just laughed and kept walking away.

"Mr. Chin, can you tell me something?"

"Yes Tim, what is it?"

"Why do you take all those insults from Al and the others?"

"Tim, words never hurt anyone. So why get upset about them? Let me tell you something. He's the only one making a fool out of himself by being that way. The other men laugh because they don't know any better. If I let him get to me, I would have to fight him. And if I did that, I could get hurt. Then again, maybe he would be the one to get hurt. No one gains anything by fighting. A bigger man will walk away. Do you understand?"

"I see what you mean, Mr. Chin. Thank you."

When we were finished for the day and were walking out together, I said goodbye and Mr. Chin asked, "Tim, would you like to have supper with me? It's been a long time since I've asked someone over for supper."

"Thank you, Mr. Chin, I would like that very much."

"Good. Do you know where I live?" I nodded. "Supper will be at seven."

As we approached the door, I saw Jill. She really looked nice. "Hi Jill, how have you been?"

"Fine Tim. How about you?"

"Fine. Have a good evening. I'll see you tomorrow."

"Goodnight Tim, and goodnight to you, Mr. Chin."

"Goodnight Jill. I will see you in the morning."

As we walked along, Mr. Chin never said a word. But it didn't bother me anymore; it was just the way he was. I had become used to his ways.

I made sure that I arrived early for supper. Mr. Chin was a very punctual man. I rang his doorbell at six forty-five. Mr. Chin opened the door and said, "Good evening, Tim. Please come in. Leave your shoes on the rack, you won't need them."

I walked with him into the parlor. I was very surprised at what I saw. His home was beautiful. It was a simple home and didn't have very much furniture, but that is what made it comfortable. It wasn't cluttered and everything was in the right place.

Mr. Chin brought two bowls into the dining room and placed them on the table. We finished the soup then he took the bowls away and placed two plates on the table. I looked at what was on them—fish and rice covered with vegetables.

"Tim, go ahead and eat. I am sure that you will like it."

When we finished eating, I was full. "That was delicious, Mr. Chin. I really liked it."

"Thank you. I am glad you enjoyed it. Would you care for some tea?"

"I don't know, Sir. I have never had tea."

"Good, then you shall have some. I am sure you will like it. Tea is better for you anyway."

As I helped Mr. Chin with the dishes, I said, "Mr. Chin, you have a beautiful home. I appreciate you allowing me to come and spend the evening."

"Thank you, Tim. You can visit anytime."

I looked at my watch. It was getting late and I knew I had to get home so I thanked him again and left.

Mr. Chin and I became very close friends. But the longer I knew him, the more mysterious he became. One night while having supper with him, my curiosity got the better of me. I had seen all of his house but one room. So, I asked, "Mr. Chin, I have a question to ask you."

"Yes Tim, what is it?"

"I was wondering, what was in that room? I have been curious about it for quite some time. I know it is none of my business and you don't have to tell me."

"Come with me."

He opened the door. Once inside, I looked around. I noticed the floors were highly varnished. There were all kinds of exotic weapons hanging on the walls.

"Come Tim, I will show you around," he said as he led me around the room.

"What do you do here, Mr. Chin?"

"I am Chinese. In my country we study the martial arts. I practice here every night."

"I don't understand. What are the martial arts?"

"The martial arts are a form of self-defense. It is also very dangerous. You can hurt or even kill someone if you make a mistake. I find it very relaxing. It takes a lot of concentration and dedication. I will show you what I mean."

I watched him move. It looked like some kind of dance to me. Then he explained what he was doing.

"Tim, each one of these moves can hurt someone. I had to learn to defend myself when I was a child. My country was at war with Japan. My family was killed by the Japanese, and I was forced to live in the mountains, or I would have been killed. I lived with a religious group of men in a monastery, and they taught me. I had to learn to survive during those times. What they taught me has saved my life many times."

"Mr. Chin, can you teach me?"

"Why do you want to learn?"

"I really don't know. When I was watching you, something came over me. I can't explain it. It felt weird."

"Karate is something you learn to protect yourself. It is not to be used just to hurt someone. If I teach you, I will expect you to use it wisely. If you misuse what I teach you, I will be very upset. I will also stop your training. Do you understand?"

"I never even thought about hurting people. Something tells me I should learn, but I don't know why. I just have a funny feeling. The feeling I get when I feel my mother's presence with me."

"I know that feeling too. I felt it many years ago when my family was killed. I will teach you. I will expect you here every night. It will be a lot of hard work and dedication on your part. Do you understand?"

"Yes Sir."

"Tim, I have a question to ask you?"

"What's that?"

"When was the last time you went out and had some fun? That is, some fun with someone your own age. What I mean is fun with a young girl your age. A date—to be precise."

"I guess I've never had the time."

"I don't think you should keep on working like you do. Between school and working, you have no life. Tim, I know this is none of my business but I had to ask," Mr. Chin said with a look of concern.

"You know Jill likes you and so does her Dad. Why don't you ask her out? I think she is waiting for you to ask her."

"Mr. Chin. Are you always right?"

"No Tim, not always, just most of the time. Besides, I am not stupid."

Mr. Chin was right. I asked Jill if she would like to go out with me. I smiled when she replied, "It's about time. I was getting ready to ask you out." I'd no sooner asked her than her father came up to us.

"What's going on, Tim?"

"Sir, I was just asking your daughter if she would like to go out with me this evening. Do you have any objections?"

"I think Jill can make up her own mind. I usually don't allow her to go out with the guys here. But, you are an exception. I think it is a good idea."

I picked Jill up at her house. I was scared. I'd never met her mother. Her mother greeted me at the door.

"You must be Tim. I have heard so much about you. Please come in. Jill is waiting."

I wiped my feet and saw Jill standing in the parlor. She was beautiful. "Hi Jill, are you ready?"

"Yes."

I watched Jill as she kissed her mother and father goodbye.

"I'll have Jill back early, Sir."

"Don't worry. Have a good time."

Jill and I saw a lot of each other, and I became very close to her. We had a lot of fun. I was very busy between work, school, and karate lessons. I had my hands full. I learned the martial arts quickly and became quite skilled. Mr. Chin was a good teacher. His style of karate was very intense. I learned what he meant when he'd said you could hurt someone very seriously if you weren't careful. I never knew why he was teaching me this particular style of karate. I wanted to ask him, but I figured he had his reasons.

Mr. Chin always gave me the impression that he could feel the future. He was really remarkable.

My life was full, but I felt there was something missing. I just couldn't figure it out. I was busy all of the time. I thought of my mother and remembered her telling me to make something of myself. I guess that is why I was worried. Where was I going? What was I going to do?

As graduation approached, I knew my mother would be proud. I had the highest marks in my class. Graduation day arrived. I sat with all of my friends. The ceremonies started and Mr. Granville, the principal, began to speak.

"Ladies and gentlemen, Class of 1960. Before we start, I would like to say something about a very special young man sitting before you today. Mr. Tim Collins would you please step forward."

Completely shocked, I stood up, wondering, What is Mr. Granville going to say?

"Ladies and gentlemen, it gives me great pleasure ... no, I am honored to speak to you about this young man. I will say this first. Never in the history of this school have we ever been this excited about one of our students. We have had a lot of students leave this school with honor, but we have never had one quite like Tim.

"Tim lost his mother last year. He made a promise to her that he would graduate with high marks. He not only made those high grades, he went further. Tim, at the age of seventeen, is graduating with the highest marks in the history of this school. Tim went to a foster home when his mother died. He has been living with Mr. and Mrs. Baker. Will you please stand up. Ladies and gentlemen, this is Mr. and Mrs. Baker. All I have to say to you is this: You have been very kind to Tim and helped him after the tragic death of his mother. I'm sure Tim realizes this. It must be hard to take a young man Tim's age into your home. Most children who go to a foster home end up in trouble. The love you have given him shows. You were fortunate in one way, Tim's mother did a great job. I want to thank you and Tim's mother because I think she is here with us today.

"What Tim is today is what you and she made of him. Tim went to work after school so he could help his mother. This is the kind of young man he is. What he has achieved is unbelievable. He went to school, worked, and has been dating a special young lady, who also is graduating here today. With all that, he has also managed to study karate diligently. Mr. Chin has been a great roll model for this young man. I have no idea how Tim was able to accomplish what he has all this time.

"I have had a steady stream of students in my office, asking me if I would do something for Tim. I am proud to be the one to give this gift to Tim from his classmates. I repeat this is the first time in the history of this school that something like this has taken place.

"Tim, I want you to accept this plaque with the gratitude from everyone here. Tim, the podium is yours."

I stood before the podium reading the plaque. I could feel my eyes filling. I knew my mother would be very proud. I could feel her presence. I heard someone yell, "Say something, Tim!"

I just stood there, unable to speak. Then I felt an arm around me. It was Mr. Granville, who said "Tim, say something."

I leaned toward the mike, but didn't know what to say. Looking into the audience, I took a deep breath and began, "Ladies, gentlemen, and fellow classmates. I really don't know what to say. I want to thank everyone here. I would like to thank my foster parents. I love you. To all my friends, thank you. I just want my fellow classmates to know that without you I never would have made it. I love all of you. I especially want to thank my mother. I miss her and love her deeply. She gave me the will and the courage to live life fully. She was wonderful. I know if she were here, she would be proud. In my heart, I know she is here. I accept this in her honor. I love this school and everyone in it. Thank you very much."

After the ceremony was over, I walked over to my foster parents. They were standing with all of my friends. We all hugged each other. Everyone was crying. I heard Bill tell Chuck, "Tim is one special kid. His mother would be proud of him today."

Jill and her father and mother came over. I hugged and kissed her. She had tears in her eyes.

"Tim, I am so proud of you."

I hugged Jill's mother and father and said, "I just want to tell you something. I appreciate everything you have done for me."

"Tim, I am just happy you chose my daughter and us to be your friends. If there is anything we can do, just ask. My wife and I mean it."

Bill and Chuck were standing next to me, and Bill said, "Well Tim, what are your plans now? I hope you're going to college. That's what your mother wanted."

"I'm not sure. I plan on working a little longer. College is expensive. I have some money saved but not enough."

"Tim, you don't have to worry. God knows you have enough scholarships available to you. Plus, we are all ready and willing to help you out," Chuck said.

"I know that, but I think I would like to do it alone. I appreciate the offer . . . I'll have to think about it."

I decided not to try to go to college right away and continued to work for a couple of years. I became an expert in karate. The fishing industry was at an all-time low so I worked at the fish house. I had to give up watching the boats because Captain John was having it rough.

One day, as I was talking to Captain John, I told him I was thinking of joining the Navy. I told him that I could save money while in the Navy and they would help me out with college expenses.

"Tim, what about Jill?"

"Jill is in college. She will be graduating in a couple of years. I have talked to her about joining the Navy. She wants me to do what is best for me. If I enlist in the Navy, I can do part of my college studies there. Then when I get out we can get married."

"Well Tim, you know what is best."

"I was going to talk to Mr. Chin about it. He is a very wise man and I respect him a lot."

"You're right about that."

I went to see Mr. Chin and as we sat in his parlor, I could see that he was wondering what was on my mind. I was never able to fool him.

"Okay Tim, what's bothering you?"

"Mr. Chin, I have decided to join the Navy. I came here to get your opinion."

"You do realize there is a war going on over there. Vietnam is going to be a hotspot. You could get killed. The horrors of war are something that no man should see or go through. But I will say this, I have trained you and I know that you can handle anything that comes your way. You are more prepared than most kids going into the Armed Forces.

"Tim, I will now tell the truth. The training you have received is far superior to what you get in the Navy. I always knew this day would come. I have trained you to kill. And what's even more important, I have trained you to survive under any conditions. I am certain you will be coming back to us."

"I think I will go home now and give this some more thought. Mr. Chin, I will always love and respect you."

"Thank you, Tim. Now go home and think. I know you will make the right decision."

It didn't take me long to make up my mind. A week later I was in the Navy recruiter's office. I signed up and requested carrier duty. I had watched every movie Hollywood had ever made about carriers.

The day came for me to leave. As I was saying goodbye to everyone, Mr. Chin came over and said, "Tim, remember what I taught you. If you do, you will be fine. I want you to have this. Do not open it now. Hide it and keep it with you until the time comes to use it. Never let it out of your sight."

I felt an uneasiness come over me. Mr. Chin knew something but wasn't telling me. He was getting mysterious again—I hated that. I hugged everybody, said my good-byes, and boarded the plane.

The engines started and we were moving. I looked at the package Mr. Chin had given and decided to open it. I removed the cover. It was the knife that Mr. Chin had had during the Second World War. I just sat there staring at it — I knew what it meant to him.

"Excuse me, Sir."

"Yes, Miss."

"You are not supposed to bring something like that on board the plane. It is against the rules."

"I'm sorry. I just joined the Navy and this knife was given to me by a very special person. I will make sure no one else sees it if it's okay with you? I'll have some coffee please?"

"I'll be right back."

When the stewardess came back with the coffee, she asked me if I was going to boot camp at Great Lakes.

"Yes. I will be there for a few months."

"Good luck to you."

When the plane landed I picked up my gear and walked toward the exit.

"Good luck, sailor."

"Thank you, Miss. Good luck to you."

"My brother went to boot camp there. If they see that knife, they might just take it from you. I would advise you to keep it well hidden."

"Thanks again, Miss."

As I walked toward the airport exit, I noticed a bus with a sailor standing next to it. There were quite a few men standing around. I approached the sailor and asked, "Excuse me, Sir. Is this the bus picking up the men going to boot camp?"

"If you're in the Navy it is? Get aboard and grab a seat. By the way, you don't have to call me Sir."

"Thank you." I entered the bus and sat down. I overheard some of the other guys talking. "Get a load of that kid. I wonder if he is old enough to be in the Navy?" I just smiled. I knew I was small and guessed this was the start of a lot of jokes about my size. We reached the base in about one hour. The bus stopped at the main gate, and a Marine came on board and checked everyone. Then we drove another half-hour before the bus stopped in front of a drab, gray building. I noticed a large sailor standing there, waiting for us. We were told to get off the bus and line up.

"Gentlemen, I want you to line up in two rows. Tall men toward the right, shorter men at the left." Once we were standing in line, he called out our names. When he called mine, he just stood there looking at me. He walked toward me and said, "My God, what the hell do we have here? How old are you, Son?"

"Nineteen, Sir."

"Let's see, nineteen years old. Have you got a note from your mother?"

He pissed me off. I replied, "No Sir, my mother is dead." He stood there for a minute without saying anything.

"Okay men, I want everyone to go into the barracks and stow their gear on a bunk. Now move!"

"Tim Collins, wait here a second."

"Yes Sir."

"You don't have to call me Sir. I just want to apologize for the note business. I was just making a joke."

"That's okay. I'm small and have been racked on in the past. I will tell you this, I will hold my own with the rest of the men."

"We'll see about that. Now stow your gear."

It wasn't long before he came into the barracks.

"Okay you guys. My name is Chief Michaels. From now on, when I enter the barracks, you better jump up and stand at attention. If you don't, your ass will be mine. You will address me has Chief or Chief Michaels. I don't want anyone to call me Sir. When I speak, your reply better be 'Yes' or 'No Chief.' Do you understand?"

Everyone yelled, "Yes Chief."

"That's good. The only thing wrong with that is I couldn't hear you. Now try it again."

"Yes Chief!!"

"That's better. From this day on, you will do nothing except what I tell you. If you screw up, I'll eat you alive. Believe me you will know what I mean! Any questions?"

"No Chief!"

"One other thing men. You are in the U.S. Navy. You will act like sailors. I expect you to live up to the standards of the Navy. We are the greatest navy in the world. That means you will be also. Do you understand?"

"Yes Chief!"

"I expect the barracks to be spotless. I will never tell you when there will be a surprise inspection. Every Friday, I will have an inspection. My surprise inspection, you won't know about, that is, until it happens. God help you if I find any dirt. This little toothbrush will be my gift to you. It is what you will end up using to clean the barracks. It will be hanging over there. It better not disappear. Do you understand!"

"Yes Chief!"

"Line up outside, men. We're going to get you your uniforms. Now move out!"

We all scrambled for the door. It was crazy. Once outside we lined up in four rows. We marched for about fifteen minutes then stopped at another gray building. Everything was painted gray. The building was located next to a large field where I could see everyone marching.

The Chief yelled, "Sailors, I want you to look at those men. They are sailors! They have all passed boot camp. You will pass boot camp! If you don't, you will be civilians. Do you understand?"

"Yes Chief!"

We entered the building in single file and were given sheets, blankets, and uniforms. When we finished, we marched back to the barracks."

"Now sailors, you will take off those civilian clothes. I want all personal items put in the box at your feet. They will be shipped home. The only things I want to see are your shaving cream and soap. If it isn't Government Issue, get rid of it. You will be shown how to store your gear. If I find it stowed wrong, your ass will be mine. Do you understand?"

"Yes Chief!"

"This gentleman is Petty Officer First Class Winslow. He will be you instructor. He will show you what we expect of you. Jack, they are all yours. I will be back to take them to chow."

Petty Officer Winslow yelled, "Attention on Deck!" We snapped to attention. The Chief left the barracks.

Jack showed us how to make our bunks and stow our gear. It was exactly two hours later when the Chief arrived at the barracks. He checked our bunks and lockers.

"I see Jack has shown you how to do things the Navy way. Make sure it stays looking like this. I expect it to look like this every time I come into the barracks. Now, fall out; it's time for chow. The Navy has the best chow in the world. It's better than what your dear mother used to cook for you."

The next day we got up before dawn. We had ten minutes to wash and shave, get dressed, make our beds, and get outside before the Chief got there. We knew he meant business.

After we lined up outside, Jack put us through our morning calisthenics then we marched to chow. When that was finished, we had our hair cut. We were marched another fifteen minutes then had our medical examinations. They took hours. When we finally finished, we were marched to chow again.

The following day we started classes. Every time we moved from one building to another we marched.

At night after we were in the barracks, I would go outside and practice karate. I usually tried to practice when no one was around.

One night I was practicing and I heard a noise. I turned around and saw some of the guys watching me.

"Tim, what the hell are you doing?"

"Nothing much, just exercising. This is how I pass the time." They laughed and yelled, "Don't you get enough exercise?" I just smiled. They left and I continued my routine.

About a half-hour passed when I heard some footsteps in the distance. When I turned around, I saw the Chief coming toward me.

"Sailor, what the hell are you doing?"

"I am exercising, Chief."

"I know that! Just what the hell kind of exercising are you doing? I've never seen anything like it."

"It's hard to explain, Sir. I was taught how by a good friend back home."

"I suppose by the same man that gave you the knife you have hidden."

"Yes Sir. When I joined the Navy, he gave it to me. He told me to keep it with me. He figured that maybe someday it would save my life."

"You do know that having that knife is against regulations."

"Sir, that knife was given to me by a very close friend; he carried it during the Second World War. It means a lot to me. I hope I can keep it. No one else knows about it. I have no plans to show it to anyone. Mr. Chin was a great war hero during the Second World War. It means a lot to me, Chief."

"Tim, keep it hidden. If I see you carrying it, I will confiscate it. Do you understand?"

"Yes Sir."

"Now, tell me just what you are doing? I have been watching you for some time."

"I know. I heard you in the bushes watching me."

"Heard me! How can that be? I was eight hundred feet away from you. There's no way you could have known."

"I have a keen sense of hearing. This exercising helps my concentration. The harder I concentrate, the clearer everything is to me. Mr. Chin taught me this form of martial arts. It saved him numerous times during the war with Japan. It can be very deadly in the wrong hands. I have been doing it for a few years."

"It looks like dancing, Tim."

"Yes Sir, the only thing difference is each move can kill a person. It is a good self-defense exercise."

"I don't understand something. Those bushes are over 800 feet away. It's impossible for you to have heard me; there's no way you heard me from that distance."

"Chief, you have been watching me for a week. The first time was east of the bushes. Then you came closer. When you walk you make a distinct sound. Plus, I can hear the change and the keys you have in your right pocket."

"That's bullshit, Tim. That is impossible."

"Empty your right pocket, Chief. That's all you have in your pocket. Some coins and a key."

I watched him empty his pocket. He looked at the coins and the key.

"Tim, it's time to go inside."

"Yes Chief, I was finished anyway. Goodnight."

"Goodnight."

After my conversation with my C.O., I noticed that he continued watching me. He would change positions every night. One night when I heard him in the woods about 800 feet away, I decided to sneak up on him. I placed my jacket on the dumpster, walked around the barracks, and came up behind the Chief. He was looking for me. He stood up and turned, and there I was.

Startled, he jumped and yelled.

I said, "Good evening."

"Tim, you scared the shit out of me. Where the hell did you come from?"

"Over there, where my jacket is hanging. I knew you didn't believe me so I decided to prove it to you."

"I believe you now. You are amazing. Mr. Chin must have been some teacher."

"Yes Chief, he was."

"What is his full name?"

"His name is Lee Chin."

"Goodnight Tim, I guess I will have a drink on this one."

That kid Tim is very special—mysterious and dangerous for a kid his age, the Chief thought as he walked away toward the Officers Club. He went inside and ordered a beer. While he was staring down at his beer, he heard a voice say, "Hi Chief, what the hell are you thinking about?" He looked up.

"Oh, it's you Sargent. Pull up a seat."

"I was just thinking about one of my men. He's something else. I can't figure him out. The kid is like Houdini. He hears me when I can barely see him."

"Whoa, Chief. I think you've had enough to drink."

"It's true. He hears me walking 800 feet away."

"That's impossible!"

"I thought so too until he proved it to me. Tell me something, Sargent. What routes do your men take when they are coming back from guard duty?"

"Why?"

"I want you to do something for me."

"Name it, Chief."

"I want you to take the two biggest men you have and when they are coming back to the barracks, I want them to try to disarm him.

"The kid exercises every night. I can't even sneak up on him. He knows whenever I am watching him. He is only 5'4" tall. He told me he studied karate from some oriental guy. I think I would like to test him. Can you arrange it? He also told me what he'd learned is the highest form of self-defense that anyone can learn."

"That's hard to believe. I have been in the Marines for years. I know hand-to-hand combat. From what you say, I would like to see this amazing sailor in action. A kid like that can get into some serious trouble with that kind of training."

"That's just it. He's quiet and never gets in trouble. He hasn't had an argument with anyone from his company. Even though they always pick on him, he never gets mad. He's incredibly even-tempered."

"What do you want me to do?"

"Like I said. I want you to get your two biggest Marines to disarm him tomorrow. I will have him guarding the ammo dump."

"I can do that. What if he gets hurt?"

"I don't think your men will get close to him, let alone take his rifle."

"Okay, if that's what you want, I'll send them tomorrow night."

"Remember, tell your men 'no holds barred,' and to be exceptionally quiet. The kid seems to have a sixth sense. This test will tell me what my next step should be. He worries me; nothing makes him mad. He's small and when I first saw him, I thought the Navy had screwed up."

"Don't tell me what to do, Chief. I will handle it. By the way, is this the midget my men talk about?"

"That's probably him. Remember, the bigger the better."

"You know, Chief, my men won't hold back."

"Good that's what I want!" The Chief started to grin as he thought, Those Marines are going to be in for a shock.

"Corporal, send Dick and Al to me."

"Yes, Sargent, right away."

"Gentlemen, I have a mission for you tomorrow night. It seems we have a contest with the Navy."

"What's that Sarge?"

"After you finish drilling tomorrow, I want you two to go to the ammo dump, disarm the sailor on guard duty, and bring me his weapon. No holds barred. Do you understand?"

"Yes Sir!"

"Take him out around eight o'clock."

"No problem, Sir. The Navy is going to be sorry."

"Everything is all set for tonight, Chief. I will meet you at seven forty-five, near the shed."

"No, near the streetlight, west of the shed. He would hear us over there."

"God, you really believe this shit?"

"Yes, you will too after tonight. No holds barred, right?"

"That's right, no holds barred."

"See you tonight, Sargent."

I showed up for guard duty at 7:00 PM. It was so quiet by the ammo dump I could hear a pin drop. I had been on duty for about an hour when I heard the Chief coming.

"Hi Tim, how's it going?"

"Pretty quiet, Sir."

"I'll see you in the morning, Tim."

"Yes Sir." I watched the chief walk away. I only had another hour to go and could hardly wait.

"Chief, is that midget the mystery man?"

"Sure is. When will your men be here?"

"They're coming now, sneaking up on him."

As I was walking around the ammo dump, I heard something close to the ground. It was a long way away. I figured it must have been an animal and kept on walking. I heard the noise again, and it seemed to be coming in my direction. I was almost around the shed when one of them leaped for me. I sidestepped and grabbed his arm. He yelled and fell to the ground screaming. By this time, the other shadow was reaching for me. I grabbed his arm and turned him around. He fell to the ground screaming. They couldn't move. Then I turned and saw the Chief and the Marine Sargent coming toward me.

"Sir, I was attacked by these two Marines. I don't understand; what is going on?"

"Everything is fine, Tim. I was testing you. You are relieved now and can go back to the barracks. Are these men okay?" the Chief asked me.

"No, they are paralyzed right now; they can't move their arms," I explained.

"What do you mean paralyzed? Are they okay?"

"They will be in a second, Chief." I reached down and applied pressure to where I'd hit them. "They're okay.

They'll just be a little sore for awhile. Tell them to rub the area."

"I don't understand," the Sargent said puzzled.

"Take off, Tim," the Chief ordered.

"Well, Sargent. What do you think now?"

"I can't believe it. They are my best men. Who the hell is that kid?"

The two Marines were rubbing their arms as they got up from the ground. "What the hell was that Sargent?"

"You're dismissed. Return to your barracks. I will see you later.

"Chief, I can't believe what I just saw. That shit took out two of my best men. They outweigh him by at least 150 pounds. Where in the hell did you find him?"

"Back east. Looks like I have to do some checking on him. He sure has a real talent. I wouldn't want to mess with him. Thanks Sargent, I'll see you later."

"You bet you will, Chief. I'm not finished with Tim yet."

The next day it was all over the base. Everyone was talking about what had happened. The guys in my company asked me about it. I told them I wasn't sure what had happened. All I knew was it was some kind of test the Chief had thought up.

"Tim, you mean to tell us, you took out those two goons? Those guys are animals. I've seen them before. They think they're something."

"Hey, let's just go for a Coke. I don't want to talk about it."

I walked to the PX with some of the guys from my company. When we entered everyone stared at me. I felt uneasy. I saw my C.O. sitting with the Marine Sargent and walked toward them.

"Excuse me, Chief. I was wondering about last night? Could you explain what happened? I don't understand what kind of test that was?"

"Tim, I can't figure you out. What I did last night was to test you to find out how good you are. You have a special talent and I think the Navy can use it. That is, if you are willing. But before we get into that, I have some thinking to do. I'll get back to you. Now get out of here and have some fun. You deserve it."

"Yes Sir. I guess you're right." I went back to my table.

"You know something, Mike," the Sargent said, "I can't figure that kid out. Just what the hell do you know about him?"

"All I know is he was raised by his mother. His father bailed out on the family when he was a baby. I understand he did some kind of work on the docks back east. His marks were the highest in the history of the high school he attended. He's not a stupid kid. He was loved by everybody when he was home. I guess you could call him the All-American boy.

"I have been watching him ever since he arrived. Everyone in his company likes him. Even with that, he mostly keeps to himself. He very seldom talks. I guess he is just the quiet type."

"He's the All-American boy, all right."

"I also know if you piss him off, he can kill you. Whoever taught him martial arts taught him well. He doesn't push his weight around."

"Thank God! I sure would like to have him in the Marine Corp, especially in combat. He could teach us a thing or two. I know he did last night. Those Marines he took out last night are the jokes of the barracks!"

I ordered Cokes for the guys I was with. I had that uneasy feeling again. Everyone was looking at me. I knew it was because of the Marines and didn't like the way I was feeling. I could sense trouble but hoped I was wrong.

"Tim, I think we have trouble coming toward us."

I looked up and saw Dick and Al walking toward me. I didn't know what to expect.

"Sailor, can we talk to you?"

"Sure, have a seat."

"That's okay, we won't be long. We just want to shake your hand. You're pretty good. I don't know what you used on us, but I can still feel the pain. We just want you to know there are no hard feelings. We were taught a good lesson. A lesson we will never forget. We would like to shake you hand."

"It would be my pleasure." I held out my hand and Dick grabbed it. I watched them walk away. The whole room was quiet.

I was glad we were able to get along. I don't like trouble. I kept thinking about the test. I didn't like it. I looked toward my C.O. and the Sargent. I'd had enough; it was time to leave. When we reached the C.O.'s table, I said goodnight and left. I was quiet on the way back to the barracks. I didn't feel like talking. My friend Jim tried to start a conversation but I didn't answer him. I kept thinking about Al and Dick. I knew what they were going through with the other Marines.

It wasn't easy for me after that. Everyone kept bringing up the test. I kept telling them I didn't want to talk about it. Unfortunately, it wasn't long before another test came my way.

In self-defense class, all the men had to learn judo. Judo was nice and I was quite good at it. But I had studied karate too long and came close to hurting my partners during practice.

"Hey Ted!"

"Yea Mike, what's up?"

"I would like you to try something. See that kid. I want you to take him out. Attack him, no holds barred."

"Are you crazy? He's no match for me. Besides, he is just a skinny kid. I might hurt him."

"Look Ted, I have my reasons."

"Okay, you asked for it."

"Remember, give it all you got."

"I think you're nuts, Chief."

"Gentlemen, I need a volunteer. What no volunteers? You sailor, get up here."

"Yea you—Tim. That is your name isn't it sailor? Judo seems to come easy to you. Why are you holding back?"

"Sir, I just don't want to hurt anyone."

"Well hurt me! If you hesitate I will hurt you. Now it's your choice."

I was watching the guys. I had that uneasy feeling again. "Sir, is this necessary?"

"It sure is. I am going to attack you. If you don't stop me, you're going to be knocked on your ass. It's your choice. Now get ready."

"I'd rather not, Sir."

"What the hell do you mean you'd rather not."

"I don't want to hurt you."

"Hurt me? Get ready. We'll see who is going to get hurt. Are you ready?"

I looked at my C.O. and somehow I knew this was another one of his tests. If this is what he wants, so be it, I thought.

"Sailor, I haven't got all day. Get ready."

"Sir, if this is a test. I want your assistant to join you in taking me out. This way I can put an end to these tests."

"You what!"

"You heard me, Sir."

"Are you sure you want to do this?"

"Yes Sir, I'm positive. It won't take long."

"Kid, you have spunk. Okay Phil, get over here. It's your ass."

They both came after me. I side stepped one of them and grabbed his arm. He started to scream and I let him fall to the ground. The other had me by the neck. I reached up and pressed on his throat, and he fell to the ground choking. That was the end of the test. It had taken all of ten seconds. I watched them squirm on the ground and told them to stay on the ground. If they tried to stand up, they would fall again.

The Chief came over and asked, "Tim, are they all right?"

"They will be as long as they stay still. Tell me something, Chief. Are you finished with these stupid games? I don't like them." I bent over to help the men on the ground. They just stared at me. They were in a tremendous amount of pain. I put pressure on the spot I'd hit and their pain subsided. I told them to rub the area, and they would be all right. It would only take a few seconds and then they could get up.

As I watched them rub the spots that hurt, I became angry and turned to the Chief. "Sir, are you finished with this foolishness. I don't like the way you do things."

"At ease, sailor!"

We went back to the barracks and the Chief had given us the rest of the day off. Everyone was quiet. I guess they knew how I felt.

"Are you two okay?"

"Yea! We're okay, Chief. Where the hell did you get that kid? Who is he? Better yet, what the hell did he do to us? I've never seen anything like it before. Where the hell did he learn that shit?" Phil asked.

"Wait a minute, you sneaky bastard." Ted said, suddenly figuring it out. "Is that the kid that took out those two Marines?"

"Sure is."

"Attention on deck!"

"What the hell is going on here, Chief?"

"Just a little test, Commander."

"What do you mean a little test? I just saw a hundred-and-fifty-pound sailor, kick the shit out of my two instructors. You call that a little test. You mean to tell me that you're going to stand there and tell me nothing. What the hell do you think I am, stupid?"

"No Sir!"

"Now talk, Chief, before you lose a stripe. You better make it good."

"Sir, I can explain. That sailor is in my company. I have been watching him since he was put in my company. He seems to be an expert in self-defense. I have never seen anything like it. Neither has Phil or Ted, Sir."

"I can see that. I just want to know what he is doing. That kid just took out what are supposed to be my best instructors. They never stood a chance. I can't believe it. Chief, I want some answers."

"Sir, the test was my idea. I am responsible for what happened."

"Is that the same kid that took out the Marines?"

"Yes Sir!"

"I suppose that was another one of your tests? I heard about it from Lt. Daly; he is pissed off at his Sargent. He feels you made a fool out of the Marines. I guess we can all agree on that."

"I didn't mean to hurt anybody's feelings. I was just testing the kid. I have been watching him practice for quite some time and knew I could never sneak up on him. He told me he could hear the change in my pocket when I walked."

"So what! Change makes noise when you walk."

"At eight hundred feet, Sir? He even told me about a key in my pocket."

"Have you been drinking, Chief?"

"No Sir, it's true. I've tried all different ways to hide from him. He always knows where I am. He scares me, Commander. All I know is he learned it from a friend."

"The Navy can use that kind of talent. Will he tell us how he does it?"

"I don't know, Sir. Tim is a funny kid. He claims a friend, Mr. Chin, taught him how to defend himself."

"With the way things are going in Vietnam, he can become very useful to us. Who is this Mr. Chin?"

"All I have found out is his name is Lee Chin. He lives in New Bedford, Massachusetts. He was supposed to be some kind of war hero during the Second World War.

"I'll have him checked out. Find out all you can, Chief. But, no more tests. I don't want him killing anyone. That's an order!"

"How can we get him to help us? He's just a boot."

"I know that Chief. I would like to see him stay on after boot camp. I think he can teach us some new tricks. Maybe even save some lives."

"He sure taught me some," Ted added. "I can still feel the pain. I have never seen anything like it. I have been teaching self-defense for years and have no idea what he did. I can't think of any place where you can learn it. I sure would like to find out more about it."

"Okay, for now we will keep this to ourselves."

"Yes Sir."

"I must admit, I sure got a kick out of Lt. Daly when he found out the kid had kicked the shit out of his men. I loved it. Now get out of here, Chief, and take these two with you."

"Yes Sir."

As I was sitting on my bunk, the Chief came in.

"Tim, I want you to come to my office."

"Yes Chief. I want to talk to you too."

"Tim, sit down. We have to talk."

"Sir, can I say something?"

"Yes, go ahead."

"Why are you doing this to me? I don't like it. I don't like being put on exhibition. The guys are staying away from me."

"Tim, you have something that no one around here has ever seen before. That is the reason for the tests. I know you don't like it and I can understand that. I promise you there will be no more tests. I would like to hear more about what you do."

"I'm sorry Chief, but I can't discuss it. I made a promise to someone never to abuse what I'd been taught. And that is what you have forced me to do.

"I will tell you this. Growing up was hard. I made a friend who is Chinese. You know his name. I promised him I would only use what he taught me for self-defense, and I intend to keep that promise. When Mr. Chin was a young boy, the Japanese killed his family. After that he went to a monastery and trained to fight. I don't think he would like it if I told you anymore."

"I promise you, there will be no more exhibitions."

"Thank you, Chief. Someday I will be a part of the fleet. This will follow me and I don't need it."

I left and went back to my barracks. Jim asked me, "What did the Chief want?"

"Just shut up. I don't want to talk about it."

"Tim, I didn't mean anything."

"Let it go, Jim."

"Sure, I won't bring it up again."

I only had a few weeks to go before graduation from boot camp and could hardly wait. I was going to the fleet and that is all I wanted. I just wanted to be on an aircraft carrier.

"Commander, you wanted to see me?"

"Yes, come in, Chief. I've been doing some checking on Tim. All I could find out was the usual bullshit. What is it with this kid?"

"I know, Commander, I checked his files. There wasn't much there. He told me where he learned the martial arts. He learned it from a Mr. Lee Chin. Evidently, his teacher is from China and the Japs had killed his parents. He was raised in China somewhere in a monastery. Tim wouldn't tell me anymore about it. He made a promise to Mr. Chin. I don't think anyone can get him to break his word. All I can say is after seeing Tim perform, Mr. Chin must have been one dangerous man during the war. I can believe it."

"I have talked to the Admiral. He knows about Tim. He laughed about the Marines. I also told him about Ted and Phil. He didn't laugh. He asked me what kind of kid Tim was. I told him all we know is what is in his files. Mr. Chin is a mystery. I told the Admiral what you suggested, and he agrees with you. Tim could be a big help to us, and the Navy. He is willing to keep him on as an instructor when he graduates."

"I think we might have a problem there, Sir."

"What the hell do you mean?"

"He doesn't think it is right to be put on exhibition. He feels that he's breaking his promise to Mr. Chin. Tim seems to be a very sincere young man. I don't think he will change his mind. For that fact, I know he won't. Loyalty means a lot to him."

"That's refreshing. There isn't much of that in this world. Do what you can and let me know how you make out."

"Yes Sir."

The Chief knew he only had a short time to change Tim's mind. Tim's training had been very intense. This Mr. Chin was the problem. I'll have to have someone talk to him, the Chief thought. How can I ask Tim to train people to kill when Mr. Chin has trained him with a strong belief to preserve life? The Chief decided to ask the Admiral to get a hold of Mr. Chin; maybe that was the answer.

I was lying on my bunk and saw the Chief walk toward me. "Tim can I talk to you?"

"Go ahead, Chief."

"I talked to the Commander and he would like you to stay on and teach the recruits after you graduate. It will mean a promotion. Plus it would mean shore duty. There are a lot of men out there who would give their right arm for shore duty.

"You are in the position to save a lot of lives. There is a war going on in Vietnam. And before it is over, there are going to be a lot of young men killed. You can change that.

"I know how you feel. It goes against everything you have been taught. I also think Mr. Chin would agree with the Navy. You will be training men, like yourself, to protect themselves when they are in combat. You can save a lot of lives."

I couldn't speak—I was shocked. I just sat there thinking how much I wanted to go to the fleet. That was why I'd joined the Navy. Training people to kill is not what I wanted to do. I didn't think Mr. Chin would like it either.

"Sir, I don't know what to say. I really want to go to the fleet. That's why I signed up with the Navy. It is where my heart is. Can I think about it for awhile?"

"Tim, we don't have much time before graduation. I will talk to the Commander and get back to you."

"Commander, Tim is going to think about it, but I don't think he will do it. He has strong feeling about the fleet. Do you think he might change his mind if he talked to Mr. Chin?"

"Chief, I think you have something there. I'll talk to the Admiral."

"Admiral, we are having a problem with Tim. The Chief came up with a good idea. If Tim talks to Mr. Chin about it maybe he will change his mind."

"Well Commander, you have a job to do. I want this Chin here right away. You are a pilot, right?"

"Yes Sir."

"Bring him here tomorrow. Now get going."

The Commander knocked on Mr. Chin's door. Mr. Chin opened the door and the Commander introduced myself. He told Mr. Chin what the Navy wanted. Mr. Chin was quiet.

"Can you come to the base? I have a jet waiting. I want you to know this first: whatever Tim decides is good enough for me. He says he made a promise to you. That is the problem. He has a sense of loyalty."

"I'll call my boss to get the time off. I will go with you. I can't promise you anything, however, as Tim has his own mind."

"That's fine, Sir."

They soon were in the air. When we arrived we went to the Admiral's office. "Sir, this is Mr. Chin. He'll talk to Tim. I'll get him."

"Orderly!???? Bring Tim to the Admiral's office."

I was sitting in the barracks when an orderly rushed in and came over to me.

"What do you want?" I asked.

"The Admiral wants you. Now!"

Everyone stared at me.

When I arrived at the Admiral's office, I knocked on the door.

"Come in, Tim. I have someone here that wants to talk to you. Take him to the PX where you can talk. I've cleared the PX for you. Your guest is in the other room."

"Thank you, Sir. But who is it?"

"Open the door and find out."

I opened the door and was shocked to see Mr. Chin.

"How are you, Tim?"

"Fine Sir, but what are you doing here?"

"You must be very important; they sent a jet for me."

"Come with me Mr. Chin. I think I know what they want."

We went to the PX and sat down. The place was empty except for the sailor behind the counter. Mr. Chin and I both had a cup of tea. I told them what the Navy wanted.

"Tim, what I taught you was to protect yourself. I can't tell you what to do. I live everyday of my life thinking of the men I killed. I know I saved a lot of lives. I had to do what I thought was right. You have to make up your mind. I am releasing you from your promise to me. May you make the right choice. Remember this, how long did you train to get where you are. That is the answer you are looking for."

We talked for hours. It was nice to see Mr. Chin, and I knew I would hate to see him leave.

Mr. Chin told me that when he finished talking to me, he had to go to the Admiral's office.

"Tim, you have some thinking to do. I have to go. They are waiting to take me back. I will say hi to everyone for you."

"Mr. Chin, I just want to say Tim is a fine young man. He has a rare talent. I have checked on you, but you are a mystery. I know you were a hero in the war and I salute you for that. I am sure Tim is going to make the right decision. Thanks for everything. There is a jet waiting for you. Thanks again, Mr. Chin.

I thought about what I should do for a week. I knew deep down they were right. I could save a lot of lives. I also knew it would take a lot of time to train the men. That was my problem, time. It had taken me years to get where I was.

Λ few weeks would not be enough time to train the men; I knew what I had to do.

I knocked on the Chief's door.

I heard him yell, "Come in."

"I would like to talk to you, Sir. I have given what we discussed a lot of thought. There is a problem, and I have reached a decision. There is not enough time to teach the men. It took me years to learn. I can't teach them in a few weeks. I would do more harm than good. It takes a lot of concentration and dedication. It took me months just to learn the basics, studying five hours every day. The men don't have that kind of time. I wish they did. I hope you can understand?"

"Tim, I never thought of that. I see where you are coming from. I'll speak to the Commander and explain it to him."

That was the last time it was brought up. Graduation day finally came. I'd made a lot of friends. I talked to the Chief before I left. He was really a nice guy. We both wished each other luck.

"Tim, I want you to know I think you made a wise decision. You were right. It would take a long time to train the men. I don't want you to think you let the men down. You're being transferred to a carrier on the West Coast. You will be operating near Vietnam. Be careful. I wouldn't want anything to happen to you. I think you are a very special young man. I know you will make out better than a lot of the men going there. I want you too keep in touch. I'll be here if you ever need me."

I went home for two weeks leave. I immediately went to see Mr. Chin. When I went into his house, we gave each other a hug.

"Welcome home, Tim."

"It's good to be home. Thanks for coming to see me, Mr. Chin. It was great to see you."

"What did you decide about training people?"

"I decided against it. I told them there just wasn't enough time to properly train the men. I wish I could have, but I was afraid they were more apt to get hurt by not be being trained properly."

"That's true. You made the right decision."

"The Navy kept asking me about you. I told them you were born in China and lost your parents when the Japanese came. I never told them where the monastery was where you learned your skills."

"You did the right thing there also. The monastery is off limits to outsiders. You would have brought grief to them. This way they can live in peace."

I had a good time on leave. I spent time with everybody. When my leave was up, I said my good-byes and left for Long Beach, California. I was on my way to the fleet. I felt good.

I'd finally reached my ship. I stood near the after gangplank, just staring at her. She was huge and beautiful. I must have been standing there a long time when I heard a voice.

I turned around and noticed a captain standing beside me.

"Sailor, she's a beauty isn't she?"

I snapped to attention and saluted.

The Captain returned my salute. "This is going to be your home sailor. I hope you like her."

"It is a dream come true, Sir."

"That's good to hear. What's your name?"

"Airman Apprentice Tim Collins, Sir!"

"So, you're Tim. I've heard about you. Welcome aboard and good luck. I think you should go aboard now."

I was a little shocked that he'd heard about me.

"Sir, you know me?"

"Just by reputation, sailor."

I saluted him and started up the gangplank. When I reached the top, I was still in the state of shock. I turned around and looked at him. He was smiling and waved; I waved back. I couldn't understand why he knew of me.

I saluted the flag and requested to come aboard. I gave the Chief Petty Officer who was standing there my orders.

The Chief was staring at me and asked, "Sailor, how do you know the Captain?"

"I don't, Sir. He surprised me when he told me he knew of me. I have never met him."

"He is the captain of this ship. In other words, he is God. You say he has heard of you?"

"Yes Sir."

"Sailor, that's a new one on me. Frank, take this sailor to the air office."

"Follow me, sailor."

I followed the seaman who halfway through the hanger deck stopped, turned around, and asked, "I have a question to ask you. That is, if you don't mind me asking.

"I heard the conversation with the Chief. Not everyone gets to talk to the Captain. Are you sure you don't know him?"

"I'm positive."

"Then I would suggest, you be careful."

We continued on. When we reached the flight deck, I was amazed at the size of it. There were planes and men all over it. They looked like ants. Everyone was busy. When we entered the air office, a few of the guys sitting there stared at me. One of them laughed, "What's the Navy doing now—recruiting babies?"

The Chief was there too and he turned around and said, "Shut up you two. I suggest you find something to do before I find some work for you. What's your name, sailor?"

"Airman Apprentice Tim Collins, Sir."

"Throw your gear in the corner." The seaman handed him my papers. The Chief opened them and looked at them briefly. "Follow me Tim, I will introduce you to the Air Officer. He's your boss. His bark is worst than his bite."

"That's enough, Chief."

"Sorry Commander, I meant nothing by it."

The Air Officer took my papers and glanced at them a second. "Well, I'll be. So you're the one. Glad to have you aboard. We'll have to talk later. I have to find out more about your experiences in boot camp."

"Sir, I would rather leave it behind me if you don't mind."

"No, problem. But, I still have a few questions. They'll be strictly between us."

"So that's what the Captain meant, Sir."

"The Captain? Where did you meet him?"

"I was standing on the dock, looking at the ship and he was standing there also. He asked what my name was. Then he said, 'So you're the one.' I asked him if he knew me, and he replied, 'Just by reputation.'"

"I will see you later, Son."

I turned around and the guys were standing there with their mouths open. I looked at the Chief. He had a puzzled look on his face.

"What do you two guys want? We have to move the chopper on 10," he barked at the men gaping at me.

"Tim, go with Ron. He will show you where to stow your gear. Make sure you get a good bunk for him, Ron. The man has pull."

"Follow me, Tim." We headed toward the aft part of the ship.

"Tim, what the hell was that about?"

"Nothing Ron, forget about it will you."

"Okay. Just remember, there are no secrets aboard ship. Whatever it is, we will find out within an hour," he said, laughing.

"Chief! Come in here and close the door," the Commander yelled.

"Sure thing, Sir."

"I am going to tell you about Tim. That young man turned down a shore job at boot camp. They wanted him to be an instructor. I got a call from the Admiral about him."

"The Admiral, Sir?!"

"That's right, the Admiral. It seems that Tim has a rare talent. He is also is very dangerous young man. He is an expert in some kind of karate. He took out his two self-defense instructors at the same time. I want you to watch him closely. He is a quiet kid and won't be any trouble. I just want you to make sure those idiots don't provoke him. They will be in a no-win situation. I was told he is very quiet and walks away from trouble. Tim had the best marks in boot camp. He's a special kid and shouldn't be onboard a ship. Why he refused shore duty, I'll never know. Treat him like everyone else, but if you see he is taking too much shit, do something about it."

"Sir, if I do, what the hell do you think the other men will do?"

"I don't care. The men are no match for Tim. I told you—he could be very dangerous."

"Okay, Sir."

When I arrived at my quarters, I was told to take any bed. I threw my gear on a bed and changed into my dungarees. Ron was waiting.

"Tim, I have to ask this. You're driving me crazy. I heard them say you turned down a shore job. I understand you were offered a job as an instructor."

"That's true. I was offered a shore job, but I prefer going to sea. That's all there is to it."

"I don't believe it. I would give my right arm for a shore job, and you turned it down. Are you ready to go to work?"

"Sure am."

The Chief was standing near a plane when we arrived on deck. He saw us and motioned for us to come over.

"Get lost Ron, I want to talk to Tim."

"Okay Chief."

"Hey fellas, you see that kid—I can't understand it. He turned down shore duty to get here. The Captain and the Air Officer have been waiting for him to arrive. I don't get it? He was offered a shore job as an instructor. Can you believe it?

"That's all I overheard. When I asked Tim about it, he just told me to forget it."

"Well Tim," the Chief said after Ron had left, "I hear you were some kind of celebrity while in boot camp."

"I don't think so, Chief. I was just another boot."

"Don't be so modest, Tim. The Air Officer told me some things about you. I have to keep an eye on you. I hear you can be dangerous."

"That's all behind me, Sir. I would appreciate it if you forgot what you've heard. I am not looking for trouble."

"Don't worry, your secret is safe with me. Whatever it is."

"Thanks Chief." The Chief had told me to see Ron and he would put me to work. As I walked toward the guys standing around Ron, I saw they were staring at me.

"I was told to see you, Ron. The Chief said you had some work for me. I guess that means I am working for you."

"Tim, this is Bill. The rest of the guys you can get acquainted with later. Right now, we have to move this chopper." I felt uneasy. The men were looking at me like I had the plague.

"Look guys, I am just another sailor, like you."

"Yea, one that turned down shore duty. We have a lot of questions to ask you."

"Forget it, I have nothing to say. Just tell me what you want me to do."

The men looked past me, staring at something. I turned around to see what they were looking at. The Chief and the Air Officer were walking toward us.

"Tim, go with the Air Officer. The Captain wants to see you."

I walked away with the Air Officer, wondering what was up.

"Hey Chief, it's about time you tell us what is up with the new guy?"

"It seems we have a man with us that is an expert in self-defense. Don't judge him by his size. He took out two Marines and his two self-defense instructors in boot camp. It seems that his company commander tested him, to their surprise. The two Marines outweighed him by a hundred pounds.

"Tim took them out like it was nothing. It only took a couple of seconds for him to do it. The reason I know this is because his Chief in boot camp is a friend of mine. The Air Officer doesn't even know that I'd heard about him. I will tell you this—give him a wide berth. If you piss him off, he is capable of hurting you. In fact he could kill you. He is very quiet and doesn't like people knowing about him. He is modest, so just treat him like anyone else."

The Air Officer and I entered the Officers' Wardroom. There were quite a few officers inside and they all looked at me when we came in. The Captain was sitting in the corner and motioned to us.

"Captain, Tim is here. I will leave you two alone."

"No, sit down. I want you to hear this."

"Tim, would you like some coffee?"

"I don't know, Sir. I feel like I am out of place here."

"Don't worry. This will probably be the last time you will have the pleasure of being here."

"Yes Sir, black if you don't mind." The Captain motioned for the steward, who brought the coffee and another cup. I looked around and saw that everyone was watching me. I felt very uneasy.

The Captain looked at the other officers. Then he stood up and said, "Gentlemen, I have the pleasure of introducing you to Tim Collins. This is his first day on board." Then he sat back down.

"Tim, I received a call from the Admiral about you. He told me about your skills. I know you are a very modest young man, but he told me some interesting things about you and I just have to find out what happened. I understand you were put through some kind of test by your company commander in boot camp. Is that true?"

"Yes Sir, unknown to me, he arranged for two Marines to disarm me when I was on guard duty. I disabled them. They were quite big."

"I heard real big, Tim."

"Yes Sir, real big. Everybody is real big to me."

"I also heard you took out your two self-defense instructors. Using the same method."

"That's true, Sir. I wish it never had happened. They offered me a job as an instructor. I thought about it, but just couldn't do it. I will tell you this, Sir. I learned martial arts from a friend and have studied it for years. I just didn't have enough time to train them. My style of karate is very intense. It takes years to master. My teacher was a close friend."

"I know. I have a report on him here. Mr. Chin was quite a war hero. He fought for us when we entered the war. He has three silver stars, one Navy Cross, and numerous citations. It seems your Mr. Chin was an expert in hand-to-hand combat. He was able to kill just using his hands.

"What I have to know is this. Are you his equal?"

"That's hard to answer, Sir. I will answer you like this—according to Mr. Chin, I am better. But I don't believe it. Mr. Chin says the only difference between us is that I can sense things and hear things better than he can. In other words, I feel things more clearly than most people, for example, I can hear you walking long before you get to me. My company commander in boot camp would hide and watch me. I knew he was there every time."

"How far away was he Tim?"

"Sometimes as much as 800 feet. I could hear the change in his pockets jingle when he walked. To me, that was always normal. Sir, sitting in the rear of the wardroom, there is a Marine and I heard him say, "So that's the son of a bitch from Great Lakes."

"Are you sure that's what he said?"

"Yes Sir."

The Captain stood up and called over to the officer in the corner, "Major, will you come here?"

"Yes Sir." I watched the officer stand up and come over to us.

"Major, I want to introduce Tim Collins. He is new aboard the ship.

"I was just wondering, why you would refer to him as a son of a bitch? You did refer to him that way didn't you?"

"Yes Sir, but how did you hear what I said. I was whispering."

"That's all right, Major. I have been talking to Tim with the Commander. It seems he has a very keen sense of hearing. I couldn't believe it when he told me he heard what you'd said. You were sitting a long way from us. I don't blame you for being mad. If a small sailor like Tim is capable of taking out two of your best. I would be mad too."

"Major—Tim Collins."

I stood up and reached my hand out. The Major smiled and said, "Pleased to meet you, Tim. I guess what they say about you is true. I apologize for that crack. It was just hard for me to believe."

"That's all right, Sir. I wish it had never happened."

"That's all, Major." I watched the Major as he walked away and noticed that the other officers sitting in the room were all smiling.

"Tim, I want you to be careful. You are a dangerous young man."

"Sir, I am not dangerous. I would never hurt anyone by accident or on purpose, unless I had to. There is one thing everyone is forgetting. I have been trained by the very best. First, I was taught never to lose my temper. And second, I don't like fighting. In a war, I wouldn't hesitate to use what my teacher taught me. But the code I live by forbids me to use my skill in a fight. I practice that code. I am the last man on this ship you have to worry about."

"Tim, I am happy to have you aboard. Finish your coffee. I hope you like it aboard this ship." He stood up to leave. I snapped to attention.

"Thank you, Tim. Commander, keep him company."

"Yes Sir."

"Tim, when it gets out, and it will, the men will have a field day with you. Don't let them get to you. Especially the Marines; their pride has been hurt."

"They won't even see me, Sir." I finished my coffee and left.

"Gentlemen, that was Tim Collins. I guess you all have heard about him. He's 5 feet 4 inches tall and he is unbelievable. Right Major?"

"I wish he were in the Marines. You mean he actually heard me whisper from over there?"

"That's right. He shocked me also. He has a sixth sense we all wish we had."

When I got back to the flight deck, one of the guys called out, "Hey Tim! What's going on?"

"Would you believe it, I had coffee with the Air Officer and the Captain? I am going to tell you something about me. I am an expert in the martial arts."

"We know. We heard about the two Marines and your instructors. We just didn't believe it."

"Just do me a favor—treat me like one of you. There is nothing special about me. Okay?"

"Fine with us. But will it be fine with the Marines? I sure would like to have seen the faces on those Marines. I bet they were shocked. How did it go after that? Those guys really think they are something."

"Pretty good. We met at the PX and they came over and shook my hand. I became pretty good friends with them."

"Let's get to work," the Chief ordered.

"Hey Chief, I have a question. Do you think it will spread around the ship about boot camp?"

"Well Tim, a ship is a really small place. It probably has already spread through the ship. I bet the Marines know all about it. You'll just have to face it when the time comes. Just don't let them get under your skin. In time, they will forget. It isn't everyday someone like you comes along. There isn't a man on board that wouldn't like to be you.

"Just remember, the guys with you are a good bunch. Teasing is a part of the Navy. What happened in boot camp has already picked up the morale around here. They will be talking about it for quite sometime. The Marines, that's going to be something else. They are all brainwashed. What you did isn't going to sit well with them so just be careful. Okay? I think it is time for me to talk with the Lieutenant."

"Thanks for your time, Chief."

When the Chief got back to his office, he dialed the Lieutenant. "Lieutenant Johnson speaking." "Lieutenant, this is Chief Mitchell. I think we are going to have some trouble with your guys concerning Tim. My C.O. told me to call. He wants it nipped in the bud before it gets out of hand. I have heard some scuttlebutt."

"Chief, have Commander Devlin meet me in the wardroom."

"Thanks."

"Commander Devlin, I think, we are going to have a problem. I have heard some scuttlebutt about Tim. I talked with Lieutenant Johnson and he wants to meet you in the wardroom."

"Okay, I'm on my way."

"Hi, Commander, have a seat."

"Have you heard the scuttlebutt about Tim and your Marines? I don't want any trouble with the Marines. Tim has promised to stay away from them. Now, I need a promise from you to do the same."

"Will he keep away from my men?"

"You can count on it. I have all ready talked with him. Tim is a quiet kid. I wouldn't want to see him hurt your men. I would like you to talk to your men before any trouble starts."

"They're not happy and I can't blame them. Marines don't like to lose. If what I heard about that kid is true, he must be something else. I can't guarantee my men won't be assholes."

"Well, they better not. I don't want Tim hurting them. He won't fight unless he has to. Believe me, your men don't want to find out the hard way."

"Okay Commander, consider it done. I will talk to my men. But keep Tim, away from them."

"Thanks for the help."

"No problem. I will speak to them tonight."

The men were buzzing all night. Everyone kept asking me questions. But I always gave them the same answer. I felt uneasy; I had a hunch there was going to be trouble.

It wasn't long before the Marines got into the act. I was in the mess hall when two Marines came walking toward me. The whole mess hall became quiet. I turned around and one of them was standing over me.

"Sailor, I hear you're a bad ass. Is that true?"

I looked around and saw everyone watching me. I looked at the Marine and said, "I don't think so."

"Are you the kid who allegedly kicked the shit out of two Marines while in boot camp. I think the stories are nothing but lies you made up. You don't show me shit."

"That's right, the stories are lies. Does that make you feel better?"

"I knew you were a coward," he taunted, as he started to laugh.

I just ignored him. Then, I heard a voice and turned to see Lieutenant Johnson. "Marine, have you any business with that sailor?"

"No Sir, I was just talking to him."

"If you're finished, I think you should return to your table."

"Yes Sir."

"Is your name Tim?"

I jumped up and came to attention. "Yes Sir."

"Mind if I sit with you for a minute?"

"No Sir, please be seated. I will get you some coffee."

I went to the coffee machine and returned with a cup of coffee, which I handed to him.

"Tim, I don't want any trouble with my men. Do you?"

"I sure don't, Lieutenant. I didn't come here for trouble."

"I have done some checking on you. At first, I didn't believe the stories. However, I called a friend at Great Lakes and he confirmed the stories. I must say you intrigue me. I also understand you have a unique talent. I want you to understand something from their point of view—you put a blemish on the Corp. They aren't going to forget it."

"Sir, what happened in boot camp wasn't my fault. I was set up and wish it never had happened. My company commander set it up."

"I think they were wrong to do it, but their motives were well intentioned. But, it's too late to worry about that now. I will talk to my men. I suggest you keep away from them."

"Sir, I intend to do just that."

"Good. Tim, may I shake your hand?"

"My pleasure, Lieutenant."

"Good-bye sailor."

I sat down. I was looking at the Marines and they were staring at me. Ron came over and sat with me.

"Well Tim, I see you have met the Lieutenant. Did you have a nice talk?"

"Yes. Why?"

The Lieutenant was standing next to his men. I could hear him tell them, "I want you to stay away from that sailor or your ass will be mine. That's an order do you understand? Does anyone have any questions?"

"No Sir."

"Sir, I have a question. Are the stories true?"

"Yes, they are. That young man is skilled in the martial arts. I want him left alone. I will eat the ass off anyone that screws with him. He is an expert in the art of killing. I checked on him. No one here has seen that type of training; that is why I don't want any trouble. That young man had a chance to become an instructor, but he turned it down for sea duty. That should tell you something. These orders come from above. You know what that means. You're dismissed."

"I wonder just how good he is. I think I can take him."

"You're nuts, Corporal. We have our orders."

"Listen Marine, I don't want to hear anymore on this subject. Get it into your head."

"Okay, Sir."

The day finally arrived when we were underway. We were heading for the Far East. I was finally out to sea and in a week or two would be in Hawaii. Air operations started right away. It was amazing to see the planes taking off and landing. Air Ops lasted all day and night. We were always on deck. First thing we did was to start launching the choppers. The planes were next. When all the planes were launched, we would recover the choppers. When it was time to bring the planes back on deck, we would start launching the choppers. Then the planes would start landing on deck. After we got them all on deck, we would recover the choppers. This went on day and night. The launching and recovering of aircraft was endless.

I hadn't practiced my karate for awhile and decided to go up to the flight deck and train. I went to the bow. The wind felt good. When I started to train, everyone was watching me. One night while I was training, I saw the Captain watching me. He usually walked the deck at night. I turned around and saw him, then snapped to attention and saluted.

"At ease, sailor. Pretty fancy stuff you're doing."

"Looks harder than it is, Sir. It is very relaxing."

"Well, have a good night sailor."

"Thank you, Sir."

"Good evening, Captain."

"Good evening, Commander. I've been watching Tim. Tell me something, just what the hell is that sailor doing?"

"I don't know Sir; it is some kind of karate. I've never seen it before. It is strange to me. I believe each move is design to maim or kill. Captain, can I speak with you privately?"

"Clear the bridge," the Captain ordered.

"I was thinking about Tim, and I need your approval on something. We're heading for Vietnam. I was wondering if Tim's training could be put to use. I would like to have him start training my pilots and flight deck directors. It might come in handy when they go on shuttle missions. Especially, the chopper pilots, in case they get shot down. The men have no formal training like Tim. They are going to be useless if they get themselves in a jam. I think Tim could be a great help to us."

"Didn't he refuse to do this already?"

"Yes, but this is different. We can get about a month of training—maybe a little more."

"I think it is a good idea. Check it out."

"Thank you, Sir."

"Chief, come to my office."

"What's up, Sir?"

"Tim, to be exact. I was wondering . . . do you think he could start training the pilots and the directors?"

"I don't know . . . I'll lay it on him."

"Talk to him. Then bring him to me."

"I'll ask him tomorrow."

"I have a better suggestion. Ask him now."

"Tim, follow me. I want to talk to you. The Commander has asked me if you could train his pilots and the flight deck directors. I think he would like to have you show the men different things. Nothing like what you are capable of doing. He would just like you to give them some basic stuff. Train them just enough to help them get out of a jam if they get shot down. We have enough time before we get to Vietnam."

"I'm not sure. I guess I can teach them the basics. That could help. When do you have to report back to the Commander?"

"Tomorrow. I will have to give him your answer, tomorrow."

"Then tell him okay."

"No Tim, you tell him."

"Okay." We both went to see the Commander.

"Tim is here, Sir. He has agreed to help."

"Good, bring him in. Tim, I appreciate this. All I want is for you to show them enough to keep them out of trouble if they get shot down. Follow me."

We followed the Commander to the wardroom. The Captain was sitting with the Executive Officer.

"Sir, Tim has agreed to help us."

"Sit down Chief; you too Tim. Have some coffee. You didn't think you would ever be sitting here drinking coffee again, did you? But Tim, things are never what they seem. I want you to teach them enough to get them out of trouble if the need arises. Can you do that?"

"Yes Sir. I only ask one thing that I have strict control over everyone, officers and enlisted men. I can't have anyone countermanding my orders. If this happens the training will be useless. I will be respectful to the officers. This is very important. You will see what I mean as we progress. Sometimes a student thinks he knows it all then he screws everything up. That is when someone gets hurt."

I looked at the Captain and Executive Officer.

"Okay Tim, you will have complete control. Tomorrow I will announce it at roll call. Commander, you can tell the pilots."

Roll call sounded. We were all waiting.

"Gentlemen, fall in. I have an announcement to make. After roll call, the directors will remain on deck." Roll call ended and everyone was dismissed. As I started to walk away, the Commander said, "Tim, you stay."

"Okay, you misfits—listen closely. Starting tonight you will start training with Tim. Be on the flight deck at 1800 hours. Tim is going to train you in some basic maneuvers. You will take this training seriously. We are heading for a war zone. What you learn might just save your worthless lives. If you don't, you will be back pushing planes. Do you understand what I am saying?"

"Yes Chief."

"Okay—dismissed."

We continued to work the rest of the day. I looked at my watch it was 1800 hours and went on deck. I noticed some of the men weren't there yet.

"Gentlemen, I am going to try to teach you some moves in a very dangerous style of self-defense. I will expect your undivided attention. If I find you clowning around, you're out. No questions asked. Do you understand? This is not a joke. At first, it will seem funny. But once you start to learn different moves, you'll like it. I don't expect you to be experts at first; I just want you to understand what you are doing."

I looked up and saw two directors and a pilot walking toward us. They were late. I waited for them to get in line.

"Do you understand?"

"Yes Sir."

"You're dismissed." I walked off the flight deck.

That was their first lesson in discipline. I wondered if they'd understood. I figured tomorrow they would understand.

I was halfway to the superstructure when I heard the Commander on the bullhorn telling me to report to him.

"Tim, that was a short session wasn't it?"

"Yes, when I say 1800 hours, I mean it. Discipline starts with the clock. I demand total discipline and concentration."

"Well Tim, this commander is going to the Air Office, he needs some coffee. Would you like to join me?"

"Thank you, Sir."

"I expect we will be hearing from the Captain soon."

I was sitting in the Air Office with the Commander when the Captain came in. "What the hell is going on! That training session lasted five minutes. I'm bullshit. Now start talking."

"It seems they had their first lesson in discipline. Tim said 1800 hours and two directors and a pilot were late. I guess they will show up on time tomorrow."

The Captain started to laugh. "I feel like a fool. Sorry Tim. You would make a great instructor. What do you think Commander? It reminds me of Annapolis—everything by the clock. Tim is on the right track. When he tells you to be here at a certain time, he means it."

The training went on for a few weeks and I could see some progress. The men were catching on fast.

At first, the officers complained about training with the enlisted men. One of them asked me to separate the men. I told him I wouldn't and he became upset. After the class, I talked to him. When I told him there were no enlisted men or officers in the class, he just stared at me. I told him the Captain had given me a free hand to do whatever I wanted and if he had a gripe he should talk to the Captain. He never said anything about it again.

We were progressing fast. I noticed the Marines were starting to watch us. They liked to make wisecracks and I could see the men were getting mad. I told them to forget about the Marines—let them laugh. I looked at them and said, "Listen men, some of you are ready to take them on now. I won't tell you who you are, but if you try to take them on, you'll be thrown out of the class. I mean just that. Do you understand what I am saying?"

The Commander had been watching the Marines. I guess he knew what was coming. He left us and went into the superstructure.

"Captain, I think we have trouble brewing."

I know. It's the Marines. Corporal, stand outside please. Close the door behind you."

"Yes Sir!"

"The men are getting pissed. I have been listening to them bitch about the Marines hazing them and they aren't going to take much more."

"What do you suggest, Commander?"

"I think a little competition is in order. I was wondering if we could set up a match."

"Go ahead."

"It won't be easy. I am thinking of Tim."

"Well, talk to the Chief. Maybe he can help."

"I was thinking the same thing. I'll do it right away."

"Hey Chief!"

"Yes Sir, what can I do for you?"

"There seems to be some trouble in the making and I want to stop it."

"How Sir?"

"Chief, do you think we can set up a match between Tim and the Marines? Will Tim go for it?"

"I doubt it, but I will talk to him about it."

"Hey Bill! Get hold of Tim. I want to talk to him right away."

"Yes Sir."

"Hey Tim! The Chief wants you."

"Okay."

"You wanted to see me Chief?"

"Yes Tim. Come in and close the door."

The Chief picked up the phone and I heard him say, "I have Tim here. Do you want to talk to him? Okay, we'll wait. Tim, pour us some coffee."

"Okay Chief, I'll get it."

The door opened and the Commander came in. "Hi Tim, got a minute."

"Yes Sir."

"I think we are about to have a major problem on our hands. The Marines are getting to the men. I don't think this is a healthy situation. I am going to ask you to do something for me. I checked it out with the Captain and he left it up to you. I want to set up an exhibition with the Marines. Maybe we can get them to join the class. I hear they are learning karate from the Sargent and if we could get them into your class, I think it would be better and the hazing will stop. Would you consider a match between you and a Marine. I know you don't like this but I think it is necessary."

"Normally, I would say no. But under the circumstances, I think it is the best thing we can do. I'm game. They need to be taught a lesson."

"Tim, before you agree, remember they are going to throw the biggest Marine they can find to take you out."

"That's okay."

"All set, Captain. I will schedule the match for tomorrow night. Tim has agreed to do it."

"Fine, go ahead and do it."

"Hey Major, I need a favor."

"Sure Commander, name it."

"I want to set up a match between one of your Marines and Tim."

"You what!"

"You heard me. I think we should before things get out of hand. You know what's been going on."

"Yes, I do and I think you're right. When do you want it?"

"Tomorrow night all right with you?"

"Consider it done," the Major said and walked away.

"Steward call Chief Michaels and have him report to me with Tim."

We entered the wardroom. The Commander said, "Captain, the match is on for tomorrow."

"Lieutenant, would you come here for a second?"

"What can I do for you, Major?"

"Get a hold of Baker; he's fighting Tim tomorrow."

"What did you say, Sir?"

"You heard me. Do it!"

"Yes sir! This ought to be something."

"Hey 'Stick'!"

"Yes Lieutenant. What can I do for you?"

"Feel like fighting tomorrow?"

"What do you mean, Sir?"

"You're fighting Tim tomorrow. It's been arranged."

"Sir, I hear he's good, but he's no match for me. I think he'll get himself hurt."

"So what? They asked for it."

"Okay, what time?"

"About 1800 hours on the flight deck."

"Commander, it's all set. Your sailor is going to get his butt kicked."

"Fine. I'll tell the necessary people."

"Ten bucks says Stick takes him."

"You're on, Major."

"Captain it's all set. I have a tenner riding on Tim with the Major."

"Gambling on board is illegal, Commander."

"Yes Sir, do you want me to make a bet for you?"

"Here is ten, Commander."

"Hey Major, want to make that twenty?"

"You're covered."

It was time for the match. "Hey Major. Is your man ready?"

"Yes Sir. By the way, remember I have you and the Captain covered," the Major said laughing.

Sargent Baker came on deck. I had never seen anyone so big. I thought, If he gets his hands on me, I am in trouble. He was the best the Marines had.

"Gentlemen, shake hands, no holds barred."

I didn't see the first punch coming. The Sargent was a dirty fighter. I fell to the deck. All the Marines were yelling. I got up and waited for him to throw the next punch. This time I was ready. Grabbing his wrist, I pressed my thumb into it. I heard him scream. Next, I pressed my thumb into the lower part of his neck. He fell to the deck, paralyzed. I stood over him and said, "Sargent, it's over." He just looked at me—he couldn't move. I walked away. It was quiet no one said a word. The Chief came over to me and asked, "Is that it?"

"Yes Sir." The Major yelled to me, "Tim, is he okay?"

"Yes, he will be all right. I will take care of it. He's just paralyzed right now."

"Paralyzed? What the hell did you do?"

I walked over to the Sargent and pressed on the spots where I'd hit him. I saw him move. "Sargent, just keep on rubbing the area that hurts. You'll be all right. Next time fight fair."

"Gentlemen, I want to tell you something. Sargent Baker is one tough Marine. When I agreed to this match. I knew he couldn't win. You could say I cheated. As I told you before, my style of fighting is very dangerous. You don't stand a chance. A little more pressure and the Sargent would be dead. Remember what I told you in the beginning of the class, dedication and discipline. That's the secret. The moves you have learned so far are dangerous. I would never use them anywhere but in combat. It should never be taken lightly. If you use it on the street, expect to spend a lot of time in jail. You know how to use it. Now, I will teach you what to expect if you use it and maim someone. Let alone kill them. This is the most important lesson I can teach you.

"First, I want to say this to you Marines. I am willing to teach you. That is, if you want to learn. The same rules apply—dedication and discipline. That's all I ask. You men are good at what you do, but I am better. You see my size and what I can do. If you end up in Vietnam, you're going to find your enemy is just as good as me. You have to be better. I have taught the flight deck directors and the pilots. Now, if you want I will help you. I hope you will forget what has happened and join in. If the Sargent had had my training, I wouldn't have been able to take him out so easily.

"Sargent, I would like to shake your hand and ask your forgiveness. It wasn't fair to you, what I did." The Sargent and I shook hands. I watched him as he walked away; I felt bad for him.

"Commander, that was one hell of a demonstration. I just can't believe it. By the way, here's your money. You earned it."

"Thanks Major. Do you think your men will join the class?"

"I sure hope so. That kid is something else. Like I said, I wish he were a Marine."

"Captain, I have something for you," said the Commander as he handed over a ten spot.

"Commander, I feel funny taking this money. I never realized just how good Tim is. Or, should I say how dangerous. It's a good thing he has a head on his shoulders. If he were a troublemaker, he'd be in the brig. After seeing him in action, I want to know more about him. Wire Washington and get a full report on Mr. Chin and Tim. I mean everything."

"I think you're right, Sir. He worries me now more than ever."

"Hey Tim! You're wanted in the wardroom again. Let's go."

The Captain, Commander, and the Major were waiting in the wardroom.

"Sir, you wanted to see me."

"Yes Tim."

"Have some coffee. That was some fight, Tim. What did you mean, you could have killed him?"

"Just that, Sir. A little more pressure and the Sargent would have been dead. There are numerous spots on the body that are vulnerable. Some of them stop a man from screaming when he is hit. It's an instant death. I haven't taught the men that yet. I don't think they are ready. The directors on the flight deck are not ready for that phase."

"I am going to talk to the men. I have to tell them what you said. I don't want them to go off half-cocked. Tim, you have done a good job, so far. I hope you will keep it up."

"I can't stop now. I have to teach them how not to kill someone. This training is for combat only."

"The Major has something to say."

"I sure do!"

"First, let me apologize, Major. The fight wasn't fair even though Baker suckered me."

"Tim, I would like to be in your class tomorrow. Is that okay with you?"

"Yes Sir, it will be my pleasure. I've never hit a Major before."

I watched the Major smile.

"Just take it easy, sailor."

We both laughed. "Tim, I knew you were against the fight. My Marines have been giving you a bad time. I think that will change now."

The Chief and I left the bridge. The Chief didn't say anything. When we reached the flight deck, I saw the whole Marine detachment coming toward us. Sargent Baker was leading them.

"Tim, I just want you know there are no hard feelings. We would like you to teach us some moves."

"That will be a pleasure, Sargent." I watched him hold out his hand.

"A little humility is good for us once in awhile. I have learned a valuable lesson. I would like to shake your hand."

I heard the Sargent yell, "Attention. Hand salute."

The Chief looked at me. "That, I would say, is quite an honor. You're a good man, Tim."

The following night everyone was on the flight deck. The deck was full. The Captain came over to me.

"Tim, I heard what happened last night and I am proud of you. The Marines are going to work together, hand-and-hand, with the Navy. That makes me proud. Thank you."

"Thank you, Sir," I replied, saluting. Then he left.

The class started. Night after night, we learned from each other. They learned the basics very quickly. As the time went by, they got better and better. I knew they could handle themselves.

One night as I was standing on the deck, looking out over the ocean, I heard a noise. It was the Major. I snapped to attention.

"At ease, sailor. I want to talk to you. I will be leaving in a couple of days with some of my men. We are going to Vietnam. I just wanted to tell you I think my men and I are ready for anything and we have you to thank. I'll always remember you. I will write to you when I get a chance. My men told me to say thanks. Vietnam is getting to be a hot spot. That's why we're being sent. But, I know my men can handle it now."

"Captain! Come here. Are you watching this? The Major is with Tim. The men from the Major's unit are coming also."

"Commander, the Major and his men are leaving for Vietnam. I guess they are saying goodbye."

"I hope they are going to be all right, Sir."

"I think they're ready—thanks to Tim."

The Major yelled, Attention!" The Marines snapped to attention.

The Major yelled, "Hand salute!" The Marines all saluted at the same time. They held the salute and when the Major said at ease, they dropped the salute. Everyone started to shake Tim's hand. After it was over, Tim was standing alone by the railing.

"Hi Tim, how is it going?"

"Fine Commander."

"I saw what the Major did. I'm proud of you. So is the Captain. I have some news for you. Starting tomorrow you're a Second Class Petty Officer. You are going to have a new job. You're a flight deck director. That is the Captain's order."

"Sir, I am an airman. What happened to Third Class Petty Officer?"

"Nothing, you have just passed over it. It is rare. The Captain wrote to Washington and they approved it. Tomorrow at roll call it will be announced. I stopped by the ship's store. After the announcement, sew these on with my blessings."

It was time for roll call. The Chief and I walked to the flight deck. When we got there everyone was present. I got in line then roll call was taken. I noticed the pilots and the Marine Detachment were there also. I looked up and the Captain was walking toward me.

"Gentleman, I have the distinct pleasure to give this yellow shirt to Second Class Petty Officer Tim Collins. Tim, the Navy and all of us here appreciate what you have done over the last few months. You gave your all to your fellow sailors and Marines. We all thank you." The Captain handed me the shirt.

"Thank you, Sir." I was about to salute him, instead he yelled, "Attention on Deck, Hand Salute!"

Everyone, from pilots to marines, saluted me. I returned their salute.

Everyone was yelling and hollering. I was in shock. All I could think of was my mother and how she would have been proud. I knew I was.

The Commander came over and said, "Tim, you will make a good Petty Officer. I guess you can say you're the youngest and shortest Petty Officer in the fleet. You worked hard for it. I am proud of you. I heard the Captain pulled some strings for you. It is rare someone bypasses one rank and goes to another. I think Mr. Chin knew what he was doing."

Time flew by. Air operations were carried on round the clock. We were near Vietnam. You could feel the tension when the pilots flew off the ship, and especially when they came back.

The planes were being loaded with bombs everyday and were making more and more flights. That meant one thing— we were attacking Vietnam. I knew men were being killed on both sides.

Most of the guys wondered what the hell we were doing there. The papers all had stories about Vietnam. They usually said we had no business being there. The war was a mess.

I felt bad for the ground troops. At least I was aboard a ship where it was fairly safe. I didn't have to fight the enemy—so I thought. Little did I know that one day I would be facing the enemy myself.

Once in a while we would launch a chopper. They would fly shuttle missions. That's when the directors got the chance to fly. The directors were the only ones allowed to go. Their job was to carry messages into the jungle along with supplies. I dreaded the day I would have to go. Ron had gone on the last mission. Snipers got him. Up until then I'd never realized how vulnerable a chopper was. The bullets could penetrate the bottom of the chopper. You sat there hoping your name wasn't on the next bullet.

I went to sick bay to see Ron. I looked around and saw him lying in the bed in the corner. He was smiling.

"How the hell are you?"

"Fine, at least I won't be flying for awhile. I guess I was lucky this time. I caught one in the leg. I never felt so helpless. All I could do was sit there."

"Tell me something, Ron, what do we do on those missions?"

"Nothing much. You just sit there until you get to your destination. Once you get there, you find the C.O. and give him the briefcase. You have him sign for it then you get the hell out of there. Tim, when it is your turn, get out fast and don't ask questions. Just get back to the chopper. One other thing—always, above everything else, forget what you see. Most of the guys there are CIA. You don't want to even talk

to them. They are crazy. You will see things that will make
you sick. They think like animals and act like animals."

"I guess you know best, Ron. I will have to find out
when I go."

"Remember, get in and get out!"

It was finally my turn to go. I was briefed on the
mission and handed a briefcase. My orders were to give the
C.O. the briefcase and no one else. We were airborne; it felt
nice being in a chopper. We were in the air for about an
hour. The jungle was all around us. We finally landed. I
walked toward headquarters and once inside I asked for the
C.O.

"That would be me, sailor. I will take the case."

I gave him the case and he signed for it. I left
headquarters and the chopper was finishing getting fuel. I
noticed a lot of men walking around carrying automatic
weapons. I also noticed the khaki uniforms they were
wearing. There were quite a few Vietnamese people walking
around too. They all wore uniforms.

I boarded the chopper. We were in the air in no time. I
was glad to be out of there. We finally landed on the ship
and I kept thinking about what I had seen. I gave the signed
receipt to the Air Officer.

"How did it go, Tim?"

"I'm not sure, Sir."

"Tim, forget what you saw. Just do your job and get
out. Don't ask questions."

"Yes Sir!"

"Good. You will live longer that way."

It was time for chow. I went to the mess hall and Ron
was there. "Hey Ron! What the hell are you doing here?"

"I'm eating, stupid. How did it go, Tim?"

"Okay I guess. Just what the hell is going on over
there?"

"Tim, no questions. Remember?"

"I know, but it bothers me. I would just like to find out a little. That's all."

"I saw, Tim. Look around. The men you saw wearing khaki jackets are CIA. They are animals. They will kill you without even thinking about it. They are training the South Vietnamese Army. I saw them interrogate a VC one day. When he wouldn't say anything, they shot him in the back of the head. They treat all their prisoners that way. To us, it's wrong. To them, it's just an end to a problem. They live by a different code than us. That is why you don't ask questions and you don't get involved. Now, do you understand?"

"I sure do, and I think it stinks."

"You have your opinion. Just keep it to yourself. Remember, the South Vietnamese have been fighting the north for years. They have seen their families killed, that includes their children. That's why they are like they are. There is no such thing as a prisoner. They can't watch every prisoner they get so they just shoot them."

"I still don't think it's right. Then again, I'm not there with them."

I watched Ron get up and leave the table. I knew he felt the same way I did. I couldn't get it out of my mind, wondering what would happen to me if I got caught, would it mean certain death?

Time passed quickly. I made two more missions into the jungle. We had been in and out of Vietnam for over a year. I was always glad to get back to the *Yorktown*. Almost four years on the carrier had gone by. This tour was almost over, and we were heading back to the States pretty soon. A year was long enough in Nam. We only had a couple of weeks left.

Flight quarters had sounded. We launched the choppers and then the planes. When the last plane was launched, we recovered the choppers and it was time to rest until the planes returned. Most of the guys just flopped on the deck and fell asleep.

It wasn't long before the planes were back. One by one, they landed. As soon as they touched down, we moved them forward so the other planes could land.

It felt good when all the planes came back. Once in awhile one of them wouldn't return; no one would say a word.

One morning as I was sitting on the flight deck, Ron came up to me and said, "Get your gear on, you're going up today. You're scheduled for the next mission."

Ron knew I hated the missions. I could see it in his face when it was his turn. I dressed and went to the Air Office. When I opened the door, the Chief was standing there. I looked at the Chief and said, "I guess it won't be long before we will be going home?"

"No, it won't be long. This should be the last mission. It is going to be a piece of cake."

"Great!"

As we took off and were watching the ship go out of sight, I guess we were all thinking the same thing—is this the one? Will we make it back?

About an hour into the flight, I could see the clearing where we were to land. We touched down and I ran to the C.O. I gave him the briefcase and he signed the receipt. There seemed to be more activity going on than usual. I wondered what was going on.

I was walking back to the chopper, when all hell broke loose. There was firing from all different directions. Mortars were being dropped all over the place. I was near the chopper when I saw a man dressed in what looked like black pajamas, carrying a bag. He was almost on top of the chopper. I could see the pilot staring at the man. I ran toward the man and grabbed him by the neck and twisted it. He fell to the ground. I threw the bag away from the chopper as far as I could. I felt someone grab me from behind. Turning around, I saw another man in black. I pulled my knife and shoved it into his throat. Someone was attacking the C.O. so I threw my knife. It hit the Charlie in the throat. The C.O. looked at me, pulled the knife out, and threw it back to me. I ran to the chopper and we took off like a bat out of hell.

We were in the air, but were still being shot at. Finally, we were in the clear. I heard the pilot yell for me to put the earphones on. I put them on. "Tim, thanks for the help. I thought we were dead. Where the hell did you come from?"

"I was walking back to the chopper when all hell broke loose."

"How many did you get?"

"Sir, I'd rather not talk about it."

"I counted three. You do realize that gook was carrying explosives in that bag. If you hadn't gotten him, he would have had us. You saved our lives."

"Forget it, Sir."

I heard the C.O. and the pilot talking. They were talking about me. The C.O. said, "Did you see Tim run up to Charlie and kill him, and then throw the satchel away? He's lucky he's not dead."

"Shut up. He can hear you."

We were approaching the ship, when the pilot yelled into the radio, "Mother hen, we have a problem. We're running out of fuel."

"Baby chick, can you make it home?"

"I'm going to try." We continued on toward the ship. She was in sight, then we were over the deck, maybe six feet, when the engine shut down and we dropped to the deck. Everyone ran toward us, and we got out of the chopper and ran in case it blew.

The Air Officer yelled, "Lieutenant, is everyone all right?"

"Yes Sir. We're fine. She was close though."

"That's enough, Lieutenant. Get down to debriefing."

I looked at the chopper. There were bullet holes all over the place. I almost shit. I wondered why no one had been hit.

"Tim, let's go. We have to be debriefed." We all went to interrogation. The Air Officer was there and I told him my story.

"Tim, have you left anything out?"

"No Sir. I gave the briefcase to the C.O. and was walking back to the chopper when all hell broke loose."

"Okay Tim, have a coffee."

The pilot and co-pilot gave their account. "Commander, Tim didn't tell you what happened on the way back to the chopper. He killed a gook with his bare hands. The gook had a bomb and was running toward the chopper. He was going to blow us to eternity. Tim caught him and broke his neck, then threw the bomb away from the chopper. The next thing we knew there was another gook coming, and Tim killed him with his knife. I looked around to see if anyone else was coming. Tim jumped into the chopper a couple of minutes later. I don't know where he was. When he got in the chopper, we took off. We were under heavy fire from the ground. We were lucky to make it—thanks to Tim."

The Captain listened silently to the pilots.

"I can tell you where Tim was," he said. "For those few minutes, he went back and saved the C.O.'s life. Evidently, he threw that damn knife about thirty feet into a gook's throat and saved the C.O.'s life. I have the message in my hand—read it."

"Tim, I know it's not easy to kill a human being, but this is war. It's different. Thanks to you, there are several men alive and that is what makes the difference. Lieutenant, are you married?"

"Yes Sir, I am."

"Tim, think about this. The Lieutenant's wife would be a widow if you hadn't done what you did. I'm proud of you. You don't have to worry, tomorrow we leave for the States.

That should make you feel better. Now, get out of here and get some rest."

"Captain?"

"Yes, Lieutenant."

"I think Tim should be decorated for what he did."

"I'll take care of that. Make out your report right away. Get it to me, yesterday. Do you understand?"

"Yes Sir!"

"I want reports from everyone."

"Captain?"

"Yes, Commander."

"Can you imagine Tim, doing what he did? That satchel could have blown him to bits—let alone the chopper. Can I see that letter from the C.O. of the base?"

"Read it."

"I don't know what to say."

"Maybe Pearl Harbor will have something to say. I am going to recommend him for the Navy Cross. The God Darn kid deserves it."

"That's for sure, Captain."

"Get me those reports."

I was sitting in the Mess Hall. Everyone was watching me. I looked up and the Lieutenant and the Sargent from the Marine Detachment were standing by my table.

"Tim, can we join you?" the Lieutenant asked.

"We heard what you did. We just wanted to say we're proud of you. We were wondering about something. We understand that you will be getting out when we reach the States. I would like to offer you a chance to join us. The Marines could use you."

"Thanks, but if I do anything, I would prefer the Navy. I love it. I think you guys are great too. But the Navy is my love. Anyway, I don't know what I am going to do. I'll know when we get to the States."

"Okay Tim. Whatever you do I'm sure it will be the right thing. It seems I am always shaking your hand. Thanks." I watched them leave.

The Chief came by and said, "What did they want, Tim?"

"They asked me if I wanted to become one of them."

"What did you say?"

"I told them no."

"Does that mean you are staying in the Navy?"

"I'm not sure of that either, Chief."

"Tim, you're one hell of a sailor! Think about it."

"I will, Chief. First, I want to go home and see some of my friends. I haven't seen them in a couple of years. Four to be exact."

"I can understand that. Just remember if you decide to come back to us, jump on a plane and re-enlist onboard the ship. We want you here."

"Thanks again, Chief."

I was sitting in the Air Office where the directors hung around. The door opened and the Chief was standing there. He said, "I need a volunteer. We have another shuttle to go on."

Everyone moaned. "This is strictly a volunteer mission. You will be going deep. You have to stop at a designated spot to refuel. That's how deep you will have to go."

No one volunteered. I looked at the Chief and said, "I'll go."

"I don't think so, Tim; you barely made it back from the last one. Besides, you're going to be discharged when we get back to the States. Have you forgotten?"

"No Sir. I haven't forgotten."

"Tim, this sounds like a very dangerous mission. This is the deepest we have ever gone into the jungle. I imagine that the chopper will be under fire most of the way. The VC will be all over the place. There is a chance that you won't be able to fuel up. That means crashing. We are banking on getting there before they find out. The outpost needs some medicine fast. That's why we going. There will be some "Top Secret" orders this time. It can't fall into the enemy's hands. You know what that means. Now, who wants to volunteer?"

"I'll still go, Chief."

"Are you sure?"

"I think I am better qualified than the clowns sitting here."

"I guess you're right, but I don't like it."

"You mean, you're worried about me, Chief?"

"Don't flatter yourself, punk."

We laughed. The Chief left the office.

"Commander, I have a volunteer."

"Good. Who is it?"

"Tim. He wouldn't let anyone volunteer. He says he is better qualified than any of the other men."

"Well, he is. But I think he has done his share."

"I told him that, Sir. He still wouldn't let anyone else volunteer."

I arrived on the flight deck and saw the pilot and co-pilot waiting. I knew then, this wasn't going to be an easy mission—they both had automatic weapons. I was handed one also.

"Thanks Lieutenant, is this for real?"

"Sure is. Get aboard."

I had been on quite a few missions, but this was the first time I'd been given a weapon. I thought, I'll be glad when this shuttle flight is over. But I definitely had an uneasy feeling about it.

We had been airborne a couple of hours and I was looking at the supplies and the briefcase, when I heard a noise.

"Hey Lieutenant! What the hell was that noise?"

"Not sure, Tim. I'm checking now."

It's funny how you can tell when something is wrong by the sound. All of a sudden, the pilot was yelling to hold on, we were going down. It happened fast. Before we knew it, we were falling through the trees.

"Captain, I have part of a message from the chopper. They're in trouble. Before we could get a fix, the transmission went dead. They have gone down."

"Commander, get some planes in the air immediately. I want that chopper found. Now move! Call communications and tell them to keep trying. Besides Tim, who is on the chopper?"

"Nelson, Peters, and Jenkins!"

"Get the planes launched; I want them back."

It wasn't long before the planes were in the air. But the Captain knew they wouldn't be able to find the downed chopper. The jungle was too thick. They would be on their own.

I woke up and looked inside the chopper. I saw Jenkins first. I checked him. He was dead. Peters was dead also. I heard Lieutenant Nelson groan. I checked him. He was in bad shape and I knew he wasn't going to make it. "Lieutenant, I'll get you out of here."

"Tim, destroy the briefcase, burn everything. That's an order. I'm a dead man. Now, get out of here!"

I forced open the case and burned everything inside. I went back to the Lieutenant. He was struggling to speak. All he kept saying was for me to get out of there. He grabbed me and pulled me toward him.

"Tim, head northeast. Then turn south. That way you can get to the coast. They won't expect you to do that. I watched him die in my arms. I took all of their dog tags with me. Grabbing everything I could carry, I left, but not before rigging a surprise for Charlie. There was no way I wanted Charlie to screw with their bodies.

I hadn't gotten far before Charlie arrived. I was hiding in the bush and could see them all around the chopper. It only took a minute before the grenades went off. The whole area went up. Everything was burning, even Charlie. I decided to leave while I had a chance.

Moving slowly through the jungle, not making a sound, I found a place to hide after a couple of hours. I wanted to travel at night because it would be safer. I had been on the move for three days and still hadn't found a clearing so I could turn south. I'd already figured out that I would have to walk out of the jungle.

I hid out during the day. The woods were crawling with VC. I figured the Navy had probably given up the search. I wondered if they had sent a telegram back home telling them I was missing in action. I had put Mr. Chin down as the person to notify if anything had happened to me. He was better suited for the job than anyone else.

"Mr. Chin, you don't look too good today."

"Jill, I have some bad news for you. Tim is missing in action. I just received a telegram from the Navy."

"I don't believe it!"

"I don't believe it either. But, I know Tim and he'll be back. I am sure of it. I had to tell you anyway, just in case."

"Thank you, Mr. Chin," Jill said as she started to cry.

"Mr. Chin, what are you doing at the station?"

"Tim is missing in action. I just got the telegram."

"That's bullshit. Tim will be back."

"I believe that also. I know Tim. He is prepared for anything. I will never give up hope."

"Do the Bakers know?"

"I was just going there."

"Can we go with you? They will take this hard."

They left the station and drove to the Bakers. Mr. Baker opened the door.

"What's up fellas?"

"It's Tim, he's missing in action. Mr. Chin just got a telegram."

"It can't be true." Mrs. Baker walked up to the door, beside her husband.

"Hi, how are you?" she asked.

"Fine, Mrs. Baker."

"Have you heard from Tim?"

"We have some bad news. Tim is missing in action. We just found out."

Mrs. Baker started to cry and Mr. Baker put his arm around her. "Gentlemen would you like to come in."

"No Sir. I think you should be alone right now. Just remember, this only means he's missing. He'll be back."

"Bill, Chuck. I know you won't believe me, but I am going to say this anyway. I felt Tim's presence the other day. I know he is alive. I don't care what the Navy says. I firmly believe he is alive. They will never convince me otherwise," Mr. Chin said seriously.

"You will hear about him. Tim can survive in the jungle. I taught him how. That's why I know for sure. The Navy hasn't seen the last of him. Mark my words."

"You know something, Mr. Chin. I believe you. We haven't heard the last of him."

"See you later, Mr. Chin."

"Goodnight gentlemen."

"Bill, what do you make of that?"

"I think he's right. Tim is coming back. Mr. Chin is no fool. He has a sixth sense about this. I would never question him."

"I think you're right, Bill."

Mr. Chin thought about Tim and what he'd taught him. Then he grinned and walked into the rear room. He lit a candle for Tim. "My shrine has never let me down. Tim is somewhere in Vietnam. He's going to do his job and come back. I'll pray for that."

It was dark. I could see the campfires the VC had lit. I knew it was time to move on. I started to walk but could hear some talking. Charlie was nearby; he was too close. I knew I was in trouble. I could tell he was walking right toward me. I decided to wait. He was only a few feet away. I waited for him to get right up to me. When he stopped it was too late; my knife quickly ended his life. There were five others coming. One by one, I killed them. I took their food and left the area. I knew it would only be a matter of time before they were missed. I had to put a lot of distance between us. I kept moving without a break until dawn. Then I found a place to hide.

I found a large tree that was rooted out. I shoved my rifle in it first. Somehow I didn't want to climb in with a bunch of snakes. But it was empty. I covered it with brush and went inside. I slept all day. When darkness set in, I was getting ready to move on again. I knew Charlie had found the bodies. Looking out of the tree, I saw Charlie was searching everything. One of them was standing next to the tree; I slid my knife into him. He never made a noise. I kept after them and one by one they fell. There were bodies all over the place. I moved on not daring to stop. I was running low on food and water. The only way to get food was to scrounge for it. I caught a snake, cut the head off, and slit the stomach. The blood oozed out. I drank it. I had to eat the snake raw because I couldn't start a fire. It would have been a dead give away.

I thought of Mr. Chin. What would he do? I just had to use my head. I saw some thick brush up ahead and worked myself into it. I was completely quiet. Hours passed. When I crawled out of the brush, the sun was coming up. I had to chance walking in the daylight. After walking for hours, I spotted a clearing. I wondered if I should walk around it.

But time was precious so I decided to cross it. It wasn't long before I knew I had made a big mistake. Charlie was thick as shit in the surrounding grass. I pointed my weapon at the closest one and shot. He dropped. The rest were coming at me so I laid down, reached for my knife, and crawled into the grass. Charlie was almost on top of me when I grabbed his leg. He fell and my knife slid over his throat. I moved to the next one. I was right on him. He looked at me, but it was too late. My knife found its mark. This stalking in the grass went on for about an hour. I had killed about a dozen of them.

I finally made it back into the jungle where I knew I could hide. I stayed there all night then decided to stay there and rest for a couple of days.

Day after day of trudging through the jungle passed. I soon found out, however, that Charlie hadn't given up. They were being very cautious. They had lost many men, but they weren't giving up. They wanted me real bad. It seemed like they were sending more and more men to look for me.

I kept on moving and found a cave where I could get some rest. I checked it out and the only thing inside was a snake. I stayed for a few days, covering the entrance with brush. One night as I was sitting in the cave, I felt my luck, was bound to run out soon. It was just a matter of time. I knew I couldn't keep going like I had been. I fell asleep.

When I woke up, I was staring up the muzzle of a gun. Several to be exact. There were six of them, all heavily armed. I knew there was nothing I could do. One of them knocked me out. When I regained consciousness, I found I was tied to a tree, under two armed guards. I noticed one of them was wearing my knife. That pissed me off. I swore he would be the first one to die. They cut me loose from the tree and we started to walk. Every time I slowed down, I was kicked and beaten. I hurt from head to toe. They seemed to enjoy hitting me with the butt of their rifles. I thought of my mother who'd taught me to walk away from a fight. But I didn't think she would want me to walk away from this one. As we walked, I kept on falling. Each time I did, I was hit with the butt of a rifle. I wondered why they didn't just kill me. I was just an enlisted man; I was of no value to them.

One of them came up to me and said in English, "We will be in my camp tomorrow. You are going to be questioned by my Major. When we have no use for you, you will die. You have killed too many of my men. I will take great pleasure in killing you."

"Why don't you just kill me now?"

"You don't ask the questions. We do."

He was laughing. I knew that I had to escape. Only one guard watched me, the rest slept. I knew it was time to make my move. If we got to their camp, I knew I would die.

I watched the guard. He was getting tired. The VC were not the best-trained men; they were mostly made up of farmers and peasants. Their training amounted to giving them a weapon and sending them out to kill Americans. But they knew the jungle and every trail that was available. After all, it was where they lived.

I worked on the ropes. Finally, I managed to get free. I made my way silently to the one carrying my knife. I grabbed him by the neck and twisted his neck. He died instantly. I took my knife and felt complete again. Silently, moving to the second VC, I plunged my knife into his heart. I had my hand over his mouth so he wouldn't cry out. Two down—four to go. I managed to kill all of them. I gathered up what supplies I could carry. I was determined to put some distance between us. When the bodies were discovered, they would begin looking for me.

I walked for hours. I ached all over; the beatings were taking their toll on me. Resting in a hiding place, I thought how peaceful the jungle was at night and how under different circumstances I would have liked it. It was so peaceful that I started to forget about Charlie. The jungle was damp and dark most of the time. The overhead foliage gave it a creepy air. The only thing I didn't like were the snakes. They were all over the place. Most of them were deadly—one bite and it was all over.

Soon, it was time to move on. Suddenly, I heard a noise and looked around, but I couldn't see anything. Remaining motionless, I knew Charlie was around; in fact, I sensed there were several of them. I figured I would let them pass. I heard the noise again. I thought, The noise is real alright, but what is it?

Finally I could see some movement. Khaki jackets, I thought, I've seen them somewhere before. Soon, they were all over the place. Then I remembered I'd seen them at some of the outposts I had been on the shuttle missions. They were crazy, and I knew they would shoot first and ask questions later. I hadn't liked them when I'd seen them at the outposts and I liked them even less now. How can I let them know I'm here? If I stand up, they will open fire for sure. I definitely don't want to startle them. When they were about fifteen feet away from the tree I was hiding behind, I spoke out loud. They hit the dirt. I yelled, "Don't shoot! I am an American sailor." I knew immediately that had been a stupid thing to say. One of them yelled, "What the hell is a sailor doing out here?" "Look stupid—I'm going to throw my gun out," I shouted back, hoping this would convince them. I threw my rifle out from behind the tree then stepped out, with my hands in the air.

"Who the hell are you? Better yet, what are you doing here?"

"My name is Tim Collins. I was assigned to a carrier and was shot down while on a mission. I have been hiding out for sometime now."

"Mac, I know who this kid is. He was on that chopper that was shot down some weeks back. Everyone has been looking for him. There hasn't been a trace of him for some time."

"How the hell did you manage to stay alive this long?" Mac asked.

"How long has it been since you were shot down? And how the hell did you get here? The chopper was shot down north of here. Are you the one who has been killing Charlie all over the place?"

"I guess you could say that."

"Let me see that knife, kid."

"I don't think so."

"Are you the only one left from the crew?"

"Yes, they're all dead. The Lieutenant was the last one to die. I burned the dispatches before I took off."

"You did a nice job booby trapping the chopper. But just count yourself lucky. If you had stayed around, Charlie would have gotten you. You would be dead."

"I have some questions for you," the guy who seemed to be in charge said. "So, you're the guy that's been killing Charlie wholesale. We came across quite a few bodies back there that had their throats cut. It seems someone is pretty handy with a knife. Is that the knife doing the damage?"

"I've had to kill a few people since the crash," I replied quietly. They started to laugh.

"I understand. There are quite of few VC with their ancestors now. I would like to chat some more, but I think we better get out of here. Because of you, and that knife, Charlie has sent in more troops to this area. We had a hard time getting around them. A lot of people are going to be surprised that you're still breathing."

"Tim, can I see that knife?" Mac asked again.

"I already told you no. I don't allow anyone to touch it."

"Where did you get it?"

"It's a long story. I suggest we do what you say and get the hell out of here."

"You're right, move out. Tim, if you get shot, I want that knife."

"I think you better keep in front of me at all times. I wouldn't want to get shot in the back."

"Don't worry, I can wait for it. I think I want you on my side for now."

We walked on through the jungle, but I didn't like it. It was too quiet.

"Hey Mac. There's something wrong. It's too quiet here. I have a hunch Charlie is waiting for us," I whispered.

I watched Mac clench his weapon.

"Are you sure?"

"I can feel them."

"Great! He can feel them. That's all we need—a psychic."

"Listen, what do you hear?" someone else asked.

"That's right. Where is the noise?" said Mac.

"Mac, I think the kid is right."

"Screw you Jack! I don't hear anything."

"The kid's right. Kneel down everyone!"

It was too late. We'd walked into an ambush. I saw Mac get hit. A bullet ripped open his chest. Bullets were flying all around us. We fired back in all directions. I saw a short guy get hit and fall to the ground. I knew we were in trouble when I saw the South Vietnamese soldiers running away like cowards. We were left alone to handle it. I felt a sharp pain; I was hit.

When I regained consciousness, I was I surrounded by Charlie. This time I knew I was in real trouble. There were just too many of them. I decided it would be easier to escape from the prison camp that they were taking me to. Besides, I was in no shape to try to escape. My head hurt. I could feel the dry blood and knew I had to clean the wound. In the jungle infections take hold quickly. But I knew they would never give me water; they only gave you just enough to keep you alive.

After we had been walking for several hours and were close to the camp, we stopped and I was tied to a tree. One of them knelt down next to me. He was holding a canteen. When he placed it on my lips, I started to take a sip, but he pulled it back. I watched the water fall to the ground. They all laughed.

It was then I knew nothing they could do to me would get the best of me. I decided that I was going to survive. I was more determined than ever to make it. A change seemed to come over me. I wasn't sure what was happening. I only knew that I just wanted to kill as many of them as possible. I could think of nothing else.

One of them walked over to a tree and took a bag off of it. Reaching inside, he pulled out a snake. He came toward me with the snake.

I thought, It's all over, now. I am going to die a horrible death. The only thing I feared was dying from snakebite. The prick came up to me with the snake in his hand and held it under my nose. He pushed the snake to within a quarter of inch of my nose, then pulled it back. He did this several times. Then he stuck the snake right into my face and it bit me.

While the VC laughed, I was waiting to die. I had no idea how long it would take for the poison to work. Then Charlie threw the snake into the jungle. And they all just kept on laughing.

In a few minutes, he came back and taunted me, "American, can you feel the warmth of the poison? You must feel the warmth of the venom?"

I didn't answer. Laughing he said, "You are lucky. The next snake will be poisonous."

"You think you're funny, Charlie. Next time I will kill you. Then it will be my turn to laugh. How does that sound?" In my mind, I saw my knife running into his stomach. I could hardly wait for that day.

A young Vietnamese officer walked toward me with a certain swagger. I knew he was the man in charge. He wasn't like the rest. He ordered them to untie me from the tree.

"What are you doing here, sailor?"

I was shocked—he spoke perfect English. I stared at him.

"I will ask you again, sailor. What are you doing here? Where did you come from?"

"I was in a chopper and we were shot down. I've been walking in this God-forsaken jungle for weeks. What else do you want to know?"

"You're liar. We' will find out the truth. We have our ways. You will find out soon enough—I promise you."

He reached into his pocket and pulled out the dog tags I'd taken from the men who'd died in the crash.

"Which one of these belongs to you?"

I heard him call out the names. When he came to mine, I told him I was Tim.

"Your name is Collins?"

"Yes, Tim Collins."

"I don't think so. I think you're an officer and you are a coward. You're hiding in an enlisted man's uniform. I have seen this before."

"Think what you like. I know who I am."

"We will find out soon enough. Like I stated before, we have our ways. You will wish to tell the truth, Lieutenant Nelson. After we've finished with you, you'll tell us everything we want to know."

I felt his fist hit me in the face and could feel the warmth of my blood as I fell to the ground. I smiled at him. He yelled for his men to hold me. They put a noose around my neck, and one of them grabbed a piece of wood and slid it under my arms. Another one pulled the noose so I was forced to stand up. Then they tied me to the tree again. That is how I stayed until dawn.

In the morning, we started our march through the jungle again. I had to keep up with Charlie. If I didn't I was beaten. After a while I became numb to the pain; I just kept walking. I told myself I wasn't going to let them get the best of me. I survived on sheer hate. The more they beat me, the more determined I was to survive.

I was always thirsty. I knew they wouldn't give me water so I waited until we crossed a stream when I would let myself fall to get a drink. I would drink as much as I could before they forced the rope on my neck to make me stand up. But it didn't matter; I'd gotten a drink. It took them a long time to figure out what I was doing. When finally they did, they beat me. Inside, I was laughing; just putting one over on them made me laugh. I really didn't care if the water was bad. I figured getting the shits was better than dying of thirst.

We finally reached the camp. It was a shit hole. I was tied to a tree again. I watched as the Lieutenant walk toward me. I knew he was going to be a pain in the ass.

"Sailor, are you comfortable?" I didn't answer. He laughed. "This tree is your home tonight. Sleep tight."

It soon got dark. Everyone slept. I decided if the guard on duty nodded off, I was going to make my move. The ropes weren't as tight as usual; they'd loosened up by my constant falling down.

The first guard stayed awake. A few hours passed, then another guard took over. I remembered this one. Whenever he got a chance to rest, he took it. There is nothing worse than getting up from a sound sleep to go on watch. Sure enough, he began to nod off then the asshole fell asleep. I was just getting ready to make my move when I looked up and saw the Lieutenant go over to the guard. He found the guard sleeping. I remained absolutely quiet. I didn't want him to know I was awake.

He kicked the guard. The guard woke up and the Lieutenant removed his gun. He pointed it at the guard. I saw the look of fear on the guard's face. Then the gun went off. The guard was dead. The Lieutenant looked over at me and said, "This is what we do to our men when they fuck up." He yelled something to the other men, and they picked up the body and threw it into the woods.

Another officer walked over to me and said, "Sailor, my name is Major Tran. I will be the man between you and your dying. I will say this only once. If you don't cooperate, you will die. You've already seen what happens. You may as well know this—we have no regard for life, even less for yours."

It didn't take me long to find that out. Even the Major's men were scared of him. I could see the fear in their eyes; they were scared shitless. I noticed that Tran's face was covered with scars. You could tell he had been fighting for some time. He didn't look like the other men. He was regular Army. Later, I found out he was from the north. He was a North Vietnamese Regular—the worst of the lot. I soon found out that Major Tran was the most sadistic man on this God's earth.

Major Tran yelled and two men came running. I could see the fear in their faces. They untied me from the tree and made me walk in front of them. We entered a grass hut and once inside, I was knocked down. I could feel the blood running down my face. I thought, This is it. I am going to be tortured. But little did I suspect just how much pain I was going to have to endure.

Looking around the room, I saw there wasn't much there, only a desk and a chair. There was also a lamp on the desk. The two goons stood next to me. The Major entered the room.

"Sailor, what is your name? I mean your real one. I know you switched uniforms. That makes you a coward. In my Army, we shoot cowards."

"Major, in your Army, you shoot everyone. Innocent as well as guilty."

"That is not true."

"Tell that to the man that was shot yesterday."

"He was asleep on watch. That means death."

"Not in my Navy. We give them extra duty to perform. That is why we will win."

"We'll see about that sailor. Now what is your name?"

"Tim Collins, US Navy!"

"That's a lie. Now, what is your real name?"

I felt his fist hit me in the face. I fell backwards and the two goons picked me up. Once I was standing, I was hit again. This went on for hours. I lost track of time.

"Tim, are you ready to tell the truth? I promise, if you do, I will make it easy for you while you're here."

"Sailor, I think you like pain. It would be easier if you told the truth. I don't like inflicting pain on people, but I will get the truth out of you eventually. So, why not tell me now? How long have you been in the Navy?"

"Four years. I was going home—my time was up."

"How old are you?"

"Going on twenty-three."

"Now that is better. What were you doing in the jungle, besides killing my people?"

"I was going for a joyride in a chopper when we were shot down." I knew he didn't believe me. Once again, I felt pain. This time the goons were working me over with a rubber tube.

Tran grabbed the tube and kept hitting me until I passed out. Before passing out, I could feel my skin open up from the blows. The pain was becoming unbearable. But I told myself I had to hang in there.

I thought about my mother. The more I thought of her, the more pain I could endure. I knew if they killed me, I would be with her once again. I looked up at Tran and smiled. He grabbed my hair and forced my head back. The more I smiled, the madder he got. It gave me something to look forward to.

"I am going to ask you again? What were you doing in the jungle and what was your mission?"

I didn't answer but continued to look him straight in the eye. I could feel the presence of my mother. I felt the tube hit me again. My blood was warm on my back. And I just kept smiling.

"You are the devil, sailor. I will, break you. You can't take this pain forever. I will enjoy killing you. I will tell you what you are doing here. You see, we already know you are an officer and your name is Lt. Nelson. You were flying the helicopter that we shot down. You have been in the jungle ever since. You are responsible for killing quite a few of my men. This is the knife you used on them. I intend to keep it and kill you with it."

"Major, that's funny. I intend to do the same thing to you." The two goons pulled my head back. Tran smiled as he slid the knife across my chest. I could feel it cutting. I held back the pain although it was almost impossible. After he'd sliced me a few times, I passed out. When I came to Tran was standing over me. "Did you have a good nap?"

"It was pretty nice, Tran. Your nap won't be so nice, believe me. Major, haven't you got the picture yet. I have nothing to say to you. So why don't you just fuck off!"

Tran grabbed my arm and cut it just above the elbow. I watched the blood flow out of the wound.

"I can see you can take pain," he said as he hit me with the butt of the knife. I passed out again.

This time when I woke up I was in a hut, tied to a stake in the center of the room. I suddenly realized I was thirsty. I hadn't had anything to drink all day. I wondered how long it would be before they came and got me again.

"Are you ready to talk now?"

I remained quiet.

"Did you murder my men?"

"You wouldn't believe me, even if I told you the truth. If you plan on killing me, go ahead. I am tired of looking at your face, asshole."

Tran came up to me and hit me repeatedly in the face. I just sat there taking the pain. Every time I passed out, they would throw water on me. Then the beating would begin all over again. The game went on for quite some time. It was Tran against me. I knew that I was getting to him. He finally stopped cutting me. The reason for this was simple: he'd pretty well cut most of my body.

The torture went on for weeks and weeks. I was beaten every night. The South Vietnamese prisoners always treated me when I was brought back to the hut.

Then Tran changed his tactics. After the beatings, instead of water he threw piss on me. He'd figured out I was drinking the water and knew I wouldn't drink piss. But this didn't work. I still kept my mouth shut. He didn't have a clue about me. Time passed. I had no idea how long I'd been there. I guessed it was months.

"Sailor you have been here for quite a while. I still have some tricks left. I don't think you are going to be able to take much more."

I smiled. Every time I smiled, I got kicked and hit until I passed out. Each time I woke up, I was back in my hut. One day I felt someone's hands over me and heard a voice. It was very distinctive. The guy was American.

"It's okay, sailor. My name is Capt. Roberts and this is Capt. Caldwell. We are Army officers. What is your name?"

"Tim Collins, Sir!"

"What the hell are you doing here? Why is Tran torturing you so much?"

"They don't believe I am an enlisted man. They think I am an officer. They just don't believe me."

"Well, you're in deep shit. If they ever do find out the truth, they'll kill you. They don't bother with enlisted men.

Enlisted men have no value to them. So, I guess you know you have to keep your mouth shut."

"I have been doing that for sometime now."

"Tim, do you know how long you been here?"

"I guess a few months."

"We've been told it's been a year."

"You're kidding, aren't you Captain?"

"No, I'm not," Capt. Roberts said solemnly.

"I just don't know how you can keep on taking the pain. Look Tim, they must think you're important, or you would be dead now. That's what has kept you alive all this time. Don't tell anyone else who you really are. Some of these prisoners can't be trusted. You're a dead man if the wrong person finds out. Do you know where this puts us? We'll all be dead if they find out. They'll figure we knew and didn't say anything."

"You got that right," Capt. Caldwell added. "If Tran finds out we knew, he will kill us all. He is capable of killing everyone in the camp. He doesn't care about anything. First of all Tim, never refer to us as sir. That's a dead give away. Just call us by our names. If you get use to calling us by our names, you'll be less likely to screw up. My name is Ken and he is Paul. You must be from the chopper that crashed last year. What the hell were you doing that far into the jungle?

"Forget it," Capt. Caldwell said, holding up his hand. "On second thought, I don't want to know."

We all shook hands. At least now, I have someone to talk to, I thought to myself.

"Tim, we've been prisoners at another camp for quite some time and were just brought to Tran's lovely camp. We are going to help you survive this camp. First of all, you have to get as much sleep has you can. Charlie gets his kicks by keeping you up. Second, do not piss the guards off. I know it will be hard. Food is scarce. We can't afford to waste anything. You'll eat shit before this is over. If you're hungry, check the floor. There is always something crawling. Water is also scarce. When it rains, drink and catch all you can. Rub the bamboo when you're in your hut—moisture forms there. You can also get some oil to tend to your wounds from the bamboo.

"Remember Tim, you will live as long as they don't know who you are. They may make you watch as they kill us. But you have to keep your mouth shut. We expect to die. It's only a matter of time. You must never give in. They will threaten you with our lives. Tell them you don't give a shit. We aren't doing you a favor; we are just looking out for ourselves. The longer Tran tortures you. The less he will be torturing us. Get the picture?

"Tim, as you already know, these bastards are experts at torture. They have been living with torture for hundreds of years. Vietnam has a history of being invaded. But being invaded is one thing, being conquered is another. These people have never really been conquered. They still have a lot of tricks up their sleeves. It is going to get worst before it gets better. Before they are finished, you will wish you were dead. I already know the feeling and maybe you already know the feeling, now. Get some sleep; tomorrow is another day. You're going to need all the rest you can get."

That night the VC left me alone and I was able to get a good night's sleep. I woke up at dawn, wondering what was in store for me. It wasn't long before the goons came for me and dragged me out by my hair. Tran was waiting.

I was knocked to the floor. My ankles were tied to a pole and I was lifted until my head was just off the floor. They left the room and I remained suspended in that position for hours. I heard the door open and opened my eyes.

Tran was standing there.

"Well sailor, is that position comfortable?"

"Not bad. I could use a TV."

Tran did not answer me. Although it was hard to do, I kept a smile on my face. The longer I hung there, the greater was the pain.

"Are you ready to talk or do you need more time hanging around?"

I smiled at him and watched him walk to the corner of the hut. He picked up a bamboo rod, smiling. When he came back, he hit me over and over. I just kept thinking of my mother. The pain was minimal when I did this. After awhile I passed out. They threw piss on me to wake me up. I was getting use to the smell. God knows, they threw enough of it on me.

"Sailor, you have been taking this pain for months. That tells me you are more than an enlisted man. No enlisted man could take that much pain. You have to be trained to take that much pain. I will reach your breaking point that I promise you.

"Hey Ken, Tran is at it again. He has Tim in the hut. That kid should have broken by now. I can't understand why he hasn't."

"I know. I have been wondering about Tim. Is he really what he claims to be. I don't think I could stand that much pain for so long. Whoever he is—he's got guts."

When I came to, my ankles were tied to a tree. Tran's goons were yelling at the men. I watched them walk into the jungle and when they came back, they were carrying a burlap bag. That only meant one thing, snakes. Now I knew what he had in mind.

I was lowered to the ground. I watched them dig a hole. When they finished digging, they emptied the bag into the hole. They moved me right over the snakes. I could see them squirming in the hole. I watched as Tran walked over to me. He smiled and looked into the hole.

I was lowered to the ground. "Sailor, meet your new playmates. I guarantee you will get close to them. I think you will answer my questions now, unless you feel like playing with my friends."

"Go to hell, you bastard! Get it over with." I started to smile again.

"Sailor, I am going to wipe that smile off your face today."

"Paul look at this!"

Standing near the window, Capt. Caldwell and Capt. Roberts watched Tran and Tim. "God, what a lousy bastard Tran is. I wonder if Tim can take this."

"I sure hope Tran, never does that to me. I hate snakes."

"That's two of us. I can't stand them either. When I was a kid, I wouldn't even pick them up."

I was hanging over the pit. I heard Tran tell his goons to bring Paul over to the pit. Two of his goons came out with Capt. Roberts. I knew what Tran was going to do. He was going to use Paul to get me to talk.

"Sailor, if you don't tell me what I want to know, the good Captain will meet my friends."

The Captain started to fight. Tran's men grabbed him. One of the goons came back with a snake in his hand. This one was poisonous. We all knew it. I saw Captain Roberts laugh. Tran motioned for his man to bring the snake closer and Paul looked at me and smiled.

"Hey Tran, can I get a better look at the snake?"

Paul looked at the snake, turned to Tran and yelled, "Fuck you asshole!" and put his hand in the snake's mouth. I yelled but it was too late. Capt. Roberts fell to his knees. It was over in seconds. What a way to go!

"Sailor, your friend is dead because of you. There was no need for him to die. All you had to do was answer my questions."

"Major, I am going to kill you. If you were smart you would drop me in that hole. If it is the last thing I do, I will make sure you suffer before you die." Tran laughed.

"Laugh now Tran, your day is coming. You are going to be my prisoner." I was taken to the hut. Captain Caldwell was standing at the window.

"I'm sorry, before I could do anything Paul . . ."

"Shut up Tim. I just lost a good friend. I know it wasn't your fault."

We both knew who was next.

Captain Caldwell looked at me and said, "You will continue to say nothing. That is how Paul wanted it. It's just a matter of time. Saying something now would be stupid. Tran played his ace. He will save me for last. He will use me to get to you. He will kill me someday, but it won't be for awhile."

Months passed neither Tran nor I gave an inch. Captain Caldwell and I were still alive. We were both being tortured now. Ken got his strength from me. I just kept smiling, driving Tran nuts. The beatings weren't so severe now because Tran had to keep me alive. I was winning.

One morning, the two goons came to the hut and I was told to go outside. Tran came up to me and said, "Sailor, today is snake day. It is time to play. I think they will eat today. I have no further use for you."

I smiled and spit in Tran's face. "Go ahead, bring on the snakes. I am not afraid to die. Remember, what I said, someday I will make you visit your ancestors. Now bring on the snakes. I am ready."

Tran's two goons each had a snake in their hands. They would put them within an inch of my face. Every time they did this I smiled. I knew that was pissing them off.

Tran waved his hand and the two goons marched me back to the hut. I was hit in the back of the head. I fell to the floor, when I woke up and looked around I saw a new man in the hut. He was Vietnamese. I wanted to kill him.

"Captain, who the hell is this gook?"

"He's all right, Tim. I know him. He's South Vietnamese. His name is Captain Nge."

"Captain, they have done a number on this kid," I heard the new prisoner say.

"What the hell do they want with him? Better yet, who is he?"

Captain Caldwell and Captain Nge washed me and gave me some water. Little did I know then how close Nge and I would become. I fell asleep almost immediately.

"Captain. Who is that kid?"

"He's the one that was shot down a long time ago. You remember everyone was searching for him. Tran thinks he's an officer. That's why he is hiding his identity. His name is Tim. He's was off some carrier and was shot down."

"So, he's the one that killed all the VC they found in the jungle. He only used a knife on most of them."

When I woke up, Nge was standing over me.

"Are you okay Tim?"

"Yea, I have felt better."

"My name is Captain Nge; I am South Vietnamese. I was shot down three days ago. That's why I am here. I was the only one brought here. I guess everybody else is dead.

"The Captain told me who you are. Your secret is safe with me. If Tran finds out the truth, you know what will happen to you.

"Everybody was looking for you. They think you're dead. Eventually, Tran will kill you. He has to—to save face. You left a lot of bodies. I hope we can do that again."

"I intend to. I am looking forward to killing Tran personally. I live for that day."

As the months went by, I had no idea of how long I'd been a prisoner. I guessed years. One day, Captain Caldwell was called into Tran's office. We heard a gun shot. The Captain was dead. He was right—Tran had no further use for him so he shot him for no other reason.

"Tim, how long have you been here?"

"I'm not sure. I was captured in 1963. I don't know what year it is now."

"It is 1970."

"God, I have been here seven years."

"Yes, about that."

"Nge, have you any idea what is over there?"

"I'm not sure."

"I was looking over there the other day. I think they have more prisoners inside that area. I overheard Tran talking about them when I was in the hut one day when he thought I was unconscious. I always wondered why we were never moved since we got here. I think I would like to check it out one night."

"Are you nuts? There are guards all over the place."

"I know, but I think I can get in and out. Besides I have something up my sleeve for Tran. Lately the guards haven't been checking on us as much as they used to."

"How do you think you can get over there without being noticed?"

"I can sneak out of the hut and crawl over to the west fence. They don't seem to patrol that section. Once there, I can get inside the other camp. If we can move around without being seen, we can escape. The only thing I have to do first is kill Tran."

"How the hell are you going to do that?"

"Like I said, I will work my way around to the other side. Once I check it out, I will figure it out. Nge, I have a knife made out of bamboo. I've kept it hid inside the bamboo flooring. I can slip out of the hut by moving these pieces of bamboo. I will try tonight."

"When the hell did you do this?"

"About a week ago; it was pretty easy."

In the middle of the night, I crawled over to Nge and held my hand over his mouth. He woke and I told him to be quiet.

"I am going now so keep an eye out." I opened the floorboards and lowered myself down. Once outside, I crawled to the other hut and moved slowly under it. I saw two guards. I wanted to kill them, but passed them and went toward the fence. After opening the fence, I crawled through. Spotting a large hut, I went inside. There were prisoners inside. I held my hand over the mouth of one. He woke up and looked at me.

"Who the hell are you?"

"I am from the other side. How many men are in here?"

"Seven Americans, some South Vietnamese prisoners. I don't know how many actually."

"Okay, I have to get back before they miss me. Make sure you keep your mouth shut. No one is to know I was here."

"What about my C.O.?"

"No one. Do you understand? The fewer men who know, the better off I am. Good luck, I'll see you again when the time's right. In the morning you will hear some commotion, but keep your mouth shut. It is time for Charlie to learn what payback is."

I left to return to my hut. I knew I didn't have much time. On the way, I saw the two guards and they were half-asleep. I knew they would be easy. I crawled up to the first one. He was leaning on the hut. Reaching up, I covered his mouth and slit his throat with the bamboo knife. I lowered him to the ground.

The second guard was even easier. He died instantly. I took his rifle and put it against his back to make it look like he was sleeping. I made it back to my hut. I hid the knife and replaced the bamboo boards.

"Tim, how did it go?"

"Good. All hell should break loose in the morning. I killed two of the guards. We have more prisoners on the other side. Tomorrow should be quite interesting."

"Tim, get some rest. I don't think Tran has that many guards here."

"You're right Nge. I don't think there are even thirty— maybe twenty-eight. That's why he keeps us away from the other prisoners. Once I remove a few more of them at night. I think we can demoralize them. I want Tran to worry about that.

Nge and I were in the hut the next morning when all hell broke loose. They found the bodies. We were all made to stand outside while they checked the huts. I looked toward the other camp. This was the first time the guards had ever opened the gates.

Nge and I could see the other prisoners coming into our compound. They were kept separate. We were all waiting to hear what Tran had to say. Everyone had a puzzled look on their face. I guess they were wondering who we were.

I looked at the other prisoners and saw the one I talked to last night. He knew I had killed the guards.

Tran stood in front of us and spoke.

"I have two dead guards. Someone in this camp did it. I will find out and make an example of him. My men are searching your huts. If we find anything, the men living in the hut will be killed. I suggest the man who did this come forward."

No one moved. I stepped forward. Everyone was watching. "Major, can I ask you something?"

Tran looked at me. "There was a guard on our hut all night. How the hell could we get out and kill your men?" Everyone was yelling. I could see Tran was getting mad. He waved his hands and his two goons came and dragged me off. The men were told to go back to their huts.

I was tied and placed in the center of the room. I heard the door open. Tran walked in and stared at me. Then he grabbed the bamboo pole and he hit me. I fell backwards and stayed on the floor motionless. Tran grabbed me by my hair. "I think you killed my men."

"Wrong again, Major. Your man was outside my hut all night. Ask him."

"I don't know how you did it. I just know you did. I should kill you just for the hell of it. But I intend to make an example of you. Take him back to his hut." Tran practiced his art of torture in a more vigorous manner. He beat Nge with the same vengeance. After each beating, we were brought back to the hut. As bad as we were hurting, we always seemed to laugh about it. Tran was getting madder and madder at us. A few weeks passed and the beatings started to dwindle.

Nge and I were in the hut one night. We were both smiling. Nge knew what it meant.

"Well Tim, are you going out tonight?"

"I think so. The guards are becoming lax, so I think tonight is the perfect night for some killing. I have been watching the guards. Tran has sixteen of them watching our side. I will visit the other side and see how many they have."

"I think I would like to go tonight, Tim."

"It will be safer for just one of us to go. I figure if I kill a few more tonight, Charlie will be scared to stand guard duty. If we keep it up, they should go nuts. Tran won't be able to handle them."

"Okay, I want to see you back here before dawn."

"No problem. Nge." I crawled out of the hut, slipped out of the compound, and made my way to the hut on the other side where the other prisoners were sleeping.

I went into the hut and crawled over to where the prisoner I had spoken to before was. I'd since learned his name was Jake. I put my hand over his mouth. He woke up and saw me. He soon had a smile on his face.

"Tim, how is it going?"

"I'm okay just sore."

"Everybody is wondering who is doing the killing. The morale has risen over here. The guys take a beating every day. But when they come back, they have smiles on their faces. All they do is talk about those two guards."

I heard a noise. I could see a shadow coming toward us. Jack grabbed my arm. "It's okay, Tim. It's the C.O."

"Who the hell are you mister?"

"You're worst nightmare if you don't lower your voice. I'm from the other side. That's all you need to know."

"If you get caught here, we'll all be killed. I think I can figure out what you're doing and I think you're nuts. You killed those guards didn't you?"

"I think you have said enough. If you open your mouth again, you're a dead man. I will make sure of that. Do you understand?"

"I don't know what rank you are, but I am a major and outrank you. That makes me in charge."

"Good then, when we break out you can stay behind. Jake, the less this guy knows, the better off we are. Kill him if he talks to any of the guards."

"Wait a minute, you! I wouldn't tell the guards anything. I hate them as much as you. I am no traitor. What the hell is your name?"

"You don't want to know, Sir! Remember this Major, we are all dead men. Tran will kill us all before he lets the Americans take over this prison. My plan is to demoralize the VC. Tonight a lot of them will die. Tomorrow, with any luck, the rest will screw off. Now Major, go to bed and shut up. If you say anything, you will die first."

"Mister, you don't scare me. So go fuck yourself."

"Sir, I think you should wait and see what tomorrow brings."

"I trust this guy," Jake said.

"I have work to do. Make sure you keep your mouth shut tomorrow if anything goes wrong." Once outside, I found the first guard and sent him to be with his ancestors. I crept into the hut where the guards slept and one by one they died. I killed ten of them in their sleep. I left the hut and started back to my hut when I spotted two more guards walking around. I couldn't resist it. I had to slit their throats. Nge was waiting for me when I crawled back into our hut.

"How many are dead tonight?"

"I'm not sure. I guess about fourteen. Ten were sleeping when I hit. Tran should be bullshit tomorrow. I can hardly wait to see his face.

I left a message for Tran tonight. One that he will never forget. I don't think his men are going to be happy either. I think they will desert first thing tomorrow. There are twelve guards on the other side. They aren't going to be any trouble."

It was almost dawn. Nge and I watched Tran's hut. We could see the dead gook leaning against it.

I felt Nge touch my shoulder. "Tim, look at the gate, near the compound. That guard sure is in a hurry."

The guard ran into Tran's hut. I was smiling. The guard and Tran came out of the hut. They were standing near the front steps, and I saw Tran look down at the guard leaning against his hut. He jumped off the porch and kicked the guard. The guard fell to the ground.

Tran had a strange look on his face.

"Major Tran! There are more dead men on the other side. I talked to the other guards, no one saw anything. The men are scared. They say there is a demon in the compound."

"I think I know what to make of it," Tran replied, glaring at our hut.

"Tim, I think we are about to have company."

"Guard! Have you been on duty all night?"

"Yes Sir, right here."

"Did you see anything last night?"

"No Sir! No one left this hut. I am sure of it. I checked the hut several times last night. If there is something wrong, it wasn't from this hut."

"Are you sure?"

"I'm positive, Major."

All the guards were scared. We could see the fear on their faces. We had no trouble sleeping, but they sure did.

They were scared to sleep even when they were off duty. I knew things were going to be different now. Tran was coming to the end. I figured the guards had one more surprise coming.

I told Nge, "Tonight, Tran dies. Tomorrow, there won't be a guard left. Would you like to have some fun tonight?"

"I sure would, Tim. I want to see Tran die slowly."

"Consider it done." We sneaked out of our hut and went straight to Tran's hut. He was asleep. I held my hand over his mouth. Nge was smiling. I grabbed my knife from Tran and smiled. Tran opened his eyes wide, and I whispered to him, "I told you I would kill you. It's your time to die." Nge wanted the first cut so I handed him the knife. He cut deep, but not deep enough to kill him. Then, I slowly cut Tran all over his body. I don't think there was an inch that wasn't cut. Nge and I returned to our hut. All we had to do was wait.

Morning came and we looked out of our hut. Everyone was gone. The guards had taken off during the night. Nge and I collected all of the weapons that they'd left scattered all over the ground.

I looked up. Jake and all of the prisoners were standing there. We smiled.

The C.O. said, "Son, I just can't believe what I am seeing. Everybody is gone."

"That's for now. I think you should tell your men to pick up everything they can use. Charlie will be back. One thing, Sir. If there are any spies in your group, kill them now!"

"That's murder."

"That's bullshit, Sir. If Charlie gets their hands on you that's murder. Now do it!"

Everybody was heavily armed. They carried food water and ammo. I watch them kill two of the men, they knew were spies. "Make sure the South Vietnamese do the same thing. I don't need surprises later."

All the men were gathered in the compound. "Listen to me. I want you men to find your way back to our lines. I won't be going with you. I have some things to do here."

"Tim, wait a minute."

"What do you want, Major?"

"I just want to say thanks. I was hoping you would come back with us. We can use you. I also owe you an apology for the way I acted the other night."

"Forget it. I have a score to settle with Charlie. If I were you, I would travel at night. One thing for sure—keep the noise down. Charlie is going to be every where. They aren't likely to forget what happened here. Have you got enough ammo and food?"

"We have plenty. Good luck, sailor. I'll tell them you're still alive if we make it back."

"Well Nge, I guess it's goodbye."

"I don't think so. How do you say it in the States? Partners, that's the word isn't it? We're partners from this day on. Where you go, I go. I hate Charlie as much as you do. Now let's move out."

We watched the men disappear into the jungle. We both knew they had to get the hell out of here quickly.

The further they got from this camp, the better their chances. Nge and I made sure we left a clear trail for Charlie to follow. We hoped they would pick up our trail and not the other men's. I wondered how many of them would make it back to our lines.

Nge and I kept moving north, further into the enemies' home ground. After several hours, we turned west and walked until darkness set in. We set up camp for the night. Nge and I talked and kept an ear out for Charlie. We finally fell asleep. Morning came. Nge told me we should keep on traveling southwest.

I asked him why.

"I have family there, Tim. They can hide us out for awhile. That way, we can get some rest."

"Sounds good to me. What worries me is if Charlie shows up, your family won't be safe. You know what they will do to them."

"They will be alright. Besides, they would like to help in anyway they can."

"If you say so, Nge. I just don't want anyone getting hurt because of us. We can keep an eye out for Charlie. The more information we gather the better off we'll be."

"Tim, if we find out what Charlie is up to, the more damage we can do. I know the trails they'll be taking. We can hide out and watch them for awhile."

We went in the direction Nge had suggested. He was right. We spotted Charlie and watched them.

They moved like they were on vacation. We followed them for hours. The further southwest we traveled, the more we saw of them. We decided to find Nge's family. In a few days, we reached the village. Nge went in and talked to his family. I kept watch to make sure Charlie wasn't there. Nge waved for me to come in. He introduced me to his family. They fed us and gave us a safe place to sleep. It felt good to be in a safe place. I must have slept for two days. When I woke up, I looked for Nge and found him talking to his uncle.

"Tim, my uncle says Charlie usually comes into the village every few days. I think we should get out of here."

"I think you're right. Thank your uncle for me."

"You're welcome Tim, I speak English. Take this medallion and hang it around your neck. Whenever it is seen, they will know you're friends."

"Thank you, Sir." We shook hands and left.

"I know where Charlie goes. My uncle told me of a place that even Charlie doesn't go. We can make that our base camp."

"If Charlie won't even go there, what the hell are we going there for?"

"The place is loaded with snakes. We will be safe there."

"Safe! What about the snakes? Are they trained just to bite Charlie; I hardly think so!"

"Don't worry, my people go there all the time. No one has ever been bitten."

"Lead the way." It took us four days to get there. Charlie was smart—the place was crawling with snakes. Every time we saw a snake, Nge laughed. "Tim, sprinkle this dust on your legs. The snakes hate it. They won't even come near it."

"Nge, I hope you have a lot of that stuff."

Nge was laughing again. "Some joke, huh Nge?"

"Don't worry, some day these snakes are going to come in very handy. They are a good source of food. I know. I've eaten them before. The blood doesn't taste bad either.

"Nge, the only snakes I grew up with were green and they didn't have fangs. Those I like."

"Well, you better get use to them, Tim. They are going to be with us for awhile. I think we should get some rest now. Tomorrow we can figure out what to do."

"First thing we should do is store some water."

"I'll take care of that. The jungle will give us all the water we want."

"That's good. Just show me where the faucet is."

We hid out for about a week. Soon both Nge and I felt better. "Hey Nge, I think we should go to work tomorrow."

"I think you're right."

We started out early the next morning. Charlie was all over the place. We watched them set up booby traps. They were expecting trouble. I wondered what they knew that we didn't.

"Tim, what do you think? Should we move the traps?"

"Sure. Let's get busy." We waited for Charlie to finish and leave the area. We switched the traps so Charlie would set them off. "I was wondering, Nge, how did Charlie know where to place the traps?"

"That's easy. You Americans are predictable and that makes it easy for them. Come on, let's get out of here."

We left and a few hours later we came across Charlie hiding in the woods. "Now, what the hell are they up to?"

Nge pointed toward a clearing east of us. "That's why, Tim. Those men are going to walk right into an ambush. Charlie has dug in. All they have to do is wait. They don't stand a chance."

"Nge, I think we can screw this ambush up. What do you think?"

"Sure do. I'll take the ones on the west, and you take the east side." We both split up and headed for the ambush site. I sneaked up on the first gook. He was facing away from me and that made it easy. He was dead before he knew it. I crawled toward the next one, and placing my hand over his mouth, slid my knife into him. He went limp instantly. I could see six of them. One by one, I crawled to them. My knife was full of blood. I was in a killing frenzy. This went on for about fifteen minutes. I was getting ready to move on to the last one when I looked up and saw he was lifting his rifle in my direction. I heard a shot and he fell. I turned and saw Nge next to me.

We looked around to see where the American patrol was. They were hiding behind some trees. "Nge, let's get out of here. I don't want them finding us." We took what we could from Charlie and left. We watched the patrol searching for Charlie.

"Lieutenant, you better come over here."

"Did you find something, Sargent?"

"I can't figure this out. All these men are dead. The blood is still coming out of them. What the hell is going on? I wonder who did this and where are they now?"

"Lieutenant, there are more of them over here. They have had their throats cut. All of them have been killed with a knife, except for that one. What the hell are we dealing with, Jack the Ripper?"

"Search the bodies so we can get the hell out of here. How many are there Sargent?"

"I counted fourteen, Lieutenant.

We watched the soldiers leave. I was smiling.

"What's so funny, Tim?"

"How the hell are they going to explain this to their Captain when they get back. I'm sure no on is going to believe them. I know I wouldn't."

We made sure they got out of the area safely, following them to the LZ, where the choppers would pick them up. The choppers arrived and they left the area.

"Hey Lieutenant, what the hell are we going to tell the brass?"

"Shit, I have no idea. I'll worry about that when we land."

They just got on the ground when the C.O. came over.

"How did it go Lieutenant?"

"I don't know. We ran into something strange out there."

"What the hell do you mean? Did you see the enemy?"

"Yes, Sir!"

The C.O. looked at the men. "You didn't lose anybody. How many did you kill?"

"None Sir. They were dead when we got there."

"Dead? Who was dead? You mean someone else killed them!"

"Sir, we were on patrol, walking in the jungle when we came across a clearing. We moved forward cautiously. We hadn't gone far when we heard a shot. It wasn't aimed at us. When we came to the area, we found Charlie lying all over the place. They had been killed with a knife. All except for one who had been shot. The bodies hadn't been dead long. The blood was still flowing from them. We searched the bodies and found these papers. We never did find the people who'd killed them. We left, called for the choppers, and came back. We counted fourteen dead VC.

"We were walking right into an ambush. Whoever killed them saved our asses."

"Lieutenant, that's a new one on me. I have heard stories coming out of the jungle before, but never one like this. I guess we have a phantom, killing our enemies now. Make out your report right away. Make it good. I'll get in touch with headquarters. I wonder?"

"What's that, Sir?"

"Intelligence sent us a report this morning. It seems some prisoners escaped from a prison camp up north. Two of the men wouldn't come back with the prisoners that escaped. The two men that escaped are the ones that set the prisoners free. They killed everyone in the camp. A knife was used to kill the guards. The prisoners who escaped were found by a recon unit. I think I will go to headquarters. Meet me at the chopper."

"Corporal, get me headquarters right away."

"Yes Sir!"

"Your call, Sir!"

"This is Major Wentworth, get me the General."

"What can I do for you, Major?"

"One of my patrols just got back. It seems they met up with something they can't explain. Charlie had set up an ambush. My men heard one shot. They checked the area and found fourteen dead VC. Thirteen were killed with a knife. One had been shot."

"Major, I just sent you a dispatch. When the chopper arrives, get me those reports right away. I think the dispatch will answer any of your questions."

The chopper was just setting down. A messenger took the dispatch to Major Wentworth. He gave the messenger the reports. "Give this to the General personally. No one else is to get them."

"Yes Sir! This is for you Sir. It's from the General."

Major Wentworth found the Lieutenant and said, "You'd better come with me!"

He watched as the Major read the dispatch.

"Lieutenant, I don't believe what I just read. It seems there is a sailor running around Vietnam killing everything in sight. The sailor was from a carrier operating around here years ago. Everyone thought he was dead. It turns out that he has been in a prison camp all these years. He was one of the two men that freed all of the prisoners. They killed over thirty of the enemy with just a knife. That's your phantom. A recon unit found the prisoners. When they got back, they told their story to Intelligence. He is out there with a Capt. Nge, a South Vietnamese Regular.

"From what I read, Tim, that's his name, had been tortured for years. It seems that all of the guards died with their throats cut. Just like the men you found."

"Jesus! Why in the hell doesn't he want to go home? God knows, he's seen enough war. I find this hard to believe."

"Well Lieutenant, think what you want. Just explain to me why all the men you found were killed in the same manner? Believe me, it's true. The General has a standing order to bring Tim back. Tomorrow, you are going out to find Tim. You are to bring him and Capt. Nge out! Lieutenant, I want you to be careful tomorrow. If these men have been tortured as long as I've been told, there is a good chance they've gone off the deep end. That makes them dangerous—to you and everyone else. I can't imagine anyone wanting to stay in the jungle when they could go home."

As Nge and I were moving through the jungle, he gave me a signal to stop. I watched him point toward my right. We watched Charlie crawl into a hole in the ground.

"What do you think Nge? How many are in the ground hiding?"

"I have no idea. There should be an exit nearby. Find the exit Tim. I will be back with a surprise for our friends."

"What the hell are you up to Nge?"

"You'll see. I'll show you later."

It didn't take me long to find the opening, then I waited for Nge to get back. He had his shirt off. You never knew what he was up to.

"What the hell have you got there?"

"Do you remember what Tran liked to do with his friends? I have five nice juicy snakes in my shirt. All you have to do is throw a grenade into that opening. When Charlie tries to come out this opening, he will be in for a surprise."

"Nge, I can hardly wait." I ran to the entrance, pulled the pin, and dropped the grenade. I ran back to where Nge was waiting, and we watched Charlie come out of the hole screaming. They didn't even have their weapons. I guess after being bitten by the snakes, they just panicked and wanted out of the tunnel.

Nge started to lift his rifle, but I stopped him, saying, "Nge, this is for the men that Tran killed using snakes. Let them suffer."

Nge just smiled.

We watched them run, knowing the poison was rushing through their system. Death would come fast running like that. I laughed.

"Come on, Nge, let's leave a sign on the tunnel."

We carved a sign stating: "Charlie used to live here."

We both laughed; we left seven dead VC behind.

It wasn't long before we ran into Charlie again. They were sitting down, resting and eating. There were four of them. Nge worked his way to the two sitting by the tree, and I managed to come close to the other two. I jumped up and kicked the first one. The second didn't move fast enough, and my knife slid across his throat. As the first one tried to get up, I cut into his throat. Nge had killed his two. We took what we needed and left. We continued to look for Charlie; when we found them we killed them. Everywhere we went, Charlie died.

"Lieutenant, why are we going back into the jungle this morning?"

"We're going back in to find the two guys that saved our asses. We're going to try to bring them out."

"Great, we'll be out there chasing ghosts. You know that don't you?"

The Lieutenant and his men searched for Tim and Nge all day. The following morning, they were at it again. But the only thing they found was where Tim and Nge had been. There were always bodies left behind. The bodies were always the same—the throats had been cut. This was how they knew that Tim and Nge had been there.

These guys are enjoying themselves, the Lieutenant thought. The Major was right they are crazy. They have been in the jungle too long. He decided to tell his men what they were up against.

"You have to be kidding, Lieutenant. No one could live during that much torture."

"They have, and they are dangerous. I'm not sure if they know who the enemy is anymore."

The Lieutenant and his men called for the choppers and were soon picked up. When they landed, the Lieutenant went straight to headquarters. He knocked on the Major's door.

"Come in, Lieutenant. Close the door behind you."

"Major, we never even got a glimpse of them. I could feel them watching us. All we found were dead VC. They are out there killing Charlie wholesale. We even found this tacked to a tree." He read the sign.

"Well, they have a sense of humor anyway," said the Major.

"No Sir, we found VC about fifty feet away. They'd died from snakebites. I figure they found the tunnel and lobbed a grenade at one end and put the snakes in at the other end. When Charlie came out, the snakes bit them. I think you're right, Major, they are both crazies."

"Okay Lieutenant, make out your report. When you're finished get some rest. You look like you need it."

"Nge, I was thinking. We have been doing a lot of killing. The death toll is getting pretty high and perhaps it is time to move on, before Charlie floods the area with men. They must be desperate to find us by now."

"I think you're right. It's time for a rest anyway." We went back to our camp and were getting ready to sleep when we both heard a noise. We pointed our rifles in the direction of the sounds. Then we heard a voice; it asked if he could come in.

We could see a shadow move. We never said a word. It was an old man.

"Please come in. Would you like something to eat?"

"No thank you, I have come here to give you a message. My son was in that camp you escaped from. He was a prisoner also. He told us what you had done. We live in the mountains and want to help. First, I have a message for you from my son.

"He asked me to tell you that Major Tran is still alive. When the guards came back, Tran was still alive and they managed to save his life. He is looking for you."

"Do you know where he is?"

"No, he moves around a lot. No one knows where he is. When we hear anything, we will get back to you. I have some food for you. If you need help, you know where to go. The mountain people will be there for you. I want you to be careful. Ten miles north of here, the North Vietnamese Regulars are very active. I have a radio for you. We found it where the NVA ambushed some American soldiers. They took a few alive. If you want to help them, they are about three miles north of you. If you leave now, you can get to their camp while it is still dark."

"Thank you. We appreciate what you are doing."

"I must go now. I have been here too long."

We watched him walk into the darkness. It only took him a minute to disappear. For an old man he moved fast.

Nge picked up his rifle; I knew where we were going. We headed north. We made good time and soon reached the NVA camp. The moon was bright. There were only a couple of guards on watch; the other three were sleeping. As I crawled toward one guard, I could see the prisoners watching me. Standing up, I grabbed the first guard and covering his mouth, I slit his throat. I waited for him to become limp, then put him down. Then I took care of the second one. The other three men who were sleeping Nge took care of. I went over to the prisoners and cut them loose. I told them to pick up the weapons and whatever food they could get.

As soon as we were ready, we moved out. I whispered to the men, "Be careful. I don't want to leave a trail if possible." We made good time; we couldn't afford to stop. Once the NVA found their men dead, they would come looking for us. I sure didn't want them tailing us in the daylight. Our camp wasn't far away, and I knew we would be safe there.

When we reached our camp, I said, "I want you men to keep quiet. If you must talk, whisper. Sound carries at night. Tomorrow, we will figure out what to do with you. I have a radio so you can call for a chopper when I find a safe place for him to land."

"How did you know where to find us?"

"That is something you don't have to know. Just be thankful you're safe."

"I sure would like to know who you two are?"

"That's not something you need to know either."

One of the guys said, "I already know who you are Tim. Your name is well known. Everyone is looking for you. They want you back so you can go home. And you, Capt. Nge, people are talking about you also. You both have become heroes."

"That's nice. When you get back, tell them we're not ready to come out. We will, when we're ready and not till then. There is someone still alive out there. When he is dead, maybe then we'll come out. Right now, we prefer the jungle and killing those bastards. Tell them that when you are back at your base."

We all went to sleep, except the man on watch. A few hours before dawn, I woke everyone and said, "Get ready to move out. I want absolute quiet. Do you understand? Charlie's out there waiting for us somewhere. I figure we will head west. Charlie won't look for us there. Now move. If any of you give our position away, I will personally kill you." We moved quickly and managed to elude Charlie for quite sometime. It was finally safe for them to call for the chopper.

The corporal had the radio and kept calling. Finally we heard a voice. The corporal gave our position and the voice said, "We thought you guys were prisoners."

"You have our position, now send the chopper. You have four men to pick up. I don't need you telling Charlie where we are." We waited about an hour and then saw three choppers coming in. I lit a smoke bomb. The first chopper set down and the other two circled in case Charlie was nearby. The men got into the chopper. "I guess there is no way you would come back with us."

"That's right. Deliver my message to the right people."

"Thanks for everything. I hope we meet again."

"Get out of here before you make me cry." As the chopper lifted off, we were already out of sight.

"Nge, I guess we better forget about going back to camp. Charlie is probably all over it by now. Are you thinking what I am?"

"Yes—Tran. I think we should try to find him. That bastard won't live this time. I will cut his head off and that's a promise, Tim."

"Do you think you can find him, Nge?"

"I sure do. If he is north of here, I know where he will be. The problem is his men will surround him. We won't be able to get too close."

"It's worth a try. Maybe we can flush him out."

"I know the area, he's in. It's been a hotspot for the NVA for quite some time. It won't be easy moving around. Tim, the NVA are much better soldiers. They are not farmers."

"I guess you could say they die just as easily as a farmer."

We were walking north when I noticed that the old man was back.

"Tim, I see you got the Americans out. I came back because I forgot to tell you something. Tran has a price on your head along with the Captain's. It is considerable. A lot of people will turn you in for it. Remember that the people are poor. They can't help themselves. But I can promise you this, if we find out the name of anyone that turns you in, he or she won't live long. The other thing I came back for is also about Tran. I was told he is up north, living just below the mountains. He has a large army with him."

"Thanks. We appreciate the information. There is something you can do for us."

"Name it, Tim."

"I want you to tell the people that I will give them $500 American for information that leads me to Tran. I figure we should put a price on Tran's head. Can you spread the word?"

"That's easy. Consider it done. Tran is going to be quite upset when he hears about this. Some of his own men would turn him in for that money."

"What do you think, Captain?"

"I think you're crazy. I also think it's a great idea. Tran better sleep with one eye open from now on."

The old man disappeared again.

"Nge, shall we head north?"

"Might as well, Tim."

We had been walking north for a couple of days when we came across Charlie. They had a couple of prisoners with them. We managed to get in front of them. "Nge, I want them to live."

"Why?"

"I want to tell them about the price on Tran's head."

"Sounds good to me." We set up the ambush and waited. The two prisoners looked like they were in very bad shape.

After Charlie walked past, Nge and I jumped them. They fell to the ground. We picked up their rifles and ammo, while they just kept looking at us. They were scared. I guess they knew who we were.

"I'm sorry, but you men will have to find your own way back. If you follow the south trail you can make it. Charlie hasn't been using it lately—not since they lost so many men. Travel by night for awhile. You will know when it is safe. By that time, your own people should pick you up. We have to head north."

"North? You're going straight into the heart of the NVA. That's their home ground."

"We know. Charlie has a price on our head so we decided to put a $500 price on Major Tran."

"Have you got the money for the reward?"

"No, but we'll get it." I saw the soldier remove his boot. He turned the heel and removed five hundred-dollar bills.

"That's a pretty good hiding place," I said.

"That's for you," he said handing me the money. "Just who is this Tran?"

I stood up and removed my shirt. They looked at the scars on my body. "Did Tran do that?"

"Yes, with a few more tricks he had up his sleeve. That's why we want him. We thought we'd killed him once, but he didn't die. So here we are. Nge and I won't leave till we see his head hanging on a pole. I think you should go now. Good luck, soldiers. You'll make it all right."

Nge told Charlie about the reward for Tran's head. They smiled. I took out my knife, grabbed one, and slit his throat. The other one was completely scared. Nge untied him and told him this time he would live. He also told him to pass the message along, or we would find him and kill him. He ran like a wild fire. He just wanted out of there. The two soldiers just stood there watching.

"Tim, a while ago, I would have disagreed with you about killing that man. Now, I am not sure after seeing what they did to you. Can I see that knife? I have heard so much about it."

"I never let anyone touch it. It means too much to me."

"Tim, how many men have tasted the blade?"

"I don't know. It doesn't matter. There will be a lot more before this war ends."

Dawn came and we sent the prisoners on their way. We followed them for a while to make sure they were all right. After a few hours, we left and proceeded north. We watched Charlie wherever we went. We pretty well knew where they were and what they were doing. Now, we had to get the information back to our lines.

"Tim, that captured radio we have—can we use it?"

"No. Charlie will be able to hear us. Nge, how far is the old man from us? Can we make it there?"

"It's possible. The mountains are to the west of us, and Charlie hates to go there. When they do, they never seem to come out alive." It took us three days to reach the base of the mountain. Charlie was camped all over the place. Nge was right. They wouldn't go up.

We waited for dark to start the climb. We passed through Charlie's lines and were halfway up the mountain when all of a sudden the people who lived in the mountains surrounded us. The saw the medallion and told us to follow them to their camp. The old man came out. "Welcome Nge." He looked at me, "Welcome Tim, what can we do for you?"

"We need a radio. Can you get us one?"

He said something to the man beside him and suddenly, he had a radio in his hand. We cranked it up. It worked fine. I called the base and heard a voice on the other end. He asked me for my call sign.

"Call sign, my ass. Get the man in charge on."

Another voice came on the radio. "This is Major Wentworth. Who the hell is this?"

"The same guy that pissed you off before. Take down this message: They're at the bottom of the mountain on the east side. Make sure the strike force doesn't hit the mountain. If they do I will shoot them down personally. The base is the target. I'm signing off now."

"Wait a minute. We want to bring you out."

"Didn't you get the message I sent before?"

"Yes, we got it."

"Then, there is nothing more to say." I hung up the radio.

"God damn that guy. He doesn't take orders well."

"No Sir, but he sure is handy to have out there, Major. Ask the men he saved."

"Shut up and get me the General."

"At this time, Sir?"

"How would you like to be on the front lines, Corporal?"

"I'll get the General, Sir." It wasn't long before the General answered.

"Major, your call Sir."

"Major Wentworth calling, Sir."

"This better be good Major."

"I just heard from our friend in the jungle. He found Charlie's camps. These are the coordinates. I was also told to make sure we hit the base of the mountain on the east side. If we drop one bomb on top of the mountain, Tim will personally shoot the plane down."

"I guess we know where he is. I'll get the strike force on their way. Thanks Major."

It wasn't long before we could hear the planes. They gave Charlie a beating. Charlie never could have survived that bombing. Not one bomb came near the village. We waited a few hours after the bombing and then the mountain people and Nge and myself went down the mountain. We took everything we could carry. "Nge, I left a note for Tran. It read: 'Say thank you, asshole. You're next.' I signed it 'Tim'. I knew that would really piss him off."

We headed north; it was tough going. Charlie was out there looking for us. Every chance we got, Charlie died. I started to worry about the trail of bodies we were leaving. Charlie could follow that trail right to us. So we changed directions and headed east. We were making good time (Charlie was west of us) when I heard some static on the radio. I checked the squelch button and the static cleared. I could hear a voice calling for us, so I pressed the button. "What the hell do you want? You know better than to call us."

"Sorry, we have an emergency. We have two pilots down somewhere near you."

"I know—we saw the chutes. We're not too far from them. So, get off the radio before you get us killed."

"Look sailor, you're still in the service."

I shut the radio off.

"Damn that guy. He just shut the radio off. Someday, I'll meet him and straighten his ass out."

"Tim, the pilots are over that hill. I hope Charlie doesn't spot them." We moved closer. There was no sign of Charlie. "Nge, cover me. I will get them." I made my way to the pilots. They saw me and I said, "Keep your mouths shut. Then, maybe you will get out of here alive. Are you hurt?"

"No, we're okay."

"Follow me and keep your heads down." We made it back to Nge and decided it was time to forget Tran and get the pilots back safely. We started to walk south and had been walking for hours when we came to a clearing. We could see Charlie hiding. "Lieutenant, you and the other pilot stay here with Capt. Nge." I left and tried to make it to the patrol that was coming toward Charlie's trap. They were moving very cautiously, heading right into the ambush. I made it to the tall grass. I crawled to within yards of the point man and whispered for him to stop. I thought he would shit his pants.

"Who the hell are you?"

"Where's the man in charge?"

"I'm right here. Now who the hell are you? Don't make me ask again."

"If you fire that weapon, you will all be dead. You're right in the middle of an ambush. Charlie has been watching you for some time. They have you outnumbered. We have another problem. I have two pilots with me. When I get you out of this fucking mess you got us into, I want you to take them out with you."

"What do you want us to do?"

"Stay in the grass for now. I'll handle it."

"You'll what!"

"I don't have time to have a conversation. Get your men ready. That means quietly! I want you to follow me. Keep your asses down and don't shake the grass too much. Charlie will be watching for that. When I tell you to stop, you wait here and stay out of sight. I have a surprise for Charlie. He placed a lot of mines over there near where he is, but we moved them. They're sitting in the middle of them now." I moved forward a little and told them to stay where they were.

I made it back to Nge. "Let's take a few of them out." We crawled on our stomach. One by one they died. Suddenly, Charlie opened fire. I threw a grenade and they started to run. They ran right into the trip wires and blew themselves up. The firing stopped. We walked toward the bodies. I heard a groan. I picked Charlie up by his hair, slit his throat, and dropped him. Nge saw one move and he shot him. We checked them all out and made sure they were dead.

The patrol came over to us. "Are you guys okay?"

"Yes, we're okay."

"That was fine work, but I don't like your tactics, Mister. Killing the wounded, I don't appreciate."

"That's fine Lieutenant, but I don't care. We live in the jungle. This way, we can stay alive a little longer. If you don't like it, the path is over there. Take it." I waved for the pilots to come out.

They came up and one of them said, "Lieutenant, shut up. You have no idea what you are talking about. These two men just saved your squad. If they hadn't stopped you, your men would be dead. I want you to call for the choppers. Charlie will be all over us pretty soon. Those explosions are going to bring them down on us. Now get moving."

"I know a safe place for them to land. Follow me."

"Thanks Tim."

We checked the bodies and made our way to a clearing a few clicks back. The chopper hadn't arrived yet.

"Tim, my name is Commander Babson and this is my back seater, Lieutenant Jenkins."

"Please to meet you. I think it's time for us to leave. You're safe now. Just keep down until the choppers arrive."

As we left the area, I had an uneasy feeling. "Nge, let's check the place out. I think Charlie is still here, waiting for the choppers to land."

We could hear the choppers; the patrol would soon be safe. I looked toward Nge; he was pointing to the brush ahead of us. I was right—Charlie was waiting for the choppers. They were aiming a rocket launcher at them. I figured they would wait until the choppers picked up the men. It would give us the time we needed to reach Charlie. Nge and I crawled toward them then I reached up and grabbed one of them, killing him. I fired at the other one and the rocket went off. It missed the chopper. All the men were in the choppers and were taking off. We stood up and waved at them. They waved back.

"That was a close one," Nge said.

"That's for sure," I agreed.

"Commander, what the hell was going on down there? That rocket missed us by a mile. Charlie doesn't make mistakes like that."

"Don't worry, Charlie didn't make any mistakes. They are with their ancestors right now."

"What the hell are you talking about?"

"I'll tell you about it over a beer tonight."

"Can I say something?"

"Go ahead, Lieutenant."

"It bothers me leaving those two men behind. We should have made them come with us."

"There was nothing we could do to get them to come out. The only way to bring them out is to shoot them. I don't think I want to do that. If we missed, we would be dead. You remember the sailor that was captured years ago. He was tortured for years. That's the guy. The other guy is a South Vietnamese Captain.

"Those two killed most of the guards in the prison camp and freed all the prisoners. They have been in the jungle ever since. Now, do you want to fuck with them?"

"Not really, Sir!"

"Ever since they were found to be alive, everybody has asked them to come out. The problem is the man who tortured them is still alive and they both swore they wouldn't come out until he was dead. You mentioned Lieutenant that you didn't like their tactics. That is all they know. They've lived under Charlie for years. Who do you think made them like that? Maybe Tim will come out someday. Then again, maybe he will die in the jungle. Either way, Tim doesn't care. He'll kill you just as fast as he would Charlie. I'd bet a year's wages Tran doesn't sleep at night."

The choppers set down and the men got out. They watched as two Marines came toward them.

"Sir, we were told to escort you back to headquarters."

"Escort Sargent? I am a Commander in the US Navy and this is my back seater, Lt. Jenkins. This man is Lt. Baker from the US Marines. Those men are his men. 'Escort!' Get out of our way. We will get to headquarters after we have a beer. Now beat it and tell your Major what I said."

"Major Sir, the pilots will be here shortly."

"What do you mean shortly?"

"The Commander told us to get out. They went for a beer. They said they would be here shortly."

"Is that right? Well, come with me."

The door to the Officers Club opened and Major Wentworth yelled, "I want every one of you out of here. Except for you three. Bartender put a dozen beers on the counter and get out. You two Marines secure the front door. No one comes in."

"Gentlemen, the drinks are on me. I'm sorry, I forgot what you have been through. I will need reports as soon as you are comfortable. I have to get them to the General. This Tim is getting to be a pain in the ass."

"I think your right, Sir. I hate anyone that saves my life."

"Look Commander. I understand where you are coming from. This kid is doing one hell of a job. But we have to get him out. Even Nge has to come out."

"Forget it, Major. Neither one is coming out. If you plan on sending some men in to get them, forget that too. They will end up dead. They saved the Lieutenant's squad from an ambush. They saved our lives. It will cost lives if you try to get them out."

"Are you saying they're crazy!"

"I can't answer that Sir. I am a pilot not a doctor. I will say this. I wouldn't want to meet them on a street after dark. I asked them to come with us; they refused. I don't think they will come out until they do what they've set out to do."

"Do you have any idea what I am going through? I have the newspapers screaming at me. Congress is screaming at me. And last but not least, the President of the United States. How do I tell them we can't capture them and bring them out."

"Not my problem, Sir!"

"Now let's talk about the enemy. They have a price on his head. They have so many men looking for him it is unbelievable. Yet Tim and Nge keep on killing everyone they send out on patrol. The patrol is found with their throats cut. I lost count of how many throats they have cut. If the papers got a hold of this, they would have a field day. War is one thing—this is revenge."

"Major, I saw Tim with his shirt off. If the papers had a picture of that, 'war criminal' wouldn't be in their vocabulary. I don't know how he could take that torture. Remember, he was just a kid when they did it to him. I think he's a hero. Fuck everybody else."

"I'm sorry, gentleman. I'm glad your back. Maybe you're right. After you finish your lunch, get checked out by the infirmary."

When they finished their lunch, the Commander and the others got themselves checked out. They made out their reports and gave them to the Major.

They watched as the Major read them. His eyes told the story without saying a word.

"Christ, these two men have killed more people than the whole Marine Corp. God only knows how many men they saved. The only thing I know for sure is that kid worked the deck of a carrier. He was never trained to survive by the Navy. This guy is a killing machine. He should be working for us. No, he is working for himself. We have to bring him out. Has anyone got any suggestions? I have to be in the General's office in an hour. What the hell am I going to tell him?"

"Sir, you will find it in my report where we went back for him."

"Back for him—you almost got your whole command killed. Plus you almost got shot down by one of Charlie's rockets. I'd say Tim and Nge saved your asses. Just shut up. I don't want to hear your excuses. You have the nerve to tell me you went back to help Tim. I think they could have finished Charlie off by themselves before you even got there. Now, just get out of here! I have to get ready to go to battalion."

"General! You have a call on line two. It's Major Wentworth."

"I want to talk to you, General. It's about the pilots and Tim."

"Get down here right away, Major. I will wait for you."

The Major went in a chopper with the two Navy flyers to headquarters, and they were escorted to the General's office by two Marines. The Navy Commander laughed, "I've never had so many escorts."

"General, the Major is here with the two Navy flyers."

"Send them in."

"Sit down, gentlemen."

The General read the reports slowly. Then he looked up at the men and said, "First of all, I'm glad you're back. I guess we can thank Tim for that. From these reports, you're lucky to be alive."

"Yes Sir, we are. Tim and Capt. Nge are something else."

"Commander, tell me about this Tim. Just what is he really like. I don't mean this entire hero shit. I know what he's done. What do you think of him personally?"

"The man is a killing machine. Wherever he goes, someone dies. He uses that knife like no one I have ever seen. He is more than an expert when it comes to using that knife. He is cunning and quiet. You don't see him until it's too late—then you're dead. He doesn't hesitate to kill. He is quicker than any man I have ever come across in my whole military career.

"As you have already read he was severely tortured. I saw him without his shirt. There isn't an inch of his body that doesn't have a scar on it. Major Tran sure did a job on him. And that's why you will never get him out until he is ready."

"How about Nge. Can we get him out?"

"No Sir. Nge is the same as Tim. They are the perfect partners. I'm sorry. You will have to wait until the war is over, or until some other reason brings them out.

"Actually, if I had to describe the two of them you wouldn't like it."

"Go ahead, tell me what you think."

"Well Sir, the two of been have been in the jungle so long that they have become part of it. They are animals preying on everything in sight. I know that's a hard description to say about anyone, but it's true. If they were stateside, God knows what they would be like. I wish I could describe them in a different way, but I just can't. They are dangerous. I met them both. Up close Tim looks like a kid. Inside, he is the most dangerous man I have ever met. I've seen him use that knife. He scares me. Killing comes naturally to him. Nge is the same way."

"Thanks for being honest with me. We still have to get them out."

"If you try, make sure you have enough body bags ready. You will need them. I think when they finally meet up with Major Tran, things will be different. I hope so, anyway."

"Commander, let me tell you something about Tim. He lost his mother when he was in high school. He worked to save money for college. He had the highest marks in school. He was the All-American boy. Everyone loved him. Now you tell me he's an animal."

"That's Vietnam Sir. What else could have changed him? He's been through more than any person I know in the service. What do you think you would be like if you went through what he did? Most men have died from a lot less. I don't know how he survived."

"When we got word Tim was still alive, I had the FBI check on him. They talked to his friend, a Mr. Chin. When they told him he was MIA, Mr. Chin just smiled. Don't you think that was unusual?"

"Not if he believed Tim was alive."

"The report said Mr. Chin was a small man and quiet. They checked his war record, and Mr. Chin turns out to be one hell of a man. He reminds me of Tim. Mr. Chin was highly decorated by both the US Army and the Chinese Government. After reading the report, I knew why Tim was so dangerous. Mr. Chin was also very adept at killing, especially with a knife. Does that sound familiar to you?

"Since Mr. Chin's arrival in the States, after the war, he has been a loner. He never married again after the Japanese had killed his wife. The first friend he had was Tim and they hit it off together. I guess you could say Tim was his adopted son. He trained him well. Tim had quite a record in boot camp. He was very impressive aboard the carrier he was on. He trained a lot of men in survival on board the ship. I talked to some of the officers he trained. They all told me the same thing: If they hadn't had Tim's training they would have been dead. Somehow, I don't think he is an animal. Thinking like one is more like it."

"Maybe you're right. But if you ever meet him then maybe you will see why I think like I do."

"The whole country wants that kid back. They think he is a hero. I have men in the Special Forces that haven't accomplished what he has. If the enemy ever catches him, they will use him for propaganda. That's when the shit will hit the fan. I just don't know what to do. I'll do anything to get him back. I even thought of drugging him when we meet up with him."

"If you do, make sure they don't fuck up, or you will have to do some explaining to the media about why he killed your men. I sure wouldn't want to be the one that tries. He's a dead man if he screws up."

"God damn it! We have to do something! I got a Senator all over my ass. It seems that Tim saved his kid's life when he was shot down. That Senator has vowed to get him back. Besides that, I have a shitload of mothers screaming to get him back. Yea, he saved their sons also.

"I would rather be on the front lines then back home facing all those mothers. Especially, if Tim turns up dead. Thanks for your report, gentlemen. You're dismissed.

"Commander, keep a lid on this. I will face the media. For that fact, leave by the back door. If you're asked about Tim, 'No Comment!' You have some leave coming—take it. That's an order. Now get out of here!"

"Yes Sir!"

"Nge, I was thinking. It's time to head north again. Charlie is all over the place and it won't be long before they catch up with us."

"I think you're right. The Marines have a small outpost north of here. If we can make it there, we can be of some help to them. Word's out that Charlie is going to hit them. They have been getting ready even while we speak. On the way, we can check on Tran. I have some friends up north. Maybe they can help us find the bastard."

We waited for dark then we headed north. Nge led the way. I would get us lost, but he knew every trail in the jungle. I sure was glad to have him along. We walked for hours and kept a sharp lookout for Charlie.

Finally, we saw small fires off in the distance. That would be Charlie. They felt secure in this area. I sure wanted to stop and pay them a visit. But whenever we saw a fire, we'd circled around it. We didn't want Charlie to know we were around. We always hid during daylight because it was safer. We came across a small village, and Nge checked it out. He came back and told me Charlie had been there and stole what food the villages had. Charlie was good at that. We entered the village. The elder walked toward us and held out his hand. We sat down and drank tea with him. They gave us food to eat. The elder told us that Charlie always talked about us. That made me worry. I wondered if Charlie knew we were nearby.

The elder laughed when I mentioned it, saying, "They are more scared of you than anything else." He also told us we shouldn't worry. The elder said to Nge, "The NVA is moving in the area planning to attack the outpost a few miles north. The outpost will be an easy target. The NVA outnumber the Americans."

We thanked the old man. We decided to leave in the morning and head for the outpost. They took us out back and showed us a place to hide. We stayed there all night while the villagers kept watch. In the morning, we picked up our stuff.

"Tim, the NVA is all over the place. They have a lot of camps up north. You will have to be extra careful. I have made a map for you. It shows the camps. It will also show you the areas where the NVA are the thickest. The outpost is not ready for an attack. The south wall has tunnels going to it. The Americans don't know about it. I have marked on the map where they are. You can catch Charlie off guard when they try to use the tunnels.

"You better be going now. It will be light soon. My son is going with you. He can show you the safest route to take."

"Thank you." The three of us left and traveled north. The old man was right—the NVA had camps all over the area. It took a week for us to reach the outpost. Charlie was busy making ladders and coffins. I looked at Nge, worried. We sent the old man's son back.

"What's the matter Tim?"

"I was wondering how the hell we can get close enough to get inside the outpost. Between the mines and the NVA, we have a problem. This place is full of mines and the NVA is everywhere. Then we have to contend with the barbed wire."

"Tim, that's easy. Let's use the tunnels that Charlie has hidden. They should be over there."

"That's a good idea." We waited till dark then crawled slowly, feeling for mines. When we found one, we'd move around it. It took an hour to get through the minefield. We probed the ground until we found a tunnel. Breaking through, we went inside. We came to the end and probed as the dirt fell on us. We had another problem. If we stuck our heads out, we would surely lose them.

I decided to yell softly. "Don't shoot. I am an American." God, I never heard so much confusion.

"My name is Tim. I have with me Capt. Nge from the South Vietnamese Army. We are going to throw our weapons out of the hole and come out with our hands up."

"What do you mean, American?" The voice was very close. That meant the tunnel was inside the outpost.

"I'm coming out with my hands in the air." I raised my arms and stuck my head out of the hole.

Marines were all around me. "What the hell are you doing here?"

"I have a friend in the hole." I told Nge to come out. The Marines never dropped their weapons. They picked up our weapons and told us to follow them.

"I think you should fill that tunnel, gentlemen. Charlie plans on using it. Have you any clamors. They would do the job quite nicely."

"Never mind the holes. Follow me."

"Suit yourself."

We followed the Marines to their C.O. "Who the hell are you men and how did you get inside?"

"Captain, we don't have much time for this bullshit. Take this map. It shows where the NVA are and also where the tunnels are located that Charlie has dug."

"How did you get this information?"

"We have friends, Sir. They told us about it."

"Now tell me who you are? Sargent, take care of those tunnels right away."

"My name is Tim Collins. This is Capt. Nge."

"So, we finally meet. You're under arrest soldiers."

"Sailor Sir!"

"Don't be cute. Everyone is looking for you. Orderly, call headquarters and tell them we have Tim and Nge here. Tell them to send a chopper to pick them up."

"Captain, I don't think you have that much time before Charlie hits you. Your east side is the weakest and Charlie knows it. That is where they will hit first. We can help you. If you give us some mines, we will set them all over the east side. When they hit, they will be in for a shock. We can do it, your men can't. You see, Charlie has two towers out there so he can watch you. Your men don't know where they are. If they go out, the attack will start right away. We can take them out and set the mines."

We left the outpost and climbed up and killed the two men in the tower. After setting the mines, we went back to the outpost.

"Well Captain, it's all set. Charlie is in for a surprise."

"So are you. They're sending choppers for you."

"Tell them not to waste their time. We won't be here when they come. By the way, you better get set for a big push. Charlie should hit tonight. You can't hold them back. I suggest an air strike right away. The marks on the map show where Charlie is storing their ammo and supplies. I think you should hit them."

"Sargent, get me headquarters again."

"Yes Sir."

"Colonel, I need an air strike right away. Charlie is going to hit us tonight. The coordinates I give you are where Charlie has hidden his ammo and supplies. Also, he has some camps nearby. Here are those coordinates.

"That's right, Sir. Tim gave them to me. How soon can you hit them? Thanks, we'll be waiting. Yes Sir, they are here and under arrest. They say they won't be here when the choppers arrive. I have them under armed guard."

"They better be there, Captain. Tie them up if you have to."

"Yes Sir."

"Tim, how bad is it out there?"

"Charlie's all over the place. These men can't hold out. I placed mines where I figure Charlie would hit. We need the air support now. By the way, I left a letter here that states Charlie is going to overrun us, especially if the air support doesn't get here in time, because you're wasting valuable time fucking around with choppers for Nge and me. If we die, I sure wouldn't want the newspapers to get their hands on the story. Do you understand!"

"Look you bastard, never mind that shit. The planes are on the way. Just do me a favor, keep your heads down."

"Well Captain, can we have our weapons back? Or are you going to fight Charlie alone."

"Here are your weapons. Sargent, stick to them like flies on shit."

"Captain, my knife, please."

"Here it is!"

We were on the line waiting for Charlie when all of a sudden we heard the planes. The ammo dumps were exploding all over as they dropped their loads on Charlie's camps. Charlie never knew what happened. The remaining ones charged us and were buried alive. We heard explosions where the tunnels were. Charlie never got through. There was fighting on all sides of the outpost. Charlie wasn't giving up. They were dying all over the place. They never reached the barbwire. The clamors were taking them out. The Marines killed them when they tried to climb the wire. We fought for a good hour when Charlie finally gave up.

I looked up and saw that the Sargent and his men had their guns on us.

"Sorry fellas, you're going home. Thanks for the help. You saved a lot of lives. We hate doing this. It's a dirty trick."

As we boarded the choppers, we were laughing. We waved to the men as the chopper took off. It wasn't long before we landed and were surrounded by armed guards. They weren't taking any chances.

"You two follow us."

We were taken to the General's office. Once inside we looked around. "He lives pretty good, huh Nge."

"Yea, I'd say it's comfortable."

"Hi General. How are you?"

"Never mind me. I'm glad to see you two. We are sending you back to the States. You won't even have time to shower. In other words, you won't be out of our sight for one minute. Do you understand?"

"Yes, we understand. Is there a place we can sit down, or maybe you would rather tie us up."

"Sargent, take them to the supply house. Keep an armed guard around them. When the choppers come, they are to be escorted to the choppers."

"General, thanks for everything. We just want to tell you this before you get into trouble. We won't be here when the choppers come."

"Pretty sure of yourselves aren't you?"

"Corporal, you have your orders."

Nge and I smiled.

"Remember, keep both eyes on them, at all times. Tim, your gear is on the table. Take it with you when you leave."

We were taken to the supply hut. I saw no sense in whispering and said, "I think we should take some of these supplies when we leave. We can use them."

"You guys know we can hear every word you say." They laughed.

"That's okay Corporal, we're sorry."

"Sorry for what!"

"For making you lose your stripes. Wake us when it gets light. We'll put the lights out after we've finish packing what we need."

The Marine laughed and said, "Go ahead waste your time."

We filled our bags. I removed my knife and cut the sandbags along the wall. The sand fell to the floor and it wasn't long before we had a hole big enough to crawl through. We shoved the supplies through the opening and crawled out. Once we were outside, we made it to the fence, dug under it, and left the base. We were laughing and walking at the same time. I felt sorry for the Corporal. I knew he would lose his stripes.

"Sargent, go get Tim and Nge and bring them here."

"Corporal, wake them up."

"Yes Sir."

"Sargent, I think you better come in here."

"What's the matter?"

"They're gone, Sir!"

"What do you mean, they're gone? Son of a bitch, how did they get out?"

"Over here Sargent. They cut the sandbags."

"General, they are gone."

"Find them! That's an order."

"They're gone Sir. They left during the night. It's too late, Sir. The choppers are here to pick them up."

"Those bastards, I should have handcuffed them. Tell the chopper pilots they are going back empty. Those two bastards did exactly what they said they would do. I should have known we couldn't hold them. Wait until battalion finds out. Things are going to get pretty rough from now on."

"General, you aren't going to believe this. Tim is on the radio."

"Give me that radio. Tim, you bastard. Where the hell are you?"

"Hey General! What the hell are you upset about? I saved your asses. The only reason I am calling you is to tell you not to be too hard on the Corporal. He did his job. There was no way you could keep us caged. General, it was your fault. Sandbags aren't hard to get past. One slice and we were gone. Thanks for giving me back my knife. Besides, your men were watching for Charlie. There was no way they'd be looking for someone to break out. I'm just letting you know that Nge and I are going to checkpoint five. It's going to be hard for your men to hit them. When we get there, we will call in their position. I will answer to 'easy one' on the radio. You should feel at home with that one, General."

"You think you're funny don't you? Someday, I'll show you funny."

"I'll call you at noon tomorrow. That is, if you're not under attack by then. Remember 'easy one.' I'm signing off now."

Nge and I moved in the direction of checkpoint five. It took us all night to get there and Charlie was dug in pretty well. We were near the strike zone. We came across a patrol. "Nge, I don't think we can get around them. I think we have to take them out." I was hoping we wouldn't have to do it until after the planes were finished doing their thing.

"Tim, they're getting closer. I'll take the two on the right."

"I've got the other two. Use your knife. We don't need the noise."

We took up positions that gave us good cover and watched Charlie walking toward us. Nge and I both knew Charlie was screwing up. They were bunched up, which was going to make it easy for us. Nge had already killed the first one, and the two I had died before they knew anything was going on. Nge just finished off his second man. We covered the bodies and left.

We were in position and could see the ammo dump. Charlie was busy hiding the ammo and supplies. They were unloading the trucks. We called in the coordinates to the General. He told us the planes should be there in a half-hour.

"Tim, get out of there; you're too close to where they are going to drop their bombs."

"Okay General, we're moving out. Nice of you to worry, Sir."

"Tim, take a look over there by the truck. Is that what I think it is?"

"It looks like an American prisoner."

"What the hell can we do about it?"

"How much time have we got Nge?"

"Ten minutes at the most."

"Then it looks like I have to get him."

"How the hell are you going to do that?"

"There's only one watching him. The rest are busy unloading the truck. I think I can get in and out before they know it. Cover me just in case."

I made my way to the front of the truck. The prisoner was staring at me and I put a finger to my lips for him to keep quiet. I grabbed the guard by the back of the neck and with one slice of my knife, he went limp. I cut the prisoner loose. I could hear the planes coming and told him to run. We both started to run into the tall grass. Charlie fired at us, but Nge wasted no time. He killed three of them before the first bombs were dropped. Four planes moved toward the ammo dump. We could see the bombs leave the plane. The first plane had a direct hit. The second finished it off. The other two planes dropped their loads on Charlie. When they finished their bomb runs, they strafed the grass where Charlie was hiding. All of a sudden it became quiet. No one was alive, except us.

We called headquarters and gave them the news. We also told them we had an American prisoner with us, that Charlie had him when we arrived.

"How the hell did you end up with him?"

"Well General, we find everything out here. Do you want him, or don't you?"

"Very smart Tim. Tell me when we can pick him up."

"I'll call you when we're out of the area. Charlie should be showing up pretty soon. They know someone tipped you off to where the dump was. Don't call us. We'll get in touch with you later."

"Okay soldier, walk behind us and keep quiet."

"I don't know who you two are, but thanks for getting me out of that jam."

"That's okay. What's your name soldier?"

"Lt. Commander Rice. I was in a chopper heading for your base when we were shot down. I was the only one that survived. I was suppose to interview a couple of guys the government finally caught up with. They're some kind of heroes. Everybody wants to get them home. Do you know them? By the way, what are your names? I should at least know the names of the men that saved my life."

"Well that gentlemen is Major Tran. And my name is Andy. That's all you need to know. We are just a couple of mud marines on a recon mission. Now, I think you should shut up and follow us before we all become prisoners."

"Nice to meet you! How long before its safe to get a chopper in here?"

"A couple of days. We have to travel by night that's why it takes that long. Are you hungry?"

"I sure am."

"Major Tran would you get supper ready for us?"

"Be right back. Anything special you want?"

"No, just the usual. Make sure you cut it up small. We wouldn't want the Commander to get sick. Commander, don't worry. Tran is a good cook."

It wasn't long before Nge came back. He had supper ready.

"We're sorry Commander, you'll have to eat it cold. We can't afford any fires." We watched the Commander eat it all.

"That was good, Andy. Where did you get the tomato sauce?"

"That's C-rations. We just add water."

"I never had C- Rations like that before. It was good."

"You better get some sleep. We leave after dark." I'd no sooner finished saying it than he fell asleep.

"Tim, you know he is going to be pissed when he finds out what he ate."

"So what? Let the Colonel tell him. By that time, he'll know who we are and have something to write about us heroes. I'll take the first watch."

"Okay." I stayed up all day. I knew Nge could use the sleep.

Night came and we started out. It wasn't long before we saw Charlie. We watched them instead of fighting them. The Commander wasn't in any shape to help. After Charlie moved away from us we camped out again. This time I slept and Nge kept watch. It was a quiet day. When dark set in, we moved out. The following morning Charlie was nowhere in sight so we called for the chopper. About an hour later we heard it. We told it where to land and helped the Commander on board. "See you guys later."

We went back into the jungle and the chopper left. We laughed. "Wait until the Commander finds out just who we are. He's going to be pissed."

"How long before we land?"

"In about twenty minutes, Sir."

"Tell me something, why didn't those two Marines come back with us?"

"Marines! What Marines!"

"The ones that put me on the plane. Their names were Tran and Andy."

The men on board laughed.

"Sorry Sir, for laughing. I think you were the brunt of a joke. Those two are the most famous men in Vietnam. That's Tim Collins and Capt. Nge."

"You mean they were the men I came to see."

"That's right Sir, Tim Collins and Capt. Nge."

"I thought they were being held back at headquarters."

"They were. But how the hell do you think you can hold them when Charlie can't. The General is really pissed

about them escaping.   Where did they pick you up
Commander?"

"Tied to the front end of a truck. Charlie had me. They
got me out just before the dump blew up. I'm lucky to be
alive."

"They sure have a lot of guts, those two."

No sooner had we started back into the jungle than we
heard a radio communication. Another pilot had been shot
down. He was giving his position on an open channel. That
was foolish; Charlie could hear every word he said. He
would have Charlie all over him before long. Nge and I ran
to his position, hoping we could get there before Charlie did.
When we arrived, the pilot was firing at Charlie. I knew he
wouldn't have much ammo left. We came out of the woods
and opened fired. It wasn't long before they were dead. The
pilot had a bullet in his arm. We stopped the bleeding and
started to move out, not daring to stop to treat him. We
made it to the base of the mountains where we could stop
and treat him. He was lucky; the bullet had gone through his
arm. We stopped the bleeding and bandaged it, then decided
to hold up for awhile.

I picked up the radio and called the General. "Easy one
to easy two." It was like the General had the radio attached
to his ear.

"Where the hell are you?" "We have the Commander
here; he sends his thanks. He's pissed because you clowns
told him your names were Tran and Andy. I don't think he's
fond of C-rations now either. What do you two clowns want
now?"

"Nothing much. We have that pilot that was shot down.
He's wounded but he'll live. Can you pick him up?"

"Yea, tell us when and where."

"Tomorrow, we'll call you. Catch you later, General."

"Wait a minute . . . Those bastards hung up on me
again. What the hell do they think I am—a private? No one
talks to me that way. At least, not until now."

We all got a good night's sleep and in the morning I asked Nge, "Do you think we should go back to the outpost? They can get the pilot out without risking our necks a lot easier than we can. Walking with this fly-boy in the jungle is like marching in a parade. He sure doesn't know how to be quiet."

When we arrived at the outpost, we knew we had made a mistake. Charlie was back. They were determined to take the base. "I think we have a problem. Charlie is back. Getting into the outpost is not going to be easy. Look Sir, do everything we do. That means no noise. Any noise from you and you'll be on your own. We got by them once. This time it's going to be even tougher. By the way, what is your name?"

"Ron Howard. I'm a Captain."

"It's seems to me, Nge, we have too many Captains. We better wait until dark. Then we will have a chance. By the way, Charlie has mines out there. When we get close to the outpost, they'll have mines also. That means we have to find them or die. If you do what we say, you'll live a little longer. Let's get some sleep for now. I'll keep watch."

Finally it was time to move. We edged our way toward the outpost. We were only about 100 yards from the mines. Ron walked in back of Nge. "If I find a mine, Nge will show it to you. That means you work around it. You shouldn't have any trouble." We moved closer. I touched the ground very carefully and we finally cleared the minefield. I was happy. Next, we had to get by the barbwire and that meant sentries with hair-trigger fingers.

We made it through the wire and I was only a few feet from the Marines on duty. This was the dangerous part. I whispered as loud as I could and someone heard me. I heard the sentry call for the Sargent. He came toward us. "What did you hear Marine?"

"It sounded like a male voice from over there." They were waiting for me to say something. I whispered,

"Sargent, I have another pilot with me. I need to get in. Charlie is all over the place."

"Come on over. We were expecting you. Hold your fire, men. Mr. Trouble himself is back."

We climbed over the wall. "How's it going Sargent?"

"Don't ask. The Captain is waiting for you. Who the hell is this?"

"My name is Capt. Ron Howard, Sargent."

"Good Sir. Someone get him a rifle. The Captain is waiting for you."

"Hi Tim, Nge. Nice to see you again. I heard you were on the loose. Who have we got here?"

"Just someone we picked up on the way. He says his name is Capt. Ron Howard. You do realize, Sir, Charlie is back with a lot more men."

"I don't know if Tim made the right move bringing you here. Charlie is getting ready to hit us. I'll get battalion on the line. Captain, have you ever heard a pissed off General before? Well, get set, you're about to! Orderly, you know the drill."

"Yes Sir, I already have battalion on the line."

"Yes General, we have the pilot here."

"What about Tim and Nge? Are they with you?"

"They're here also. I am calling you because we are going to be hit tonight. Maybe tomorrow morning. Charlie doesn't want us here. Tim tells me they are all over the place. We are badly outnumbered and could use an air strike if they hit tomorrow."

"Call me as soon as you know for sure. Tell Tim and Nge to keep their heads down. Tell Tim also, there is one pissed off Commander here. He keeps screaming about C-rations. Tell him to keep his jokes to himself. He keeps asking me what Tim gave him to eat. If he ever finds out, the shit will hit the fan. Over and out."

"What the hell did you feed him?"

"The specialty of the house—the only thing you can get when you're in a hurry. The jungle doesn't have that much to offer. We told him it was C-rations. Anyway, raw snake and blood is good for you. He needed the energy. I hope they tell him. If it is good enough for us, it's good enough for him. Out here we can't pick what we eat. Anyway, we needed a laugh."

"Sargent, get the men ready; everybody is on the line. Charlie will be here sometime tonight."

"Hey Sargent, have you got a place for me. I think I can be of some use!"

"Stick with Tim and Nge; maybe then you'll come out of this alive."

"Come on Captain. I'll show you a good spot."

"You mean there is a good spot here?"

"No Sir, but it sounds good. Just be careful. Charlie fights real hard."

It was almost dawn when we saw Charlie moving. They started to shell us. That lasted for about a half-hour. When it stopped, Charlie moved in. We fired and they kept falling, but they kept coming. The fighting was hand to hand on the east. I ran over there. I saw Nge fighting harder than ever. I got beside him and kept shooting until I was out of ammo. We were down to using our knives. We sliced and moved constantly. We could hear the bullets buzzing our heads. We picked up Charlie's weapons and kept shooting. Finally we could see the choppers. They kept circling and firing. Soon, Charlie gave up and ran back to the woods. The choppers followed them shooting and killing them wholesale. Nge and I searched for any that were still alive. As soon as we found one, we'd kill him. The pilot was watching us.

"What the hell are you two doing? Those men are wounded. They are the enemy, but they are still human beings." We heard a shot. The Marine returned fire, killing Charlie.

"I guess we don't have to answer you now. Those bastards would rather die than be captured. They will kill you even if they have just an ounce of breath. I suggest you check someone that is still alive, before he puts a bullet in you. This is not California, Sir. This is hell and they are the devil. Now, get out of our way so we can do our job. I have seen what they do to prisoners. You would wish you were dead shortly after they started to torture you." A chopper soon arrived to take Capt. Howard back to headquarters.

The Captain walked over to us and asked, "How are you two doing?"

"Fine Sir, we just finished mopping up."

"I heard. I was wondering if it was necessary?"

"It is to us, Sir."

"Why weren't you on the chopper?"

"Do we have to answer that again, Sir?"

"I was going to call for another chopper. I guess I can tell the General, you escaped after the fight. What the hell! We're all in shit because of you two anyway, a little more doesn't matter. Come on, we'll have some coffee."

As soon as we reached the bunker, the radioman handed the Captain the handset. "The General is on the line."

"We were hit hard. I lost a lot of men. No, Tim and Nge are all right. God knows where they are now. General, what the hell do you want me to do? I didn't have time to watch them. I've got bodies all over the outpost—my men and Charlie. They must have left after the fight. You know them. I don't think anyone is going to hold them if they plan on leaving. I'm tired of being yelled at; court-martial me if you want. At least that will get me out of Nam."

"Okay Captain, I guess you're right. I'll send some choppers to get the wounded out."

"Well Tim, what's next?"

"Thanks for everything. But I think I am going to head south. Can we catch a ride on one of the choppers?"

"Yea, what the hell are you up to?"

"Captain, I wouldn't worry about your rank. The General isn't going to keep us there long. We need a rest. That's the best place to have a rest, without endangering anyone. They won't even know we're on the base."

"Somehow Tim, I believe you. Good luck and thanks for everything."

"How the hell will he be able to bust you or anyone else if he can't hold us! We checked out on him once before— that really pissed him off. Maybe this time, things will be different. Besides, Tran is still out there. We will never quit chasing him. Even if this war ended, I would still be here."

"I sure hope you get him first. I would hate to think of you being out here after the war."

"Tim, if we get on that chopper, there will be a welcoming committee waiting for us."

"Nge wrap your head in these bandages. I'll do the same. When we land, we'll disappear."

Nge just laughed. The Captain watched, shaking his head. He turned around and left. The choppers finally came. We waited for the last of them to prepare to take off then we got on board.

"That was some fight you guys had."

"Sure was. I'm glad it's over. My head hurts."

"Don't worry, we will have you back before long. The nurses are pretty cute there. They'll fix you up."

We landed at the base and everything was hectic. We walked toward the hospital then took the bandages off. We found a place to sleep near the ammo dump. At least no one could see us there. We ate in the mess hall everyday. No one really paid any attention to us. We were just two more men. We decided to do some shopping for some new clothes. One night after dark, we broke into the supply house, got what we needed, and took off. We had two new rifles and all the ammo we could carry. I guess we'd been there for about a week or so, when one night while we walking, the General walked by us. He stopped and turned around. "Hey soldier! Don't you believe in saluting?"

"Yes Sir, but I don't think this would have been the right time." Nge and I laughed.

"What the hell are you two doing on my base? How long and how the hell did you get on?"

"The choppers, Sir. We came in with the wounded and hid out."

The General yelled for the MPs. "Soldiers, I want guards around these men every minute. Find a place that can hold them until I can get them out of here. Two weeks, I can't believe it."

The guards marched us to the stockade. It was made of chicken wire. They had men patrolling on all four sides. We laughed. After dark, we figured we could leave by the top. Four guards meant two a piece. No problem that the guards took our weapons. I knew we could get some more.

"Good evening General!"

"Good evening, my ass. Get the XO in here now."

"What's the matter, General?"

"I just found Tim and Nge here on the base; they have been hiding here for two weeks. Can you believe that!"

"They needed a rest. That's what they told me," the Captain said laughing. "I'm sorry General. But you have to agree—they're something else. Where have you got them, Sir?"

"The guardhouse."

"That's made from chicken wire. How do you expect to keep them there?"

"Shit, get them here on the double."

Tim and Nge were brought to the General's office. There were four guards on them. "Sargent, you will watch these men all night. If they have to piss, someone better be there. Even if they have to hold it. Do you understand? I better see them in the morning."

"By the way General, how is Capt. Howard?"

"He's okay, just shook up from the fight and what he saw. He won't tell us what it was he saw. I can guess though."

"Do you think I could see him?"

"Tim, do I have your word of honor you won't try to escape."

"General, I will give you my word this way. I will not try to escape without letting you know first. That also goes for Capt. Nge. I'll give you my word that way."

"I don't know, Tim, but I guess I can take your word. Sargent, you're dismissed. Tell Nge the same. Don't cross me Tim. I am taking your word at face value."

"I'll let you know when I am ready to leave."

"You can see Captain Howard. I also want you to get a checkup. Take Capt. Nge with you. Now get out of here. I will tell them at the hospital you're coming."

"How the hell are you, Captain?"

"Pretty good, Tim. I will be a lot better when I get out of here. I never realized how rough it was out there. If it weren't for you, none of us would be alive. I will never forget you. The General asked me about you. I told him what I just told you. I also told him that if it weren't for you, that outpost would have been overrun. I told them what you're like in action. I didn't tell him about Charlie; I left that part out. I think I understand. I just hope I never have to do something like that. Tim, I am not passing judgement on you. I am just talking about myself.

"I never knew what war was like. Hand-to-hand combat, I never want to do that again. Looking into someone's eyes before you kill them is awful. I can still see the eyes of the ones I killed. At least in a plane we never see the enemy up close. I don't think I can ever drop another bomb."

"Just remember this, Captain, if you don't drop those bombs a lot more men will be killed. What you do means a lot to the men on the ground fighting. I think you will be all right. Just look at it that way. I have to go—the doctors want to check me before I leave this place."

"That reminds me. How did you talk the General into letting you loose on the base?"

"I told him I would let him know when I was leaving."

"He believed you?"

"Yes Sir."

"He's a fool."

"I'll be back to see you before we leave."

"Okay Tim, thanks for everything."

I smiled and left.

"Nurse, my name is Tim and this is Captain Nge. The General wants us to have a complete physical. Can you point us in the direction of the doctor?"

"Follow me. I will take you to his office."

"Dr. Mindus, these men were sent here by the General. They're supposed to have a physical."

"I know; I have been waiting for them. I just want to say I am proud to meet you. Would you go into those rooms and take a shower and put the Johnnys on."

"What the hell is a Johnny, Sir?"

"Nurse, help them out. Give them what they need."

She showed us the way to the showers and handed us some funny looking pajamas. We washed and put the Johnnys on. Nge started to laugh. The nurse asked if we were finished. We yelled yes. When she entered the room, she laughed.

"What's so funny, Miss?"

"I'll turn around. You have them on backwards."

We turned them around. We went into two separate rooms. The nurse was taking my vital signs and asked me to pull my Johnny down. When I did she just stood there staring at me.

"What's the matter?"

"I'll be right back, Tim."

"Doctor, can you come with me. I want to show you something. I want you to check Tim. Look at his body."

As the doctor looked me over, he said, "You've been through a lot, Tim. That's over now. How long did it take those bastards to do this?"

"I don't really know. I guess years. It was just one man. I will find him and kill him before I go home."

"Forget about him, Tim. Let it go."

"I can't. I owe him."

"Okay Tim, follow me." It took a couple of hours for all the tests and the shots they gave us. After they'd finished, they gave us new clothes and boots. It felt funny having new boots on my feet. I was told they would stretch and become comfortable before long.

"Nge, if we get separated, you know where to meet me. I don't trust these doctors."

We were released from the hospital and went to the Officers Club. We had a beer. It sure tasted great.

"General, the doctors are here. They want to talk to you about Tim."

"Come in. How did they make out?"

"They are both in good condition. We gave them both some shots. Considering what they have been through, they are in perfect health physically, but mentally I don't have any idea. They have to get treatment for their mental condition. They are too dangerous to walk around stateside."

"Doctor, there is nothing wrong with them. The only thing wrong with them is they have been fighting too long. I will never allow you to lock them up. Furthermore, you wouldn't be able to keep them under lock and key. No doubt, they are dangerous, but if you lock them up, they would probably kill your orderlies to get out. If not kill, they would fuck them up.

"They gave me their word that they would not try to escape. Do you think I believe them?"

"I sure wouldn't, General."

"Why do you think I am letting them run freely on the base? Because, otherwise they would escape and might hurt a lot of people. They just need some freedom right now. When they are rested, they are going to leave. No one can stop them unless they kill them. That is highly unlikely to happen. Now, take your asses out of here."

"General, we won't be responsible for them."

"Responsible, are you crazy? They are responsible for themselves. Now, get out of here and go back and take care of the sick."

Nge and I walked back to the General's office and saw the doctors coming out. We laughed. I could just imagine what they'd told the General.

"Come in Tim, Capt. Nge. Have a seat. Nge, I have talked to your C.O. and he wants you back under his command. I am forced to return you. I don't like it."

I looked at Nge. I knew what he was thinking. Just then the telephone rang.

"Yes, this is the General. What do you want? Well, it's about time. I'll tell Nge."

"You don't have to go, Nge. You've been assigned to us. You are a captain in the U.S. Marines."

I smiled. "Tim, you're still an ass. One that I would salute every time I see."

"General, we haven't had much news lately. Can you tell us what's going on. In the jungle we don't really hear the latest scuttlebutt."

"Well Tim, I don't think we are going to be in Nam much longer. The people home are giving the government a bad time. They want the war to end. I will tell you the truth. We are being screwed and there is nothing we can do about it. This war has become a political bombshell. If we were left alone, we could finish it. Those assholes in Washington are afraid they won't get elected again. They are trying to get our men out because everyone is screaming about the war.

"I have orders to ship you both to the States. Nge, you're going to become a U.S. citizen. You are going to rest here before you leave. Give yourself a week to do nothing but relax."

We both knew we would never be on that plane. Tran had to die. I was more determined to kill him than ever.

"You two have a week to have fun. The orderly will show you where to stay. If you need anything, let me know."

"Sir, there is one thing. We feel naked without our knives. There is still a war going on."

"I still have your word, don't I?"

"Yes Sir, you do. We will tell you when we are leaving."

"Sargent, I want you to make sure they have their weapons."

The Sargent hesitated.

"Sargent, I gave you an order. If I repeat it you're going to be a private. The Sargent will be with you for awhile. He'll show you around."

"I guess that means you don't trust us."

"No. It simply means, you will have company. Tim, you have to realize this base has Charlie inside the perimeter. They are working here. We just don't know who they are. That's why the Sargent is with you. If you don't want him, I'll dismiss him."

"Sargent, I think you can use a short vacation. You can come with us. Let's find the Officers Club. We can start off with a beer."

"That's a problem Tim; neither one of us are officers."

"So what? Nge is a brand new Captain in the Marine Corp. That makes us his guests. Isn't that right, General?"

"No, but I'll call them. I would prefer you there. Somehow, you and Nge in the enlisted men's club means trouble."

"Thanks, I appreciate that General."

"Come on Sargent. We have some drinking to do."

"Sargent, I think moderation is the word. Do you understand?"

"Yes Sir."

We sat down in the Officers Club and had three beers sent over. Everyone was watching us.

We started to drink the first round when I wondered how we were going to pay for it. I hadn't seen money in years. Then one of the officers told us the beers were on them. There would be no charge. We said thanks.

"How do you like that, Sargent?"

"Great, the only thing is I feel like a fish out of water."

"Sargent, I have a favor to ask you."

"Okay Tim, what is it? I know you are planning on leaving, and gave your word to the General. I also know you'll keep it. If I can help you, within reason, I will. But I won't do anything that will cost me my stripes. Do you understand?"

"When we leave, I promise you, we will let the General know. I believe in my word. Besides, I wouldn't want to get anyone in trouble. I've already found a weak point in your lines. We'll have no trouble walking out of here. How often does Charlie hit you?"

"Quite often, and if he finds out you're here, he will hit us every chance he gets. You two still have a price on your heads. You will have to be careful wherever you go. Charlie is mixed in with us.

"Your quarters have to be checked every night. You will be sleeping with other Marines. That doesn't mean Charlie can't infiltrate your barracks. They are sneaky bastards. We have lost a lot of good men to them. They can even get in there during the day. Make sure you're armed at all times. I suggest you check your bunks before you get in. Snakes have an uncanny way of showing up."

The Sargent showed us the way to the barracks and I wondered just how safe we were. At least in the jungle, it was different. "Sargent, where do the South Vietnamese sleep?"

"They are watched pretty closely. Charlie still manages to get in. There are a lot of good soldiers. Then again, some of them are dedicated to the north. When they are found out, they are eliminated, that is usually after the mortars hit us."

We entered the barracks and checked our bunks. They were clear so we crawled in. About an hour passed and I heard Nge moving. We weren't use to sleeping in a bed, and Nge was having trouble sleeping. "It's not like sleeping on the ground, is it?"

"Don't worry Nge, we won't be here that long. I think the jungle is a lot safer."

"I hate these bunks. What worries me most is Charlie. I keep getting a funny feeling."

"I think they are going to pay us a visit tonight. Being in here makes me feel confined."

"I know what you mean. I'll take the first watch."

We were right. It had only been a couple of hours when we saw a shadow walk by the window. We grabbed our knives. Guns would be worthless. There were too many people in the barracks. "What do you think Nge?"

"Four, maybe six. I'll take the front door. You take the side." We moved toward the door.

"Let them come in. They know our bunks so that should be the place to get them."

They entered the room, quietly. The first one stood over my bunk. I grabbed the rear man and covered his mouth, then slit his throat. I reached for the one standing over the bunk as he was reaching for the blanket. I grabbed him and shoved the knife in his back. There was never a sound. I looked at Nge; he grinned. All of a sudden the door open.

There was one left, he started to fire. Nge and I threw our knives, and they both hit Charlie. He went down.

There had been a lot of noise. Nge and I went back to bed. The Marines were running all over the place. The Sargent yelled, "What the hell is going on?"

"Nothing Sargent, we're going to get some sleep."

"Sleep? What the hell are we going to do with these bodies?"

"Oh, by the way, can you get our knives for us?"

"Yea, I guess so."

The door opened and the General came in. "What the hell happened here?"

"Don't ask them, they're going to bed."

"Tim, Nge, get out of bed. What the hell happened here?"

"Nothing much, General. They paid us a visit. We were waiting for them. They came and they died."

"Why wasn't I told? I could have lost some of my men. From now on you're sleeping in another barrack, under guard.

"Your men were in no danger. If they'd known, they probably would have shot themselves in this confined area. Can we get some sleep now, General?"

"You men get these bodies out of here."

We watched as they moved the bodies outside the barracks.

"You two think you're pretty cool. I don't."

"No Sir. We just know how Charlie thinks. Your men should learn from this."

"Sargent, I want men at all the doors, and on the side of the barracks. If that's not enough get more men. I sure will be glad when you two are gone."

"Come on, General. We were just getting to feel at home."

"Sargent, have your men clean this mess." I turned around and saw a South Vietnamese officer standing there.

"Well Major! We have some of your men here," the General said.

"I can see that. I will have them removed."

"That's okay. My men are doing it now."

"I'm sorry, General. This won't happen again. I won't allow my men anywhere near the barracks. I will issue an order to kill anyone who comes near Tim and Nge on sight."

"Very good, Major. That might help."

"You men get some sleep. You two, be in my office tomorrow. Sargent, pick a bunk, you'll be sleeping here tonight."

"Tim, Nge, I have a question for you? How did you know?"

"It was easy. Charlie had to get us right away. So we played dumb. Charlie is always thinking. Sometimes, they forget and screw up. This was one of those times. Remember, they still have a price on our heads. The one that gets us will be a hero."

"That was quite a distance to throw a knife, especially in the dark."

"Thanks Sargent, we work in the dark most of the time."

"It's going to be interesting having you two here."

"I don't think so, Sargent. I think our time here is almost over."

"There's no need for that. Take your time."

"No, Sargent. The next thing Charlie will hit us with will be mortars. That's why we will be sleeping outside. I wouldn't let your men sleep in here tonight." We were right. The mortars started to fall on the barracks. Charlie had the distance down perfectly.

"It's a good thing we weren't in there, Tim"

It was 0800 in the morning. The General finally arrived.

"At ease, men. From now on, you'll be berthed in the supply depot. I'm sorry. This has to be done. I would also suggest that you don't move around too much. I believe we haven't seen the last of Charlie. The rumors about you are correct. Wherever you go, the body count goes up."

"General, the Sargent had a good idea. He told us that he was going to move his men tonight. He seems to think Charlie will be sending in more mortars. I agree with him. He was right last night. They would be dead now if he hadn't moved his men."

"I think he was making good sense. I think we will find you a different place to bunk tonight. The supply dump won't be safe."

"If that's the case, Sir, we will have to leave after the shelling tonight."

"Sargent, these two men are under arrest. They are to be under guard until the plane arrives."

"Yes Sir."

"We will stay here until Charlie hits us tonight with more mortars. Then we will be leaving."

"There will be four men watching you, how do you plan on getting out?"

"They won't even see us go." The General looked at me and then turned around and left without saying a word.

"Tim, behind those barrels are supplies and some brand new weapons and ammo. There will be a box of grenades there also. That's all I can do for you," the Sargent said.

"Thanks, Sargent. It's been a pleasure."

"The men on duty—I will have a talk to them."

"No need for that. They won't be hurt."

"I will meet you here after dark and show you the way out."

"That won't be necessary, either. We already know how we're getting out. If I were you, I would mount some 30s on the jeeps. I found the wire cut and that means Charlie is coming in that way tonight. We will stay here until after the fight, then we are on our way. We're going to get some sleep now."

"Okay men, you know what to do. I want 30s mounted and covered on those jeeps. Bring everything we need. Keep your mouths shut."

Nge and I went to sleep. We heard some talking outside. It was the General.

"How's it going men?"

"Fine. They're sleeping inside."

"Okay. Goodnight men."

The men watched the General looking at the jeeps. He turned around and said, "What the hell is that on the jeeps?"

"Our ponchos, Sir! It looks like rain tonight."

"You men have been here too long. The stars are out. It's a nice night."

He walked toward the jeeps, then shook his head and left.

"Man, that was close."

At about 2100 hours Nge and I came out with our rifles. We could hear movement. The men mounted the jeeps and waited. The mortars started to fall, and the whole base came alive with Marines running everywhere. Then the shelling stopped. Charlie came through the section of fence they'd cut, and the men on the jeeps opened fire. It was like a turkey shoot. They kept coming and fell all over the place. The fighting lasted about an hour. There were bodies everywhere. The Sargent thought how stupid Charlie had been. If they had gotten in and separated, things might have been different. The General came running up to the men, yelling, "Where are they?"

"Don't know, Sir. We were busy over here."

"Wait a minute. Busy over here! What the hell are those 30s doing on the jeeps? I suppose you thought of that Sargent. How did you know Charlie would be coming in right here?"

"Well Sir, we found the fence cut. So we figured that something might happen here."

"That's good thinking. Maybe my explanation is better. I'll give you one word. No, make those two words—Tim and Nge. What the hell do you take me for? They told you! Sargent, I want you in my office in ten minutes."

"Yes Sir."

"If you don't want to be a private, I want the truth. Now!"

"Sir, we found the fence cut and we figured we had to do something. We didn't have much time."

"I guess your men will have the same story to tell?"

"I can check, Sir."

"No, just get out. I will meet you back there with your men."

The Sargent saluted and left. He walked back to his men.

"How did it go, Sargent?"

"Don't really know. How many dead here, Corporal?"

"I lost count when I hit two hundred."

The General came up to the Sargent and said, "Sargent, how many are dead?"

"Over two hundred, Sir."

"That was a good guess. By the way, we have two radios missing."

"I know, General. I tried to find them."

"Do you think Charlie stole them?"

"I have no idea."

"I can't give you men a medal for this. How would I write it up? Five men decided Charlie would hit near a fence they found cut—out of all the fences surrounding the base. Especially, when the five men were guarding Tim and Capt. Nge. I do know how to reward you. Tomorrow, bright and early, you and those four men have latrine duty."

The Sargent and his men got up bright and early and started to clean the latrines. Everyone laughed, then pitched in to help.

The General came over and said, "I see you have a lot of help. Just make sure that those 30s you stole are cleaned and put back where they belong."

The Sargent looked up and saw the radioman running toward them, yelling, "General, I have Tim on the line."

"Hi General. I have some news for you."

"Let me give you my news first, Tim. I have five Marines on latrine duty. Can you guess who they are?"

"No Sir! Have I ever met them?"

"By the way, are we talking to each other on the new radios that are missing?"

"They might be. They have a long range. Nge and I are about twenty miles from you and I can hear you clearly."

"That's nice. Now what do you want?"

"I just wanted to tell you that Charlie is heading your way. He must be mad for some reason. He has about a dozen tanks well camouflaged driving down the road. They look stupid—all that brush, and they're moving. Could they be pissed about last night?"

"Where are they? Never mind the jokes."

"General, you have to ease up. Oh, thanks for the wine. We are watching Charlie and drinking a bottle of wine. It's good stuff."

"That was my last bottle, you bastard. How did you get it?"

"Now, now, don't be that way. Do you think you can drop some bombs on the tanks before they get to you. I think that would be nice."

"Just give me the coordinates. Make sure you don't spill any of that wine. You owe me one, remember that. I will expect you to return a bottle. That is, if we ever meet again."

"General, here are the coordinates. Tell the guys I'm sorry about the latrine duty."

"Yes, I'll do that."

"Corporal! Call battalion and tell them what's going down and give them these coordinates."

"Yes Sir."

The General looked at the Sargent and his men and said, "So much for radios, huh men?

"I wonder how he got my last bottle of wine. Especially since the only two people in my office last night were you Sargent, and of course, me."

"No Sir, four is the correct number."

"Well, who were the third and the fourth?"

"That's easy, General—the orderly plus the thief."

"Okay. By the way, you men did a good job last night. Things could have turned out differently."

"Thanks General."

"That's all right. Get back to work on the latrines. I am going to inspect them personally. Doesn't that make you happy?"

"Yes Sir!"

"What do you think is going to happen to us, Sargent?" one of the men asked.

"Who cares? We're still alive. The General will get over it. Just keep out of his way."

"Do you think he believes our stories?"

"I think everything will work out fine. Especially after the fire fight last night. Thank God for Tim's tip. We could have got our pants kicked off."

"Talking about Tim, I hope he's all right. They're pretty close to the bombing area."

"Tim, I hope those planes get here fast. I don't like Charlie getting too close to the trees. If they stop they'll be hard to spot."

"If that happens, we'll just have to tell them when to drop their loads."

"Yea, and Charlie will be right on us."

"Keep your mouth shut and don't drink too much of the wine. The General said the planes are on the way."

"Look to the east; here they come." The jets were flying low. The first pass they missed the target. I picked up the radio. "Easy one, calling easy two. The tanks are off the side of the road. Drop your bombs 100 feet east from your last drop."

"Okay easy one, we see them; keep your heads down." They made another pass. Charlie was shooting at them. They dropped their loads right on the tanks. The tanks exploded and Charlie was torn to bits. The jets kept coming back and strafing the area. It was beautiful. The sky lit up from the explosions. The whole battle lasted about ten minutes. What was left of Charlie could be seen running. They wanted out of the area.

"Easy two, calling easy one. Thanks for the help."

"No problem, give my regards to the General. Tell him I need another bottle of wine. You guys did a good job. We had a ringside seat. Good luck to you."

"What do you think Nge? Should we go down and check it out?"

"You like living dangerously. Maybe we can find out where Tran is."

"I'll go in and you stay back and cover me."

I checked the bodies, at least what was left of them, and it appeared that no one was alive. Everything was burned to a crisp. Then I heard a noise. There was one left alive. I kicked his rifle aside and picked him up. He was an officer. Nge and I took him with us. When we were quite a distance away, we treated his wounds. We questioned him and after about a half-hour he told us that Tran was in the high country. He knew we were going to kill him. At least he was right. Nge finished him off. We took the papers that he had with him. I figured we would hold onto them until we met up with a patrol.

We headed into the high country, watching for a patrol, but there was none anywhere to be found. We slept during the day and walked by night. A few nights passed when we heard Charlie. "What the hell are they up to?" It wasn't long before we found out. They were setting up another ambush. Only this time, they had some heavy-duty weapons. I could see at least two fifty-caliber machine guns. The patrol didn't stand a chance against them. There were about ten men waiting for the patrol. This time our boys were up against the NVA, seasoned troops.

I knew we had to do something. It was just getting light with only a few minutes of darkness left. I pointed to Nge to take the south side while I took the north. That just left the men on the 50s. If we could take the others out first, we could then eliminate the 50s. We crawled to each man and one by one they were killed. It only took about ten minutes.

Nge was near one 50 and I was just to the rear of the other machine gun. We decided to lob a grenade at them. We pulled the pins and threw them. They went off killing all of the men that were left. We checked the bodies to make sure they were dead, then hit the ground to make sure the patrol didn't waste us.

They were moving toward us very carefully. I yelled for them to come in. I stood up and they said, "What the hell happened?" Nge and I smiled.

"Nothing much. Just another day in Nam."

"You don't mind if we look around?"

"Be our guest—take a good look at those 50s. They are brand new, Russian made. Could you do me a favor, Lieutenant?"

"Name it."

"Take these papers back to your C.O.. Have them sent to the General. There is some valuable information in them. There are also some maps. I think you should take those 50s with you."

"Our pleasure. What the hell are you men doing out here?"

"Sightseeing, Lieutenant. There is a clearing about a mile back where the choppers can land safely. Make sure you take the ammo for the 50s. You might just be able to use them. See you next time."

We disappeared as fast as we'd arrived. We followed the patrol to the clearing and watched the chopper pick them up and take off. We proceeded toward the high country.

"Hey Lieutenant! Where the hell did you get those 50s?"

"We met up with a couple of guys. They saved our asses. Charlie, or should I say the NVA, were waiting for us. These two guys took them out and left us with these 50s, plus some dispatches from Charlie."

"You're new out here, aren't you Lieutenant?"

"Yea, so what?"

"Those two guys that saved your asses—the whole Marine Corp and the Army are trying to find."

"Don't tell me they were Collins and Nge."

"Okay Lieutenant, I wont. I'll let you figure it out."

The choppers set down at base. As the Lieutenant looked out the doorway, he saw the General. The Lieutenant snapped to attention and saluted. He returned the salute.

"Where did you get those 50s, Lieutenant?"

"We were walking into an ambush and heard a couple grenades go off. When we got there, two men were standing there. They asked me to bring the 50s back and to give you these dispatches. Then they took off."

"Sargent, take these dispatches to Intelligence right away. You men take those 50s with you."

"Sir, there's ammo in the chopper they asked me to bring back." The General looked inside the chopper.

"Lieutenant, where are those two men now?"

"They said something about going to the high country."

"Damn it. They're going after Tran."

"Who the hell is Tran, Sir?"

"The one man you don't ever want to meet. You did a good job bringing back those 50s. I didn't know the NVA had any this far south. Go to debriefing and then get some rest.

"Just for the record, Lieutenant. You're lucky to be alive. If Charlie had opened up on you with those 50s, none of you would have made it back. Next time you go out, remember those guys you talked about might not be there to save your sorry asses."

Nge and I were getting close. We could feel Charlie in our bones. We came across a village. We watched it for awhile, but didn't notice any unusual activity. Right outside of the village was an old man sitting by the road. Nge went over to him. I saw Nge motion for me to come. I was very careful because some of the Vietnamese couldn't be trusted. You never knew who they were.

The old man looked at me and smiled. I said, "How are you, Sir?"

He got up and looked at the medallion I was wearing. "I know you. You are the one they call Tim."

"Yes Sir. This is Nge. We saw your village and are looking for information about a man called Tran. He is a Major in the North Vietnamese Army."

"I know him; he has been here. He takes our food and rapes our women. He is an evil man. He is also very anxious to get his hands on you. I heard his men say he doesn't sleep thinking of you. The last time he was here, he killed some of our young men. We couldn't tell him anything, but that didn't matter, he killed them anyway."

"I'm sorry to hear that. I wish that there were something we could do for you."

"There is. Kill him!"

"That's why we are here. We're looking for him. I have sworn to kill him and am not leaving Vietnam until I do. I promise you, when I meet up with him, I will kill him for the harm he has caused your people."

"I would invite you to share my food and home, but I can't because some of my people would turn you in. They are afraid of Major Tran."

"Sir, we have food. Could we give you some? You're welcome to some."

"That would not be wise. If we were seen with American food, they would know you were here and that would mean death to a lot of my people. I will take you to a place where you can hide and get some rest."

"That would be nice."

"Follow me. Where you are going you can watch the VC. That way you'll know where they're at."

We walked with the old man for about a half-hour. The old man was right. We had a good view of Charlie. The old man was getting ready to leave and turned to say, "Be careful. Tran is desperate. He doesn't stay in one place too long. He was here about a week ago. Since then we have not seen him. He goes to some of the other camps. He is trying to make it hard for anyone to get at him."

"Where are you going, Nge?"

"I know you offered our food to the old man, but I forgot to tell you we are out. So I will gather up supper."

Shit, I thought, that means snake again. I sure am tired of it. Nge came back with a big one. He slit it and the blood drained out into a cup. Then he sliced the snake. We had supper and fell asleep. When we woke up, the old man was back.

"Tim, I heard Tran is up north about twenty miles. There is a small VC camp there. If you follow the stars toward the north, you will find the camp. Stay well off the road. About 100 feet out, they have booby-traps."

I was picking up my gear when the old man handed me a bag. I looked inside—rice and dried fish. He smiled. He knew we were out of food.

We thanked him and started north. Twenty miles in the jungle is a long way. I could feel my heart pounding. We were getting close to Tran and I could hardly wait. His day was almost here. Every yard we traveled was bringing us closer. We circled around quite a few villages as we didn't want Tran to find out we were nearby. If he did he would have everyone looking for us. We finally arrived at his camp. There weren't very many men there. They hadn't even posted any guards. The only one we could see was half-asleep near a tree.

I kept thinking that there was something wrong. If Tran, was here, surely there would be more men, especially on guard duty. I whispered to Nge, "I will take the guard out. You start on the huts to the south."

I crawled toward the guard. When I reached him, I covered his mouth, slit his throat, and waited for him to go limp. When he did I entered the first hut. There were six men in the hut sleeping. By the time I'd finished, they all had their throats cut. We worked each hut with precision. Soon they were all dead. All, that is, except the one we wanted—Tran. He wasn't to be found.

Nge and I were sitting near a hut, when we heard someone walking nearby. We hid behind the hut. We missed one, I thought. The fool doesn't even notice the guard isn't around. When he was about two feet from Nge, he reached up and knocked him down. I yelled, "Don't kill him. We need to find where Tran is." We tied him up. He had a scared look on his face. We asked him where Tran was, but he wouldn't answer. We asked him several times. The light was coming up and then I had the shock of my life. The bastard was the one that had killed the Captain with a snake, right before our eyes in the prison camp. I told Nge to get a snake.

"Nge, do you remember him?"

"No."

"He likes to torture people; he really enjoys holding a snake an inch from a prisoner's face."

"Now, I remember him. I think I will bring him a nice big one."

Nge came back with a huge snake. He showed it to the prisoner. We asked him where Tran was, and he told us that he didn't know. We made sure the snake kept coming closer and closer to his face. Finally he broke, "Tran has moved to the southeast. He had orders to go there." For some reason, we believed him this time. I looked at Nge, "Payback time." We tied the snake to the prisoner's neck then let it go. The snake bit him over and over. He screamed and screamed, then fell to the ground. We felt good.

We left the camp, certain that Tran would soon get word about what happened.

"When Tran finds out, I figure he'll go crazy," I told Nge. We wanted him to worry when we would show up. We headed southeast. Tran was easy to follow—he was on a murdering spree. Killing everyone in the villages wherever he went. We made good time. Tran was getting nearer and nearer.

We stopped at a village and they made us welcome. We were fed and allowed to rest awhile. We stayed a couple of days. Anymore time would have been dangerous. As we were getting ready to leave, a runner came up and said, "Tran knows you're in the area. He has all of his men looking for you. They found their men dead along the way. Their throats had been cut. That's how he knows it's you."

We said our good-byes and started out. Heading south, we came across a small enemy patrol. We circled around them. The jungle was getting thick with Charlie; they were always in sight. We had a hard time maneuvering around them. Tran knew we were there, somewhere, and it must have been killing him not knowing where. We spotted a large group of VC and figured Tran had to be with them. All the information we had told us he wouldn't travel light.

Deciding to watch them, we followed them for miles. We knew they would have to make camp soon. We thought that if we took out some of his men, maybe he would make a mistake. "If we wait until dark, we can make our move. We'll take out a few of his men on guard duty."

"That sounds good to me. If that doesn't flush him out, nothing will. We'll wait until they go to sleep then take out the group toward the west of the camp. After we finish, we'll leave a false trail leading north. Then we will circle back."

We made our way stealthily to the two sentries. Soon, they lay on the ground with their throats cut. One by one, the sentries died. Cutting their throats proved to be easy; not a noise came out of them. Before we'd finished, twelve of them were dead. We left the camp and deliberately headed north, leaving a trail a Boy Scout could follow. We circled back and waited. We were on the south side of the camp. Most of the men had left to find us. When we made sure they were well away from the camp, we killed a few more. Just before he died, one of them told us where Tran's hut was. I checked the hut out, but it was empty. We left the camp in a hurry. We wanted to put some distance between Tran and us.

"Tim, what the hell did you do when you went into Tran's hut?"

"I cut up his bunk and his clothes. That should really screw his mind up."

We watched Tran and his men come back. They found the other four dead men. Then Tran went into his hut. He came out yelling and screaming. We watched Tran murder one of the guards because of what we'd done to the hut. We were right—Tran was losing it. I figured he was going to screw up and then he would be mine.

We found a place to hide. Charlie was out in full force, looking everywhere for us. We were always in a different location. We kept away from them unlessl we wanted to send a message. That usually meant someone dying.

We played hide-and-seek for about a week. We would strike at night, kill a few, and then run. We never had to use a rifle. Our knives were the quickest and quietest way of doing things. It drove Tran crazy. Everyday he would shoot one of his men. I guess he figured that they would shape up by doing that. The number of dead was getting higher. I knew Tran would be called back to his headquarters before long. No officer can lose that many men without reprisals. I just hoped we could get to him before that happened. He made sure that he was always surrounded by his men. What I wouldn't have given for a high-powered rifle with a silencer.

"Nge, I was just wondering. Maybe we should cool it for awhile. We can use the rest. We're liable to screw up if we don't keep our shit together. We're getting tired."

"I think Tran will be heading north shortly. We should move out and get there first. That way, we can get some rest."

We packed our gear, so we could get an early start. When daybreak came, we moved out. Charlie was nowhere to be found. Our plan had worked; they were still looking for us down south as we headed for the U.S. outpost. It took us a few days to get there. When we did, we became worried because we couldn't see anyone walking around. It wasn't right. Why would they leave the safety of the outpost? Nge and I waited for nightfall and then crawled into the outpost. We were hiding when Nge spotted Charlie. We waited to see how many were there. Two were sitting by a fire, one was sleeping, and the other one was guarding the bunker. We made our way toward the fire. We killed those two first, then the sleeping one.

We wondered about the guard in front of the bunker. Who was he guarding? We moved closer to the bunker, then hit him with the butt of the rifle. Inside, we found the Sargent tied up.

We untied him and gave him water. Nge dragged the guard in. The Sargent went for him, but we stopped him.

"What happened here, Sargent?"

"We were overrun and the men were captured. They killed everybody—one after another. They thought it was funny. They were making a joke of it. I was unconscious and when I came to they were shooting the men. The tied me up and beat me. I guess I was being saved for later. That bastard was in charge. He ordered the shooting."

Charlie was coming to. He moaned and when he saw us he tried to run. I knocked him to the ground. "Are there anymore of you?" He didn't answer. I looked at the Sargent and said, "Would you like to have the honors?"

The Sargent picked him up by the throat and choked him until he turned blue. Charlie was coughing and choking as the Sargent asked him again, "Are there anymore of you and where are they?"

Charlie told us, "Don't worry, they will be back."

I stood up and removed my knife. The guard saw it. He became quiet; he knew that knife."

"Well Charlie, I guess you know who I am. Is Tran coming back here? If so when and how many men will he have." Charlie spilled his guts, and every time he saw the knife, he squirmed.

"Sargent, do we need him anymore?"

"No, we don't!"

"Hold this, Sargent. I have to piss."

I heard the guard gurgle. He fell to the ground. "Sargent, I hate to ask you to do this. Can you get the dog tags from those men out there?"

"No problem, I can handle it." He came back a few minutes later. You could see by his face, he was taking it hard.

"Hold onto them. We will get you out of here as soon as we can."

"I would prefer to stay with you and Capt. Nge."

"Thanks, but that is impossible. You need to get back and tell the story to the General. I saw a deep hole out there. We're going to bury them."

"Sorry Tim, I won't bury them. Let the ants and rats eat them."

"No. We're going to bury them headfirst. We will put the shoes of our dead on them. Then we will cover them and leave the shoes showing. We will rig them with grenades. When Charlie comes back, I am sure they will want those shoes. When they take them off, the men who owned the shoes will have company, to screw over when they get to wherever they go."

"Now that sounds good, Tim."

I was thinking of Tran, but he would have to wait. I had to get the Sargent out right away.

"We're going to head for the mountains. The people there will help us."

"Are you crazy? The mountain people will kill anyone that even comes close to their villages."

"Don't worry Sargent. They are our friends."

"That's news to me. We have orders to keep out of those mountains. Even Charlie doesn't go there."

"That's why we can. So let's move out. We don't have that much time. The mountains are between Tran and us. So keep your mouth shut. The only talking will be by hand signals. We will travel by night."

We got away from the outpost and made our way toward the mountains. Charlie was every where. We only killed when we had to. We finally reached the mountains and weren't that high up when the people surrounded us. We waved to them, and they told us to follow them. They led us to their leader. He picked up my medallion and told us to come with him.

As we walked toward a hut, the old man came out. He smiled and shook our hands. "Tim, we have heard about what you are up to. You have killed a lot of our enemies. What can we do for you?"

"We need some rest and we're hungry. And he needs medical attention."

"Sargent, are you the only one left from the outpost?"

"Yes Sir. I am the only one left. They killed everyone else. I guess I was going to be next when Tim and Nge arrived."

"Sir, we noticed that Charlie has some of your people working the rice paddies below the mountain."

"Yes, we are allowing it until the harvest, which should be soon. Then we will go down, harvest the rice, and kill them all."

"Pretty good thinking, Sir."

"We have our moments, Tim. Come now, we will help you."

We stayed with the people for about a week. It was getting close to the time of the harvest.

"Sir, when you go down the mountain to get the rice, we would like to help you. That way we can be part of you and your people."

"That will be fine, Tim. Tomorrow we will gather our people and take care of Charlie. Now get some sleep."

When we woke up everybody was ready, and we walked down the mountain. When we reached the wooded area before the rice field, we noticed four guards. The mountain people walked over to them and killed them. They picked up the rice and headed back up the mountain. I made sure they cut the throats of all the NVA. That way, Tran would think Nge and I had done it.

When we reached the village, the villagers were putting the rice away. Nge and I decided that it was time to move on. The old man told us we didn't have to go. But I was thinking about Tran and how when he found his men dead, he would be after the villagers. I knew they didn't like coming up into the mountains. But now it was different.

Tran would be looking for us and in his half-crazy state of mind I figured he would attack the villages. We had to make him think we had done it, not the villagers. We explained the situation to the old man and he agreed. We thanked the people and left.

We headed north, that way Tran would follow the trail of bodies we left. We had traveled for about a week when we came across another rice paddy. This one was different, however. The men working it were Americans—prisoners. There were three guards watching them. We crawled toward the guards, knowing the clearing would give them a chance to fire. We each took a man. We fired and they dropped. The third one came running toward the prisoners. We fired at him and he went down.

We stood up and looked at the three Americans; they were in bad shape.

"Can you walk?"

"Yes Sir. We will be glad to get out of here. We have been prisoners for a year. They move us from paddy to paddy. We're never in one place for too long."

We gave them food and what medical attention we could. Now I had three men to slow us down. We were forced to call for choppers. Moving about two miles north, we found a clearing that didn't look dangerous. We called for the choppers and gave our coordinates. As we hid in the tall grass, we were surprised to see Charlie coming toward us. That's all we need, I thought. Choppers coming in at the same time as Charlie. We knew we had to take them out.

We waited for them to get closer; there were six of them. When they were right on us, we opened fire; five died right there. But the sixth one managed to get away. I hoped the choppers would come before he returned with reinforcements. We had no choice but to wait. It wasn't long before the choppers arrived and we helped the three American soldiers get aboard.

"Get out of here quick. Charlie should be here any minute."

"Aren't you coming?"

"No, we have something to do. Now get out of here."

Charlie showed up and started to open fire as the choppers were lifting off. Nge and I ran through the tall grass after losing them and made our way north. We just kept going north. We waited a couple of days before we decided to set up camp. We were trying to find a place to hide, when we came across a village. "Do you think it is safe to go in?" I asked.

"I've been here before; the people are friendly. They have helped me in the past," Nge answered. Nge went into the village to check it out. I watched him enter the village. He had been gone a long time and I began to worry. Then I saw him come out. He waved and I went into the village.

I saw an old lady sitting with Nge and asked her if there were any VC in the area. Looking up, I noticed an old man standing next to us. "No VC here. You are welcome to eat and stay with us." As soon as we sat down, the villagers brought us food.

Nge said, "The VC doesn't like coming this close to the mountains. If we go high enough we should be safe."

"Have you seen any Americans in this area?" I asked.

"The VC has a lot of prisoners not far from here. They use them for slave labor, then kill them."

"Can you tell us where they are?"

"I will draw you a map. They won't be hard to find. What are you going to do with them once you get them out? They are in bad shape."

"I don't know. But I just can't leave them there. I guess they will have to find their own way back."

The old man drew us the map. I could see they weren't far. That was good. He made a mark on the map to show where the Americans were being held. "I will have some men go with you. The only thing is you'll have to wait for them. They live in the mountains and are good fighters. They should be here tomorrow at noon. See this mark? That is a base camp about two miles from where the prisoners are located. They're well armed. There are about a hundred men there."

I knew we would have some problems. No one knew how many Americans were there. The mountain men arrived. They had enough weapons to start their own war. We left and walked for hours, camping at night. We finally didn't have to worry about sleeping since the mountain men stood watch while Nge and I slept. They woke us up in the morning and we left. We walked for another day and when we finally stopped, we could see the camp. The old man was right. There were a lot of VC. We bypassed them and decided to booby-trap the road about a mile from where they had the prisoners. We wired grenades and clamors in the road. If Charlie crossed them, they would lose a lot of men. We made our way to the rice fields and spotted about twenty prisoners working them. The VC had ten men watching them.

Nge and I started for the huts, but the mountain men told us to wait where we were. We watched as they took out the VC one at a time. They checked the huts then waved for us to come in. The prisoners came out of the paddies.

"Are you men all right?"

"Yes, but who are you? How do you expect to get us out?"

"We'll worry about that later. Pick up the rifles and everything you can use. We have to get out of here."

"These men will lead you out. You'll be safe with them. They will feed you and give you medical attention when you get to the place they have waiting for you." We watched them leave. They were soldiers again. You could see it by the way they walked.

Nge and I headed for the next camp. We had made good time. "When Charlie finds their men dead, they are going to come straight here. So whatever we do, we have to do fast," I told Nge.

We checked out the prison camp area. The prisoners were in bamboo cages. The guards were watching them. Making our way quickly to the guard near the cages, we grabbed him and slit his throat. Then we slipped into the hut and killed everyone inside. We went to the cages and let the men out. "You men grab what you can from Charlie. We are going to get you out of here. We have to move fast. We have one more place to go. There are more prisoners about a mile from here and we want to get them out."

"I know where they are," said one of the prisoners. "They are working on a bridge east of here; quite a few prisoners are being held there. Charlie comes by every morning in a chopper with supplies. We will have to take it out."

"Can anyone here operate a chopper?"

"Yes Sir, I can. But I don't know if we can get off the ground with this many men."

"That's your problem," I said. "Figure a way to do it so no one gets left behind."

We made our way to the bridge. We could see the men. There was a radio shack, which we decided had to go first. We figured the men in the huts would be asleep when we attacked.

"We can free the prisoners then take off. That's if the chopper comes."

We waited for the chopper to show up. It finally came and we watched it land. "Thank God, it is a large supply one."

The guards woke up the prisoners and made them unload the chopper. We were all set. Nge took out the radio shack, and the mountain men and I hit the huts. The rest of the men took care of the guards outside and the pilots. Everything went like clockwork. We made everyone get into the chopper. The pilot yelled that we'd better fuel up first or we wouldn't get off the ground. Some men jumped out and fueled the chopper. Nge and I watched the blades slowly turn and then the chopper was in the air. It was having trouble getting any altitude so they threw out the weapons and everything else they could. Finally, they were high enough to head toward our lines. But I was worried— the Americans were a long way away.

Now we had to make our way back to the mountains. Charlie knew we were here. The booby traps we had set on the road were exploding. We decided to head west to bypass them. I suddenly noticed that there was one man who'd been left behind. "Why aren't you on that chopper?" I demanded.

"I couldn't go. You see there's another camp northwest of here. A lot of American prisoners are there."

"Well, you better follow us. Just keep up. Where is this camp?"

"Just head northwest and we'll will run into it."

"Okay, let's go. Eat this on the way. Charlie is going to be all over us any minute." I heard one of the mountain men say, "We can go this way. Charlie stays out because of the snakes. If we wear legs covers we can make it."

"Leg covers! Where the hell are we going to get them," I asked.

"We can make them. I'll show you how. This way we can save a lot of time."

"Okay, let's go."

We got to the area the mountain man had told us about, and I said, "Hey you, what the hell is your name?" "Corporal Baker."

"Let's get the leg covers on."

We were shown how to make them. Everyone had a pair on their legs in no time. The mountain men laughed at us.

We moved into the area and there were snakes all over the place. Every so often we could feel them striking at our legs. "Thank God for these leg covers," I thought. After about an hour we were out of the snake-infested area and removed the covers. We kept going and soon arrived at the camp. It was a fairly large camp. We got into position and then opened fire; Charlie was running all over the place. We kept firing. They were dropping right in front of us. I saw Nge throw a grenade in the hut; bodies flew out. After about an hour, the fighting stopped. We checked for the Americans and found them hiding all over the place.

"Are you men okay?" I asked.

"Yes Sir, we sure are glad to see you."

"Are there anymore of you around here?"

"Just some hiding under the bridge." We watched as about fifty men came out. "What the hell are we going to do with them?" I asked Nge.

Grabbing whatever we could, we left. We never stopped; Charlie was sure to come after us. We traveled as long as we could, but some of the prisoners couldn't move anymore so we stopped. We fed them, gave them water, and treated them. We decided to stay the night. Nge and I were talking about the men and what the hell to do with them when one of them laughed and said, "That's easy, Sir. About two miles from here is an airport. There is an old DC-3 there. I can fly it but the only thing is we have to take the base. It's a Russian base."

"Russian, what the hell do you want to do? Start another war."

"You got it wrong. It's an old base. Charlie mans it now. The old DC is in the hangar, and about forty men. We can fuel the plane, take off, and get to the sea. There is enough room for everybody. We can take the mountain men that are with you. It's the only chance we've got."

"Okay, tomorrow we will head there. How long will it take for us to reach the base?"

"Maybe a day. I have been taken there several times to fix the plane. They don't have any mechanics that are worth anything. So I got the job. I made them pay me in food for the men."

"We'll hit the base tomorrow."

"Tim, don't you think we should hang loose for a while?"

"Normally, I would agree. But we have too many men with us. How can we hide? I can't endanger the lives of innocent people. The prisoners will just have to move when we do. If they can't make it, so be it. But I can't risk the lives of so many for so few. If the plane is there then our problem will be over."

We left at dawn. The men were a sorry lot. The ones that could helped the sick. Everyone was armed, just in case Charlie showed up. We continued deeper and deeper in the jungle.

We finally reached the airstrip. I told Nge to take out the hut with the radio. I planned on killing as many guards as I could. Luckily, there weren't that many. But what worried me was the barracks. How many of the enemy were in there?

The pilot crawled toward me and said, "The plane is covered by brush. The mechanics are usually sleeping near the plane. Over to the left is the truck with the fuel. That is the most important thing. We have to protect it. Without gas we're screwed. The guards near the truck have to die first."

We were ready to go. Nge was already at the hut, waiting for my signal. The pilot and I got close to the mechanics and then fired, killing both of them. Nge dropped a grenade in the hut and after the explosion he ran in and opened fire. They were all dead. The mountain men hit the barracks at the same time. We could hear firing from both sides then it was quiet. Some of the men moved the gas truck to the plane and filled it. When she was topped off, everybody got onboard. The wounded were put on the plane first. Some of the guys raided the mess hall, looking for food and water. I got the signal from the pilot. After what seemed like an eternity, the starboard engine finally started. What a beautiful sound!

But the port engine wouldn't start. The pilot got out and checked the engine. "Charlie was smart;" he said. "He always left a wire off. I forgot," the pilot said. I found it and put it back on. Soon the port engine fired and both engines were running smooth. Now the only problem was getting the plane off the ground with so many men on it. I figured that was the pilot's job. I sat down next to him. "How long before we are airborne?"

"That, my friend, is a good question?" The pilot started to rev up the engines. They just kept getting louder and louder.

We're not moving."

"Tim, I need speed and wind to get this plane off the ground. If these engines don't burst, we will be lucky. I'd hate to get down to the end of the runway, just to end up in those trees. So, do me a favor, say a prayer and shut the fuck up."

As the plane started to move, everyone was quiet. We began to pick up speed, but we weren't getting off the ground. Finally, we started to lift off the ground. The pilot brought the stick back as hard as he could. We barely cleared the trees; I could feel the plane shutter as the wheels hit them. Everyone cheered. "I'll check on the men. By the way, what the hell is your name?"

"Lt. Warren, Sir!"

"Don't call me sir; I am only a petty officer."

"You're what?"

I laughed and went to check on the prisoners.

"How are the wounded?" I asked Nge.

"They are fine. All they're talking about is getting out of that hellhole!"

"Get them fixed up the best you can and make them get as much rest as you can. They need it. Have you figured out where we are going?"

"Probably, to hell. I don't know how he is going to get this plane down. There are no landing strips around here."

One of the mountain men heard us. "I think I can help you, Tim. On the coast east of here is a small village. They have some kind of boat hidden. If we can land in the water, we can make it to shore."

"How do you know about a boat?"

"I was on it when I was a kid. The sailors used to take me out on it. That is until Charlie killed them. The people of the village took the boat out of the water; it's hidden in the brush near the edge of the water. I think it might still work."

"Well, I guess it is worth a try."

"Just travel east, make sure the mountains are to your left, and you won't miss it. It's a small fishing village. There will be boats nearby.

"Thanks. I'll tell the pilot."

"Lieutenant, can you put this crate down in the water?"

"I probably will have to anyway."

"There is a small fishing village east of us. Keep those mountains on your left and you'll come to it."

"I hope we come to it soon. We are getting low on fuel."

"Lieutenant, that's your problem, just make sure you get this plane there! There is a ridge in front of us. Maybe once we're over it, we can see the village. If we have to ditch the plane in the water, how long will we have to get the men out before it sinks?"

"I don't know—a couple of minutes, maybe longer. It all depends on how hard we hit. Then it is up to the men. I suggest you go back and warn them. Once we stop, they are to move out. Leave everything behind but their asses."

We made it over the ridge. There was the ocean. I looked to the starboard and could see the village. The plane headed for the village.

"Lieutenant, make sure the plane lands far enough away from land. I want it to sink in deep water."

"That's going to make it rough for the men in their condition."

"Yea, but the people in the village won't end up dying because the plane can be seen from the air. That's the decision I have made. Now do it."

"Okay, everybody get set for the roughest landing of your life. I will open the hatch and everyone is to get out and start swimming for shore immediately. The wounded better be helped. I don't want to lose anyone. We can do this."

I heard one engine shut down. The second engine was running rough. We were low to the water then we hit with a bang. We were thrown all around. I got to the door as the plane stopped. I was throwing men out. The healthy were helping the wounded. I checked the plane and saw that everybody was out. Then Nge yelled, "Where's the pilot?" We both ran forward. He was unconscious, so we grabbed him and jumped into the water. The people of the village were picking up the men in their boats. It wasn't long before they had us too, including the unconscious pilot. We were sitting on shore, when the plane sank out of sight. The old man of the village came over to us and told us the men were okay and the wounded are being cared for. "My people are feeding them now."

"You are Captain Nge and you must be Tim. We have heard what you have done. You are not safe here. Once they find out you stole the plane, they are going to head straight for the coast. We have a boat. It will be crowded with so many men. It's been here for years. Have you anyone with you that can fix it? I don't know if it will start."

"Is there anyone here who can fix the boat?"

"I can, Sir. I was a chief on the PT boats during the big one. This should be no problem. The only thing that worries me is fuel. Where are we going to get it?"

"Just get the boat ready. We'll find some fuel."

The old man said, "My men are moving the boat into the water. The fuel you need is in barrels hidden under the sand. I'm sure there is enough to fill the tanks."

The boat was put into the water and covered up. The Chief started to work on the engines. After a few hours, they started to fill the tanks with the gas.

"Tim, now is the time of reckoning. You'd better pray also," the Chief said. The engine kicked over; it was trying to start. The Chief got mad and hit the bloody thing with a hammer. The port engine started then he started the starboard engine; they were purring like a cat. He ran it for awhile but we didn't dare take it for a test ride. The people of the village put water and supplies on the boat.

Everyone got on board; it was really crowded. If it hit a storm, the thing would probably go under. But no one cared. They were free and that's all that counted. Nge and I said our good-byes to the prisoners then watched them until they were out of sight.

The beach was cleaned up so that Charlie wouldn't suspect anything. Nge and I, along with the mountain men, decided to head back to the mountains. We knew Charlie wouldn't be far behind. Whenever Charlie showed up, we hid. We didn't want to kill anyone because they would know we had been at the village. Moving in the daylight was dangerous but we had to take the chance.

We had been moving southwest for a day, when we heard a man running. We hid until we saw it was one of the mountain men. We stood up and yelled. He came to us.

"Tim, I have a message for you. Tran has gone north to Hanoi. I was sent to tell you this."

"Hanoi!"

Nge and I just looked at each other. We couldn't believe it.

"Well Nge, I guess we can't get to Tran now. Maybe our luck has changed."

"Charlie will be all over the place. There will be few places to hide."

"Then, we will have to take care of them. I have nothing better to do. This is a good a place to die as any."

It wasn't long before we met up with Charlie. They were all over the place. But this time they were careless. They had forgotten about us with Tran in Hanoi. We moved around more and more at night. Every time we saw a fire, we would kill everyone there. The price on our heads kept going up. Night after night we stalked the jungle. Killing and killing. It seemed like it was never going to stop. I started to think about the boat and whether they made out okay. I also wondered about the prisoners we'd sent back in the chopper. Did they get back to the Americans or did they crash?

"Hey Lieutenant, how long have we been floating out here?"

"I have no idea. I hope someone sees us pretty soon. We have no gas and the food is getting scarce. It better rain soon so can get some water to drink. I just hope Charlie is not out here. We can't defend ourselves. I think we should start praying—that's the only help we're going to get."

They were drifting southeast, too far out for patrol boats. That was one good thing. A week passed and we were still drifting. "Maybe we will get lucky and land in Australia?"

"If we do, there will be nothing but skeletons on board. Do you think someone will spot us from a plane?"

"I have no idea. The only thing I know for sure is we're not drifting back to Nam. That alone makes me happy. I guess dying free is better than dying in that filthy prison." All of a sudden the men were yelling and waving.

"What the hell are they doing back there?"

"There's a plane up there. He's flying low. No wait, there are a few of them. Send up a flare."

The flare went up and they all began to pray. "What the hell are we going to do if it's the enemy?"

"Die with dignity. That's what we will do."

"Captain, I think I see a flare off the starboard quarter."

"I see it. Let's go down for a better look."

The planes turned and dove on the small boat. They could see men waving.

"Captain, do you see what I am seeing?"

"Yes, and I don't believe it! That boat is overloaded and drifting. I am going to call the ship."

"Mother hen, this is chick one. We have visual on a small craft with what appears to be a bunch of Americans on board. They are drifting. Here are the coordinates. We will wait here for the choppers."

"How is your fuel, Captain?"

"It's getting low."

"Then return to mother. The choppers are leaving now. We will have cover coming in a few minutes. So get back now."

"Yes Sir." The plane made a pass and waved its wings to the right and left.

"Lieutenant, they are coming; they know who we are."

"Captain, how many are onboard the craft?"

"I'm not sure, maybe forty or fifty."

"I can't believe it!"

"I am returning. I see the jets, but where are those choppers?"

"The choppers will be there shortly, Captain. Bring your planes back to the ship."

The planes headed back to the ship and saw the choppers heading for the boat. On landing, the Captain was instructed to go to the bridge.

"What did you find out there?"

"Sir, I have no idea. All I could see was a small boat overloaded with Americans."

The choppers picked up the men off the boat. One of the chopper pilots called in the boat was full of prisoners from a camp up north.

Finally, one by one, the choppers touched down. And once they were down, they brought the jets back on board. The men were unloaded from the choppers and rushed to sick bay.

"Commander, I have no idea who they found out there. They are in sick bay, being treated. The most I know now is that they were prisoners. And can you believe this? Tim is still out there. He set them free. First, they stole a plane and ditched it, and these men came out on that boat. They have been floating around for weeks."

"Let's go to sickbay. I want to talk to the men personally."

"Who is in charge here?"

"I guess you could say I am, Sir. I am Lieutenant Jacobs. We were prisoners in Nam."

"We have been prisoners for some time, Sir."

"I can't believe this. What about a couple of guys named Tim and Capt. Nge?"

"They're still there, Sir. They refused to come out. They said they hadn't finished what they had to do."

When they left the sickbay, the Commander said, "Captain, I can't believe this."

"Neither do I. But they're here."

"Get a message off. This is going to shake up some asses."

"Radioman, I want this message to go off right away."

The message was delivered. An hour passed then the ship was ordered back to Japan. The Captain went back to sick bay to speak to the men again.

"What about the other men, Captain? Apparently, Tim had them sent to the mountain people so they could make it back."

"That must be the group that made it back a few weeks ago. They are back home. They never mentioned you people being alive," the Captain said to Lieutenant Jacobs.

"No Sir, we were still prisoners when Tim freed them."

"What about Tim? Where is he?"

"He's still there. I guess he is still killing Charlie. He has a score to settle and he isn't giving up."

"Who is Lt. Davis?"

"I am, Sir."

"The doctors say you can answer questions now; follow us to the wardroom."

"I'll get dressed, Sir."

"Lieutenant, I don't care if you are bare-assed. Follow me."

As they entered the wardroom, the officers stared at Lt. Davis, then stood to attention.

"At ease men, this is Lt. Davis."

The men started to clap their hands.

"Thank you, gentlemen."

"Stewards, get us some coffee. Lieutenant, what about Captain Nge and Tim?"

It took an hour for Lieutenant Davis to tell his story.

"That is amazing, if I wasn't looking at you, I would never believe it."

"Did you know Tim was a crewmember on board this ship? It was from this ship that he was lost. It would have been great to have him back. By the way, Washington will be notified about your men. We will notify your families and tell them you're all safe."

"Well, Tim and Nge are still there. As long as he has that knife, he is going to kill."

"We have heard about that knife. It has seen a lot of blood."

"I have seen it used. He kills like no one I've ever met. The stories are all true."

"Sir, the men and I would like to go on deck. We have something to do."

"What might that be?"

"We want to thank Tim and Capt. Nge. I know it sounds stupid, Sir."

"I don't think it's stupid. Take your men up there at 1800 hours."

"Thank you Sir."

At 1800 hours, the whole ship's company was standing at attention when the prisoners came on deck. As they walked toward the port elevator, the loud speaker announced, "Attention On Deck."

Everyone saluted, looking out at the open sea, the prisoners all said, "Thanks Tim. We hope you make it back."

Lieutenant Davis turned and said, "Thanks Captain." When everyone dropped the salute, the Captain looked at the men and said, "Thank you men." Then everyone started to cheer. The prisoners could feel their eyes filling. The sailors offered them cigarettes and not one of them asked the prisoners about Nam.

A sailor came toward the prisoners. "Sir, I bought these cigarettes for you. I also want to thank you. I had a brother in Nam. He never made it back. I am proud to meet you." He saluted and turned away. Lieutenant Davis didn't know what to say. But, he was also proud to meet the sailor even though he didn't even know his name.

"Captain, have you ever seen anything like this?"

"Never, and I have been in the Navy for twenty years. But I hope I never see anything like it again. I can't imagine what those men have been through."

"I wonder if the guys got out, the ones we sent to the mountains?"

"If I know my people, they got them out. We would have been told if they were still here."

"I guess you're right."

"I guess all we have to worry about now is Tran?"

Everywhere we went we came across Charlie. We were on a killing spree. We knew Tran was going crazy. He was losing a lot of men. We kept killing every day. The days turned into weeks, and the weeks into months. Nge and I lost track of time.

"I think tomorrow, we should try to make it into the mountains. Maybe we can hide out there for awhile."

We broke camp before dawn and headed for the mountains. We ran into Charlie on the trail. When the shooting stopped, we checked the bodies out. One of them was alive. He kept saying, "The war is over." He didn't want to die. I slit his throat. Nge and I left the area. Every time we met up with a small patrol, we ended up killing them. The war might have been over but it wasn't over for the people. We came across a lot of villages where Charlie had killed the old and the women for absolutely no reason. America's war was over, our war wasn't.

When Nge and I reached the mountains, we kept climbing until we came across some villagers. They took us to their village. The old man greeted us. "Tim, what are you doing here? I haven't seen you in a long time."

"We are still looking for Tran. I promised you I would kill him, and I'm going to fulfill that promise. Tran must die. He is still killing the people in the villages whenever he arrives at one."

"Tim, you're wrong. It isn't Tran. He has gone."

"Gone where?"

"He is living in the States."

"That's impossible. How could he get there?"

"I'm sorry, but your people took him there."

"Not my people!"

"Yes, Tim, the CIA got him out of Vietnam. Now he is living in the States."

"The CIA—those bastards! They're not my people. If it's the last thing I do, I will get even with them too."

"Tim, you have been living in the jungle too long. You have to stop killing. The war is over. Now you can go home."

"No Sir, this is my home now."

"No, this is not your home. You must return to your people. Tran was taken to the U.S. to traffic in drugs. He will be killing your people like he did mine. He will be using heroin instead of bullets. Only this time, he will be making money. He will also be protected by the CIA. That is why you must go home. We found out Tran and the CIA have been in the drug trafficking business for years. That's why they let him into the States."

"How am I going to get there?"

"It will not be easy, but I think there is a way. I heard a story awhile back about some dignitaries coming to Vietnam to see if they could find their missing MIAs. I understand they are in Hanoi right now. That is your way out. I heard they are negotiating with Hanoi for the release of prisoners that still might be here. They were supposed to be here a long time ago, but Hanoi wouldn't let them in until now.

"Tim, you have to go. That is why you will leave in the morning. You must get Tran. This time, on your turf. You will have to be real careful, the CIA is involved now. That means you will have two enemies to deal with."

Dawn came early. We left for Hanoi. As we walked through the jungle, I realized I was going to miss my people in Vietnam. It had become my home. The people were my family. Then I thought of Tran. I could feel the hate running through my body.

It took almost a week for us to get to Hanoi. We had to find out when the plane was leaving. We came across a village, but I was leery about stopping. After dark, we got closer. We could hear them talking. We overheard them saying the plane was leaving in two days. We backed out of the village.

"We have enough time to get there. We have to think of away to get you on board," Nge said. We started for the airport.

We could see the plane. It had United States of America painted on it. We could also see the guards around the plane and knew it was going to be hard to get on board. Especially, with two Marines guarding it. Killing the NVA was one thing, but I wasn't about to kill any Marines.

"Tim, if we kill a few guards on the other side of the field that should distract them so we can get to the plane."

We hid in the woods until it was dark then moved in slowly. We killed four of the guards and moved toward the plane. We noticed the guards standing on the top of the stairs, near the door. There were also four NVA guards standing around the plane. We made it to the first two and slit their throats. We picked up their bodies and took them inside the hangar and dumped them in a big box we found in the corner. The other two NVA guards began to look for their comrades. We grabbed them from behind, slit their throats, and put them with their friends. We walked back toward the plane and saw the Marines looking for the four guards. They had their weapons at ready when someone called them. Nge said good-bye to me. I asked him to come with me.

"I can't, I have to stay here. Get Tran. Then I will be happy. Now get aboard quickly." We hugged each other for the last time. I silently made my way to the stairs of the plane. The Marine guards were still talking to the NVA officer. I could hear the NVA officer yelling. The Marines were telling him that the four NVA troops were missing. They came back to the plane and checked all around it. By then, I was inside looking for a place to hide. There wasn't much room anywhere so I went into the cockpit area. That was even worst. I took out my knife and open up a panel. There was nothing but wires in it, so I backed into it and closed the door. I tried to turn the bolts that secured it from inside, but could only get three of them. The fourth was loose. That will have to do, I thought to myself.

I was worried about Nge. If I knew him, he was killing more of Charlie just to cover for me. I held the medallion that I had been given, thinking of all the people that had helped me all these years.

I also kept hearing Nge's last words to me: "I'll see you in the States. That's a promise." He knew where I lived; I'd talked about New Bedford quite a bit over the years.

All of a sudden, I could hear the crew talking. Charlie was on board the plane. I heard the two Marines saying, "We noticed your men missing and told the officer. No one has boarded this plane but the crew and you, along with your men." The pilot yelled, "This is American territory, you don't belong on board. I am asking you to leave."

"We are going to check this plane whether you like it or not," replied the NVA officer. He told his men to check everything. The Marines went with them. He ordered a panel to be opened. The Marines opened it and looked inside. "Go ahead, check it out for yourself it's empty." They did and the Marines secured the bolts. Charlie was checking all of the overhead compartments. Everywhere they checked they came up empty. "There, we told you no one has been aboard."

"What the hell is this all about?"

"Beats me, Sir. They're ready to kill. That's how mad they are. It seems they are missing some men. So take some advice, Sir, don't piss them off."

I heard the co-pilot tell the pilot, "This bolt is loose."

"Tighten it, but don't let them see you do it."

I heard the screwdriver turn the bolt. I could hear people coming aboard. It was the news media and the Ambassador and his party. When they got aboard, they were told to sit down. The Ambassador got up and asked, "What the hell is going on?" The NVA officer told him to shut up and sit down and when he didn't they pushed him down.

"Captain, I am going to tear this plane apart. The men that killed my men have to be on board," yelled the NVA officer.

"That's bullshit. You're just trying to start an international incident. Some of these news people are from foreign countries. They will be writing about this. What reason would they have to kill your people. You're full of shit and you know it!"

"The man we want is on board somewhere and we know it. We will find him and then we will take care of you. That's a promise."

"Major, there is no place left to search. You have gone over everything. There is no one on board except the people on your list. Check it again. I demand to be allowed to leave. I said whoever you're looking for is not on board. Now, shit or get off the pot. Major, get that gun out of my face. If you plan on shooting it, do it. I am tired of looking at it. I don't care how long you search. There is no one here who isn't supposed to be. Now, I demand to leave! Check with your superiors. We are guests of your country—not your enemy. I want permission to leave, now!"

It wasn't long before the Major came back. "I want you and this plane out of my country." He looked at his men and yelled, "Everybody out. Now! And, I hope you do come back because I will make sure you and your crew disappear—just like my men did."

"Maybe they deserted, Major."

"Get out now!"

I could hear the Major yelling at the Ambassador, "You American dogs don't deserve to live." One of the reporters tried to get up and the Ambassador grabbed him.

"Major, get off my plane. If you don't this plane will be considered high-jacked in the eyes of the United States government."

The Major left the plane. I could hear the pilot give orders to the crew. The engines started. We were moving and it wasn't long before we were airborne.

"Captain, am I glad that is over. I have a question, for you."

"What might that be?"

"Why was that screw loose, Sir?"

"You got the screwdriver? Open it."

I heard them turning the bolts. The door opened and I smiled at the co-pilot.

I heard the pilot say, "Who the hell are you?"

"I guess you could say I am a stowaway, Sir."

"Get out of there. I don't want any of the wires broken."

I crawled out and they took a look at me. They saw the knife. The Captain told me to give it to him. But I just grinned and said, "Not unless you want to die. This knife has been by my side for years and no one gets it. Or if they do, they die shortly after. If you have to land this plane, make sure it is out of Vietnam airspace. I will not be taken alive. I will kill you faster than the Major. I wouldn't hesitate. I mean no one any harm. I promise you no one will be harmed. I just need a ride home."

"What the hell is your name, son?"

I looked at the co-pilot as he sat staring at me.

"Well, I'll be. It can't be!"

"Art, what do you mean it can't be!"

"I know this man. He is Tim Collins. Everyone is looking for him from the President down to the mothers who have sons alive today because of him. The Vietnam Government has a price on his head, preferably dead."

"No wonder the Major was bullshit. How many men dead men did you leave behind?"

"I think about a dozen getting to the airport. Even more if the Major does what I think he will do. There should be a trail of dead gooks leading away from the plane. Does that answer your questions? If they send up any jets telling you to land and you do, they will kill everybody on board. Believe me when I say this, I have seen them do it."

"Thanks a lot! I really needed to know that."

"Whatever you do, don't transmit my name while we are in the air. They'll shoot you down in a minute."

"Any other news for me?"

The door opened and the stewardess walked in. She took one look at me and then at the Captain. "I see you found the stowaway."

"Ask the Ambassador to come up here. No one else is to know what is going on. Especially the news media."

I watched her as she started to leave the cockpit. She turned and saw me looking at her. She smiled.

"Mr. Ambassador, the pilot would like to see you in the cockpit."

"Is there something wrong, Miss?"

"No, Sir, the Captain would just like to see you for a moment."

Everyone watched as they went to the cockpit.

I heard the door open and saw the stewardess standing next to a very distinguished looking elderly man with gray hair.

"Who the hell are you, mister? Are you the reason for all that bullshit back there?"

"I guess you could say that, Sir. I had to kill some of their men to get onboard. I hid them in a box in the hangar. I guess they have found them by now."

"Mr. Ambassador, I would like to present to you one Tim Collins."

"Tim Collins! You mean the Tim Collins everyone has been looking for all these years."

"I guess I am, Sir."

The Ambassador became very quiet. He stood there speechless.

"So, you're Tim. I finally get to meet you. You don't know me, but we have heard of you. My name is Sterner. Does that name mean anything to you?"

"No Sir. Should it?"

"You saved my son's life. He was shot down. You saved him and got him back to our lines. I owe you a lot. If you need anything, let me know. I will back you."

"Captain, is this still Vietnam airspace?"

"Yes Sir, we have about an hour left to go before we are clear."

"Under no conditions are we to turn back even if it means we crash. Do you understand? Now get us out of here. Put the boots to this old girl. I want a lot of distance put between Hanoi and this plane."

The seat belt sign went on and everyone became curious.

The stewardess went into the cabin.

"What the hell is going on? The seat belt lights are on."

"Just fasten them, please. The Captain has decided we should pick up speed to get out of Vietnam airspace."

"Okay Shirley, now tell us the truth."

"Sir, all of your questions will be answered in due time. Now fasten your seatbelts."

"Why is the Ambassador in the cockpit?"

"There is nothing I can say right now." The whole plane was buzzing.

"Ambassador, I think you should get back to your seat. We have company. Tim find a place on the deck for now."

Two Migs were on each side of the plane. "I guess we better start saying some prayers now. Those Migs know we're near the line. It isn't going to matter to them."

"I told you so."

"Shut up Tim. I have to think."

"Try the radio maybe we have some planes in the area."

The two Migs were calling us. We didn't answer. The pilot was hitting his ear, trying to tell them the radio was out. They were telling us to land.

Finally, we crossed over into international airspace, but the Migs were still with us.

"Hey Captain, look ahead of us. There are four of the most beautiful sights I have ever seen."

The radio blared: "Captain, do you need any help with the Migs?"

"We sure do. We are glad to see you. What brings you here?"

"Radar Sir. We saw the Migs alongside you so we decided to check it out."

"This is Captain Riley of flights one and two. Calling the Migs following our plane. Do you need any help at this time?" The Migs turned to the port and left.

"Thanks Captain. The Ambassador would like to talk to you."

"Can you stay with us for awhile. I would appreciate an escort?"

"Don't worry. We are going to follow you back to the base. What did the Migs want, Sir?"

"Meet me tonight with your squadron and I will buy the beers and tell you."

"That's a deal."

"My pleasure!"

"Ambassador, will you take Tim and find him a seat."

"Follow me, Tim."

As we entered the cabin, everyone was watching. As soon as we sat down, everyone started shooting questions at us.

"Gentlemen, I want you to meet Tim Collins. He was our stowaway. I believe most of you know his name."

"Ambassador, give us the story. This is the greatest story to ever to fall into our laps."

"First, I have to get a promise from each and everyone of you. The story cannot be released at this time. We have to keep a lid on it for security reasons. If the Vietnam Government finds out Tim was on this plane, they will never help us in any future endeavors to find our people."

"Sir, this is just too big a story. Do you realize what you're asking? The public has the right to know. This is just too big."

"I promise you, we will have a story for you. Just give us a break. Tim has been through enough. If this story gets out, Tim's life won't be worth a dime. I promise you if any news gets out, the newspaper responsible will never get another story first hand. There are still men over there who we want to get back. We can't jeopardize that."

I watched one of the reporters get up from his seat.

"Sir, you have my word. I will not print one word of this until you give me the okay. But I do have something to say. You see, fifteen years ago I was a prisoner in Nam. I want to shake your hand Tim. I was one of the men you saved. Your story is safe with me. I figure I know why you left Nam. Good luck with that problem, Tim. Now is my chance to thank you. If anyone of you men let this story get out, I will see to it you are blacklisted. I will make sure you don't work for a respectable newspaper ever again."

"Thanks. I am glad I helped you once. What is your name?"

"I am Paul Williams. And Tim, I promise you, no reporter will betray you."

"Mr. Golden is my name. I had a son saved by this man that means the man who leeks the story will never be allowed near the White House ever again. Trust me I have the power to do it."

"I will hold the story and so will everybody here. I know my editor would want it that way. Especially, under these circumstances."

"Tim," the Ambassador said, "forgive me, but we have to get you cleaned up and shaved. We also have to get you something to wear. Gentlemen, can any of you give Tim some clean clothes. I think he would like to shave too."

"I can handle that Sir, we are the same size. I owe him more than clothes. Let me help."

"Shirley, can you take Tim to the lavatory and show him how it works?"

"Sure Sir. Follow me Tim." I watched her move. It's been a long time since I've seen anything like that, I thought to myself. She is beautiful. Shirley opened the door and explained how everything worked. I started to wash. I had my shirt off when I opened the door. Shirley was there with the razor and shaving cream. She just stared at my body.

She looked at me and said she was so sorry. I grinned and said, "Don't be, that's how they play in Nam. I am used to it now. It shocks everybody at first." She came close to me and kissed me on the mouth. I stood motionless.

"Thank you, Tim. I will let you finish."

When I'd finished washing up, I changed clothes. I felt like a new man. I came out of the washroom and sat down with the Ambassador.

"You look great. Shirley told me what happened in there."

"She feels bad. I told her there was no reason to feel bad. What happened, happened."

"I'll get you some coffee, would you like something to eat?" Shirley asked.

"Yes please."

"We have steak and mashed potatoes if you like?"

"Would I! I haven't had steak in God knows how many years. I have lived on snakes for so long a steak would be great."

"I'll be right back."

She placed the tray in front of me. I ate it all. I drank the coffee. Then it hit. My stomach felt funny.

A man came up to me and said, "Tim, I am a doctor. Drink this. You're not ready for that kind of food yet. In a couple of weeks, you'll be able to eat a whole cow." I drank whatever it was he gave me and soon felt better.

The pilot came back to where I was sitting. "Tim, I have to have that knife. I will give it to you later, I promise."

"Captain," said the Ambassador, "I will handle this. Tim, the Captain is right. You can't have the knife on board. You have been in the jungle too long. I promise you, I will make sure you get it back when the plane lands. It will be safe with him.

"Captain, no one is to be given that knife when we land but me. Do you understand? In other words, that is an order."

"Perfectly Sir! No one but you!"

"Tim, you have been in the jungle too long. You have done more killing than anyone I know. It's time to make peace with yourself. I will make sure you get the best medical help available. But that is not going to be hard; there are a lot of people out there ready to help and I am one of them. I didn't tell you this but I have been fighting to get you home for years. I am glad your home now. Let us take care of you. You are going to have a new life. I promise you that."

I knew he was wrong—Tran was out there, with the CIA. My war was just beginning, but I figured I'd keep it to myself for a while. The stewardess came back and asked, "Would you like some more coffee?"

"Yes Shirley, that would be nice." She poured the coffee and I watched her walk away. When she came back she bent down and whispered in my ear. "Tim, you can watch me anytime."

I smiled, "I'm sorry. It's just that it's been years since I've seen a beautiful woman. I didn't mean to embarrass you."

"Tim, you didn't; it makes a woman feel good when men notice things like that."

"Thank you, Shirley."

I was so relaxed I fell asleep.

"Mr. Ambassador, what do you think?"

"You have no idea, what Tim has been through. That man should have been dead years ago. I will never know why he didn't die. It is going to take a long time for him to be able to be on his own. God help the person that crosses him!"

"If you're smart, Mr. Ambassador, you won't give him back that knife. It is part of him just like your heart is. He has killed so many people with that knife he is not going to be able to stop. Killing has become part him. So natural, he just does it. He has killed hundreds of men with just that knife. It was his trademark in Nam—slitting the enemy's throat. Like I said, he was very good at it and I am afraid he is going to get himself in trouble."

"Thanks for the advice, but I don't believe that. Since I met him he has been a gentleman. He is quiet and very polite. What you describe is not what I see."

"That's true. But just wait till you see him in a dangerous situation then you will see another Tim."

"Tim will receive the best medical treatment available to him before he goes home."

"Have you talked to him about why he has come out of the jungle? Especially, without Capt. Nge. They are like brothers so why isn't Nge with him? My guess is that Tran is in the States."

"Who the hell is Tran?"

"Tran was a Major in the North Vietnamese Army. He is the one who tortured Tim. I bet Tran is in the States and that's why Tim is on this plane. He swore he would never leave Vietnam until Tran was dead. I suggest you bring the subject of Tran up. I also suggest you look into Tim's eyes. Then you will see what I see."

"Thanks Bill, now find your way back to your seat. I have some thinking to do." The Ambassador looked down at me; I seemed to be sleeping so peacefully.

I opened my eyes and smiled.

"Tim, you heard every word Bill said."

"Yes Sir. I am a light sleeper. You have to be able to hear a pin drop to survive in the jungle."

"How much is true, about what Bill said?"

"Quite a bit of it. I left Nge behind because he wanted it that way. We heard Tran . . . Excuse me, Mr. Ambassador, you seem to be a trustworthy man. If I tell you why I left, will you keep it to yourself for now?"

"I'll promise you this Tim. I will keep it a secret as long as you prove yourself to me. I don't want to unleash a killer on the general public."

"Sir, I don't kill unless someone is trying to kill me. Then I will react."

"That's normal. But just remember there are laws about when you can and cannot kill. I think you should read those laws. Now, what about this Major Tran?"

"Yes, he is in the States and I intend to find him. I will also kill him. The CIA took him into the States so he could deal in drugs. He was a murderer in Nam and now he is going to bring in heroin and kill in the States. He's going to get rich doing it. I will find him. I know the States is one hell of large place to hide in and once he finds out I am here, he will come after me. The CIA is going to try to protect him and that means I am a target for both the CIA and Tran.

"But nothing in the world is going to stop me from getting him. Put me in a hospital, lock me up. I will be out before you know it. It's been done before. Charlie was good at it. As far as my being a homicidal maniac, I am not. An animal, yes, I have had to be. That was the only way to survive in the jungle. You had to learn how to live like an animal. Strike whenever you had to. It became a way of life for me.

"Tran is different, however. He kills because he loves to. I didn't—I killed because I had to. Slitting throats, that was a message to Tran. In the jungle you moved by night; noise would kill you. The knife was a quiet way to do the job. I became very proficient with it. I figure when you put me in the hospital for a complete physical, the CIA will pay me a visit."

"I will handle the CIA, Tim. I will see the President about it. You will be safe."

"I hope you're right."

"Tim, have a drink of this. It will help you sleep."

I looked at the glass. It smelled good. I drank it and soon fell asleep. When I woke up, I asked the Ambassador what it was.

"That was brandy."

I laughed. "I'm use to drinking jungle juice. You know it as moonshine."

"I was in the Second World War, Tim. We made our own also. We made it from coconuts. It tasted like shit, but we drank it anyway. It was all we had. We will be landing pretty soon. I want you to remain on the plane."

I looked out the window when we touched down and saw several jeeps with armed guards standing by them. "Sir, what are my chances of flying back with you. I don't want those goons touching me. I would be stuck here a long time and time is something I don't have."

"I don't know for sure. Let's see what I can do. Stay on the plane. I'll handle this."

The door opened and a Marine officer came onto the plane. I watched him talk to Shirley. She pointed in my direction. He walked toward me followed by two other Marines.

"Mr. Ambassador, my name is Major Simpson. I have to take Tim with us."

"What are the armed guards for Major?"

"Security reasons, Sir."

"Well Major, Tim is going back with us."

"I'm sorry Sir. My orders say he comes with us."

"That's nice. Now, I am going to say this only once. He is going back with me and that is my order to you. Do you understand, Major? This is a diplomatic plane. I am the diplomat in charge. Now get off my plane."

"Take him men. I felt their hands on me. I was forced to take them both out. They were on the floor holding their arms. I saw the Major reach for his sidearm.

"I wouldn't do that Major. The consequences might be too great for you to handle. I have done nothing wrong. You told those two men to grab me. I have some rights I believe."

All of a sudden the newsmen were taking pictures and yelling, "The TV camera is rolling."

"Major look around. The news media has it all on film. How is it going to look on the news tonight?" the Ambassador asked the Major calmly. "'Marines Fight with War Hero.' I can hardly wait."

"I'm sorry, Mr. Ambassador. Newsmen or not, I have my orders. Captain, show these gentlemen from the plane."

"Major, you tell your boss to come here himself. Now leave!"

The Marines left the plane. "Jack, get the President on the telephone! Use the hot line."

"Yes Sir."

"The President will call you back in a minute. They are trying to reach him."

"Thanks."

"Tim, you sure are a lot of trouble."

The Marines were soon back on board. "I am General Talbot and I give the orders here, Mr. Ambassador. Tim is going to come with us. That's final. Come on sailor, you're going with us."

"Tim, stay seated. General, you think you're the only one in charge."

"Your call is ready, Mr. Ambassador."

"Thank you. Phil, how are you doing? I guess you have heard about our stowaway. I seem to have a little problem with General Talbot. He thinks he is in charge of this airplane. He's onboard with three Marines armed to the hilt. They want to take Tim off the plane. I told them no. They tried to use force. Yes, Mr. President, the news media filmed it. It's going to look real nice on the news. 'Marines attack War Hero on Air Force Two.' I don't know where their orders come from, I think it's this Talbot character. I'm sure he will want talk to you."

"General, the President will talk to you. That is, if you have time."

"Mr. President, my orders come from the Pentagon. Yes Sir, I will tell them. But we were doing it for his own safety, Sir. Yes, Air Force Two is safe—I agree. I will send two Marines with the plane. That's correct, no weapons. I will handle it right away. Thank you, Sir," General Talbot hung up.

"Tim can fly back with you. I will have two Marines sent over right away."

"Mr. Ambassador, I think I would like to have these two assigned to me."

"They're hurt, Sir."

"I'll take care of them General; they will be all right. After all, I did it to them."

"Okay, they will go along with Tim. Major relieve them of their weapons."

"General, leave their 45s with the airplane Captain if you don't mind."

"Will there be anything else, Mr. Ambassador?"

"No, that will be all."

They left the plane. I bent down and pushed my thumb into the part of their arms I'd grabbed. They got up and moved their arms.

"Feeling better Marines?"

"Yes, what the hell was that?"

"Just something I learned along the way. I hope you two are ready for some goof-off time."

"We sure are."

"This is the Ambassador."

"Thank you Sir."

"Don't thank me. Thank Tim."

"Tim, thanks for everything."

"Forget it. I hate generals."

"A trip to the States in Air Force Two. I can't believe it!"

"Find a couple of seats. We will be taking off pretty soon. Our first stop will be California then on to Washington. Hey! I just want you to know the chow is great on this plane. What's even better—it's on the U.S. Government."

"Tim, can I talk to you?"

"Yes, Mr. Ambassador."

"I was thinking about what you said about the CIA. This country can't afford a scandal. I think this could be a major one. Especially, if those reporters find out. Bill is suspicious already. I was talking with the President and he agrees. What I am asking you to do is keep it quiet."

"Sir, you can count on me. After what you have done for me, it will be a pleasure to help you out. I don't want to be the one to embarrass anyone."

"Tim, call me Henry. I think I would like that."

"Henry, it is. Those two Marines are going to find out what's going on. Especially, if they are with me when the CIA shows up."

"I think I can handle them for you."

"While I am in Washington, do you think they can be assigned to me. I figure they will be more apt to keep their mouths shut, especially if the duty is a good."

"Leave it to me. I will talk to them before the news media has a chance at them."

"That's a good idea. Did you know there's a bar on this plane? I don't think anyone is using it."

I got up and asked the Marines to follow me. They did. A couple of reporters stood up.

"Excuse me, gentlemen. I would like to be alone to talk with the Marines. You know Nam stuff."

"Okay Tim, go ahead. I guess it would be nice talking about old times."

"Thanks." We went straight to the bar.

"Three beers, please." We sat down away from the bar.

"Look men, I have a problem. It's a dangerous one. Also, it could be dangerous for you and embarrassing for the country. No one knows this and they can't find out, especially the news media. The reason I came out of the jungle after all these years is Major Tran. He's the one that tortured me and killed a lot of men, both Army and Marines."

"We've heard of him."

"Believe it or not, the CIA brought him into this country. That's why I am here. I intend to get even with him. I have a score to settle. That's why it will be dangerous. Tran wants me dead and the CIA has to cover their asses. I have had you reassigned to me. Your orders will be sent to your C.O. I figure we can have some fun while here in Washington. I don't know how long we will be here. Just look upon it as a party."

"Tim, you can count on us. Those bastards will never get near you."

"Be careful what you say to the news media. They aren't stupid. Just tell them you have no idea why you're here. Keep to that story. You're here to help me get to Washington that's all. You are going to be in danger, even in the States. When Tran finds out I am here, he is going to come looking for me. He'll kill anyone to get to me. That even means you two."

"We can handle ourselves."

"I know that, but Tran is something else. You have never gone up against anyone like him. This is not going to be easy. He fights without any mercy. He is a mad dog. If you get a shot at him take it. Believe me, there will be no burial, no ceremony for him. Before you see him, his men will be all over you. And the CIA will be the first to come. However, I am banking on Tran loosing it before that happens. I almost got him once that way. The only reason I didn't was he went north on me then came to the States. I hope he doesn't try anything for awhile. I need time to train you in his tactics.

"Now, let's finish our beer before the reporters get wise." I'd no sooner finished than one of them showed up.

"May I sit down? My name is Bill."

"I know who you are. I wasn't asleep when you were talking to Henry."

"Who did you say?"

"The Ambassador!"

"You lost me for a second. I didn't know anyone called him that."

"Would you like a beer?"

"I'm buying. I'm sorry about what I said. You do know where it was coming from. Your reputation is overwhelming. Tim, you've been in the jungle a long time. I was wondering why you're here without Nge."

"Nge remained by his own choosing. He has family there. Maybe someday, we will meet again."

"Does that mean you two have a plan?"

"Gentlemen, do you see how a reporter can put words in your mouth. I said that maybe someday we would meet again. I hope so. He is like a brother to me. That's what I mean. If you print anything that is not true I will turn into the jungle animal you referred to. Now I think you should leave—that way you won't get hurt. If you ever want an interview, bring your editor. Then maybe I will consider it. The Ambassador, I mean Henry, is down below."

"Good-bye, gentlemen. Tim, you don't scare me."

"Actually, I wasn't trying to. I was only repeating your words. I never in my life tried to scare anyone. If I had to do something like that, the end result would only take a minute. Please tell the Ambassador, I am ready to give the interview I promised him."

Moe and Eddie moved to get up. I laughed and said, "You're with me. So sit your asses down." We could hear the reporters running up the stairs. They all started to ask questions at the same time. The Ambassador came to the table. I stood up. "Sir, would you please sit here with us?"

"Thank you, Tim."

"First thing, gentlemen, I will point to one of you and that person will ask a question. If you ask questions at the same time, my three pals and I are going to have a beer and not answer any of your questions." The Ambassador laughed. Shirley was in the corner with a smile on her face.

"Is the editor of the *Tribune* here?"

"Everyone turned around and looked at Bill.

"You know he's not here."

"Then you're excused, Bill. You may leave."

"That's not fair, Tim, and you know it."

"Was it fair when you came up here and asked me questions then put words in my mouth. I told you then, I would only give you an interview, if your editor were here. I don't see him. To all of you other reporters, Bill thinks I am a mad dog. He also thinks I've been in the jungle too long and I am an animal. Maybe he's right. I had to eat things that no man should ever have to eat. Like those venomous things that slither on the ground. I guess you call them snakes. I would drain the blood out of them so I could have something to drink; it was either that or die. So until your editor is here, please leave. Bill also thinks that I slit the throats of so many people because I liked it. Noise in the jungle can get you killed, especially when you're surrounded by the enemy. That is why a knife becomes so useful. Yes, I used it skillfully. I was taught how and I was glad I knew how."

Bill left. I knew he was mad. I figured he'd print what he wanted no matter what I said. The other reporters would ask a question when I pointed at them. They got an honest answer. This went on for an hour. One question intrigued me: "How many people did you kill?"

The Ambassador then told the reporters that would be all. They stood up and clapped. I felt good. I knew they understood. I told the Ambassador I would like to answer that question first, being the mad dog that I was accused of being.

"The answer is I really don't know. I would guess it was in the hundreds. I would like to ask all of you one thing. If you were in a war and had to kill, would you keep a running count? Would one of you like to ask me how many Americans the Vietnamese have killed. I would have to answer the same way, I really don't know. I would have to guess. So, perhaps that makes me a mad dog. Thank you for your time."

I sat down with the Ambassador and the two Marines.

"Tim, you're quite a guy. And no, I never thought you were a mad dog. Just one hell of a sailor and one hell of a man," the Ambassador said.

"Shirley, may we have some refreshments and please join us. I am tired of looking at these ugly bastards." Everyone laughed.

"Mr. Ambassador, you are a man of words. I toast to you."

Shirley laughed. "This has been one hell of a flight. May I never have another one like it. This is one memory I want to cherish forever. Here's to you Tim!"

"Thank you Shirley. I would like to make one to you. Here's to the only stewardess that fed a man and made him sick." We all started to laugh.

"I guess I did do that. I am sorry."

"Well Mr. Ambassador, I think the *Tribune* is going to be mad at you. I hope they understand why I did what I did to Bill."

"Tim, I have been a politician for most of my life. I admire what you did. And believe me, when I talk to his editor, he won't believe a word I say because he knows what a liar I am. Then we will both go out to dinner. Tim, did you brief Moe and Eddie about the CIA and Tran?"

"Yes Sir !"

"Don't worry about Shirley. She is the only woman I ever met who could keep her mouth shut. I have no secrets from her. I just want to remind you of the danger you'll be in. I have arranged for the FBI to help you. They can be trusted. The agent's name is Gifford. He's been around a long time and he doesn't like the CIA. He lives near you in South Dartmouth, which will make it easier for the two of you."

"Don't worry, Mr. Ambassador, I can take care of the CIA. I have seen them in action. They work best when your back is turned. My back will never be turned to them."

"Tim, I will do everything I can to find out where Tran is. You know that this must remain with just the people here."

"I know, Sir. You have a lot to lose if they find out you are helping me."

"I don't care about me. I am thinking of my son and all the other boys Tran screwed up. He shouldn't be in the States free and clear. He is a war criminal and should be dealt with. If I get him before you, he will be given the death penalty. Somehow, I don't think that will happen."

"Sir, the word I got was that Tran and the CIA were in bed together. Tran has set up a vast drug network."

"That's just great. That's all this country needs, another scandal."

"There won't be one, Sir."

"Tim, I can't be a party to murder. You know that if you get word where he is it will be from an unknown source."

"I don't think the entire CIA is involved. I think there are just a few renegades—out to make a fast buck."

"I hope so. Maybe then the CIA will help us, but I think it is unlikely to happen."

"I think this meeting is over. I've had it."

We all went down below. I noticed Bill was pissed. Everyone was giving him the cold shoulder. He was sitting in an aisle seat.

"Bill, I want to tell you something. You asked me how many men I'd killed. I don't know. Aren't you going to write this down?" Everyone was listening.

"I don't know how many men I killed or even how many I saved. I was never brought up to kill. I was always taught to walk away from a fight. My mother raised me that way—God rest her soul. She hated violence. I hate violence also. What I did was forced on me. Let me show you what Tran did. I haven't shown this to anyone on the plane." I removed my shirt. Everyone hung their heads. "This was done over a few years; it was done to me almost every day. This is why I stayed in the jungle. Someone has to stop Tran and that person turned out to be me.

"Charlie never took prisoners. He killed them right away unless they could use them for propaganda. They usually killed them right away or tortured them first for fun. I have seen it. They were experts at torture. Why I never broke, I will never know. I don't even know how long I was a prisoner. I just stayed in the jungle and fought them. And it was worth it. God protected me. I guess you could say he had his reasons.

"You asked me about my knife. I'll answer you now. Fighting in the jungle, at night, that was the weapon of choice. That is, if you wanted to live. Noise could get you killed. You had to sneak up on your enemy and kill him."

"Tim, you don't have to say anything," the Ambassador said.

"I know that Mr. Ambassador. I just think Bill should understand. I want him to know that I only killed to save lives. God knows I did do that. Someday I will pay for the killing I did—right or wrong. God is waiting for me. They were animals and I had to learn to be one too. If I hadn't, there would have been a lot more people killed. Charlie thought I was an officer that is why they kept me alive. That is why I was tortured every day for years. All during the time they tortured me, all I did was smile. It was my secret for surviving during each session. I kept thinking of my mother and how wonderful she was. That, gentlemen and ladies, gave me the strength to fight back. It drove Tran nuts. I saw him shoot his own men for no reason. That is what I would call an animal.

"Yes, I took the dog tags of the men on the chopper. They were dead. I wanted their parents to know they weren't missing in action. And that is why Tran thought I was an officer. I took those tags back from Tran when we escaped from the prison camp. I have them here," I said as I held them up. "I have carried them with me for all these years. Mr. Ambassador, I think you should give them to the parents. I was never able to get them back to them. I was always to busy getting live ones out. Tran killed some Americans in front of me; it was his way of breaking me. I told him I was just a petty officer many times, but he didn't believe me. I saw him take a live snake and shove it in the face of a Captain whose name is on one of these tags. He died a horrible death. That is what you dealt with out there. They were all that way. If you wanted to survive, you became an animal.

"Right now, I am tired. I am tired of killing. I just want to get on with my life. Every time I take a shower I will see these scars." I stood up and dropped my pants. They looked at the scars all over my legs. "But I can live with this. I survived for a reason—whatever it was. I will always have a reminder. That is my story. Bill, you can print whatever you want to print. I know the truth."

Bill stood up. "I am sorry, Tim. I was a fool. Please accept my apology." We shook hands. The Ambassador sat without saying a word. I sat next to him.

"Tim, I am really proud of you. That took nerve."

I looked up, Shirley was crying. "Hey girl, is there any coffee left?"

She bent over and kissed me. "Sailor, there sure is. I'll get you some. I'll be right back."

"Tim, you puzzle me. I did some checking on you when I found out you'd helped my son. I was asking questions about you. I just couldn't figure you out. You were the All-American boy. High marks in school. You were a loner but well liked. I know you were taught the martial arts by a Mr. Chin, but to do what you have done just doesn't fit your profile."

"First, let me tell you about Mr. Chin. He was a wonderful man. I worked with him in one of the fish processing plants in New Bedford. We became very good friends. He taught me a lot. He was a war hero during the war with Japan. He taught me to think for myself. I learned a lot of his ways and will go back to the old ways when I've finish with Tran. What he taught me will be a lot of help in my recovery. I don't want to remember how to kill. I just want to get on with my life. I am really a simple and humble person. Tran made me what I am. And for that, I will have to deal with him. Whatever might happen at that time, I can't answer now. Only time will tell."

"Mr. Ambassador, I have a message for you from the President."

I looked at the reporters; they were all ears when they heard the word President.

The Ambassador read the note. Everyone was quiet.

The Ambassador stood up and announced, "I have just received a letter from the President. I think you should read this, Tim."

"It seems the Vietnamese Government has lodged a complaint with our government. They claim someone on board this plane killed about a dozen of their men. That is why we were held up in Hanoi."

The Ambassador leaned over and whispered in my ear, "Deny it."

"Tim, do you know anything about this?" the Ambassador asked me.

"No Sir, I didn't have anything to do with it. I figure it must have been the men that were with me. You have to remember their war is still going on. They are being killed for no reason at all. When we were walking through the jungle to get to Hanoi, we passed through villages where people were being raped and killed for no reason."

"Tim, may I ask you a question. This will be off the record. If that is true, why did you come out?"

"I had to. If I'd stayed, the Vietnamese Government would still be looking for me. And more innocent people would be killed because of it.

"I'm sorry," I said tired of the whole thing, "I don't want to talk about it anymore."

"What about the men you saved? There were hundreds. What I am especially interested in was when you attacked a Russian base and stole a plane."

"Okay. We had so many Americans we had no way to get them out. So one of the men mentioned the base. We went there and attacked the base. We stole the plane and you know the rest."

"Tim, one more question. How many men died?"

"We lost none. The enemy, they all died. They fought hard right to the end. The American prisoners that were freed said they would rather die than go back to being slaves. They were glorious and I am proud of them. That is all I am going to say. I am sure when you talk to the survivors they will give their version. One other thing, if Charlie had lived we, none of us would have made it to the coast. We would have been shot down. We couldn't risk it. I had too many prisoners to get out safely. It didn't matter anyway; they chose to fight to the death."

"Tim, is Captain Nge alive?"

"I don't know. I just pray to God he is. There is a price on his head too. So, I think you should forget about him. I am sure the prisoners we helped onto the boat will tell you about the battle.

"Captain Nge and I made it back to an old outpost. When we got there, we found Charlie had taken it over. We were worried about the men that had been stationed there. Little did we know that the war was over. We found North Vietnam Regulars at the outpost; they were guarding one prisoner. You have to remember the war was over. We found a lot of our men dead; they had been shot in the head. They had been used for slaves then they were killed for sport. We found out what had happened from the Sargent who had survived. He buried his comrades-in-arms. He didn't want us to help him. We watched the last NVA survivor until the Sargent came back."

"What happened to the last NVA soldier?"

"I guess he died of a heart attack." The reporters laughed.

"You mean he died in combat."

"I mean he died of a heart attack. We scared him to death. Leave it at that. If you must think about the killing, think about the men being held as POWs, the killing of Americans for sport.

"That will be all, gentlemen. No more questions. Just take a good look at these dog tags. They used to belong to four of our young men. If you have any questions about Tim's tactics. Take a look at these tags. That should answer your questions. They could have been your kids. If you want, I can arrange for you to be there when their mothers are told."

We finally landed in California. We left the plane while it was being refueled. I was having coffee when the brass came in. Everyone wanted to hear about Vietnam. I was tired of talking. The Ambassador introduced me then told them we had to leave because the plane was ready. I was walking out when I noticed they were saluting. I turned and stood at attention. I returned the salute and left.

After a four-hour flight, we were in Washington. The Ambassador and I were the last ones to leave the plane. The Captain was standing next to Shirley.

"Tim, this was an unusual flight. I just want to say thanks for everything. I think I have to give this back to you. I must tell you this—I hate the sight of it."

"Thank you, I feel better now. I wish I could say I hated it too. Maybe someday that will happen."

"Well Shirley, I want to thank you for everything."

"Tim, I just have to do this." She reached up and put her arms around me. She gave me the longest kiss I'd ever had. I just looked at her then gave her a smile.

"Thank you, I will never forget you Shirley; you've been great."

The Ambassador grabbed my arm and said, "It's time to go."

As we stepped off the plane, everyone was cheering. There was a band playing. The President walked over to us.

"Mr. Collins, welcome home. I want to shake your hand."

"Thank you, Sir. It's nice to be back."

"Tim, I have something to say to you. You will never know how much you have done. In back of me are some of the men you saved. They are here today to pay honor to you. Some of them have their parents with them. I have talked to most of the parents and they want to meet you. I know you must be tired and I promise you it won't take long."

"That's okay, Mr. President. I will be proud to meet them." I could hardly believe my eyes. Everything was so different. I met the parents of the men I'd helped, one by one. They shook my hand and started to cry. It was a somber time for all of us, but I knew their tears were tears of joy. After meeting the last of the families, the President looked at me and said, "Tim, in all my years in politics, I have never seen anything like this. If you don't mind, I think we should leave."

"To tell the truth, I think that would be a good idea. I don't feel as though I deserve this. All I did was help my brothers in arms. Any soldier or sailor would have done the same."

"Tim, things are different here since you left. There are young people that are not going to welcome you. They are going to call you a lot of names and insults. I just want to warn you. There is nothing much we can do about it. But I think you can handle it, especially after what you have been through.

"If there is ever anything I can do for you, you know where to reach me. Right now, a limo is waiting to take you to the hospital. They are going to give you a complete physical and get you on your feet. I guess you will be there for a few weeks. I will have a guard with you at all times. And I think you brought a couple with you. The Ambassador called me about it and I had them reassigned to you. They will be with you as long as you want. You will be hearing from Mr. Gifford, the FBI agent. You will need his help. He is a lot like you; he's a renegade. I am having him flown in from So. Dartmouth. I understand he lives in a neighboring town to New Bedford. He is there to help protect you. I think you will get along with him. Here's the limo. Please get in and we will get you to the hospital."

We both got in, along with some Secret Service men who sat in the rear with us.

"Mr. President, where are my two Marines?"

"They are in the car behind us."

"I'd rather they were here with me. That is, if you don't mind?"

"Fine with me." The Secret Service men got out and walked to the other car and asked the two Marines to ride in the President's car.

"Hi Moe, hi Eddie. This is the President of the United States."

"Sir, we would come to attention, but that is impossible."

The President laughed. "I think a handshake will do men."

They shook hands and told the President they were honored to meet him.

"Just take good care of Tim."

"Yes Sir! We plan on it."

"Do you have any civilian clothes with you?"

"No Sir, we left in a hurry and weren't able to get any."

"I'll take care of that. I will send someone over from the White House and you can give them your sizes. They will get some clothes for you. I guess the White House can afford to pay for them."

We left the airport. I looked at the buildings out of my window and couldn't believe my eyes. Everything seemed so different. It didn't take long to get to the hospital. We weren't allowed to get out of the car until the all-clear sign was given. I felt like I was in prison, but knew it would only be for a short time.

The President whispered in my ear, "Tim, I hope you get rid of that knife. They frown on weapons in the hospital."

"I will, Sir. But I think I will keep it for awhile. I'll keep it well hidden. You don't miss much, do you Sir?"

"No Tim, that's why I am the President. The Secret Service should have taken it from you. They could be fired for not discovering it."

"I hope that doesn't happen, Sir."

"It won't, but I will have to chew their asses out. I will do it privately.

"Tim, don't take it personally but they have you listed on your medical records as very dangerous and emotionally unstable because of what you have been through. That will change once they talk to you."

Inside the hospital, the nurses and doctors were waiting for me.

"Good morning. My name is Doctor Johnson and I will be taking care of you, along with your nurse, Sandra Souza. She will be the only nurse you will deal with. If anyone else tries to tell you they're going to check you, call security right away. That goes for doctors also. If there is a change you will be notified and introduced to them by Sandra or myself."

Sandra told me to follow her. "I will get you settled in. The two Marines will be in the room with you. We have fixed it up with three beds. You can fight over the TV. You can hang your clothes in the closet. Put this Johnny on."

"Haven't you got anything else? I hate these things. They are cold and uncomfortable."

"That's too bad. I am sure you wore less in the jungle. Now change, sailor!"

The two Marines laughed.

Sandra said, "Don't laugh too hard. I have some for you two also."

I changed and didn't like it. I took a shower. I heard Sandra come back into the room. As I came out of the shower wrapped in a towel, I saw Sandra staring at me.

"What's the matter, haven't you seen scars before Sandra?"

"None like that. The bastard that did that has to be one sick animal."

"He is!"

"That must have taken him a long time."

"Yes, a few years. He didn't want to do it all at once. It was his way of playing. Someday, we'll meet again."

"I hope not, Tim. Well, you're safe now. You have your guards with you so don't worry."

I was thinking about what she said and it made me wonder how long it would be true. I figured the CIA would be calling on me soon. That much was for sure!

"I'll get you some coffee, and some for your friends."

"Tell them to come in, please. They don't have to stay out there. The door locks from the inside doesn't it? Thanks a lot Sandra."

She opened the door. "Okay, you two can stay inside with Tim. I am getting some coffee for you."

"Thanks nurse."

"Sandra's the name."

I was sitting on the bed and Moe and Eddie were sitting in the chairs when someone knocked on the door. Moe got up and asked, "Who's there?"

"Your coffee, that's who."

Sandra came in with the coffee.

"How comes there are only three cups?"

"Why do you want more?"

"You drink coffee, don't you?"

"Next time, Tim," she said as she left the room.

"Tim, answer a question for us. Just how much danger are you in?"

"I told you on the plane. You will find out soon enough."

"We don't know how long we will be assigned to you."

I laughed.

"What's so funny, Tim?"

"You are. You're assigned to me as long as I want. The President is having your orders cut now. I've already arranged it."

"You have to be kidding."

"Wait and see. If you don't want to stay, that's okay."

"That's great. This is good duty."

"Don't be too hasty. I expect a visit from the CIA anytime. They have to make a move. I am going to set a trap for them starting tonight. See that door that leads to the adjoining room. Tonight, that is where you will be sitting with the door ajar."

"It sucks to have to live this way. I hope that Tran is dead just so you can live normally again."

There was a knock on the door and Eddie opened it. The doctor was standing there. I had my hand under the pillow; that's where I'd put my knife.

"Well Tim, it's time for your physical." Moe went with me while Eddie stayed behind. He took my knife so no one would find it. He stayed in the adjoining room.

"Tim, we're going to start with a series of x-rays. Then, some blood work." I laughed.

"What's so funny?"

"Blood work, doctor. I have drunk so much snake blood, you might be shocked at what you find."

"I will warn them."

The x-rays took about two hours. I guess they took enough pictures to open up a gallery. Then came the blood work. God, I didn't know I had that much blood in me.

On the third night, we sat in the adjoining room with the lights off. My room had the TV going. We heard a noise and I whispered, "Here they are." We waited for the door to my room to open. We saw the two shadows near the bed. They removed the blanket and saw the pillows, but it was too late for them. We knocked both of them to the floor. We heard some noise outside and Moe opened the door. Security had arrived and they handcuffed the men. I told them they could leave for awhile. They did.

"Well gentlemen, what took you so long? I could ask you a lot of questions. But that would be a waste of time. Eddie call the FBI, they will talk to them." Not ten minutes passed and Agent Gifford came in with another agent. "Are you all right, Tim?"

"Yea. Take these creeps out; they belong to the CIA."

"No problem. We'll handle it."

The following morning the Ambassador came to see me.

"Tim, I guess you made it through last night. I talked to the CIA about it. They don't know who these men are. They are being printed and pictured. I'll get back to you with whatever information I have. Take care. Good job men."

Between the FBI, the CIA, and the doctors, I was going crazy answering questions.

The doctor came in and said, "Tim, I have some good news for you. You are physically fit. For that matter, you're amazingly fit. I guess all that snake blood was good for you."

"That's great. When can I get out of here?"

"Oh, those are just the first tests. Now, we have to check you out emotionally."

"When does that start?"

"Right now. This is Doctor Lisa Radcliffe. She will be helping you get better mentally."

"I have read your file. I think we have some serious problems, Tim."

"You may have problems. I feel fine."

"Tim, you're a walking time bomb. You could explode at any time. Now, open your shirt, I have to see those scars."

I opened my shirt. She looked at the scars. "Okay, button up your shirt now. They did a hell of a job on you, didn't they?"

"It's not bad; I've cut myself worse shaving."

"Tim, we don't need jokes. I want to help you."

"I'm sorry, Lisa. That's just the way I am."

Just then the door opened. It was Sandra; we'd become very close.

We smiled at each other. Sandra said, "I'm sorry, I didn't know you were here, Doctor."

As Sandra turned to leave, she said, "Remember tonight Tim. Gin Rummy and just don't let me catch you cheating. Your ass will be mine if I do. Doctor, you're my witness."

"Tell me Tim, what do you think of Sandra?"

"Come on, Doctor. I am no kid so stop treating me like one. Sandra is beautiful and I like her a lot. Now are there any other questions?"

We talked for a few hours then she said, "We will continue tomorrow. Is that all right?"

"You're the doctor."

After she left I wondered when they would make their next move. I decided to check the room thoroughly. I looked in every nook and cranny. Sure as hell, I found some bugs. They were well hidden.

When Moe and Eddie came into the room, I motioned them to keep quiet and pointed to the bugs.

"I am supposed to play Gin Rummy with Sandra tonight. Can you tell her I am too tired after talking to that shrink half the day. Eddie, I could use a beer."

"No problem. Moe get a hold of Sandra and I'll get the beer."

We slammed the door and I rustled the sheets and pillows. We went into the other room quietly, and it wasn't long before two more goons came into the room. We came out of the adjoining room and jumped them. I had a firm grip on my knife. I could see a gun in the hand of one of them. I sliced his hand and he dropped the knife. Moe and Eddie had the other one. We shook them down. The other man also had a gun, which we took away. All of a sudden, Gifford was in the room with his men.

"Gentlemen, let's see some ID." They didn't say anything.

"CIA huh? You'll talk when we get you back to the office."

Just then the nurse and doctor entered the room. They checked the men over.

"This one needs stitches right away. Sew him up here Doctor. They're going nowhere," Gifford said.

"Sandra, I'll need a needle and some stitching materials."

When she came back the doctor cleaned the wound and stitched the man's hand. It took twenty stitches to do the job.

Sandra looked at me. "Too tired, huh? You knew they were coming. Why didn't you tell someone? You might have been hurt and I wouldn't like that to happen."

"Well, if you had been here, you could have been hurt. We had everything under control."

"Tim, where did the knife come from?"

"Give it to me. It is not allowed in the hospital. Sandra you know that."

"Doctor, I didn't know he had it."

"Well, we're taking it now. Hand it over."

"Sorry Doc, it stays with me. I won't be without it."

"I'm Agent Gifford. I am authorizing Tim to keep the knife. Without it, he's not Tim. I will be responsible for him."

"Okay, it's your ass."

The next day when Lisa came to see me, she said, "Well, it seems you had a good night, Tim. Let me see the knife!"

I handed it to her. She looked at it and said, "How many men have died because of this knife?"

"You mean, how many of the enemy have died trying to kill me? The knife was weapon of war. My war. Last night I could easily have killed those men. But I didn't. I am not at war now. I am just trying to live. If I were a mad dog, like you think, they would be dead now. So, get off my case or give up seeing me. You have an attitude problem. I bet you were one of those who were against the war. Well, I was there and had a job to do. If you'd checked my file, you would have seen I was against violence. I am still against violence. Those men came to me. I didn't go to them. If you can't handle the case, have yourself removed. Your attitude has sucked ever since I met you. How can you evaluate me when you have so much hate in your heart!"

Just then Sandra came into the room and said, "Dr. Radcliffe, I think you should leave. We will have another doctor evaluate Tim. Now get out before I call the head doctor."

"We'll see about that!" she said as she stormed out.

Agent Gifford came into the room. I told him to be quiet as I pointed to the bugs. He took one down and placed it in the sink with water.

"Tim, that one over there is ours. This one belongs to the CIA. I heard your conversation with Dr. Radcliffe. I'll handle the matter."

We heard Sandra being paged to go to the office. Dr. Radcliffe had put in a complaint about Sandra being too close to the patient and it affecting her job.

We went to the office too. Agent Gifford didn't say anything. We both listened. Dr. Johnson asked Sandra if the accusations were true.

"Yes Doctor, Tim and I are close. But that has nothing to do with the way she was treating him. I heard the whole conversation. She has him already diagnosed as 'Emotionally Unstable.' That's bullshit. Tim is as sane as we are."

"I see. Well, I have to think about this. Sandra, I want you to go on leave for a few days."

"I don't think so, Sir," Agent Gifford interrupted. "I am FBI Agent Gifford."

"I know who you are."

"I want you to listen to this tape. It will only take a few minutes." Agent Gifford played the tape.

"Dr. Radcliffe, is that your voice?" Dr. Johnson asked.

"Yes, it is."

"Well, that tape doesn't agree with your accusations. Before you say anything else, I want to make it clear that your attitude, as Tim put it, sucks. There will be a hearing on this matter to see if you should be let go."

"Don't bother. I will have my files out of the office in the morning."

"No, you will take your personal items out right now. I will have security help you."

We watched as Dr. Johnson picked up the telephone and called security. When he finished telling them what he wanted, he turned toward Sandra and said, "I still think you should take a couple of days off. But that does not mean you can't visit anyone in the hospital."

"Tim, I think a new doctor is in line for you."

The next day a Dr. James talked to me.

"I read your file and I know what's been going on. From what I can see you are ready to leave here. I don't think you're a mad dog. I think you have your life under control so I am going to suggest you be discharged from the hospital. It will take a couple of days to do the paperwork.

"Tim, good luck to you. By the way, I was asked to give this to you. I believe it has the address and telephone number of a friend." We shook hands and he left my room. Agent Gifford came in with some more information.

"Dr. Radcliffe is being questioned; we think she was a plant to have you committed. They would have gotten away with it if it hadn't been for our bug in your room. Tim, it's time to get rid of that knife."

"Yea, when hell freezes over."

"By the way, where are the guns you took off those goons?"

"They're on the bed in my room, I guess."

"Tim, I know those two goons. They are two tough bastards. I was told you were good and I guess you are. They are not usually so careless. They were sent here to give you a message. Would you mind telling me what it is?"

"They told me to get well, and for me to stay out of their business. Anything else you want to know?"

"You're a liability to them. They won't be so casual next time."

"And neither will I."

"Tim, I'm not kidding. I know these two from Nam. They are animals. Human life means nothing to them."

"I've met their kind before. They usually end up dead."

"You're going to be getting out of the hospital soon. That means you'll be a target everywhere you go. I can't protect you, unless you help us."

"Thanks Gif, I will keep that in mind. Now, can I get some sleep?"

"By the way, the two Marines will be leaving when you're released from the hospital. They are going back to their unit. The Ambassador told me to tell you. He also wants us to find this Major Tran. We've never heard of him. We have no record of him being in the country."

"He's here all right."

"I have a picture of someone we think is this so-called Major Tran. Look at it and tell me if it's him."

I looked at the picture and hate overwhelmed me. "Yea, that's him."

"If that's him, he's in New York. Or I should say, was in New York. He disappeared."

"He's good at that Gif."

"If we'd known who he was when the picture was taken, we would have locked him up. We are looking for him everywhere. He just can't be found. All we know for sure is that he is somewhere on the East Coast."

"Why don't you check the drug dealers? That's why the CIA brought him into the country."

"We don't know that for sure."

I laughed. "For what other reason would they bring scum like that into the country? When I get out I will prove it to you! He'll turn up. I have ways of finding him and he knows it. That's why he is intent on killing me."

"Great! I have to protect you from the CIA and this Tran. Is there anything else I can do for you?"

"Yes, let me get some sleep."

"How the hell can you sleep at a time like this?"

"What else can I do, worry? That would be stupid. Goodnight Gif!"

"Yea, goodnight Tim. Sweet dreams," Agent Gifford said as he slammed the door behind him. Moe and Eddie laughed.

"Sir, Agent Gifford is here to see you."

"Send him in."

"Sir, they made a move on Tim last night. We have two men in custody. They aren't talking, but I know who they are. I met them in Nam. Their names are Russell and Mitchell."

"Jane, call the CIA and get Holmes for me."

"Holmes is on the line, Sir."

"Holmes, I have two of your men in custody. What do you want us to do with them?"

"Two of my men! What the hell are you talking about?"

"Don't play dumb with me. I am going to send them to you, but if I see them again, it's going to be very embarrassing to your people at the CIA."

"Wait a minute. I'm not lying. I have heard rumors, but that's all. Branch, we go back a long way. I have no reason to hurt this Collins kid."

"Do the names Russell and Mitchell mean anything to you?"

"Yes, they haven't been around for quite some time. We've been trying to find them. I'll send my men to get them."

"Too late," Branch said as he was handed a message. "They were bailed out—I just found it out. I don't know who bailed them out. I was about to release them to you. Now you tell me their renegades. Well, this makes quite a picture. I suggest you try to find them. This could involve the White House. They don't want anything to happen to the Collins kid, as you put it."

"I'll get back to you. I promise you we have had nothing to do with any of this."

"Well Gif, I think we are in for a bad time. As much as I hate to believe Holmes, I think he is telling the truth. We have two CIA renegade agents loose out there."

"Linda, get me Jenson, now! I want him in my office immediately."

"Yes Sir."

"Sir, Mr. Holmes wants you in his office right away."

"Sir, you wanted to see me?"

"What the hell is going on? Russell and Mitchell have surfaced. They are trying to kill Tim Collins. They let themselves be caught by the FBI. Now they're back on the streets."

"I haven't any idea what is going on. Russell and Mitchell have been gone for months. They just disappeared. I hate to say this but there are three other agents missing. They were all friends in Nam. They disappeared last month. I think they might be with Russell and Mitchell."

"Find them and get rid of them. I don't need the trouble that's heading our way. Now do it. Get every man you can on it. I have to call Branch at the FBI."

"Sir, Holmes is on line one."

"Thank you."

"Branch speaking."

"This is Holmes. I just found out about three other agents missing. We believe they are with Mitchell and Russell. Their names are Wood, Parker, and Jackson. Those three have been missing since last month. I have everybody

I can spare working on finding them. You do realize if they don't want to be found, you aren't going to find them. They're very good at what they do. They're trained in Black Ops."

"What is that?"

"Black Ops. Just say they are very well trained. Keep your friend Collins well hidden. I wish I could help you more. I will send you their files."

"Thanks for the help."

"Yea, I've been some help. I'll see you later."

"Gif, come in here."

"What's up?"

"I have the names of those agents on the loose, plus three more. Holmes gave them to me. At least he gave me five of them. There is a sixth one out there. He hasn't told me about. Maybe he doesn't know who he is because he is still on the payroll. That means a mole in the CIA."

"You know what this means. Those men are ruthless. They have been trained for one thing. They were part of a special unit in Nam."

"Tim, today is the day you go to the White House. The President wants to see you. They sent you a new uniform to wear for the occasion. A car will pick you up at 7:30 PM. I guess they are having some kind of ceremony planned for you. After all, you are a hero."

"I really don't feel like a hero. I just wanted to survive."

"Hero or not, you're going. You can take Sandra if you want. Call her."

I dialed the number; it rang twice. I heard her voice.

"Are you busy tonight?"

"Are you asking me out?"

"Yes, I am."

"Where are we going?"

"The White House! I guess they're having a dinner for me tonight. I would like to have you attend it with me."

"This is a fine thing. How much time have I got?"

"We have to be there at 7:30. Just throw anything on."

"That's the White House, that means the President and God knows who else will be there."

"Can you be ready? I'm sure you can find something to wear."

"Okay, I'll find something. Thanks for giving a girl so much time to get ready."

"I just found out myself. We'll pick you up in a limo. That's what they told me."

"Get off the phone. I have a lot of work to do."

The car finally arrived and I gave them Sandra's address. When we got there, the driver went to the door. It opened and Sandra walked down the steps. She was beautiful.

"I could kill you for this."

"Sandra, you look great!"

"Hey Gif, what do you think?"

"Much too nice for you!"

"I'll take that as a compliment, Gif."

When arrived at the White House, it was already crowded. Everybody was there. The place was full of reporters—lights were flashing all over the place. I guess you could say we made a Grand Entrance. I was embarrassed. I noticed a lot of military men from all of the branches of the service. I even recognized some of them.

The Admiral was walking toward me with the Ambassador. They had their wives with them. I was introduced to both of them. One of the wives said, "Tim, who is this lovely lady your with?"

"This is Sandra Souza; she is the nurse that helped me while I was in the hospital."

"Then, we all owe you our thanks. Come dear, I will introduce you to the ladies." I watched Sandra walk away. I could see she was nervous.

"Relax Tim, everything is going to be fine. Admiral, will you see to it that Tim meets everybody?"

"My pleasure. First of all, Tim, I want to thank you for everything you did. May I shake your hand?"

We shook hands. "I am proud to be here tonight. There are lots of people here that you helped. I am sure you will want to see them."

We walked around for quite sometime. I was reunited with the prisoners I'd helped in Nam. I even met their parents. It felt good seeing them alive. Finally, the Admiral came back to get me.

"Tim, it's time to sit down. Follow me to the platform."

Several dignitaries were there. Sandra sat next to me. She was smiling. The President and his wife came out and everyone stood. The band played and the President went to the podium with his wife. He asked everyone to sit down.

"Ladies and Gentlemen, we are here tonight to pay a great honor to a man who all of America loves. This man is one of America's greatest heroes. We all know his name. First, the Secretary of the Navy has something to say."

"Ladies and gentlemen, I have the honor to present Tim Collins, Petty Officer Second Class. I am proud to present him with the Navy Cross. While on a shuttle mission in Nam, the outpost was attacked. He saved three crewmembers in the chopper from being blown up. He attacked the enemy soldier determined to blow the chopper up. He killed the attacker and threw the bomb away from the chopper. Then he saved the life of a CIA Agent just before he got back on the chopper and left the base. I am proud to award him the Navy Cross. Thank you Tim, from a grateful Navy. I will pin the medal if you allow."

He pinned the medal and saluted me. I stood at attention and saluted him. I went to sit back down.

"Tim, we're not finished yet. From this day on, you are a lieutenant in the United States Navy. By an act of Congress, here are the papers to prove it."

The ceremony continued on for about an hour and then the President stood up.

"This is the last of the medals we are going to give you, Tim. I don't think you can carry anymore."

Everybody was laughing. "Tim, I would like to have my wife help me pin it on you." The first lady stood up. "Tim, I am so proud to do this honor with my husband. Before we pin this medal on, I would like to say thank you to your mother, who has passed away, for giving us such a great son. And thank you to your foster parents, who are here tonight along with two of Tim's friends who are police officers in the City of New Bedford and are sitting in the front row with his foster parents, along with the spirit of his departed mother. It is with great pleasure that my husband and I award Tim with the Medal of Honor." The First Lady placed it around my neck. "We salute you Tim." Everybody stood up and the flashbulbs were blinding.

"Tim, the people here would like to hear from you."

I stood at the podium, looking down at my friends. I smiled and bowed to them. "Thank you for being here."

I then looked at the crowd. "I am speechless. I don't know what to say. I accept these medals in the name of this great country and its people, especially my friends sitting up front and my foster parents. I especially want say to my departed mother, thank you for your love and teaching me to be a man. I am proud of you all. But someone is missing. Wherever you are Mr. Chin, I love you and thank you for all you taught me." I looked up and said thank you to everyone and sat down.

Everyone was shaking my hand again as I walked toward my foster parents and friends.

"Tim, we never gave you up for dead. We prayed for you every night."

I turned around and saw the President and his wife were standing next to us.

"Lt. Tim Collins, would you introduce these people to my wife and me?"

"These are the Bakers, my foster parents. These two gentlemen are police officers from my hometown. They watched over me when I was a teenager. I will always love them for being there for me. Mr. Chin, I guess, could not be here."

"No Tim, he is with his wife. But I have a letter from him. I was asked to make sure I read it to you."

"Dear Tim, I know you aren't dead. I missed you everyday you were gone. My home is yours. I made a place for you to live and be proud. There is a room downstairs, under the stairs. When you see it, you will know just how much you were loved. I know I am going to be with my wife. I only wished she could have met you. She also would have considered you her son. May you live a long life.— Mr. Chin.

I held back my tears.

The President's wife put her arms around me and gave me a hug. Sandra was standing with us, and I held out my hand and she grabbed it, then hugged me. Soon after that the evening ended. I asked my family and friends if they were staying. They laughed. "We can't, we have our own private jet. Air Force One is taking us home. It actually managed to land in New Bedford." As we said our good-byes, I knew that my life was worth something.

We took Sandra home and she asked me if I wanted to come inside. Gif told her, "Not this time. Security reasons, in case you have forgotten."

"Sandra, there will be a time in the future for us. When I get back to New Bedford, I hope you will come see me. I promise I will come back to see you when it is safe."

I was called back to the White House. The President wanted to talk to me. When I arrived, I was taken to the Oval Office. The President was sitting behind his desk.

"Tim, I would like to talk to you. I am the President of these United States and it galls me that a man like you has to put up with what happened the other night. I am going to do everything in my power to find this Tran and the CIA agents who brought that animal here. We are going to do everything we can to protect you. I am ashamed that something like this happening to you. I have started a full investigation and intend to get to the bottom of it. When we do, they will be dealt with harshly. Tran will answer for his war crimes. I intend to see to it.

"But your killing him will bring nothing but grief to you. I hope you understand. I am not telling you not to protect yourself. I am only asking you to leave it to us. Agent Gifford is the one man that can do it. Give him a chance. He is the best we have. I won't lie to you, Tim; this government cannot stand another scandal. I will tell you this, if there is a scandal, we will back you. We won't hide what the CIA did or whoever it was that brought that animal to the States. And when we find out where Tran is and he is apprehended, the men who are involved will be dealt with no matter how high it goes in the government. I understand that five or six CIA agents are involved. They are what we call renegades. They actually are no longer part of the CIA; they're on their own. They are criminals now. That's what makes them even more dangerous.

"I want you to put your life back together. God knows you deserve it. I understand you will be going home soon. When you do, the police will be notified, and Agent Gifford and his men will be with you at all times. I hope you can go back to New Bedford and start your life over. When you are released from the hospital, I will have a jet take you to New Bedford. The FBI will be monitoring you, but they will not interfere in your personal life. I wish I could tell you that they wouldn't be seen, but that would be stupid of me. Especially, under the circumstances.

"There is one more thing. I wish you would get rid of that knife. There is blood on it from the war. That was necessary then, but now it is different. I hope you will never have to use it again."

I hesitated then reached under my shirt and took the knife out. I stared at it for a moment and then said, "Mr. President, would you do me a favor?"

"Name it, Tim."

"I would like it to go to the Navy. Maybe they can display it with the rest of their souvenirs. I think Mr. Chin would like that. I would like his name on the plaque with mine, if possible. He deserves it."

"Admiral, what do you think?"

"I will pay for the case and memorial myself. The Navy and I would be proud to do it."

"Now Lieutenant, I have a favor to ask of you."

"What might that be?"

"Your uniform, the one you wore as an enlisted man. I would like to include that in the memorial."

"I will have it sent over today, Sir. Thank you for everything."

When I left the President's office, I felt naked. But I knew I had done the right thing.

"Well Mr. President, what do you think?"

"I think Tim is in for a lot of trouble. I am glad he can handle himself. I have no doubt that eventually he will kill Tran. I just wonder how many will die before that day arrives. I gave him my personal number at the White House. I hope he uses it if he ever needs me."

As I was walking out of the White House, I thought of something. I'd never seen the grounds. So I asked the Secret Service agent, if it would be possible. He said no and was sorry.

"Can I use the telephone, Sir?"

"Go ahead, Tim."

I called the President on his private line. "Sir, I was wondering if I could get a tour of the grounds around the White House. I have never seen it."

"I will send the Admiral down."

"Admiral, Tim would like to see the grounds. Can you escort him?"

"Yes Sir, my pleasure."

"That's power, Tim. All it took was a call to the President."

"Come on Tim, I'll show you around." After my guided tour, I thanked the Admiral.

"Tim, I am an old man. But I am not a foolish old man. What was your real reason for the tour? Please don't tell me you're a tourist. I couldn't swallow that."

"I was curious. But I had another reason. I was just wondering if a person could bypass the security."

"It's never been done, Tim. Do you think you could do it? Now I am curious."

I just smiled, thanked him, and left him standing there.

"Mr. President, I did what you said. I gave Tim the tour then I asked him why he wanted it. He told me the truth. He said he was wondering if anyone could breach the security. I told him it's never been done. Then I asked him if he could do it, and he just smiled and said goodbye. I think he can. If I was you I would have it checked again. I would look for some obvious thing that we might have overlooked."

"Do you really think he could break into the White House?"

"Not to steal, but maybe to see you if he didn't want anyone to know he was here."

"I will have it done immediately, Admiral. Maybe you're right. He is smart and very cunning."

I asked agent Gifford if I could see FBI headquarters. He told me they had tours all the time.

"Not the tours, Gif. What the people don't see."

"I will ask the Director. Maybe he will okay it."

"Sir, Tim would like a tour of the FBI building. I mentioned the regular tour and he said no, he would like to see what the people don't see."

"What the hell is he up to?"

"I don't know, Sir. I wouldn't trust him. He already told me he had a personal tour of the White House."

"What the hell were they thinking? Go ahead. Arrange it. You give him the tour personally then report to me. I want to know what he is looking for."

"Sir, I don't think that's a good idea. You know Tim can get in anywhere he sets his mind. He proved that in Nam."

"I think our security is a lot better than Nam."

I was given the tour. I didn't ask any questions, but looked at everything, especially the cameras and the alarm systems. Agent Gifford knew that they had made a mistake, especially when I asked him questions about the CIA. He wanted to see that building also.

So a tour was again arranged. I did the same thing, just looked at everything. Gifford figured I had found a flaw in the system of both the FBI and the CIA.

"Tim, let me get this straight. You've had a personal tour of the White House and the FBI and also the CIA. Now why did you want to do this? Never mind the bullshit. I want the truth. You're not interested in tours. Now, I would like the truth."

I laughed. "Agent Gifford, do you think I have ulterior motive?"

"You bet your ass I do. Now what is it! I know you found flaws in our systems and could get in very easily. You have me curious. That's all."

"I'll tell you the truth. I think there is a mole in one of those three places. If I ever needed to get in to see him, I would know how."

"Then you have found a flaw in the system. The government paid and pays a lot of money for that system. Plus what it costs for manpower. Now, I am told you can break in without being caught."

"I never said that Gif."

"That is bullshit. You know I am going to have to tell the Director."

"Go ahead, all you have is suspicions. You have nothing else. You're only going to cost the government more money."

"Tim, you're something else. I think we better get back to the hospital."

"Okay boss!"

I was to be discharged in a couple of days. Sandra was working again. I looked at her. "How was last night?" She smiled.

"Everyone here saw the papers. My picture was all over, especially with the President and the First Lady. They have been teasing me all day. They call me Miss Lucky."

"When do you get off tonight?"

"In about an hour."

"Would you like to have supper with me?" The other nurses said, "If she doesn't, we will." I laughed.

"I think I would like that. Is this formal?"

"No. Just wear anything. You can even pick out the restaurant."

"Okay, I know a nice quiet place. Will *he* be dining with us?"

"Nah, he's too old."

"I heard that! No Sandra, I don't think I will be dining with you, but I won't be far away. That's for sure. You can have a good time. I can keep my mouth shut when I have to."

"Yea, I wouldn't want to be hanging by my thumbs on that one." She turned and walked out of the room. She always looked back. I guess she wanted to make sure I was watching. I always was and she knew it.

It was seven o'clock when we picked Sandra up at her house. She just couldn't get used to the limo. Her neighbors were always watching. They were calling to her, "Have a good time, Sandy."

"Where to Miss?

"Chuck's on Pennsylvania Ave."

"That's a nice place. They don't have much security."

"We'll be all right.'

The driver laughed. "I know we will, look out the back window. There are three FBI cars with us. I guess they will check the place out before you go in."

"Tell me something, how long have you worked for the FBI?"

"What makes you think that Tim?"

"I guess because I am stupid. That gun you carry hidden is easy to spot. You should have your suits tailored to fit the gun then you would be less conspicuous."

Sandra and I laughed. We pulled up to the restaurant and the FBI pulled up behind us. Two agents went inside. When they came out, they nodded to me. When we sat down, I noticed the agents were sitting there having dinner. I looked at Sandra and said, "I guess were alone, huh?"

"Yea, but it's okay. I understand. I don't blame them."

I kept looking around. I had that uneasy feeling. The waiter came by and took our order. I noticed a couple in the corner. They never looked at us. Everyone else did. That made me a little suspicious. We sat and talked while eating, and the night passed quickly. Just before desert, I excused myself and walked into the bathroom. I looked around. In the corner was a door. I opened it and looked inside. It was empty except for a mop. I went inside and kept the door ajar. I heard the bathroom door open and a man walked in. He looked around. Taking out a gun with a silencer on it, he started to check the toilets by looking under the doors.

When he got to the last one and started to bend down, I opened the door and caught him unprepared. I pushed my finger in his neck. He went down and I took his gun. I removed his belt and tied him to the plumbing under the sink. It only took a minute before his girl companion came in. She saw him and pointed the gun at the door. When she realized I wasn't there, she turned and saw me. Before she could shoot, I shot her.

I took her gun and walked back to the table. I then went up to the FBI agents. "I think you should have these guns." They were shocked. I pointed to the men' s room. They found the two people. The girl was dead. The guy they handcuffed. Within seconds the place was crawling with FBI. Sandra and I were having desert.

"Okay Tim, what the hell have you done?"

"Nothing."

"Just knowing you tells me something went down."

Everyone was watching. The ambulance came and they carried the woman out first on a stretcher. The FBI had removed the man.

A woman sitting next to us asked us what had happened.

"I don't know; it must have been the food."

Sandra looked at me, smiling, "Very funny, Tim."

Gif came over and said, "That's it Tim; time to go. Okay, how did you know they were after you?"

"Simple, they never once looked at us. Everyone else did. Then I saw the bulge in his suit coat."

"Why the hell didn't you tell us?"

"Gif, figure it out. The restaurant was full. If they had opened up with their guns someone could have gotten hurt. Then again, I didn't know if anyone else was in there."

"Yea, talking about that I figure we should get out of here. I'll feel better with you two at home."

"How did they know we were here?"

"They've got Sandra's house bugged is my guess."

"Sandra, did you tell anyone where you were going tonight?"

"Wait a minute . . . I was talking to Gayle on the phone and I mentioned Chuck's.

"That's it. Don't worry. I will have a team there in a couple of minutes to clean the bugs out." When they finished, they'd found six bugs in the house.

"This pisses me off! You do realize that. Do you have any bugs in my house, Gif?"

"Yes, we do."

"Well, I want them out now."

"Sandra!"

"Never mind the 'Sandra'! I want them out now!"

"Tim, do you plan on spending the night with me?"

"I'd like that."

"Good! Now Gif, I want them out now. Where the hell is that gadget your men used." Sandra picked it up, looked at it, and checked the bedroom. She could hear the beeps.

"Your men can wait outside. I hope you freeze your asses off. Haven't you heard of the word privacy?"

"Sandra, the bugs are for your own protection. They might grab you to get Tim."

"That's bullshit! Bugs in my bedroom. There are a lot of other rooms you could have put them."

"Okay, we're sorry. It's just the way we work."

"That's not how I work. Please leave. Breakfast will be when we get up. I'm sure your tape will tell you when we're up."

"Sorry Sandra, we're going to leave now."

They left and we locked the door. "Honey, they didn't mean anything. They are just doing their job."

"I guess you're right."

We went into the bedroom. When morning came and Sandra was cooking breakfast, we yelled for them to come in for breakfast.

Tim was laughing when Gif and his men knocked on the door. We all had breakfast together.

"Gif told me he was sorry about the bugs."

"Sandra, if we had too do it again, I just want you to know we would."

"I understand—just don't bug my bedroom."

"That's a deal. Put the bugs back in place. Except the bedroom."

We watched them place the bugs in the telephones and the other rooms. Sandra still felt violated.

"What is going to happen to the guy you arrested last night?"

"He will be turned over to the CIA. They can handle their own better than we can. They will extract the information they need. That way we can find out how many we are up against. I think, maybe six or seven agents went sour. If I remember correctly, they won't know too much. That's how they work. One hand doesn't know what the other hand is doing."

We were in the car heading back to the hospital when Gif said, "Sometimes I wonder about you Tim. Were you in the jungle or are you just devious?"

I laughed. "Gif remember this, Washington is just like the jungle. You have to keep an eye out for what doesn't belong there."

"I guess you have a point there."

"I don't think Tran is going to wait too much longer; the CIA is screwing up. That's what happened in the jungle. His temper almost got him caught. We drove him crazy. That's when he started to make mistakes. He is going to do the same thing again. That's when he will show his face. But it will take some time."

When we got to the hospital, Gif went to the room with me and checked it out. The room was clean. No one was inside.

"I'm leaving now. Get some rest. My men will be monitoring you all night."

"Hey, you guys keep your ears on. They made a move on Tim at the restaurant last night."

"Tim, make sure the curtains are drawn. I don't want them taking a pot shot at you through the window!"

"Okay Mom."

"Screw you. You better start to take things more seriously. It's your life were talking about. You're the one that's going to end up on a slab if you're not careful."

Gif stopped by FBI headquarters. Director Branch was there.

"Had a busy night, huh Gif?"

"Yes Sir, they made a move. We have one downstairs, but he won't say a word. The bastard would rather be dead than talk."

"He would be dead, if he did talk. He told me he wants his lawyer."

"He didn't like it when I told him the CIA was picking him up. He screamed for his lawyer. I left him yelling his head off."

"Jane, get me Holmes on the phone right away. I think he will be home."

It wasn't long before Jane announced that Holmes was on line one.

"This is Director Branch. We have one of your men here. He refuses to talk. He wants a lawyer. I suggested to him that the CIA would handle it. He wasn't happy. Do you want him? By the way Holmes, the girl that was with him is dead. I suggest you send a clean up crew to the hospital before the news media finds out the truth about what happened. If it's not too late already. Goodnight."

"This is Holmes. Get Jenson in on the line."

"Jenson, get over to FBI headquarters and pick up one of our missing agents. Bring him to the usual place. I want some answers."

Jensen arrived at FBI headquarters. "My name is Jenson, CIA," he said showing his credentials. "I am here to pick up one of our agents. Mr. Branch okayed it."

"You mean Mr. Mason?"

"Yes, that's him. Mr. Gifford detained him."

"I'll get him for you."

"Mr. Gifford, the CIA is here for Mason."

"So that's his name."

"That's correct, Sir."

"I'll be right up."

"Nice to see you again, Mr. Jenson. Follow me and I'll get Mason for you."

They went down to the interrogation room and found Mason sitting there.

Mason looked up and said, "Fuck you, Jenson. I want a lawyer."

Jenson laughed. "I am your lawyer." Mason was cuffed.

"Thank you, Mr. Gifford. You'll be hearing from us."

Gifford went home and had no sooner entered his house than the phone rang. "Gifford speaking."

"Agent Gifford, I have some bad news for you. Mason's gone. Jenson is in the hospital. He was shot in the chest. They're operating on him now. We don't know if he is going to make it. The doctors are going to let us know in a few hours."

"I never should have let Mason go with Jenson alone. Come to think of it. Why did he pick him up alone? How stupid could I have been. He must be the mole. Get the Director on the phone and tell him what happened tonight. I am going to the hospital."

By the time Gifford got to the hospital, Jenson was dead. He suddenly thought of Tim and ran to his room. Tim was sitting on the bed smoking a cigar.

"I was worried about you. The guy who tried to hit you last night is gone. The CIA agent who picked him up is dead. He was shot in the chest and died on the operating table."

"That's good news, Gif."

"What do you mean good news?"

"Take a look in the bathroom."

Gifford opened the door and found two bodies lying there. Mason was one. The other was Parker.

"What happened?"

"I heard them come in. Your men must be stowed somewhere. They looked toward the bed. I had the lights off. I was forced to break the neck of the first one. The second probably had a blood clot on the brain."

"That's cute, where did you hit him?"

"Where it would do the most good! That's three down. How many left, Gif?"

"How the hell do I know? The bastards just keep coming."

"The faster they come, the more of them will die. I think it's up to them now. The question is how many are going to have to die before Tran makes his move?"

It was time for me to leave the hospital; I was going home. The President had a jet waiting for me. Sandra came with us to the airport. She had tears in her eyes.

"Sandy, I'll be back. Just make sure you don't come to New Bedford to look me up. Tran is still out there. He has to make a move pretty soon. He can't get back to his business with me out there. I don't think it is going to take too long before he shows himself."

"Sandra will be watched all of the time, Tim. We will have men protecting her."

"I don't care about Tran or the CIA. It's you I want. I want you safe. That's all." She reached up and kissed me.

"You are the best thing that has ever happened to me. I will call you. Give Gif your new number when you get it. He'll get it to me. Remember, never answer your regular phone. Let the answering machine do its thing. Then call them back on your private phone. No one gets that number—not your friends, not the hospital. They will have men watching you at the hospital. You'll be safe. If I know Tran, he isn't going to stick his neck out. Especially, if you are not answering your phone. He is more interested in me. When he finds out I've left, he won't bother you. I have to go now. I love you."

When we arrived in New Bedford, Gifford drove me home. We stopped in front of Mr. Chin's house, now my home.

"Tim, you do realize that you're going to put a lot of people in danger. I suggest you limit your contact with your friends. You are going to make one hell of a target and that puts your friends in danger. We can only do so much. Right now, we're doing everything we can." I looked at my watch. It was just past midnight.

"Gif, I want to go for a walk. Why don't you have my house checked out?" I gave them my key.

"You know what to do," Gif told his agents. "Check on the bugs we got in there. Make sure you can hear clearly from each room. I guess we will be on the docks."

We walked toward the docks. I really missed being here. It felt good to be home. We were crossing Union Street and I saw Pat's was open. "How about a beer, boss?"

"Look, we haven't checked the area out."

I laughed. "Pat's is the one place in the world that I will be safe. I know the owner."

"Tim, you haven't been here in almost twenty years."

"I'll bet you Pat is in there."

"Loser pays for the beer, Tim."

"You're a sucker, Gif. Pat would never sell this place. He's king down here. He'd have to die before giving it up. Besides, I didn't tell you this. He has an apartment in back."

"Like I said Tim; you're a devious bastard."

We opened the door. There were so many new faces. We went to the bar and ordered two beers. The bartender opened the cooler and gave us the two beers.

"Pat's paying for them, okay?"

"You know Pat?"

"Sure do."

"Then you know damn well, he hasn't paid for a beer in years. So pay or get out!"

"I said Pat's paying." Three of the guys sitting at the bar asked the bartender if he was having a problem.

"Yes, I have a couple of chiselers here."

"I'll bet you guys, twenty bucks apiece that Pat will buy the beers. That makes forty dollars if you lose. I will give you forty dollars if I lose." I showed them my money.

"Tim, if I get in a fight in here, your ass will be mine."

I laughed. "Get that dumb Irishman out here."

The bartender left. He opened the back door to the apartment and yelled, "Pat, I have two chiselers here and they told me you were paying for the beer. They're drinking the beer now."

"What! I'll be right down."

"What the hell is going on? That's all I need tonight is a couple of chiselers."

"Pay the man for the drinks, fellas, before I get mad and break up the place with your asses!"

Gif was looking at the guys standing up.

"Look kid, just pay for the beer and get out."

"Okay, but before I do, I was wondering what Mr. Chin would say if he knew you were treating me this way?"

Pat's face went flush.

"It can't be. Is it really you?"

"Pay for the beers," the bartender said, glaring at us.

Pat looked at the bartender and said, "Look stupid, the beers are on me. For that fact, give everyone a beer. This is a special occasion. Now move and give everyone a beer."

"Before you do that bartender, where's my money?" They all paid me the money. I left it on the counter. We were all given a beer.

Pat kept looking at me. "I can't believe it. I heard you were back. Fellas, I am making a toast to the man I tried to kick out of here years ago. This little shit came in here to see Captain John about a job. Now he's home a famous war hero. Gentlemen, meet Tim Collins. A man I am proud to say is my friend." Everybody in the bar just stared at me.

"You're that Tim Collins!"

"I guess I am. But let's keep that to ourselves for now. I don't want anyone to know I am home. I have to drop in on some of my old friends."

"You can count on us. I was in Nam. I know what you did better than these assholes sitting here with me. I am glad you made it out. It took you long enough. I also know why it took so long. If you need anything, I am the man on the docks that can help you."

"Here's your money back. I wasn't playing fair."

"Forget it. You won it. I'm proud to lose it to you. Anyone else wouldn't have made it out of the bar."

"Gif, this bar has its own arsenal. Right Pat?"

"Right Tim. By the way who is your buddy in the suit?"

"This is my friend Gif. He's a FBI agent."

"He's what? "I was only kidding about the arsenal. We don't have any weapons here. I won't allow my customers to have such things here."

Gif laughed. "Forget it. You never know when you may need it, especially if Tim is here. There is one thing you can do for us. If you suddenly have any strangers coming in asking about Tim, let us know right away."

"We can handle them."

"No Pat, that's what we don't want."

Gif leaned toward me and whispered, "How much can you trust these guys?"

"Gif, I trust them. They are a tight-knit group. They can all be trusted. I would trust them with my life."

"That's what you're doing Tim."

"Let me tell you this gentlemen, the guys that are looking for Tim are professional killers. You wouldn't stand a chance against them. They don't care about human life. Let alone theirs. You'll put the key in the lock one morning to open up, and this whole place will be in another county. Just play it cool. Call Tim, he'll give you his number. But don't even let them see you pick up the telephone.

"Tim won't be coming in here that much; it's too dangerous for him. Come on Tim, I want to get some sleep. I have had enough of your sense of humor for one night."

"Okay, I'm getting tired anyway." We said our good-byes and left.

"Hey Gus, you were in Nam—how bad off is Tim? I heard the bastard that tortured him cut him up pretty bad and Tim has sworn to kill him."

"I will say two things. If this guy Tran is around here so is the CIA. And that means that Tim is up to his neck in trouble. If I were you, I would do like Gif asked. Don't be a hero. If it's the CIA looking to kill him, they'll kill you without batting an eye. Tim is the only one who can handle them. Just make sure they don't see you grab a phone, especially after they've asked you questions."

"Tim, I have been in touch with the police. They are going to keep an eye out for you. Make sure you tell them what they are up against—the best killers the government could train. They have no idea what these men are like and I want you to emphasize it upon them.

"Your friends on the force have been told about the weapons these men have at their disposal. The police have never seen some of them. That makes the police vulnerable. I'm not kidding; I don't think they really understand. Those bastards would blow up the station just to get to you. They wouldn't care if there were innocent civilians in the building at the time. Once they know where you are living, they will do everything they can to get you. I have men watching your house twenty-four hours a day. If anyone even stops near your house, they have orders to detain them. That goes for the postman too. I mean anybody.

"I would hate to see half the block being blown up. I don't think the police really believe me. I hope they don't find out the hard way and I don't want one civilian killed while were here."

I woke up early. I wanted to see my mother's grave and Mr. Chin's. I walked to the cemetery. I slid the gate open and walked into the cemetery when I suddenly heard a voice. It was Chuck. He was a Captain now. "Hi Tim, I figured you would be coming here. I'll walk with you." We didn't say much. When we reached my mother's grave, I just kept staring at her gravesite.

"Mom, I am back. I love you and miss you very much. But I always knew you were with me. Thinking of you helped me survive; it kept me alive. I could feel you with me, all those years. Now I am back and will take care of you. I'm so glad you were my mother. I love you very much. I have to see Mr. Chin now. Chuck is here with me. I'll be back to see you everyday."

Chuck never said a word. As we were walking, he told me where Mr. Chin was buried. I knelt down and read the tombstone. His name was on it with that of his beloved wife. Under their names was printed "Parents of Tim Collins, our beloved stepson." I started to cry. "I didn't know he thought of me that way." I looked at Chuck.

"Mr. Chin was always proud of you. He never gave up the idea you were alive. Even when the letter came saying you were missing, he just smiled and said you would be back. And somehow, we always believed it."

Looking at his grave, I said, "Thank you for everything you taught me. I am back now and still need your help. Unfortunately, my past is here with me. I am afraid that people are going to get hurt—innocent people. I need you to guide me. I miss you, Mr. Chin, and will be back every day to see you."

Chuck and I left the cemetery, and as we were walking toward the police station, I had an uneasy feeling again. We stopped, I turned and started to look around.

"What's wrong?" Chuck asked.

"I'm not sure. I have the same feeling I used to get in the jungle. I can feel trouble coming."

"Come on Tim. The station is around the corner; you'll be safe there."

When we got to the station, I opened the door. Bill was standing inside and came up and gave me a hug. "Tim, it's great to have you back." The other guys were looking at us.

"I am here for a reason. I have to see the Chief."

"Come with me. We will take you to his office. He's waiting to see you." Chuck knocked on the door. We heard a voice tell us to come in.

The Chief looked up when we entered and said, "Tim, welcome home! I'm glad to see you. We missed you around here. I bet it's nice to be home."

"That's why I am here. Agent Gifford talked to you?"

"Yes, he did. We will do everything we can for you."

"I don't think you understand. I am here to warn you. The men that are looking for me aren't your average killers. They are trained professionals. Your men could get hurt— most likely they will be hurt. Let me tell you about what your men are in for. These men shoot first and don't care about anyone who is in the line of fire. Your men can't do that. But if they hesitate, they will be killed. These men don't even care if they die; it's the mission that counts. Your men carry nine millimeters. They carry machine guns. They would think nothing of dropping a grenade into a cruiser. Some of the weapons they have at their disposal you have never seen."

"What are you trying to say, Tim?"

"Just this. I am the only one that can stop them. You have to shoot first and make sure they are dead. Wounded, they will still come after you."

"Tim, that's murder."

"Yes, I know that. That's why I am here telling you this. I don't want your men killed. In Washington, the other night I had to kill a woman. She tried to kill me. Your men wouldn't have been able to do that. What I want from your men is simple. If they hear of anyone asking questions, strangers I am talking about, tell them not to approach the strangers. Instead call me. The FBI will handle it and that way your men will be safe."

"Tim, my men are professionals. They are highly trained."

I looked at the shelf and picked up a law book. "This is their training. Where does it say shoot the bastard and then when you're looking at him eye to eye, put another bullet in him!"

"We can't do that."

"But I can! Believe me they will do it to your men if they get in their way. That is how they are trained."

"Who the hell would train a man to do that?"

"The government, in other words the CIA. These men are renegades and the CIA wants them. If they get them, these guys will never be seen again. That's the way it works. Chief, I am serious. They are the most dangerous men you will come across. Even if you had them surrounded in a house, they would get out. They have every weapon imaginable. They even have rockets and explosives— everything they can get their hands on. I wish I hadn't come back here, but I wanted to see my mother and Mr. Chin and everyone else. Plus, I knew Tran would make a try for me. He's the man I want and have to get. He is the kingpin of the drug trade. He is a sadist and would cut your men to pieces and put their bodies on your front steps."

"Look Tim, you're back, and there is nothing I can do about that. But while you're here, I want you to stay away from crowds. I can't afford any of our citizens getting killed. I will talk to the Mayor right away. I don't know how he is going to take this, but I really don't care. This is your home, and you have a right to live here. What are you going to do when you leave the station? Where are you going?"

"For now, I thought I'd go down to the docks and the fish house. I have some friends to see. By the way, I have someone I want you to meet." We walked to the front door of the station. I opened it and waved. They started up the steps.

"Sir, I want you to meet Agent Thompson and Agent Wilson. They are my bodyguards . . ." The window on the door shattered. I was on the ground looking out. We never heard where the shot came from.

The police were running all over the place. Outside they were looking for the gunman. I went over to them.

"It's over, men, they have already left the area. You won't find them."

"Tim, aren't you nervous? Someone just tried to kill you. You're standing here like it was nothing."

"Sorry Chief, I am use to it."

"Tim, you are starting to piss us off," Agent Thompson said to me. "Where you go, we go! That's the rules. You're lucky they didn't get you this time. That attempt was made because they knew how to find you. Someone is telling them."

"That's nonsense. They knew I would go to see my mother and Mr. Chin. It was just a matter of time before they found me. They must have seen me walking toward the station with the Captain," I tried to explain.

"Chief, can I use your phone?" Agent Thompson asked.

"Right there on the desk." Agent Thompson called Gif and told him what had happened. You could hear Gif yelling at him. Thompson hung up the phone and said, "He'll be right down."

I laughed. "He's pretty mad, huh Thompson?"

"Fuck you Tim! You aren't making it easy. By the way, where is the bug we put in your clothes?"

"It's under my pillow."

It only took Gif about twenty minutes to get from So. Dartmouth to the station and when he did he was fuming.

"Tim, what the hell do you think you're doing? You could have got my men killed. Sorry Chief. This bastard can't be watched all the time. He likes to disappear. Did he talk to you?"

"Yes, he did."

"Now do you take me seriously?"

"I sure do Agent."

"If you could have your men drive by his house every so often, I would appreciate it. But keep them out of this as much as you can. I am surprised they didn't use a rocket on you. Come on—you're going home."

"I want to make a stop first."

"A stop, are you crazy!"

"I want to see some of the people on the docks and at the fish house. They're not going to make another move now. They missed and that means they have to make new plans."

"Okay, the fish house is the only place you're going. This way we can cover your dumb ass."

"Bill, I want you to use car number six."

We left the station from the garage. "Bill, why is number six so special?"

"The windows are bulletproof. We use it for special occasions."

"Hey Gif, you're special."

"Yea, I'm special all right. I moved my family out last night."

"Gif, I'm sorry. I didn't think it would come to that."

The orders came from headquarters and I agreed with them. They need a vacation anyway. My wife wasn't happy. But she never is when it comes to my job. She always gets over it when we're back together."

"Victoria, send Capt. Benzer in."

"Chief, you wanted to see me."

"I want you to tell the men at roll call what we are up against. I also want you to emphasize we don't need any heroes. We need cops that are alive. If I find out they are out there trying to be heroes, I will have them sitting behind a desk. That's after I suspend their asses."

"Right away, Chief."

The Captain was present at all three shifts for roll call. The men were lined up.

"What's the Captain doing here Sargent?"

"Shut your mouth and listen to what he has to say. If you don't you could make a widow out of your wife."

"I have some orders from the Chief. You all know Tim Collins is back. Everyone here should know about him. I guess some of you have been to Vietnam so you know who he is better than anyone. Tim is in shit up to his neck; you all know what happened here earlier today. They tried to hit him right here at the station. That's the problem. We will be patrolling around his house, and if you see something suspicious, you call in and let the FBI handle it.

"You are to do nothing at all. Just call it in. You have no idea what you're up against. I will tell you this. The men who want Tim dead are highly trained CIA assassins. Bob, you have a question?"

"Yes Sir, if the CIA wants him dead, how come we know about it. The CIA can't operate in the States."

"That's correct. But these men are renegades and are operating on their own. They are mercenaries now. They are highly trained to kill. They have weapons we have never even seen at their disposal and would think nothing of dropping a grenade into your cruiser, with you in it. Life means nothing to them. Not even their own.

"If you see or hear of a stranger asking about Tim, call it in. Do not try to be a hero. We have a direct line to the FBI. The Chief has sworn that no matter what the outcome is, he will suspend anyone who acts and after your suspension is over, you'll be working a desk. Do not be fooled, he means it. That's why I am here telling you this.

"I know some of you guys were in Nam. But forget it. These guys are better trained in killing. Even if you are wounded, they will still try to kill you. We can't do it. We have to obey the law. That would be murder but not to them. Remember it is a way of life to them. They have combat weapons at their disposal, even rockets.

"The only one that can handle them on their terms is Tim. Don't let his size fool you. He is better trained than they are in hand-to-hand combat. I knew him when he was just a little younger than you; I was proud to know him then I am proud to know him now! He survived in the jungle with the enemy searching for him for years because he became an expert at killing.

"Any man who is given the Medal of Honor from this country is special. Remember that! The President and the First Lady gave it to him. Now get out of here. Bob, you will patrol Tim's house—keep your eyes open. I don't want you there all night. I want you to drive by every fifteen minutes or so. You will not be receiving any calls. If someone gets a call two blocks away, I want you to check out Tim's house. Do not leave your cruiser to check the house. I will have someone relieve you for coffee. Do you men understand what I want and expect of you? Are there any questions?

"Good, I take it you all know what to do. Be careful out there tonight. I don't want any dead cops because they didn't know how to follow orders."

The Captain repeated this to all the shifts. He was worried about his men, especially those who had been to Nam. They knew of Tran, and it made it hard for them to obey the orders. They knew the name and hated him.

"Tim, I have talked to my boss and he thinks it would be a good idea for you to get lost somewhere."

"Gif, why would I do that? I want Tran and those CIA bastards. No matter where I go, they are going to show up. Can you imagine what would happen in a large city like New York or Boston, a lot of people would die. This city isn't that big, plus I know where everything is. I know the best spots to hit someone if I have to. Here I am less of a target because I am familiar with the area. I can also get information we can use."

As we arrived at the fish house, I saw John, Jill's father, watching the cruiser come into the yard. Gif said to get inside quickly; he didn't want us outside at all.

"John, remember me?"

We shook hands. "I just came by to see you again. How is Jill?"

"Tim, she is married and has a couple of kids. She's married to one hell of a nice guy."

"Hey John, I am not here to try to get her back. I just want to see an old friend."

"Come on. She has been talking about you all the time. Here she comes."

Jill was running toward us and called out, "Tim, is that you?"

"Sure is." She threw her arms around me and gave me a kiss. "It's so nice to see you." She started to cry.

"What are the tears for?"

"It's so good to see you. I also heard what happened to you so just shut up and let a lady cry." Jill took my arm and said, "Come with me, I want you to meet my children. They both work here. I told them all about you. I can hardly wait for you to meet my husband, Ralph. First, I'll take you to meet my two boys.

"This is Tim Collins, boys, the man I told you about. He is coming for supper tonight. I want him to meet your dad."

"I don't think that would be a good idea Jill. I have a target on my back."

"My name is Agent Gifford and I think Tim is right. It is too dangerous for anyone to be near him at this time."

Jill and her father looked at me. Jill said, "We eat at 6:30. Be there. I don't care about anything else. We have some talking to do. You can bring your friends."

"I guess it will be all right," Gif said. "But we will have to leave early so we can make sure no one is following us."

"Thanks Gif. I appreciate it. Jill, after tonight, I don't want to be anywhere near your family. I wouldn't want anything to happen to them."

"That's fine. I understand."

Cruiser number six picked us up at 5:30. We traveled toward Cape Cod on Rte 6 to make sure no one was following. There are lots streets to turn into on Rte 6 to make sure we weren't followed. When we arrived at Jill's house, her husband opened the door.

"Tim, I am proud to have you has a guest in my house. Please come in, supper will be ready soon." We sat in the parlor. Everybody introduced themselves to each other.

As we were sitting at the table having supper, one of Jill's sons said, "I heard they did a number on you in Nam. The kids in school are all talking about you. They say you're a real War Hero. You saved a lot of lives and killed a lot of the enemy."

"Tim, that is enough. He doesn't want to be reminded of those days," Jill scolded.

"Is it true, Mom, that you named me after Tim?"

"Your dad and I both decided on it. Tim was such a nice boy. We hoped that by naming you after him, you would be too. I guess we were wrong."

"Mothers, they have all the answers—all the time."

"Let me tell you this boys. My mother was always right and I always listened to her. I learned a lot from her. That is why I survived all those years in Nam. I think your mother is going to be a lot like my mother.

"I know your mother and father will do the right thing with you. Be proud of them always." Jill suddenly left the room and her husband went after her.

"Kids, what do you think about that?"

"Tim, we always listen to our mom. We both love her a lot."

I thought of my mother when they said that.

"Jill, is everything okay?"

"I just can't stop thinking about Tim. Honey, not in that way. But what he has been through. I heard his whole body was sliced up when he was tortured. Seeing him now—he is not the Tim I once knew and loved. My dad has told me things about him since he came back to the States. Tim is a killing machine. Vietnam made him into something he should never have been."

"Come on, honey. We have guests."

I looked at Jill as she came back to the table. "Don't worry, Jill. I have seen a lot of grief, but I can handle it. Seeing your beautiful family makes me proud of you and your husband. I wish this family all the best there is. I want to tell you something, Jill . . ." They all looked at me expectantly, "I am famished; how about you kids?"

We all laughed and finished our supper. We sat in the parlor and talked for awhile. Then it was time to leave. As we said goodbye, Jill put her arm around me and kissed me. "Tim, I wish you the same happiness that we have."

"Someday. I met someone in Washington, she is a nurse. I hope when this business is finished, we can get together."

"Well, just make sure you bring her here."

It was quiet in the car as Gif and I rode back to my house.

"Honey, Tim is a nice guy. I am glad you're friends. I hope he can come back again sometime. I am worried he might get hurt. That is why I want to say this. Normally, I wouldn't mind you talking to him if you were in town and met accidentally. But now, I wouldn't like it. Not because I'm jealous either, that's not it. But people are going to die. It could happen to anyone around him and that scares me. We have two kids. Now that worries me. After this mess is cleaned up. I won't care."

"Thank you Ralph. You just showed me why I love you like I do."

Gif and his men checked the house. Once inside I went to bed.

"Mayor, Sir, the Chief is here to see you."

"Send him in. What can I do for you Chief?"

"Have you heard about Tim Collins?"

"I was going to call you about him. I think the city should do something for him."

"No way, Mayor!"

"Why not?"

"Some dangerous men are after Tim. They tried to kill him yesterday. They shot out the front window of the station. Luckily, no one was hurt."

"Well, what the hell are you doing about it?"

"Nothing Sir. The FBI doesn't want our men involved."

"Screw them; he lives here. He will be protected like any other citizen."

"That can't be done, Mayor. The men that are after him are trained killers. They would blow up the station to get to him. Anyone near him is taking a chance of getting killed. Tim and the FBI told us that themselves. They have a plan. They want us to just drive by the house once in awhile. That way, none of our citizens will get hurt. I think they're right. They are doing everything they can. The CIA renegades after him have no consideration for human life. The CIA is out there trying to find them. Then there is this drug dealer Tran; he is the one that tortured Tim. They are waiting for him to show his face.

"Tim talked to me. He scares me. He told me straight out that if our men meet up with any of the men hunting him, they would kill our men without blinking an eye. He also said our men have never seen this type of man. He told me if you are lucky enough to shoot one of them and he is still alive, you have no choice but to put a second bullet in him because that man will still try to kill you. You can't hesitate."

"That's murder, Captain."

"I told Tim that and he laughed. This is the new Tim. This Tran made him that way. But I also know Tim is still the clean-cut kid he was before the war."

"That Captain is a contradiction. You're telling me Tim is two people at the same time."

"I have heard of his reputation in the jungle. I've heard that when he has to fight, he is someone else. He is going to have to fight here and that's when we will have to pick up what's left."

"This is bullshit! The kid comes back to us a hero and we can't even help him. Okay, do what the FBI wants. But I still want you to watch Tim. I think we are going to see a high body count before this is over although I hope not."

"I'll keep you informed, Mayor."

"Tim, as I said, I've talked to my boss and he thinks you should leave the area for a while. It wouldn't be for long.

He thinks it would be the safe thing for you to do and I agree. It isn't safe for the people here. You have friends that could be in danger. Can you imagine what it would be like here in New Bedford if some of the people were killed before this shit ends?"

"Gif, I am safer here. I plan on keeping out of sight. Let them come here to get me. You're here and that's what counts. They are going to have a hard time getting to me. I will be able to see them first."

"Okay, I will pass the word back. I want you to be careful, stay inside during the day. I received word today that they are going to try to hit you again. I just don't know when. I heard it from an undercover agent in Fall River; the word is out that it's going to be soon.

"There is a small community of Vietnamese people there. They are a hard-working people. Then you have your jerks that would love to make a name for themselves. But that's the same wherever you go."

"Gif, I think this one will be from Tran. He's tired of the CIA missing. I think he is scared and is going to try to have it done himself."

"Are you sure?"

"Positive. I'll bet you breakfast tomorrow on it."

"How are you going to pay if you're dead?"

"Then you pay. Gif, I've got work to do."

"Be careful tonight. I'll have my men in the van listening all night."

I was alone but I could feel Mr. Chin's presence. I went into the room where Mr. Chin had taught me martial arts. I thought of the letter he had written to me before he died. What was it he was trying to tell me? I remember he talked about a room he'd made especially for me. Looking around, I located the room and went inside. I could feel Mr. Chin's presence even stronger. I looked around and saw a small stand with a box on it. I opened it and found a knife like the one I had when I went to Nam. He was looking after me again. I also discovered I could leave the house without being seen, go out at night without endangering anyone. Opening the tunnel door, I looked outside and saw two men coming toward the house from the rear. I recognized them—they were Vietnamese. So that's what Tran had sent. I slipped out and crawled toward them. They had a couple of sticks of dynamite and were just about to light them when I grabbed one by the throat and slid my knife across his throat. The second one tried to run. His throat was sliced as easily as his friend's. I went back into the house and kicked the lamp over.

An FBI agent ran toward the house and I heard one yell for the other to come outside. They found the two bodies and called it in.

Gif called the police. We waited outside for them.

"Okay Tim, how come they were found with their throats cut?"

"I don't know. Ask your agents; they have every room bugged."

"To the best of our knowledge, Sir, he never left. We heard him walking around. Then he went to bed, and a couple of minutes later, he kicked the lamp over. We checked the yard and found them lying there."

"You know what I think Gif? The CIA renegades did it. They mustn't have liked the idea that Tran sent them to kill me."

The police arrived and checked the scene. The Captain came over to me and asked, "What the hell happened?"

"I have no idea. I was in bed and got up to go to the bathroom then stumbled on the lamp. The next thing I know, there are a couple of Vietnamese guys dead in my backyard. Hell, the FBI has it all on tape."

The police had the bodies removed and the Captain came back to me and said, "Tim, you're full of shit. You know it as well as I. But I guess you're going to get away with it. It sounds like a clear case of self-defense to me, especially finding the explosives next to the bodies. You don't think I will find your prints on the stuff?"

"No Captain, I'm clean. I was in bed sleeping."

The next day the incident outside my house was all over the front page of the newspaper. I stayed inside all day. The reporters were in front of the house waiting for me to come out.

I heard a knock on the front door; it was Gif. "Hi Gif, how are you today?"

"Fine, you bastard. I would love it if you'd taken some prisoners. We could have questioned them."

"Do you really think they would have told you anything. I sure was happy your men were taping me."

"Tim, we both know what happened. I am not going to ask you how you knew. I called my informant, and he hasn't heard anything yet."

"That's too bad. Maybe he could have helped us. Come on. I was just fixing breakfast—eggs and bacon. I'll only be a second."

"That's fine; it will give me time to think."

As I was cooking the bacon, I asked if Gif he had heard anything about Captain Nge.

"Not yet, they are working on it. Remember Tim, they are looking for a guy that is in hiding. No one is going to talk. We are going to have to get lucky to find him. You know that, but I promise we will keep on trying.

"My main concern right now is you. I am worried they are getting desperate and might come after you fast and furious the next time, both the CIA and Tran's men.

"Tim, this is pretty good. I didn't know you could cook. Did you learn to cook in the jungle?"

"No, most of the stuff we ate was raw. Fires were off limits. Anyway, snake don't taste that bad after awhile. To tell the truth, the snakes tasted a lot like bacon."

I watched Gif look at his bacon, then laughed.

"Gif, the package for the bacon is in the garbage if you want to check it." He laughed.

"I almost had you going."

"There is no telling what you are up to, Tim. I want to warn you. We can only protect you for so long when you're pulling shit like you did last night. Tomorrow might be different."

"Don't worry. I can take care of myself."

"I'm worried about me. I'm close to retiring. That's what scares the hell out of me. My informant called it seems Tran is pissed about the two men failing. We are trying to trace the calls to the dead guy's home."

"Forget it. Tran would never be stupid enough to call them on his phone. He would send messengers to Fall River. That's the way he works. Tran is doing exactly what I want. The more men he sends who fail, the madder he is going to get. Then he will slip up."

"Tim, you're forgetting about the guys from the CIA."

"No I'm not. They are coming next. I have been thinking about it and think they are going to come from the direction of the woods in the back of my house. This time, with rifles and silencers."

"I'll alert my men."

"I wouldn't do that. These guys will pick them off. With silencers, they wouldn't be found until morning. What matters more is to catch them red-handed."

"Tim, are you suggesting that I allow you to go out after them? If you are, you're, crazy!"

"You can put a wire on me. Have one of your agents walking around my house. They'll never know the difference. Just make sure they don't stop at the windows, for any length of time. I have checked the area and it is the perfect spot to ambush someone. It's a sniper's dream. The only problem is I will be hiding nearby. I can build a blind to match the area then I can get them for you. There are only three of them left. The head one Russell won't come out.

He can't afford to get caught. But the others are expendable. I think I can do it. Remember, I am at home in the woods."

"Okay, go ahead. By the way, how are you going to get out without being seen?"

"Same way I did the other night."

"Tim, I didn't hear you say that. You guys back up that tape."

That night I hid in the woods, but they never showed up. This went on for about a week. Finally, one night I heard something moving. It was a dog. Just what I need, I thought. The dog was sniffing around, when all of a sudden he ran into the woods. I saw two men standing there with rifles. I watched them take aim, but they couldn't get a clear shot. Just as one of them raised his rifle to take the shot, I jumped up and grabbed his throat. My knife went to work. The second one turned on me; I threw the knife and he fell. I ran over and removed my knife, then slit his throat. That took care of the missing CIA Agents. There was only one left and I would meet him when I meet Tran. I hoped that day would be soon.

As I walked back to the house, the FBI agents came up and asked, "Are you okay, Tim?"

"I'm okay. They are dead. Here are their rifles, silencers, and all."

"Sorry Gif, I wanted to take them alive. At least one of them, anyway."

"You got the one on the right first. So how come you couldn't take the second. He has a wound from a knife in his stomach and his throat has been slit," Gif said, looking me in the eye.

"Your agent forgot to keep walking. The first one was lining his sights on him. I had no choice. It was either those two or your agent. Which would you have preferred?"

"Screw you, Tim."

I wondered when they would try again. Each night I went out without the FBI knowing. I figured I'd go to Pat's for awhile. It was just the usual guys. Pat had a place for me by the rear door; he told me he would feel more comfortable with me sitting there. Gus sat with me. The door opened and in walked a couple of Vietnamese guys. They sat at the bar and ordered a couple of beers.

Pat's bar was located in back of police headquarters. When they asked for a beer, Pat asked for some ID. They showed him a license and he gave them the beers. Pat grabbed two more beers from the cooler and walked toward Gus and me.

"Tim, do you see what is sitting at the bar?"

"Yes, I bet they're here for me. Don't worry Pat. We'll be okay." Gus saw them and laughed.

Gus stood up and walked toward them. "What the hell are you two doing in here? This bar is not for you bastards. I was in Nam and that makes you anything but a friend."

One of them said, "Go easy, buddy. We don't want any trouble. We're looking for a friend of ours. He is supposed to live around here. We sure would like to see him. Having a beer for old times would be nice."

"Somehow you're full of shit."

I could see Pat on the phone. He hung it up.

Pat told Gus to sit down and keep his mouth shut.

When Gus came back to the table, the two Vietnamese guys saw me. They said something in Vietnamese, which I understood. One of them reached inside his sweater, but I was up and slicing with my knife. The other tried to grab me, but Gus had the guy by the neck and twisted. He fell to the floor.

Pat yelled, "I called the FBI." He'd no sooner got the words out than the door opened. Gus and I were finishing our beers at our table when the agents came in and saw the bodies. "Tim, what the hell are you doing here?"

"Gif is on his way down right now. I guess we can't question these two either."

Pat called the cops. One thing about the cops—all they have to do is run out the back door to get to Pat's. They came in the same time as Gif. Gif looked at the bodies and shook his head.

"Tim, when are you going to learn! We need them alive."

The cops took statements from everybody. They tried to confiscate the guns, but the FBI took them.

"We need them for our reports."

"What reports?"

"You know, the reports. The ones we make out when a crime is committed." Capt. Benzer came in. "I just received a call at home and came right down." He looked at the bodies and said, "Tim, you do nice work huh?"

"Captain, it wasn't my fault."

"I'm sure it wasn't."

Gif told the Captain that there wouldn't be any reports. But the Captain said, "My men will make them out, give them to me, and keep their mouths shut. That is standing orders. The reports will be sealed in the Chief's office. The guns we will need. They also will be in the Chief's office. When the call came in, I made sure there was no record of it. That's the best we can do."

"That's fine. What about the news media?"

"They don't even know what's going on."

Pat unlocked the back door and four men came in.

"Where are the bodies?" Pat pointed to the left and they brought a van to the door. The bodies were removed. They cleaned the floor and never said a word. The cops were watching, amazed.

One of them said, "I don't believe this. Who the hell were those guys? Where did they come from?"

Gif smiled, "Son, you have just seen our government at work. They are from the CIA. They are what we call clean-up men. They'll do anything not to embarrass the CIA.

They are living around here someplace. God is the only one that knows for sure."

Pat being Pat said, "Shit, maybe I should have had them varnish the floors."

I laughed, "Pat, don't ever change. Take some advice, Pat, forget what happened here tonight. Talking about it wouldn't be good for business. Let alone your health."

"Who cares? I am seventy years old, and I love the excitement."

"Well, that's enough for tonight. Why don't you guys go home? I want to close up."

We all left the bar. Gif told his guys to look for the car the Vietnamese men had come in. It wasn't long before they found it. They had it towed and printed, and then it was taken to the junkyard and smashed into a block. The car was registered to one of the dead men and was traced to an address in Fall River.

"You know something, Gif? I am going to go to Fall River one of these days."

"Tim, let's get this straight right now. Fall River is out. It's a nice city. I don't want the Mayor on our ass. The Vietnamese community there is made up of some nice hard-working people. I told you this before. The police there have no idea what's going on, and I want to keep it that way."

Capt. Benzer was at the station talking on the telephone with the Mayor. "They tried to get Tim again. This time at Pat's. No Sir, there won't be any reports. The news media doesn't even know it happened. The bodies are gone. Four men came in and took them away; they even cleaned the place for Pat."

"Captain, I think this is going to come back at us. Is there anything we can do? You and I both know this has got to stop. The bodies are mounting up. Sooner or later it will be in the papers again. We can't keep it a secret for long and when it hits, we'll all be in shit up to our necks.

"You know that Costa woman from the New Bedford *Times* has a lot of friends. She is one hell of a reporter; she has a nose for this shit. If she finds out, she'll cover this story like she never did before. This is news. 'War Hero's life has had several attempts on it. Cops do nothing.' That will be the headline. I sure don't need that shit. Christ, if it ever gets out what is happening to Tim, we'll have every Vietnam Vet walking the streets armed to the hilt. Get Agent Gifford in my office tomorrow. I want to talk to him."

"He's here now. I'll set up a meeting for ten o'clock tomorrow."

"Good. Now let me get some sleep—if I can!"

"Hey Gif, the Mayor would like to see you tomorrow at ten."

Gif laughed, "That's fine. I'll be there. You want me to bring Tim?"

"That's up to you. He asked for you, but I think it would be a good idea. It might ease the Mayor."

We arrived at the Mayor's office promptly at ten.

"Sit down, gentlemen. I am starting to get worried. The bodies are mounting up. I know you are cleaning them up as soon as something happens. What I am worried about is the news media. We have a reporter that works for the *Times*. She has a nose for the news. If she finds out, I will be massacred. She works the crime beat and I'm surprised she hasn't found out all ready. Cops can't keep their mouths shut. Sooner or later it will break and the headlines are going to kill us."

"Is she an honest reporter?"

"Yes, that much I am sure of. She is well respected."

"Then let me talk to her. I have never met a reporter that wouldn't do anything for an exclusive story."

"That's fine; there is only one catch. She works for the only newspaper in New Bedford."

"That doesn't matter. There are others around someplace—even Boston. What about TV? "Maybe you can get her here right now."

"Here? Are you nuts! If her boss gets wind of her coming here, he'll ask her a thousand questions."

"Call her. I'll handle it when she gets here."

"Okay. I will send for her now."

The Mayor pressed the button on the intercom.

"Yes Mayor. What do you need?"

"Call the *Times* and get Ms Costa for me."

"Yes Sir."

"Line one for you Sir."

"This is the Mayor. Can you come over to my office right away? But I need a promise from you now."

"No promises Mayor!"

"Okay then forget it."

"Okay, I'll be right there."

"Ms Costa make some excuse to your boss. No one is to know you're coming here."

"This sounds interesting. I guess I will shut up and come over there. I'm on my way."

A few minutes later she walked into the office. She looked around, saying, "You, I know. From all the attention you're getting from the news media. This one wearing a suit looks like FBI. So, what's this all about?"

"I am Agent Gifford. I live in South Dartmouth. That's why I have been assigned to this case. My job is protecting the young man to my right."

"Protect Tim, that's a laugh. He won the Medal of Honor. He can take care of himself."

"You don't understand, Ms Costa, that's why I need you to promise not to write about what' s going on. When we can let it out, I promise you the exclusive story. And I keep my word. I don't have any idea when this mess will be over. But on that day, I'll give you the complete story—word for word. If the story leaks out now, however, a lot of people could die. Some might even be your friends and neighbors."

"You've got my word. One thing though, if the story gets out, I still get the exclusive rights to the story for my paper. If Tim is the man I think he is, the story will leak. That's the deal."

"Fine, we have an agreement. Ms. Costa, there have been several attempts on Tim's life. So far, about ten people have been killed. Three in Washington and the rest here in New Bedford."

"Your Honor, how the hell have you been able to keep this quiet, this long?"

"Tim has some friends here in New Bedford. All of the hit men are from out of town. We were afraid innocent people would get hurt if Tim walked the streets. Once they tried to hit him in front of the station. They shot the front door out."

"I saw the door busted later that day and was told someone had slammed it, and it broke. How in the hell have you been able to keep your men's mouths shut?"

"Be nice. Not all cops have big mouths," the Mayor replied.

"Yes, you're right. I know one." Gif took over.

"This is the interesting part, Ms Costa. Some of the hit men used to work for the CIA. They are known as renegades; they left and turned to mercenary work. Usually, no one knows when agents are gone, until someone looks for them and suddenly can't find them. There were about seven, six are now dead. Thanks to someone in this room—not mentioning any names. But the main one is still out there. Then, there is Mr. Tran. He was the one that tortured Tim in the prison camp. Tim, just so she knows we're not kidding, lift your shirt."

I stood up and lifted my shirt. She saw the scars and hung her head.

"Ms. Costa, that is why we need secrecy. If Tran's name gets out, there will be a blood bath here in New Bedford. It will also be embarrassing for the government. This part of the story you'll never be able to print. I think you will understand. If you don't print it when the story breaks, I can promise you a job with a newspaper dealing strictly with the White House. That is if you want it.

"Ms Costa, this is not a bribe. I am offering you this and no one else. I am a very good friend of the owner of one of the biggest papers in Washington. I will make sure the President knows of your help in this matter. Of course, he might not make the next election. But if he does—good. You never know."

"Let's forget about Washington. What's this part you're about to tell me?"

"Okay, those CIA renegades, as we call them, have nothing to do with the CIA now. That is the truth. They were the ones that brought that bastard Tran into this country to traffic in drugs. Just the things I have told you now could get you killed if it got out. Tran would have it done. We are trying to find him now. He has been like a ghost. We'll get him. He has tried to kill Tim about three times but hasn't succeeded. Well, what do you say? Will you help us?"

"I was never here." We watched her stand up. "Tim, I want you to be careful. I think you're in deep shit."

We watched her leave the office.

"You're right Mayor, she is one hell of a reporter. She is not stupid. I'll keep my part of the bargain."

"She will be all reporter from this day forward. She's not going to miss a trick."

"Tim, you'll have to be even more careful with your actions. That means, instead of people dying, I would like to question them," Gif warned me.

"Tim, I am speaking to you as the Mayor now. I am worried. So far we have been lucky. The only people that are dead, I could care less about. But if one citizen gets killed, I am not going to be able to keep it quiet. Ms. Costa isn't going to keep still for it either. You know what that means. The city will be in a complete panic. The city council will be on my ass. I can only get away with "No Comment" just so long."

When we left the Mayor's office, Gif said, "Tim, you know he's right. Maybe you should get away for awhile. I have a cabin on the Cape. It's at the Myles Standish Reservation. That would be a good place to invite a certain young woman. It's got everything except TV. It's not to far from Plymouth. I can have Sandra flown up without anyone finding out. A couple of weeks there might do you good."

"That sounds good to me."

"I'll arrange it right away."

"What about her job?"

"Don't worry, I'll handle it. I'll get you there tonight." We left after dark. It only took about an hour to get there. The roads to the cabin were country roads. No one followed us. Once inside the cabin, Gif started a fire.

"I will be back in about a couple of hours. I have to get some food and things. Make yourself at home. You can find where everything is. There is a telephone in every room, even the bathroom."

I looked around the cabin then walked outside. The thought of being in the woods like this scared me at first, but I realized this wasn't Nam. This is what I thought the country should be like. I could hardly wait for Sandra.

I sat on a log near the water. I thought, I could get use to this. I heard Gif drive in.

"Come on unload this stuff with me."

While we unloaded the trunk, Gif told me the Director was arranging for Sandra to fly up and should arrive in Boston in a few hours.

"Someone will meet her and bring her here. Tim, there won't be any bugs in the rooms. You'll be on your own. This time of year there shouldn't be many people around to bother you. We won't be here also. If you need anything, the phone in the bedroom is a direct line to my house in South Dartmouth. It also goes to Washington."

It was two o'clock in the morning when Sandra showed up. The first thing out of her mouth was, "Are there any bugs in this place, except for the kind that crawls?"

Gif laughed, "No Sandra, there aren't any bugs here. I know that for sure."

"That's good to hear because if I find one, I'll burn the place down."

"What do you think, Tim? Would she?"

"I'd bet on it. All you'd have left would be cinders."

I'm going to leave. Tim, check the broom closet; there is a key above it."

"Yea, I know. I found it but couldn't figure out why anyone would lock a broom closet."

"That's just in case of an emergency. I built it a long time ago. I had visitors show up here from a case I was working on. I wasn't here, my wife was. That's when we put it in. It is well supplied. Lift the floorboards and you can get out.

"Well I'll be . . . that sly old Mr. Chin! Now I realize how you got out of your house without us seeing you. When you get back. I want to know where it is. Now have fun. There are enough stores inside to last you a couple of weeks. I don't want you two going anywhere. I should cut the tires on the motorcycle in the garage."

"Thanks Gif. I appreciate this."

"No problem. Sandra, keep an eye on him. He's to darn devious."

Gif called us a few times. He always used a payphone. He was pretty smart. He's been with it for a long time. Sandra and I had a great time. We fished and had an isolated life. We even drove the motorcycle in the woods— that took some getting use to. I had never been on one. Sandra called it a dirt bike. I had an ulterior motive. I wanted to know the countryside in case we had to leave in a hurry.

Sandra and I sat under the stars every night. One night she came out with blankets and we slept under the stars. By morning we were freezing. Time meant nothing to us. We were sitting by the fireplace when the phone rang. It was Gif.

"Tim, I want to warn you. Tran is looking all over for you. My informant told me he is pissed."

"Gif, be careful when Tran is like that he's very dangerous. I've seen him murder his own men for no reason at all. So be careful. Do you think we should get out of here?"

"No, that's the last place on earth he could find you. The Director said to keep you there for a couple of more weeks. He talked to Sandra's boss and everything is fine."

I told Sandra what Gif had said. I could see she was worried.

"Tim, is it ever going to end?"

"I think I have to make it end. When we get back, I will force Tran to make a move."

"How the hell are you going to do that?"

"I have nothing but time to think about it."

"I don't think so. I have other plans for your time. It doesn't include Tran either."

I didn't sleep much after that. I was worried Tran would find us. Then I remembered what Gif had said about the time he'd had visitors. I realized this place could be traced back to him.

It was about midnight when I heard something outside. I got out of bed and told Sandra to get dressed.

"Be quiet and get dressed." I reached for my knife and went to the broom closet. I unlocked it and took out a couple of 45s. There were some extra clips inside and I shoved them into my pockets. I lifted the floorboards and we were outside in no time at all. Russell was visible in the moonlight. He had three of Tran's men with him. They kicked the door down and started to fire with automatic weapons.

I asked Sandra, "Can you use one of these?"

"Yes, my dad taught me."

I gave her one of the 45s and told her to remain quiet. As I was crawling back toward the house, one of the men came out. He was walking toward the garage and I met him halfway and silenced him forever. It wasn't long before the other two came out. When they saw the body, one of them came toward me. I knew I had to move fast. The other one was almost to where Sandra was hiding. After shooting the first guy, I ran toward Sandra. But I was too late; she'd shot him. I checked him; he was dead.

Russell came out of the house with an automatic rifle. I told Sandra to keep quiet. I didn't move because; I didn't want Sandra getting hit from a stray bullet. Russell got in his car and drove up the road. The bastard had set the cabin on fire. Sandra and I got on the dirt bike and took off.

The most logical route to take was through Carver. Instead, I went through the woods and came out in some small town. I called Gif and told him what had happened.

"Where are you?"

"We made it to Wareham, near some rotary and a bridge."

"Stay hidden. I know the area. It will take about a half-hour or so to get there. Just stay out of sight. I'll meet you at the rotary."

"Sorry about your cabin. The fire department and police are going to find the bodies. I didn't have time to get rid of them."

"Tell me later; I'm on my way."

Gif arrived in about an hour with three or four of his men.

"How the hell did they find you, Tim?"

"I was thinking about what you had said—the part about you having some visitors show up at your house—and realized they could trace that back. I wasn't able to sleep after that and heard a noise. I woke Sandra up. We left by your floorboards. Once outside we saw Russell and three of Tran's men. I managed to kill two and Sandra got the third with your 45. Russell took off in his car. I think there was one other with him. We got on your dirt bike and headed in the opposite direction. Traveling through the woods, we came out on some highway. Then I headed east to make sure Russell wasn't waiting for us. That's when I called you."

"Now what about the cabin? You said something about being sorry."

"Yes, Russell burned it down. I wish I could have stopped him."

"Screw the cabin; my wife never liked it anyway. Now, we have to find a place for you."

"They don't know who Sandra is. We have to get her back to the hospital and home."

"I don't like the sound of what Tim is saying."

Sandra said, "Neither do I. What are you going to do?"

"Gif, get her home safe. Then we are going to talk."

"You're right Tim. You four men take Sandra to the airport and make sure she gets home safely. Then get back here. Tran wants a war—he's got one."

I kissed Sandra goodbye. She told us to take care of ourselves. "You too, Gif. I hate to say this but I think I am beginning to like you. I wouldn't want anything to happen to you."

We watched them leave.

"Tim, what the hell have you got up your sleeve? I want the truth! No more bullshit! I am going to retire shortly and don't want to go out knowing I screwed up my last case."

"I want my life back. It's time for me to go after Tran. He could have killed Sandra. That is where Tran made his mistake. I have friends in Fall River; this medallion will be my introduction to them. It was given to me by the mountain people in Vietnam, and they told me anyone who sees it will be a friend.

"Now I am going out and get Tran. I don't care how many men he has. It's either him or me. This can't go on. I think he is in the area. I also think they know where he is.

"Tonight, I am going to Fall River. Gif, you can't come along. I have to do this myself. You would scare them off."

"Good luck, Tim. I will be waiting to hear from you. Call, I don't care what time it is."

I waited until it was good and dark then drove west on Rte 195, taking the Fall River exit. I found where the Vietnamese people lived. I parked my car and walked toward a little bar where I had been told they might help me. I looked around outside. It was quiet. When I entered the bar, everyone looked at me. I asked for a beer. The bartender, who was an old man, didn't say a word, but just stared at me. He put the beer in front of me. He started to walk away, but came back and said, "Aren't you in the wrong bar." I answered him in Vietnamese. I could see he was puzzled. I told him I was looking for Tran and that really did it.

He was scared; it was written all over his face. The three guys in the corner got up and walked out. I asked the bartender again about Tran.

"I am looking for him." I heard the bartender mumble, "You're looking to die a young man." I opened my shirt and he saw the medallion. He looked around. There was no one left in the bar.

"What is your name?" he asked.

"You know who I am. Don't you?"

"Yes, those three men who left work for Tran. I would like to help you, but I just don't know where he is. I know he's not far away. He's been in here. I hate it when he comes in. It's rare that he comes here. He usually sends someone in when he has a job for them. I want you to know that Tran has a price on your head."

"I figured that. I have met him before. I want to kill him as bad as he wants to kill me. There is someone else I'm looking for."

"I know that name too. You're looking for Russell. Him, I can help you with. He is going to be at your place in two nights. He is determined to kill you.

"Tim, those men are waiting outside to kill you. You better leave by the side door. The alley is dark. That is where they should be." He opened the door without making a sound. I stepped out with my knife in my hand. I could hear them talking in Vietnamese. They were joking about killing me and spending the money. I walked up behind the first one and grabbed him by the mouth. My knife sliced through his skin. I dropped him and stuck my knife into the second one, but he turned and got off a shot before he fell. He missed. Then I thrust my knife straight into the third one's heart. All three were dead. The old man came out, saw me standing there, smiled, and went back inside.

I started to walk away from the alley when a police cruiser pulled up.

"Drop that knife," they yelled. I dropped it and they told me to put my hands on the roof of the cruiser. After searching me, they put me in the back seat of the cruiser. The old man was standing near the cruiser and I spoke Vietnamese to him. He nodded and left. I had given him a number to call. Shortly, Gif arrived at the bar.

The Sargent asked him what he wanted and Gif showed him his credentials.

"Please to meet you, Sir. I have your man in the cruiser, under arrest for now. We caught him with this knife. The knife has the victim's blood on it. He never even bothered to clean it."

"Let him out. I want the cuffs taken off him. He isn't going anywhere."

"I just can't do that."

"I suggest you get someone down here that can. Have your men searched those three for weapons?"

"Not yet Sir, we'd just got here when we heard a shot.

"You heard a shot and arrested the man carrying a knife. Seems to me, you have the wrong guy under arrest. I suggest you get your C.O. down here before it becomes a lawsuit. I would hate to have to be witness against you."

The Sargent picked up the radio and requested that a Lieutenant come to the sight right away. The detectives showed up. The Sargent started talking with the Lieutenant and they turned to look at Gif.

"What's your story?"

They were screwing up the crime scene.

"Did anyone find a gun on the man in the cruiser?"

"No, he had a knife. The three of them died from knife wounds."

"Your Sargent told me he heard a shot. That tells me that one or all three had a gun," Gif explained.

One of the detectives came out with three guns in a plastic bag. "We're getting these sent to the lab for printing."

"Release Mr. Collins immediately," Gif ordered.

The Lieutenant looked at me and said, "Tim Collins!"

"Release him now, Lieutenant!"

"Sargent, take the cuffs off the prisoner, right now!" the Lieutenant barked.

"Sir, who are you and what are you doing here?" asked one of the detectives as he walked up.

"FBI—I am agent Gifford. Who are you?"

"I am Captain Larsen, Chief of Detectives. That man is going nowhere until I question him. He just killed three men and I want to know why."

"It appears to me that he was protecting himself, a knife against three guns. I would say you don't have much to hold him on. If you want to question him, come by my office in New Bedford tomorrow. Right now he is coming with me."

"Lieutenant, have you got his name and address?"

"No Sir. Can I talk to you alone a minute?"

They moved away from us and I could see them discussing something. They came back and the Captain said to me, "What happened here, mister?"

"The three men attacked me. I was defending myself."

"Just like Nam, huh Collins?"

"That's not called for," Gif said angrily. "He was doing a job in Nam. He came here to see if he could find some of his friends."

"If you believe that, I will sell you some swampland in Florida. Tim, I admire what you did in Nam, but I don't admire what you are doing now. Scuttlebutt has it you're on a killing spree. Wherever you go someone dies. This is Fall River not Nam. We can't and won't tolerate it. If you screw up, I will nail you."

"I am sorry, Captain that has been tried before with very little success."

"Agent Gifford! Get him out of here. I don't want to see him in Fall River again. Tomorrow, I'll talk to the mayor."

"Captain, have you ever been in the service?"

"That's none of your business, Mr. Gifford."

"I'll run your name tonight. I'll know tomorrow what you did during the war. You were probably one of those bleeding hearts. I'll be back to see your Chief. Or, can't I come to your city? This is your city isn't it? Remember this, Tim almost died many times to make this your city. You have the nerve to tell the war hero of all times to keep out of your city. Wait until the newspapers get a hold of this. Tell your God darn Mayor I'll be back tomorrow. And I think I'll have Tim with me. I want to see you try to throw him out of your city. You'll be lucky to be a Captain tomorrow.

"Now get out of my way, before I forget I'm a gentleman. By the way, tell your mayor Tim can call the President of this great country anytime he wants. He has his personal number. You can tell your mayor he can call the President too. That is, if he can get through to him. He might be interested in talking to him tomorrow. Especially, about what is going on. Now get out of our way."

As we walked away, I looked back—every cop standing there had their mouth open. I said goodnight but no one answered.

Later as we were driving home Gif asked, "Tim, what happened there tonight?"

"Those three men work for Tran. When I came in to the bar, they left. I did find out Tran is going to make another try for me in a couple of nights. Maybe we can catch Russell in the act."

The next morning Gif came by and said, "I called Washington to check on Jack Larsen. The report I got stated he wasn't even in the service. He went to Canada. I can't wait to put him in his place."

Gif received a call from Washington. The Director wanted to talk to him.

Gif told him about Capt. Larsen and me.

"Canada, be careful what you say, Gif. I am sorry about your cabin. Don't worry, we will pick up the tab, that's the least we can do."

We drove to Fall River and parked our car across from the city hall. When we went inside, Gif showed his credentials and the guard told him where the Mayor's office was. We went inside and Gif said, "I want to see the Mayor."

"Do you have an appointment?" When Gif showed her his credentials, she smiled and said, "He's expecting you."

"Your Honor, Mr. Gifford and Mr. Collins are here." The door opened. The Mayor was standing there. "Come in please. Sit down and make yourself comfortable. Would you like some coffee?"

"That would be nice, black please." His secretary came in with the coffee, and Gif said, "That's fast."

"I wouldn't know what to do without her. I think she can read my mind at times. I know why you're here. Capt. Larsen called me this morning. He is on his way here. You were right. The only prints were of the dead men. Tim, I am pleased to meet and have you in my office. I am also proud to have you visit us.

"But what scares me is why you're here. Tran is not in the city as far as I know. If he shows up, I will have him arrested. I have already given that order to the police. I can't have you here killing my citizens. I know this was self-defense. If you are attacked, I expect you to defend yourself. However, I just hope you aren't coming here with that in mind."

"No Sir, I had to come here to try and get some information. I was asking the owner of a bar a question when the three men I killed left. They were outside waiting for me as I went out the back door to the alley. They attacked me and I had to defend myself. This man Tran that I am looking for comes to Fall River. He has a price on my head. So I came here to try to get some information."

"Did you Tim?"

"No Sir. The people are too scared to talk."

"I understand that—where they come from they would be killed in a minute."

Capt. Larsen walked into the Mayor's office. "Have a seat Captain. You will help the FBI and Mr. Collins out, with whatever they want. I think you owe them an apology. What this man has gone through is more than any man I have ever seen or heard about, and I will not stand for you to treat him in such a manner. As a Captain you should be smart enough to know what the word respect means. I don't know what your problem is. I checked with the men on the scene, but they were reluctant to say anything. I finally got a couple to give me their version. If you ever treat anyone like that again I will suspend you and reduce you in rank. That will be as low as the law permits. Do you understand!"

"Yes Sir! May I leave now Sir?"

"Didn't I just tell you something about an apology?"

"I apologize, gentlemen."

We left the office together. The Captain was mad.

Gif said, "Captain Larsen, I have something to say. I checked on you last night. You have never been in the service. You went to Canada to make sure you didn't go. Whether or not you thought the war was right or wrong, you have the right to express your feelings. Men fought to give you that right. If I ever hear of you screwing with your men, the ones that served your country, I will personally come back to the station with several copies of your record. I will hang them up myself. Now, do we understand each other? Be a man and show some respect. You're lucky I never gave a copy of your youthful trip to Canada to the Mayor. By the way, did you know the Mayor served two tours in Nam? Now, I suggest you get out of our way."

As we started to walk away, Gif said, "Tim, you have to be more careful. We can't keep up with you. I know I agreed to this, but I am getting a little worried. Now that it is going to hit the newspapers, how are we going to keep the whole story from coming out? Let's get back to the Mayor's office. Maybe we can stop it. He doesn't want the publicity."

We made it back to the Mayor's office and he was still in. "We have a problem, Mayor. We can't afford to let the story get out."

"I figured that. If the story comes out, it will state it was a gangland killing. No sense in panicking the people. Remember, part of my job is lying. I hope your cops can keep their mouths shut. I talked to the Chief in New Bedford. He was vague about a lot of the things that are happening. He told me he would fire the men that leaked the story out. I understand you have a reporter that knows quite a bit."

"Yes, she has promised to keep quiet. She can be trusted. I would tell you more but that would be dangerous for your city. New Bedford is worried, that is, the Mayor and the police. You wouldn't want what has happened in New Bedford to happen in Fall River. Believe me, when I say this—I would be careful of Capt. Larsen."

"Do you know something I should?"

"Well, let me tell you this. I checked him out. He's clean except when the Vietnam War started he ran to Canada. I told him if he ever treats those men working under him like he treated Tim, I would release the information to his men. I also warned him you'd spent two tours in Nam."

"That son of a bitch was a draft dodger?"

"That's right. Just keep it quiet for now. You don't want him shooting off his mouth. Thanks for the help your honor."

When we got back to New Bedford, Ms. Costa was waiting for us.

"Hi, would you like some coffee."

"Yes, I think we could all use some," I answered.

"I understand there was some trouble in Fall River. They wouldn't give me much information. All the information I could get was a gangland-type killing. Since when is slitting people's throats gangland-type killing?

"What about it Tim? I'll get the coffee. How do you take it?"

"Black, with no bullshit." Ms. Costa laughed.

"Tim, I am serious. Maybe I am making a mistake."

"No, you aren't. What happened there can happen here. Or, should I have said, has already happened here. If you break the story, there will be hired guns all over New Bedford. We have the problem centralized right now so I hope you won't bring things out into the open. We hope to be finished in a few weeks or less. Then the whole story will be yours."

"Mr. Tran, a Mr. Russell is here to see you."

"Bring him in."

"Well, Mr. Russell, it seems that all your best men, Tim has killed. What the hell are you doing to get him?"

"Well Major, I understand he took your best men out too. How many men have you lost? It will only be a matter of time before I get him. Remember, he eluded you for years. He drove you nuts in Nam. This is my turf and I will get him."

"We have a lot to lose, Mr. Russell. I don't intend to lose anymore. If they catch me, I go to jail for life. I might even be hung. Now get him, or I won't need you any longer."

"Tran, don't even think it. If anything happens to me, you're going to get caught. So don't threaten me. I cover the bases, just like you."

"Mr. Russell, you have failed too many times. Let me show you what happens to my people when they fail."

Tran took a gun out of his belt and pointed it at the man standing next to him. He squeezed the trigger. The man fell to the floor.

"Call someone to clean this mess. Do we understand each other Mr. Russell?"

"Don't threaten me, Tran. Tim will be dead in forty-eight hours. I promise you. Just buy the newspapers in a couple of days. You'll read all about it."

"I hope so. You can leave now Mr. Russell."

Russell left the house; he knew he had only one day to get Tim, to put his plan in action.

When he got back to New Bedford, he made a call. "Are you ready for tonight?" The voice on the other end said, "Yes. Nine o'clock fine with you."

"Fuck the time, just do it!"

I was home lying on my bed, remembering what the old man had said. I decided to call him. He answered the phone and I told him who I was. He yelled back, "I want the beer here at nine. Do you understand?" I hung up the phone and looked at my watch. It was eight-thirty. I knew I didn't have much time. I shut off all the lights in the house except for the bedroom light. I hung my pillow from the curtain rod. The drapes were closed. I went into the cellar, opened the door to the tunnel, and went outside. I waited in the woods. Sure enough, they came, carrying a rifle with the silencer. They stood next to a big oak tree and saw the silhouette in the window. The shorter one raised the rifle and took his shot. The pillow went flying. As they lowered the gun, I came out of nowhere and knocked them to the ground. As one of them fell, he tried to aim the gun at me. I kicked him and shoved my knife in his gut. The second one tried to get up. I grabbed him by the hair and dragged him to the house. The FBI was all over the house. When they saw me, they took the prisoner inside.

Gif was called. He must have flown to the house. He was there in no time. I was sitting having coffee when he came through the door, "Where is he?"

"Who?"

"Look you prick. Where is the prisoner?"

"Your men have him. Aren't we feisty today?"

"I have been waiting a long time to question one. Now we have him and I will get the information I need. Thanks Tim for not killing him."

"By the way, you remember where I killed the other ones? There is a body there. Can you get someone to clean it up? Or you can leave it there. It doesn't matter to me either way." I was laughing.

"Frank, make the call."

It wasn't long before a van pulled up. The cleaning crew had arrived. "Don't you guys ever get tired?" I asked.

They didn't answer me. I thought, Screw the CIA. I wouldn't be having this trouble now, if it weren't for them.

"Gif, if you can't make him talk, let me have him."

"Thanks Tim, this one goes to Washington. They'll make him talk."

"Seeing is believing. That's all Gif."

They asked the prisoner about Tran, but I knew they were wasting their time. It was quiet for a few days, but I knew they wouldn't give up. It was only a matter of time before they would be back.

I was ready for them. This time, I was determined to do whatever it took and wasn't taking any prisoners. I was in the house alone and could here something outside. I had all the lights off and had left the back door unlocked. Two men entered the room. It was too late for them. I had the second one by the face and covered his mouth; I felt my knife go into his back. He never made a sound. I gently lowered him to the floor.

The first man was looking for me and I followed him to the kitchen. He thought I was his partner. I grabbed him by the throat and said, "Goodbye asshole," and slid my knife across his throat.

The door opened and I put on the lights. I told the two FBI agents there was another body lying on the floor in the other room.

"Damn it Tim, now we have another mess to clean up. Can't you take anyone alive? I'll make the call."

It wasn't long before they were cleaning the place of the bodies and the blood. It was the first time the CIA said anything. "We're getting tired of cleaning up after you."

"That's too bad. If it weren't for the CIA, this wouldn't be happening. We didn't bring that animal in."

"Is that right?"

"I suppose the CIA agents who brought Tran in weren't on your payroll. Well, just get that shit out of my house. I'll tell you this. It's not over, yet. The more of Tran's men I kill, the madder he is going to get. That's when you're going to see bodies. If I find him first, there will be fewer dead men for you to dispose of."

Gif came in and said, "Tell me something Tim, how many men are you planning to kill?"

"That's up to them, isn't it? It depends on how many men they send here. If I were Tran, I would change my tactics. He already knows I can't be hit here. Now he has to do something else. He's not spending much time on his business, right now.

"Gif, doesn't it seem strange to you that they know where we are all the time. I was wondering if they have a mole somewhere. They seem to be getting information pretty fast. The CIA says they want to help. We call them after the attacks. Could someone in the FBI be working both sides?"

"I don't want to hear that Tim; these guys have been with me for a long time."

Gif paused for a minute. He was quiet and I knew he was thinking to himself. I'd hit a nerve.

"Damn you Tim. I only have one new man with me and his credentials check out."

"Shit, I can have any credentials I want made in an hour. I guess the government is slow."

"Let's find out. It's time I tested him, just to show you. What can we do to catch him? That is, if it is one of my men?"

"That's easy. Tell him when he's alone I will be on the docks tonight. You can say I slipped up and told you I was going for a walk after midnight. If someone shows up there then we know for sure."

"Sometimes you piss me off Tim!"

"You guys keep a watch on Tim. I have to go into town. Grant you can come with me. I don't want anyone out there alone."

"Okay Sir. Where are we going?"

"Bring the car around. I'll meet you out front." When Gif finished what he had to, they went to the police station. He said to Grant, "I was going to tell them to stay away from the docks tonight around midnight. That fucking Tim wants to go for a walk. He is tired of being in the house. If we keep the cops away, then no one will get hurt. I don't want to read in the paper about some cop getting killed instead of Tim. Tim can handle himself on the docks. He's at home there as much as he was in the jungle. The only way anyone can get him is on the water. Tim is very well covered except for one area, and I'll make sure he makes it quick when he walks through that area." Gif got out to go into the police station, and told Grant, "I'll be right out."

Going inside he met Capt. Benzer at the desk.

"How are things going, Gif? I hear Tim has been busy lately."

"Is there somewhere we can talk?"

"Sure, follow me."

They went into the Captain's office and had a cup of coffee. Gif told him what Tim thought.

"I agree with him, Gif. They know too much. Someone has to be feeding them information."

"Your department has a police boat, doesn't it?"

"Yes, a fast one."

"Good. Can you have it hidden under the State Pier around midnight. We are setting up a trap for the guy waiting outside for me."

"Consider it done. Isn't he one of your agents?"

Gif didn't answer, he figured the Captain was smart enough to know what was going down.

"Just make sure your men keep their mouths shut. If there's going to be a hit, I think it will come from the water. Remember sound travels over water. Make sure your men don't forget it!"

Gif and I walked to the docks and when we got to the area we had to cross, sure enough, there was the flash of a gun. We both hit the ground fast. Then we heard the motor of the police boat, as the police gave chase. We could hear both boats firing at each other. Then one of the boats was hit. We heard on the radio that the police had one of the men. The other was dead. They radioed that they were going to tow the other boat to us. Gif got up and started to talk, but I was gone. Gif ran up the road a ways and found me sitting with another one of the men.

"Gif, take him back to my house. I'll show you how to interrogate a man—the way they did it to me."

"Tim, I can't be a party to this sort of thing."

"You don't have to. I will do it. No one needs to know. All you have to do is call for the clean up crew."

"Just don't tell me what you have in mind. I have to live by the law."

It was easy for us to get away from the docks without being noticed. We went inside and tied the hired gun to a chair.

Gif told two of the men to go to the station and take their time coming back with the other prisoner. The two men left. Grant was told to go with them. Gif called Frank back and said, "When you're ready to come back with the prisoner, cuff Grant. He is working both sides. Place him under arrest. We'll send both of them to Washington. Have a jet ready at the airport. You know the number. I want you to come back here. Let the other men take Grant and the prisoner to headquarters; make sure the tapes are all shut down in the van before you leave."

"What the hell are you two going to do?"

"Tim wants to question this one."

"I guess when I come back, I will have to call the clean up crew."

"I don't think so. Not this time anyway."

"I hope you're right. I'm on my way. Good luck, Gif."

I spoke to the prisoner in Vietnamese.

"Tim, I want to hear what you're saying, speak English."

Tim laughed, "Okay Gif, I can do that for you."

This went on for couple of hours, but we were getting nowhere. Frank came into the room and asked, "Any luck?"

"No, they would rather die than speak. This is weird. I think life is precious and they don't even care. It's unbelievable."

"Gif, could you watch him for a moment. I think he is ready to talk." The Vietnamese guy smiled.

"We'll see if you're going to smile in a minute," I said as he left the room. But the prisoner just sat there with a smile on his face. I came back with a box and put it down.

Smiling, I opened the top and pulled out a snake.

"Tim, what the hell is that!"

"Our friend knows; he has seen them before. They live in Nam. This is how they questioned Americans to extract information."

"Look Tim, I have let you get away with a lot because of the way things were. But this is something else. This is illegal right down to that damn snake. Is it poisonous?"

"One bite and you're dead a couple minutes later."

"Well, just don't drop it. Let's get out of here, Frank. We don't want to be a witness to this. Tim I want him left alive!"

They left the room and I continued questioning the prisoner about Tran and his whereabouts. After a few minutes, he finally told me that Tran would be coming up here next month. That's all he knew.

Gif came in and said, "Tim, I want you to get rid of that thing. We got our information."

"Relax Gif. Frank, do you know how Tran questioned our troops when they were captured. He would take the snake and put it about an inch away from the prisoner. He would do this for hours. I'll show you what our boys felt." I shoved the snake about an inch from the guy's face. He couldn't move to either side. He screamed in fear.

"I had this done to me. I used to spit in Tran's face. He had me to the point where I didn't care if I lived or died. One snake bite would've put an end to the torture."

"Tim, do me favor and get rid of it."

"Okay Gif." As Gif turned away, I let the snake bite the prisoner and then broke the neck of the snake.

"Tim, are you crazy? You just killed him in front of the FBI!"

"Yea, prosecute me. The bastard knew what was coming. For him to know that, he had to have been there when they did it to our boys. Sons of the mothers who are grieving today. I don't care—he deserved it."

"Where in the hell did you ever get something like that?"

"Last night, I got it from a friend in a nearby city. He was more than happy to get it for me. He knew what I wanted it for. You see he lost his family over there, probably in that manner. We are civilized in this country. Where that man came from during the war, things were different.

"Gif, I used to have to eat these things. That was all the food we could find. Once the head is cut the venom is gone. We would bleed it then eat it raw and drink the blood. That's Vietnam. I hope I have one when we catch Tran.

"I have to make a call. You might as well get that piece of shit taken care of. The people I am calling are going to party tonight. I wish I could join them. I have to tell them the pet they gave me has just been fed."

"Tim, I think you really need help," Frank said.

"No Frank, that's not true! I need Tran. Then I can live a normal life like you guys do. It is my only wish and if that makes me crazy, then that's what I am. Remember, they taught me these tricks. Thank your lucky stars they never had you as a houseguest. If they had you would be just like me. That is, if you'd lived that long.

"I hope the day comes when I can put this behind me. But as long as Tran and Russell are alive I have to be what you see and dislike so much."

"Hold it, Tim. We don't dislike you. We are proud of you. But we just don't understand a lot about you. But I think we are learning. It's going to take time. Just think about us watching what just took place. It is something we've never seen before, and personally speaking, I hope I never have to witness something like that again."

"I don't usually talk about Nam. I will tell you something else. What you just saw is tame compared to some of the things I have seen. I have seen a dozen snakes in a hole—maybe four feet deep. I've seen an American soldier, eighteen years old, put into the hole, head first, just so the snakes could do their thing.

"Wait a minute Gif, you too Frank." I left the room and came back with a dog tag. "This is the dog tag from that soldier. I was going to give it to his parents, but I can't. How could I explain to them how he'd died. I think of him every night, so don't tell me I am cruel. I have been forced to live differently than you. I have feelings, but not for shit like that. What the hell do you think they would do to your family if they had them?"

"Tim, give me the dog tag. I will see the family gets it. They will never know where it came from. I promise you. I will have the director of the FBI send it and will make sure he comes up with some other story for them, after I tell him what you just told us."

"Tim, I'm sorry for what I said," Frank apologized.

"Forget it Frank. You had no way of knowing what some of these people are like. Wait until you meet Tran. He is the number one bastard of the world. He makes Satan look like the good guy." The clean up crew arrived. As they started to pick up the body, one of the men looked at me. He knew what had been done and that meant he had seen it before.

"Tell me something," I asked, "have you been to Vietnam?"

"Why do you want to know?"

"You seem to know what went on here. That's why?"

"I have been to Nam and I know what went on here. I have seen it before. I didn't like it then and I don't like it now."

"I've seen the CIA do it."

"Maybe, not this one though."

I watched him clean the mess. He continued to stare at me.

"While your staring at me—have you ever had it done to you?"

"No I haven't."

"Good. I have had it done to me several times. Now it is my turn. When I get Tran it will be over."

He didn't say anything else and left with his partner.

"Have you heard anything about Grant?"

"I talked to the Director. Grant is in Washington; he's not about to talk. He's sitting in jail now. Somehow, I think he is in bed with Holmes from the CIA. We haven't really anything to prove it, but at least he'll do time for Federal law violations."

"Sir, remember when I put the bug in the telephone booth next to the police station on the corner. I found Grant calling Russell. I just listened to the tape. Holmes's name kept popping up. That's the link."

"What the hell is Russell doing with Holmes? Make a copy of the tape and get it to the Director. I want it delivered to Branch by hand. If we can prove Russell is tied in with Holmes, we will have them all. The only one left will be Tran. What are you still doing here? Go get a copy of that tape made! I want you on the plane to Washington. Let the Director play it for Holmes. We should get some results that way."

Frank went to Washington and as he went to the Director's office, he kept thinking of Holmes. What a way to end a man's career. I walked into the Director's office and said, "Sir, I have a tape you might be interested in hearing. It's Grant telling Russell about our operation to trap the men trying to hit Tim. The special part is Russell was going to tell Holmes when the next hit on Tim was going to take place. I just came across the tape that's why we didn't know before. Russell and Holmes are in this together. That's how Tran got into the country."

Frank played the tape. Director Branch was speechless. Frank, you're coming with me. We are going to see Grant. When we played the tape, Grant became worried. "I am willing to talk if you cut me a deal."

"Deal, my ass. The only thing you'll get is a shorter time in jail. That's the deal." Grant agreed and spilled everything. A stenographer took down his statement word for word. Grant signed the statement. "Holmes is about to come down from his ivory tower."

Frank and the Director went to the CIA and asked for the Assistant Deputy Director. We played the tape.

"Gentlemen, I don't think that is enough to convict Holmes."

The Assistant Deputy Director was then given a copy of Grant's statement. He read it. "Gentlemen, follow me please." They went to the CIA Director's office. "What can I do for you gentlemen?" Holmes asked as we came in.

The tape was played. Holmes remained silent for a moment and then said, "Well, I guess you think I did something wrong. But this tape alone means nothing. Now get out of my office." He was handed Grant's statement; it took a couple of minutes to read. Holmes held his hands over his face and said, "What do you need?"

"Tran for a start!"

"I have never met him. My contact with him is through Russell. Find him, and you get Tran. Russell calls me when it's an emergency. I heard Tran is somewhere off the coast of New England. Where, I really don't know."

"You're going to keep your job for a little while longer. When Russell calls, you'll arrange a meeting with him."

"He'll never fall for that."

"That is your problem. Find a way. We are going to have your phone tapped and my men will be here with you. Then you will resign. I will have your resignation ready for you in an hour."

Branch told the Assistant Deputy Director, "I want to know where Captain Nge is. When you tell us where he is, then I want the CIA to get him out."

"That won't be easy, Sir. He is still wanted by the new government."

"That's another problem you've inherited. I suggest you get a search warrant and go through Holmes' house and garage. If he is tied into the drug trafficking, I want him."

"Mr. Branch, how the hell do we do this without a scandal?"

"I will help you if I can. So far, this whole mess has been kept quiet. If Holmes is dirty, then screw a scandal. If you clean your own house, it will look good for the CIA. If I do it, you will have to pay the price. Whatever it is."

"I'll see what I can do."

Branch and Frank left the CIA. On the way back to headquarters, the Director was quiet for a while then said, "Frank, you know what is going to happen to Holmes. Once he meets with Russell, and we get him, Holmes is going to have an accident. Frank get back to Gif and tell him what is happening. Tell him I will get in touch, as soon as I learn something. Tell him I have the CIA working on finding Capt. Nge. Frank, what do you think of Tim?"

"At first, I thought he was a nut case. Now I know he is one hell of a man. He is dangerous and scares me. But if I ever needed anyone to back me, he would be who I would want. I had him wrong at first."

"He is hard to keep under control!"

"Sir, that is an understatement. If he doesn't want you watching him, you never will. We are still trying to figure out how he is getting out of the house. We know there is a tunnel. We have tried everything, but just can't find it. Mr. Chin made it for him. They are two of a kind."

Gif and I were watching TV and eating a pizza when Frank got back.

"You're just in time Frank. Grab a beer and have some pizza. We're watching the game. It's been quiet here. How did you make out in Washington?"

"Grant is in jail. We played the tape for him and he wants to make a deal. Director Branch and I paid a visit to Holmes. At first he laughed at the tape. When he read Grant's statement, he changed. He's going to set up a meeting with Russell. Once we have Russell, Holmes is going to resign."

"Resign! I don't think so."

"The Director thinks that there will be an accident waiting for Holmes after we get Russell. I guess that's how the CIA works. They are afraid of a scandal. The new Director of the CIA is going to try and find Capt. Nge. He promised he would do everything he could."

Tim looked up and smiled. "That's the best news I've heard all night."

A few days later, Russell met with Holmes and was arrested. He didn't come easy. Two agents were wounded. Russell had had someone with him so the FBI covered the incident up by using the name of the man that was killed. The FBI said the dead man was wanted and he fought it out, rather than spend years in jail. It made a good cover story.

Gif looked at Tim, "Now it's only Tran we need to get."

"I'll flush him out. I have done it before. Gif, I need to be alone to do it. That way no one will get in my way. If I need you, I will get in touch."

"Somehow I don't like this Tim."

"Gif, stay away from Fall River. I have business there."

"Damn it, Tim. I thought that's where you were going. Remember what Larsen said. I don't trust him."

"I'll keep out of his way. I will be going there tomorrow."

At eight o'clock I walked into the Little Saigon. I walked up to the bar. The old man was there. He motioned for me to go into the back room with him.

"Tim, it's been quiet here. None of Tran's men have been in. I don't think they are going to come back here. Right now they don't trust me. I'm glad; I don't need them here. My regular customers have been talking about you. Every so often, one of them drops a hint to me. There is a bar a block away on the north side. The owner is a friend of mine and he tells me Tran's men are hanging around there."

"Good, I will pay them a visit tonight."

"Be careful, they are scared. That makes them even more dangerous. You'll stand out like a sore thumb. My friend tells me they always sit in the back room. There's only a table and four chairs there. If anyone is sitting there, it will be Tran's men.

I will be back in about fifteen minutes. If the police come in here after I return, I never left the place. Your friend over there, will he tell the police I was here all night?"

"You can count on it, Tim."

I left the old man, walked north and found the bar. I looked into the window and saw the only one sitting there was the bartender. He was the owner. I opened the door. When he saw me, he quickly walked toward his office and pointed to the room where Tran's men were. I looked in and saw three men. They started to reach under their coats. I had my knife out and slashed the first one. Then, I flipped the table over. Within minutes they were all dead. The owner came out of his office, looked inside and smiled.

"Good job, Tim."

"When you call the police, I was never here. Do you think you can get the word on the street that I am looking for Tran? Until I find him, make sure you say he is going to lose a lot of men."

"I can handle that. Now get out of here. I will call the police in exactly five minutes. Go to the Little Saigon. You'll be safe there, bedsides once the police see this they will know it was you. Clean your knife before you leave."

I went to the sink to clean the knife. The old man was going through the dead men's pockets.

I laughed and he looked up at me.

"No sense on letting the police have it!"

"Help yourself. Just leave a couple of bucks inside their pockets. That way they won't think you cleaned them out."

The old man was laughing, "Screw the police. I'm taking it all. I'll tell them they had a tab. I will make one out. Now you better leave."

"Make sure that message gets on the street. I will be back every so often to play."

"Okay Tim, now will you leave. I have to call this in."

I left the bar and went to the Little Saigon. The old man had a half-empty beer on the bar. About five minutes passed and I guessed the owner of the other bar was on the phone reporting a brawl. A couple of minutes later the cruisers could be heard going down the street. I had been sitting at the bar for about ten minutes when Capt. Larsen came in.

"Tim, I want to talk to you, right now!"

"Go ahead, I have no secrets from my friend here."

"How long has he been sitting here?"

"All evening. Why is there something wrong?"

"Did he leave the bar at all tonight?"

"No Captain. He has been sitting here all alone with me."

The Captain left.

"My guess is that he's going to bring your friend here to identify me as the guy that did the killing."

"Don't worry, he won't do that. He hates Tran as much as I do."

Sure enough Captain Larsen came back with a few of his men and had the other bar owner with him. "Have you seen this man tonight? Was he the one that killed those men in your place?"

"No Sir. He was never in my place tonight. For that fact, Tim has never been in my bar!"

"If you don't know him, how do you know his name?"

"Captain, you asked me if he had been in my place tonight. I answered you. Tim is known by a lot of people. We read the papers. His picture has been in the *Times* several times. Now, do you have anymore questions for me because I have to clean up my place."

"By the way, where were you when the fight broke out?"

"I was in the toilet, taking a shit. Would you like to check, Captain. I forgot to flush the toilet."

We watched the old man leave.

"Tim, stand up I want to search you."

"Captain, give it up. One phone call to the Mayor and you'll be a patrolman." I stood up. I pulled my shirt up and told the Captain I wouldn't help him again. "Do you see a knife?"

"No, not now. But I will see you later and I promise you, it will be in the near future."

"The next time you search me, have a warrant. When I leave here, I will make sure I have witnesses. That way you won't break the law. Right, draft dodger. Old man, I will tell you a story about our Captain when he leaves. Or, would you like to hear the story again, Captain?"

"Tim, you won't have the FBI protecting you forever. Someday I will teach you a lesson."

"Is that a threat? I would be happy to oblige you. Personally, I don't like to fight with sissies. But in your case, I would make an exception. Tell me something Captain, how the hell did you make it to Captain? Did you kiss the right asses? Next time I visit your station, I will ask your men. I don't think they like you. Which, I can understand. I don't like you either. So get out of my way. I am leaving. If you put a hand on me, I will throw you right out the window! Good night Sir." I walked out the door and got into my car. I could see his men watching me. I was on Rte 195 heading east when I saw a car in back of me with the blue lights on. I pulled to the side of the road. Two cops got out and walked toward my car. I got out of my car.

"Tim, we were there at the scene of the killings. We saw you leave the bar about five minutes before the call came in."

"Did the Captain put you up to this?"

"No Sir, we just want to tell you that we were both in Nam. We heard about you when we were there. We are with you. The Captain will never find out anything from us. If he knew we were here, he would be bullshit! If you ever need anything, my name is Norman and he's Kenneth. We work together. We know about Tran, if we find out anything, we will get in touch with you through the FBI. Our lines are all taped at the station. That's why we can't make any calls from there."

"Thanks guys. Here's my phone number at home. If you find out anything, call this number. The FBI will be listening so don't leave your names. They will know who you are. Thanks again."

"Good luck Tim!"

By the time I arrived in New Bedford, Gif was waiting for me. "I just got a call from the police chief in Fall River. He told me about what happened there. Tim, be careful of Larsen. I am doing some more checking on him. This guy is too full of hate. Or he has another reason. Frank is checking on him now. He is definitely after you. What the reason is no one knows. But I think he might be in with Tran somehow. We are checking his financial records. Maybe that will tell us something.

"Russell is in jail in Washington. He isn't saying much, but he'll come around. He won't allow himself to be the fall guy—especially for Tran.   When Holmes gets scared enough, he's going to talk.   He has already made one mistake. He set Russell up. We haven't told Russell that yet. We're letting him cool his heels in jail.

"These guys don't care about life. They do care about jail. Tomorrow, Holmes is going to face Russell, that is when Russell will talk. We have Holmes in custody. We are going to keep him in custody until he gets Russell mad enough to spill his guts. The new CIA director talked with the President. He appointed him right away. He also told him to find Tran and to find out where Nge is."

Grant, Russell, and Holmes were in the same heavily guarded room when Branch and the new CIA director walked in together. "Gentlemen, you are all going to be charged with attempted murder, drug trafficking, and a list of other charges. I have seen to it that two of you will remain in jail. Mr. Holmes gave us a statement. He told us how you, Russell, masterminded the scheme with Tran to kill Tim Collins. Holmes, you are going to testify to what you know. I am going to arrange bail for you. Grant you're going to do some heavy time. Russell you will also. The only winner, here is Tran. Russell, you brought that animal into this country. Holmes didn't find out until he was already here then he covered it up."

"Covered up nothing! I gave him a hundred thousand dollars for his help. Since then he has gotten ten times that much. He has a safe deposit box in Alexandria."

"We're going make sure Holmes goes home. Holmes, get out of here; they are ready to bail you out."

"I don't have a safe deposit box. Russell is lying. I allowed Tran to come into the country because I was told he knew where the MIAs were. I didn't know about his war record. That would be stupidity on my part."

Holmes left the room. The other two remained. "What I want from you gentlemen is the address of Tran."

"Mr. Branch, I have never met him. Russell is the only one that has. I was just paid for information. I never killed anyone; tell him where to find Tran, you fool."

"Screw you, stupid. Tran will have us out of here in no time. I'll still be alive and you'll be dead. How does that sound Grant? Tran will see to it you die."

"Russell, you're forgetting something."

"Look Director Winslow, I'll be out of here in no time. So don't try bullshitting me."

"I wouldn't even try. I'm just thinking what Tran will say when he hears you implicated him and Holmes in the money transactions. Talk about dying. Can Tran reach you in jail? I was just wondering. I don't think he'll put up a dime to get you out. If he does, it's to kill you. Now who is stupid!

"All we want is Tran. We can't afford the scandal that you have put us in. The President is more worried about a scandal and wants us to avoid it, if we can. Think about that."

"That's all I have to do to get out of here? Tell you where Tran is?"

"That's right. Of course you will stay in protective custody until we find him. That is for your own protection."

"He moves around a lot. Right now he is somewhere in Maine. I understand he is pissed because of the men he is loosing. Word is he is getting a place on Martha's Vineyard in a couple of weeks. That's all I know. Is that good enough?"

"For now it is. Are you sure you don't know where in Maine he is?"

"If I did, you'd know."

Holmes was released. They didn't want to release him, but had to so they could get the money. He had to hide it near his home. There were bugs on his phones, in his house, and cameras all over the area. If he made a move for the money, they'd get him. He wouldn't be thinking clearly because of the jail time he was facing; it would make him careless. The FBI figured he would go for the money and then they'd have them all.

But what no one figured on was Tran—that he'd eliminate everyone he could reach.

Holmes was going home when a car pulled alongside him. Two men open fired. Tran was one step ahead. When the police got there, they found the money—over a million dollars. At least it proved Russell wasn't lying. The FBI decided to move Grant and Russell to a safe house. At about three in the morning Gif got a call. There had been an explosion at the safe house; everyone was dead.

"Gif, this is Director Branch. Tran got everybody. He blew up the safe house. He is the only one left. Russell told us that Tran plans on moving to Martha's Vineyard in a couple of weeks. He's pissed because of the men Tim killed. When we find out where he is, we will get him. Make sure Tim knows. It will make him feel better."

"Sir, if Tim knows where Tran will be, you will never get Tran alive. I don't think we should tell him. Tim will get to him before we can. He's still out their killing Tran's men. He leaves every night and comes back when he has killed someone. He thinks he's forcing Tran to make a move. I wouldn't be surprised if Tim already knows where Tran is. The Vietnamese people in Fall River cover for him. He plans on killing Tran's men until he shows himself."

"Okay Gif, you know best."

"Tim, there is a possibility that Tran will be in the area. Washington has got wind of it. Maybe we'll be able to get him finally."

"I know he's coming, he has to. I have been working in his area for too long. He is losing men rapidly. When this happens, he loses face in the eyes of his men. That's why he'll be here. When he does show up. I will know. Then it will be either him or me."

"Tim, don't do anything foolish. Let the FBI handle it."

"I can't promise you that. I have to get even with Tran for a lot of people. This is personal. I will let you know ahead of time whatever I plan on doing. You can be a part of it or not."

"That's fair with me Tim. Are you going out again tonight?"

"I have to. If I quit now, Tran won't show up. I have to keep up the pressure. He's hiding somewhere. What I am doing is forcing him to show himself.

"Gif, don't worry, I'll be back. Those assholes in Fall River aren't smart enough to get me. They have no idea of what it is like to hunt someone down. They have lived in the city too long. I'll see you later tonight. Get some beer in here will you. You guys have been drinking me dry." With that and a laugh I left for the hunt.

The phone rang Gif picked it up, "Gif, speaking."

"Gif, Capt. Larsen is working for Tran. You should see some of the deposits he has in a bank. We found the accounts in a bank in Portland, Maine."

"Maine—that's where Tran is."

"No, he has gone. I found out from an informant that he is recruiting some men from New York and Chicago for the final showdown. Is Tim with you?"

"No, he is out again."

"Can you reach him?"

"Not until I get a call from the police. That's after he does his thing. I don't dare call the police in Fall River. If they know Tim is on his way there, they'll get him on the road. We just have to wait. The only cop in Fall River I worry about is that Capt. Larsen. Wait a minute, I heard Tim talking to a cop named . . . what the hell was that name? I think he used the name Norman, when he was talking to him on the telephone. Let's see if I can reach this Norman."

"You mean to tell me you're going to call the station and ask for a patrolman with the name Norman?"

"That's right. If there is more than one Norman, I'll hang up."

"That might work."

I dialed the Fall River Police Department, a female voice answered.

"Fall River Police, this call is being recorded."

"Miss, maybe you can help me. I am looking for a patrolman by the name of Norman. I don't know his last name."

"Who am I talking to, Sir?"

"I'm sorry miss, I wish to remain anonymous. This is very important. How many Normans do you have working tonight who are patrolmen?"

"Just one, Sir."

"Can you give him this message and tell him to use a payphone. I really have some information for him. Have him call the regular number. He'll know the number. Thank you. Please this is urgent."

"I'll do it right away."

"Car 12, come in please."

"Car 12, responding."

"Call the station right away. I'll be waiting for your call."

"Norman, this is Ann. I had a call from someone; they seemed upset. They want you to call them at the regular number right away."

"Thanks Ann, I owe you one."

"Ann, was that car 12?"

"Yes Captain."

"What did they want?"

"I don't know Sir. Someone just wanted to talk to Norman."

"Did they leave a name?"

"No Sir, that's all the information I have?"

"I'm going out for awhile. Call me on the radio if you need me."

"Yes Sir."

Norman dialed the number and Gif answered. "Are you Norman? Do you know Tim Collins?"

"Why do you want to know that?"

"Look, I don't know you. I just have to get a message to Tim. My name is Gif. Have you ever heard the name?"

"Yes Sir, I met you when Tim had some trouble here a couple of weeks ago. How do I know you're that Gif?"

"Simple, how did I know you called him about fifteen minutes ago?"

"Yea, I'm that Norman. What can I do for you?"

"What I am about to tell you can get you killed. Tell Tim that Captain Larsen is working for Tran. Tell him Larsen is a dirty cop. I want him to forget about Fall River tonight. I want him to come back home. Larsen will kill him if he gets the chance. Can you find him?"

"I think so. He usually shows up at the Little Saigon. I'll check to see if he is there."

"Be careful, Larsen is working."

"I know Sir, I saw him in the station when I left to go on patrol. Thanks for letting me know. I'll find him and give him the message."

Norman headed straight for the Little Saigon. When he entered the bar, he asked the old man if Tim was in.

The old man asked, "Who are you?"

"My name is Norman."

"Follow me, please."

They went upstairs to where I was sitting.

"Tim, Gif called. He told me to tell you Capt. Larsen is dirty. He's working for Tran. That's why he's been on your case. He wants you to get out of here and head back to New Bedford."

"Thanks Norman, be careful. If Larsen even finds you're in this place, he'll figure it out. I'd hate to see you dead."

"Just get out. I can take care of myself."

"You go first, Norman. Then I'll go out the side door. That way no one will see us together."

"Okay Tim, good luck."

When Norman went outside, Capt. Larsen was there and stopped him asking, "What the hell are you doing in there? Who were you suppose to meet tonight?"

Larsen turned his head and looked behind him.

"No one of importance, Sir. It turned out, the information was wrong."

"Follow me. I don't like talking here." Norman and the Captain entered the alley.

"Look Norman, I don't want you hiding anything from me. I can help you get ahead. Who were you suppose to meet?"

"No one, Sir." Captain Larsen drew a weapon from his ankle and said, "Who were you supposed to meet tonight? It was Tim, wasn't it? That's too bad. If you'd kept your nose out of it, you would be alive tomorrow."

Captain Larsen pointed a 38 at Norman, when all of a sudden, a hand came from behind and grab him. The blade of a knife shone in the moonlight and slid across Larsen's throat. He fell to the ground.

"Man, that was close! Now what the hell do we do? You just don't cut the throat of a Captain and walk away."

"I'll call Gif. You call it in." I went back into the bar and asked the old man for the telephone. I called Gif. "Thanks for the warning. I just killed Larsen. You were right, he was dirty. He was about to kill one of his own men. Norman is calling it in now. I think we can use your help."

"Be there in fifteen minutes. Keep your mouth shut until I get there. Tell Norman to have the Chief there if possible."

"Okay Gif, thanks a lot."

I walked outside and into the alley. "Norman, can you get the Chief down here right away?"

"Car 12 to headquarters. Ann, do me a favor, call the Chief and get him down here right away. Larsen is dead."

"I'm on the telephone right now."

"Chief, this is Ann. I have an emergency. Your presence is being requested at the Little Saigon. It seems that Capt. Larsen is dead."

"Call them and tell them I'm on my way! No one is touch anything. Not even, the homicide squad. Have you got that straight?"

"Yes Sir!"

"All cars going to the Little Saigon. No one is to touch anything until the Chief arrives. That goes for homicide also."

"Lt. Francis calling. What do you mean, don't touch anything. I am in charge of this crime scene!"

"No Sir! I am right now. I have orders for you to follow from the Chief. You are to seal off the area. That's all. The Chief should be there any minute."

"This is bullshit!"

"Lieutenant! You have your orders."

"Put the Sargent on the radio."

"Yes Sir."

"This is Sgt. Hawes. What's your problem Lieutenant?"

"Ann, I want her placed on report. I want her relieved immediately."

"Lieutenant, she is not on report. She is staying on the radio. You and your men will do nothing until the Chief gets there. Do you understand! Read the rules of the department, Lieutenant, the dispatcher is to be obeyed when she or he gives an order."

"This is the Chief speaking. Lieutenant you're relieved. Tell Baker he is in charge. I will see you at the station later. Tell Baker to seal the area. My ETA is about two minutes. Keep everyone at least a block away."

The Chief arrived and looked at the scene. He examined the body and said, "Tim, somehow I thought you would be here. What happened? The FBI can't get you out of this mess. That's a Captain there with his throat cut; that's his blood spilling all over the place. You mean to tell me you are still carrying the knife. Give it to me."

"Chief, if Tim hadn't killed Capt. Larsen, he would have shot me."

"Patrolman, what the hell are you saying?"

Norman was about to answer when Agent Gifford joined us.

"Hi Chief, I guess you're not having a good night?"

"Agent, I really don't need any shit from you. I have a Captain lying here with his throat cut. Look on the ground. That's blood coming from his neck. Your war hero did it. What makes matters worse is my patrolman started to say something about Larsen trying to kill him."

"That makes sense, Chief. Your patrolman is lucky to be alive."

"Gif, do me a favor and brief me about what you're talking about. Are you saying Larsen was dirty? If you are, I hope you have proof. If you don't, your boy is going to jail."

"We checked Larsen's bank accounts. It seems he has quite a bit of money in another state. A lot more than he could ever make as a Captain. The bank accounts are in Portland, Maine. Do you know who was living in Maine? Major Tran! There were several cash deposits made to the accounts we're talking about."

"That proves shit! I need more."

"I called your patrolman Norman tonight. Unfortunately, I didn't know his last name. It took time to reach him and I am sure the Captain asked who wanted Norman. I suggest you ask the young lady who was dispatching tonight. Then answer this. What the hell was Larsen doing here in the Little Saigon?"

"Officer, what did Larsen ask you tonight?"

"He wanted to know what I was doing in the bar. I told him I was looking for someone. He asked me if I'd found him and I told him no. Then, he insisted on knowing who I was looking for. I told him an informant. He asked me again what the name of the informant was, and I told him I didn't know. Then he asked me to follow him into the alley. So I did and that's when he told me that I should mind my own business. Next thing I knew, I was looking into a barrel of a 38. He also told me that if I had stayed out of his business, I would have been alive tomorrow. That's when Tim grabbed him. Sir, Capt. Larsen had that 38 about three inches from my nose. I knew he was going to kill me. Thank God Tim showed up. I didn't even hear him. That's what my report will show. That is my story and if I am asked what happened, that is what I am going to say. That pig on the ground was going to kill me."

"Norman, I want you to go to the station. You are not to talk to anyone. Tell Ann she is to be replaced and is to make a copy of the tape. Then, the two of you are to make out your reports. If I hear anything about you talking to any reporters, I will personally make your life a living hell."

"Agent Gifford, it's not a nice thing to find out you have a dirty cop under your command. Tim, I'm sorry. I want you to know, however, that I don't appreciate the body count we have had lately. This is not Nam. It's time you stopped this hunt or sooner or later you are going to kill the wrong man. It's happened before. I'll need a report from you also. I am sure Agent Gifford will help you make it out. Would you mind going to headquarters to do it? Tell them I want you put in an office where you won't be bothered. Please, no press releases. I'll figure out later what to tell them."

"Chief, I want you to keep Tim's name out of the press release."

"How the hell am I going to do that?"

"I'll think of something. I sure wouldn't want him talking to the press."

"Do me a favor! Get both your asses out of my sight. I don't know how much more I can take. Make sure you sign the report Tim. Agent Gifford, would you tell the Sargent to hold all the reports until I get there. I don't want anyone seeing them, especially the cops on duty!"

"No problem Chief. I'm use to doing things like that. We have the same problem from time to time.

It took a couple of hours for us to do the reports. We asked Ann how she liked dispatching.

"I did until tonight. When Capt. Larsen gave me the third degree, I was scared. I didn't know what to think. Then when Norman called me, I knew the shit was going to hit the fan. I will never forget this night, that's for sure. Did you see the reporters and TV crews outside the station? When I get home, I am taking the telephone off the hook. I might even go into hiding."

"Maybe you should ask the Chief for a few days off. The both of you should disappear for awhile."

"That's all we have to do! The Chief is pissed now."

"So what! If you're off for a few days, the reporters can't get to you. I'll tell the Chief when he gets back."

"Yea! That's all we need."

The Chief finally came into the room.

"Are you people finished with the reports yet?"

"Yes Sir, we just finished them."

"I want you to get lost for a couple of days. Stay away from the media. I don't want your faces around the station or anywhere the news media can get to you."

Gif and I started to laugh.

"Am I missing something?"

"No Sir, Agent Gifford just told us the same thing. We we're going to ask you about us getting lost."

"Here's another laugh for you—the time you are off will deducted from your vacation time. Laugh that one off. Now, give me the reports." He read my report then the other reports.

"I hate to say this because of what happened tonight, but I am glad you're all okay. It hurts to have a dirty cop on the force. It makes us all look bad."

"Officer, how long have you been helping Tim?"

"I really haven't, Sir. I just told him if I could ever do him a favor I would. Chief, I am not an informant. Ken, my partner, and I were in Nam. We heard about this Major Tran and that's why I offered to help, if we could.

"Chief, you have no idea what Tran is like. I have seen what was left of some of the men he tortured. He would move them into areas where he knew we would find them. It was an awful thing to see. If it meant my job, I would help Tim. One other thing, I would make sure I stayed within the law. I don't think I could do what Tim is doing, but I am not sitting in judgement. I know this, however, if I'd survived what he did, I guess I would be the same. Tran is an animal. He will bring drugs into this country and won't think twice about how many people die."

"Okay, you people did a fine job; now get out of here. The back door is clear. Use it!"

"Tran is coming, Chief. He is bringing in men from New York and Chicago. These men are hired killers. At least they won't be coming to Fall River."

"Are you sure Gif?"

"Yes, I am. I'm positive. He likes to stay near the coast. We just have to figure out when he is coming. I am sure Tim will have that information soon. When we get it, we'll call you and tell you when it's over."

"Major Tran, we have just received word that Larsen is dead."

"How did he die?"

"His throat was cut. Like all the others."

"Tim again! I want him dead! Send enough men this time to do the job. If any of them come back alive, I will kill them if they tell me they failed. Now get out and take care of the matter. I don't want excuses; I want results. When are the men coming in from New York and Chicago?"

"I expect them anytime. The ones from New York will be here in a couple of days, those from Chicago a couple of days later. I figure about a week and they will be in place."

"Have you found a place on Martha's Vineyard?"

"Yes Major, it is out of the way. The closest building is a Coast Guard Lighthouse."

"Is that wise, being that close to the Coast Guard?"

"Yes Sir, that is the last place anyone would look. There aren't any houses anywhere around. One Guardsman mans the lighthouse most of the time."

"Good. When can we move in?"

"Anytime you want, Sir."

"Good that will give us time to prepare things."

"Okay, get out. I have to plan a reception party for Tim."

The telephone rang. Gif picked it up.

"There are about six men coming in from New York the day after tomorrow. The following day there will be at least four more. They are going to be Tran's bodyguards! I'll keep an eye on them."

"Don't let anyone spot you. Report to me when you find them. Let me know where they are staying and what they are doing. Especially where they go! That's where Tran will be."

We were watching TV when the phone rang. I answered and said, "When will they hit? Thanks, I'll take care of it."

"Okay Tim, what's up? Or should I say when are they coming?"

"Word's out that there are at least seven more men coming tonight and they will be here sooner than I expected. Tran is desperate. He wants me dead even more and that means they won't care about anything. They know if they fail, they're dead."

"I'll post two men across the street in the hedges. They will cover the front. I'll have a man on each side of the house. The rear we will cover."

"I'll be in the woods. If any try to run, I'll be waiting for them."

"I'll call Benzer and warn him to keep his men out of the area." Gif called Benzer and told him the plan. He wasn't happy.

"Don't worry, my men are sharpshooters. They will be using silencers."

"Silencers? Where the hell did they get them?"

"Don't ask. Tim got them."

"I'm sorry I asked already. What time do you expect them?"

"We're not sure. I hope it will be late. I figure they will be here after midnight when the houses in the area will be dark. I think this will be Tran's last try for a while. At least, until he can get another plan in motion, if this doesn't work out. God knows what will. I'm tired of this assignment. It's been going nowhere. Everyone is dying and still no Tran. I am surprised the newspapers haven't had a field day with us."

"Good luck, Gif."

"Thanks, we'll need it. They are sending about six or seven men tonight."

Twelve o'clock came and we were still waiting. Around 1:30 AM, we saw a van drive by the house. It drove to the corner and turned right.   We watched them park in the wooded area. I called Gif on the radio.

"There are six of them plus the driver. I will take out the driver when the men separate." I started to crawl toward the van when the men split up. The driver had his window open. I reached in with my knife; he was dead instantly. I crossed over to the woods and could hear the silencers go off. It lasted only a few seconds. One man started to run on foot. I was waiting and he ran right into me. I grabbed him and told him in Vietnamese that he was a fool. Those were the last words he ever heard.

I went back to the house and found Gif there. He counted five bodies.

"I thought there were supposed to be six?"

"There were seven of them. One is in the woods and the other is slumped behind the wheel of the van."

"I'll tell Benzer everything is okay. Frank, you make the call to clean up the area. Did anyone see any lights go on?"

"Nothing Sir. They're all sleeping thanks to these rifles."

"Benzer, this is Gif. We finished our business everything went fine."

"No prisoners I take it."

"Can't take fanatics willing to die."

"Well, that means one thing Gif. When Tran finds out he'll be down here. What happens then?"

"I don't want to even think about it."

"Tim, what's next?"

"Gus—I think it's time to pay him a visit."

"Gus. That nutcase! I don't like this Tim."

"Don't worry, he's okay. He's a good man to have on your side."

"Maybe when he's sober."

I didn't wait for the clean up crew. I went to Pat's bar and found Gus."

"Give Tim a beer, Pat."

"Let's sit at a table, Gus. If you had to hide and wanted to be alone, where would you go to do it?"

The western side of Martha's Vineyard—somewhere close to the lighthouse. They only have one man on duty. I take him lobsters all of the time."

"Next time you're there, can you find out if there is an empty house nearby?"

"Shit, I can tell you that. About a half-mile away is the only house on that side of the island. I can also tell you that there is no one living there now. It's on a cliff and very windy. That's why they have trouble renting it."

"Next time you see the Guardsman, ask him to let you know when someone moves in. Especially, Vietnamese."

"Tim, are you saying what I think you are? I don't want to be left out of this."

"Gus, this is going to be very dangerous. Tran has brought in some big guns from New York and Chicago."

"Big guns! I'll show you big guns when you need them. Tim, I won't be left out. I want to be the one that helps you get that bastard. You will need some tools and I can get everything you need at a moment's notice."

"When the time comes, I will be looking for a boat to take us there."

"Meet the lady of the seas. She's lethal. She can also carry a load. Let's go to the boat; I want to show you something."

We walked to Gus' boat.

"See that plate? Guess what goes there? The lady wears a fifty when I want to play."

"A fifty! What the hell are you doing with a fifty?"

"I shoot sharks with it."

"Gus, I have to go. I don't want to hear anymore."

It was quiet for a couple of days; no one made a move toward me. The FBI watched the men Tran had shipped in. All of a sudden, they were gone. I wondered if Gus had talked to the Guardsman at the lighthouse. As I was walking toward the docks one day, one of the fishermen yelled at me. "Gus just came in. He wants to talk to you."

That's why I hadn't heard from him. He had been out fishing. I saw his boat and he was unloading the lobsters he'd caught.

"Tim, I just left the lighthouse. The Chief who keeps it running told me they rented the house up from the lighthouse. I asked them if they were Vietnamese.

He laughed and said, " 'Some are. I have a funny feeling about them. I noticed a lot of guys there. They looked like mercenaries to me. They walk around the house all day and night. I can see them from the top of the lighthouse with binoculars. They are heavily armed. I've seen guards there before. The rich always bring their own security force, but this is different. These guys are more than security. I make it a point to keep my distance from them. Once in awhile, they come down to the lighthouse to talk. They ask a lot of questions. I don't tell them much. I'm all alone here.' "

"Thanks Gus. I'll let you know when we will need your boat." I left the docks and walked back to my house. I was finally going to get that bastard. I could feel the anxiety building up in me. My day was finally coming.

I opened the door to my house and Gif was there with his men. "Tran's here," I said. They all looked up.

"What did you say?"

"Tran is on Martha's Vineyard. I just got word. The missing men are there guarding the place day and night. I know how to get him. I can come in from the lighthouse. There is a pier there that is far enough away so they can't see me."

"Tim, you can't go alone. You're going to need help."

"Look Gif, I appreciate your help. You have been a good friend. What I have to do is not in the FBI Manual. You're too close to retirement. Besides, Gus is coming with me. I am going to use his boat to get there."

"Tim, I have been through a lot with you and am not going to be left out now. You are going to need all the help you can get. Gus will not be enough. Besides, he is unreliable. You don't even know how many men Tran has with him. You fucking well know he is going to be heavily guarded. Besides, I have to make sure you stay alive. That means I go! End of discussion. Frank, I will leave my credentials with you while we're gone. If anybody calls for me you know what to do."

"Gif, are you sure you know what you're doing?"

"Don't worry Frank; I'll be coming back. I'll probably lose my retirement, but it will be worth it to finally get this bastard. I have to go. Tim, you know Tran will be on full alert. He knows you want him as bad as he wants you. He must know the last group he sent to kill you failed. So we have to move quickly."

"Okay, we go tonight. We can check the place out after dark. Gus said he has some things we can use. Just don't question him about it."

We arrived at the docks as Gus was fueling up the boat. When he saw us he said, "Tim, are you nuts? He's FBI."

"He's one of us tonight."

"I'll be done in a minute. Then we can leave."

"Where the hell are all your lobster pots?"

"I left them over there on the docks. The old lady is going into a different kind of business tonight. I'm ready, jump aboard."

The engine started and we set off.

"It will take about an hour or so to get to the lighthouse. There's coffee down below."

"I guess that means I get the coffee."

"Hey, I'm the Captain."

Gif and I went down below.

"Tim, this guy scares me. I wonder what he's got onboard."

"Whatever it is, we will need it. If I know Gus, he has it all. Do you know he has a fifty that he can attach to the bow?"

"A what?"

"A fifty-caliber machinegun. He showed me the mount for it; he kills sharks with it."

"There goes my retirement!"

We had been underway for about an hour, when we heard the engine stop. We went on deck.

"What's the problem Gus?"

"No problem, I have some things you can use. Lift that canvas on the stern. Take what you need."

We lifted the canvas. Gif stood there in state of shock.

"Gus, everything you have here is against the law."

"No shit!"

We picked up everything from automatic weapons with silencers to rocket launchers. He even had a box of grenades. He had enough ammo for everything onboard. He could actually start his own war.

I started to load the weapons and Gif helped.

"I don't believe this Tim. Has anybody stopped to think about the Guardsman living at the lighthouse? He is going to be able to see us and see everything we're carrying."

"Don't worry, he'll keep his mouth shut. He lost a brother in Nam."

"By the way, under the canvas on the portside, there are two sets of night-vision wear. Take them with you. You're going to need them."

"Is there anything this boat doesn't have? I could use a tank. I had to ask," Gif said.

Gus and I laughed.

We were soon underway again and in about fifteen minutes the dock came in view. We could see the Chief standing at the end of the dock. We coasted in and he helped tie up the boat. We watched him staring at the weapons. "What the hell are you guys up to? You're ready for war."

Gus said, "I'll answer that. I am going to introduce you to one man. This is my friend Tim Collins. I guess you have heard of him?"

"Yes, I have. Let me shake your hand. I lost a brother in Nam. If you need help with what you're going to do, I'm willing to go. Who is it you're going after? That is, if I may ask?"

"Have you ever heard of Major Tran?"

"Who hasn't? The bastard killed a lot of prisoners during the war. You mean he's in the house over there?"

"He sure is. And tonight is the night he dies."

"Good luck Tim. I wish I were going with you."

We started for the house, taking the long way around so we wouldn't meet up with anyone unexpectedly. Gus stayed by the boat in case someone came. The Chief was in the lighthouse. I didn't want him involved anymore than he was. We were about three hundred feet from the house and could see the guards. They walked back and forth along each side of the house. They would meet at the corners and talk for a minute. We could see people inside the house. That was a problem. We didn't know how many. The night-vision glasses gave us a clear view of the yard and everybody there. We decided to wait until we knew for sure how many were in the house.

Gus and the Chief were talking. Gus looked up and saw they had company.

The Chief looked up. It was one of the Vietnamese guys.

"Good evening. Who owns the boat?"

"I do, I am a lobsterman. I always bring lobsters to the Chief. You live near here?"

"I'm on vacation."

"I hope you have one great vacation. Martha's Vineyard is beautiful. You will enjoy it. By the way, would you like some lobsters?"

"Yes Sir, I could use some. I'll buy them."

"Chief, is this a friend of yours?" Gus asked.

"Yes, you could say that. He keeps me company every so often."

"Then come aboard and I will fill a bag for you."

The guy stepped on the rail and Gus held out his hand. He grabbed it and jumped on deck. Gus' knife went into his stomach. He stood there looking at Gus for a second and then fell to the deck. He was dead.

"Chief, help me put the canvas over him just in case anymore of his friends show up."

The Chief started to cover him up, and saw a Russian-made pistol in his belt. He removed it and said, "You no good bastard. I'm glad you're dead." Gus and the Chief sat on the deck smoking a cigar. The Chief loved them. He always said, "A good cigar is better than a woman anytime."

"Gif, you take the north side. I'll work around toward the south. When the guards bunch up, let them have it. No one will hear anything. Then we'll wait for the guards to change shifts and get the next bunch."

We saw the guards standing together at the corner of the house and opened fire; they fell to the ground. Not one sound was made. They died instantly. It took about an hour before we saw the next four men come out to relieve the guards. When they came across the dead men, we open fired again. They dropped to the ground.

Gif and I made our way into the house. We saw six men watching TV. When they saw us, they started to stand, but we mowed the room with bullets. Again, not a sound was made. They were all dead. They never even got their guns out. We checked the bodies. Tran wasn't there. I went upstairs and could see a light under the door of one of the rooms. I checked each room, but they were empty. That meant Tran was in the last room.

I walked toward the door and put my ear against it, listening. I could hear someone walking. I kicked the door open and was face to face with Tran. He had a shocked look on his face.

I had finally met up with him. Finally, Major Tran, I thought, you're on my turf. Tran moved toward the table and I hit him with the butt of my rifle. He went down and I kicked the table over. The gun he was reaching for was too far away for him.

"Tran, I fucked up the last time, but now I intend to kill you and believe me it will be painful. I have a lot of friends that want you dead. I am going to slice you up until you bleed to death. The longer you suffer, the better I'll like it."

He tried to move. I kicked him as he held his stomach. Dragging him to the bed, I tied his hands and feet. When he came to, I was sitting in the chair. I took out my knife. He just stared at it.

"Do you remember this knife?" He didn't answer. "This one is an exact duplicate of the one you used on me. If you're wondering about your men, they are all dead. You're the last one to go. I saved you for last."

I slid my knife across his chest. He screamed. I shoved a rag into his mouth. I kept slicing him until I was covered with blood. I couldn't stop myself. I kept thinking of all the men he killed. I sliced and sliced until there wasn't anything left of him to cut.

I could hardly find a pulse, but he was still breathing. I was just about to finish him off when I thought of Sandra. I couldn't do it anymore. I was finished. "Why can't I kill him?" Then I remembered what Sandra said. I knew why I couldn't do it.

I went outside to meet Gif.

He saw the blood all over me and couldn't talk.

"Gif, it's time to go."

"Are you okay Tim?"

We made it back to the boat. The Chief and Gus looked at me. We gave Gus back the guns. No one said a word. I walked to the edge of the boat and jumped into the water. I washed Tran off of me. When I'd finished, I climbed aboard the boat.

"Chief, I expect you will have the police all over you sometime tonight."

"Hell Tim. I can't see anything from here. That's all they'll get from me."

"Thanks for everything."

"No, thank you Tim. I know my brother will sleep in peace."

Gus started the engines, the Chief let the lines go, and we pulled away from the docks. We had been out for about thirty minutes when Gus yelled, "Shit, I forgot something." He turned around and said, "Hey, under that canvas—would you mind throwing that shit overboard before it stinks up the place!"

We took the canvas off the pile and found a body.

"Where did you get this Gus?"

"He showed up and tried to get some lobsters. I gave him the house specialty. You can throw him overboard. He'll float out to sea. The tide's running in that direction."

We tossed him overboard and washed the deck. We soon reached the dike leading into New Bedford harbor. We went through and then tied the boat up to the dock.

Gif asked me what was in the briefcase I had removed from Tran's house.

"Shit, I almost forgot. Gus, this is for you. Buy yourself a bigger boat." He opened the case. It was full of money.

"Tim, what the hell would a guy like me do with this much money?"

"What do you think, Gif?"

"I never saw a thing, Gus, think about it. You can live like a king. Get yourself a bigger boat and have fun."

"I just want to tell you guys something. I'm not a nutcase."

We smiled and left. I turned around and said, "We never thought you were."

Gif laughed and said, "Just a little strange maybe. Take care of yourself Gus."

"I think I would like to be alone for awhile, Gif. I'd like to sit down here. I have some thinking to do. I'll meet you back at the house. Gif when you get back to the house, would you call the clean-up crew. Remember, Martha's Vineyard is a tourist town. What just happened over there could hurt business for them."

"Sure thing, Tim. I'll do it right away. Gif, make the call before you call your boss if you don't mind."

I watched him walk out of sight then I went to the pay phone. I called Ms. Costa and told her if she wanted the biggest story of her life, she should get a photographer and go to Martha's Vineyard. "The last house before you get to the lighthouse is the one you want."

"What's there?"

"Just get your ass moving. You better rent a chopper, make sure you hide in the brush, and take your pictures. You better bring enough film for the cameras. You'll need it. Make sure you bring the video camera. You'll need it also. Ms. Costa you just might get a Pulitzer Prize for this exclusive."

"Tim, you got Tran!"

"You're wasting time. Make sure you keep out of sight." I went back and sat on the docks. I could hear a chopper heading toward Martha's Vineyard. I then called the State Police on Martha's Vineyard and I told them about the bodies. They only have one State Trooper stationed there.

The following morning I watched the news and it showed the CIA cleaning up the bodies. They even had pictures of what the inside of the house was like. The State Trooper got there just after Ms. Costa. The CIA agents were caught red-handed moving the bodies.

The front door opened and Gif walked in. "Tim, you bastard, you called the news media."

"Well Gif, didn't we promise someone an exclusive."

"Tran isn't dead Tim. What happened?"

"I thought of Sandra and what she'd said and couldn't do it. So I figure a war crimes trial would be nice. Come over here and sit down and listen to the news. They were talking about Tran, the animal from Vietnam. This was the name the news media had given him." Gif and I burst out laughing.

"Tim, you do know there are going to be repercussions from this. This shit is going all the way to the White House. You have embarrassed a lot of people."

"Tough shit! I think when Tran stands trial for war crimes, the White House will come out smelling like a rose. The CIA, I really don't care about. Politicians are good liars and know how to cover things up. But I hope they keep their promise to me about Nge. They better get him out. Sit down and watch the news. I'll make breakfast for us."

We had breakfast and laughed, "Costa sure got her story. She was a hero in the eyes of her boss."

Now, I just had to wait for Nge to get here.

The telephone rang. It was Sandra. All I could think about after hearing her voice was: Now we can start our lives together.

Printed in the United Kingdom
by Lightning Source UK Ltd.
105489UKS00001B/170